# COW GIRL

Kirsty grew up in South Yorkshire, idolizing comedy writers like Sue Townsend. Having studied languages at Nottingham Trent, her love for theatre led her to write and direct several comedy stage-plays, which received favourable reviews at the Edinburgh and Brighton Fringe festivals.

Kirsty now lives in South-East London with her partner and two children.

*Cow Girl* is her debut novel, and won the inaugural Comedy Women in Print Unpublished Prize 2019.

Facebook.com/kirstyjaneeyre/

@KirstyJaneEyre

eyre.kirsty

# KIRSTY EYRE

# COW GIRL

HarperCollins*Publishers*

HarperCollins*Publishers*
1 London Bridge Street
London SE1 9GF

www.harpercollins.co.uk

Published by HarperCollins*Publishers* 2020
1

A catalogue record for this book
is available from the British Library

ISBN:
B format: 978-0-00-838224-7

This novel is entirely a work of fiction.
The names, characters and incidents portrayed in it are
the work of the author's imagination. Any resemblance to
actual persons, living or dead, events or localities is
entirely coincidental.

Typeset in Minion by Palimpsest Book Production Ltd,
Falkirk, Stirlingshire

Printed and bound in Great Britain by
CPI Group (UK) Ltd, Croydon CR0 4YY

**MIX**
Paper from
responsible sources
**FSC** **FSC™ C007454**
www.fsc.org

This book is produced from independently certified FSC™ paper
to ensure responsible forest management.

For more information visit: www.harpercollins.co.uk/green

To my mum, the real Kay Oliver

# PART ONE

# FARMERCEUTICALS

# CHAPTER ONE

# #SAVEOURDAIRY

I crouch beneath the mottled underbelly of a cow, her speckled udder dangling inches from my chin. It's a wool-grey January day. London's Covent Garden is awash with farmers, its cobbles splattered with dung and dusted with hay. The fifty-five-foot Christmas tree has started to lean towards a Gourmet Sausage van, which chugs and whirrs, the smell of Bratwurst and diesel intermingling with the stench of manure. Stall after stall of riding boots, fishing rods and artisan oatcakes line the edges of the piazza, their wares fingered by tourists and farmers. Five Holstein Friesians are penned outside Mulberry, a cacophony of grunts echoing under the rafters of the Royal Opera House arcade. Tongues lollop through the metal bars against shop windows. A jet-black cow with white knee-sock markings is being led over to the enclosure. Overwhelmed, she backs into a stall of handmade jewellery, sending fake pearls bouncing across cobbles.

I should be focused on the task at hand, but I'm both

3

desperate for the loo and wondering where on earth Dad is. He was meant to be here two hours ago and the drive from Derbyshire shouldn't take this long.

A man in a #SaveOurDairy fleece stands at a table piled high with cheese. 'British dairy farming is on the brink of collapse,' he shouts through a megaphone. 'Premier Milk is to drop its "A" milk prices again, meaning a further drop in profits.' The megaphone whines with feedback. 'Every week another dairy farm closes. Support our dairy farmers!'

A pigeon struts underneath a show-caravan in pursuit of a sandwich crust and I wonder if I can join it, the prospect of lying under a Scenic Getaway Motorhome for the next hour becoming more attractive by the minute. I hate dairy farming events. It's not just the slogan-chanting country folk or the backlash from my vegan friends. It's more that, having grown up in the countryside, I've been subjected to enough falconry displays, hound parades, jousting gerbils and country cads to last a lifetime. Were it not for Dad, I certainly wouldn't be here right now, poised beneath a stranger's cow.

'Buy our "Milk for Farmers" branded milk!' the #SaveOurDairy man yells.

Bev and Kat approach in black leather jackets and a swirl of winter scarves. Bev's Mohican only serves to accentuate their height difference. Today, it's not its usual lurid pink, but that sort of murky blue-green that bad tattoos go in the sun. She runs her hand over it, and I worry for a moment that she's going to ask me whether I like it.

'Bill!' Kat's Kiwi tones fill the piazza. It sounds more like 'Bull'. 'Did you want one?' She waves a hot dog at me, mustard dripping down her arm.

4

I gesture apathetically to the udders above me. 'I've got my hands full.'

'Any news from your dad?' Bev says, massaging her Mohican.

I want to bite my fingernails, but I've been stroking a cow. 'His phone is switched off.'

'Three, two, one . . .' The #SaveOurDairy man blasts his horn, startling shoppers and tourists alike.

A giant digital display starts its three-minute countdown. Gently, I clamp the base of diagonal teats between my thumb and forefinger, squeeze firmly and pull down. A dribble of milk plips into the bucket. *Squeeze and pull down.* Another drip. I've clearly lost my touch, proving Dad's 'it's like riding a bike' theory wrong. *Squeeze and pull down.* Another drip. The latex gloves are three sizes too big and wrinkle like old lady's stockings. I should have brought some from the lab. Where the fuck is Dad?

'You've got this, Bill!' Kat shouts aggressively.

Maria joins them from the refreshments queue. She's head-to-toe in active gear, in spite of her aversion to exercise. 'Come on, Bilbo! I thought you grew up on a farm?'

Marigold swings her bulky head round, all forelock and attitude. Her nostrils flare, puffing out clouds of warm breath, which spiral in the cold air. She holds my gaze through big, watery eyes, before turning back to her hay net. The guy next to me is having more joy with Daisy, milk spattering against his pail. Four neat, pink teats. I should know what to do, but I blocked that chapter out of my life thirteen years ago and am too worried that Dad is in a pile-up on the M1 to retrieve it from my memory bank.

Maria leans over the enclosure rope, her breath heavy with free-range pulled pork and curried gherkins. 'Pull your finger out! I've got a tenner on you winning 7/1.'

Marigold swishes her tail and a matted dreadlock of hair, manure and urine whips me across the cheek. It stings, like lemon juice on a paper cut. And at that moment, I hear Dad's voice loud and clear. I'm seven again and he walks Roberta, the most docile of the herd (long legs, and a black splodge the shape of Australia on her left buttock) into the yard. 'Bump the bag,' he says, gesturing to her udder. *Bump the bag*, of course.

Gently, I buffet my head against Marigold's soft, warm udder to simulate a calf feeding. Once. Twice. Three times, before reaching for the teats and gripping the plastic bucket between my ankles. I squeeze and pull down. A stream of milk spirts out diagonally, first onto my shoe, and then into my bucket. *Squeeze and pull down. Left, right. Left, right.* I'm up and away, steady at first. *Left, right.* Until I find my groove. A little bit faster. *Left, right.* I move in closer, head cocked to one side, street entertainers and the Apple store rotated ninety degrees. Faster. *Left, right.*

'Mar-i-gold!' Maria chants, her rose metallic Reeboks disappearing in and out of view behind Marigold's undercarriage.

*Left, right.* Faster still, until I'm expressing like a steam train, fingers like pistons, sequentially squeezing a powerful jet of milk from each teat. Gentle but firm. Faster and faster until it's a blur, I'm a child again, and this is one big game. Marigold chomps her way through her hay. I see Bev's black leather lace-up boots. Kat's burgundy suede ankle boots.

'Mar-i-gold! Mar-i-gold!' the girls chant.

Feet I don't recognize come into view. Suede loafers. Ankle boots. Nike Air Max.

'Mar-i-gold! Mar-i-gold!' The chant carries.

Walking boots. Wedges. Garish pink Crocs.

'Mar-i-gold! Mar-i-gold!'

Vans. More Nikes.

The crowd gets behind me. 'Mar-i-gold! Mar-i-gold!'

I'm milking like my life depends on it. Like Dad's life depends on it. Which it does, in a fashion. *Left, right.* Why isn't he here yet?

'Five, four, three . . .' A voice booms over the megaphone. 'Two, one.'

The horn blasts again, a man in wellingtons accosting the girls with a book of raffle tickets. When I clamber out, there's still no sign of Dad. The bucket of frothy milk feels warm against my chest. I'm just about to dip my finger in and taste the cream, when two familiar figures emerge from an animal trailer in his-and-hers Parsons-Bonneville Premier Vets polo shirts and jodhpurs. Dread drifts into my stomach. There's only one thing worse than being stuck at a dairy farming awareness campaign, and that's being stuck at one with Lorna and Guy, the darling couple of rural Derbyshire.

I duck back under Marigold, put down the bucket and take an interest in the gluten-free beetroot muesli sample I got given when I registered. In my peripheral vision, I see their shiny riding boots marching towards me in synchronized strides. They have the gait and precision of a pair of dressage horses. She's seen me. Lorna Parsons: my dad's vet and mistress of everything bovine. Lorna Parsons, who outed me to a bunch of octogenarians at my grandma's bridge club. Lorna

Parsons, who has known me since we were kids and has never ceased to humiliate me. I try not to think the words 'bull sperm incident' . . .

She approaches me, square shoulders, athletic frame, mousy-blonde hair scraped into a ponytail, arms laden with rosettes. The silvery-pink horseshoe-shaped scar on her forehead shimmers in the light. Heat rushes to my chest. I stand up clumsily and only go and kick the bucket over, milk spewing across the cobbles and crawling into the cracks.

'Billie!' Her owl eyes single me out.

'Hi.' I hold onto my empty bucket and look around for my friends.

'You remember Guy?' She pulls her cap down over her forehead.

Guy adjusts his Rolex watch and extends his hand. 'Long time, no see, Belinda.'

'She prefers *Billie*,' Lorna says, with an air of superciliousness reserved for both of us; Guy for not remembering, and me for wanting to be called *Billie*. 'Shame about your dad's migraine.'

'Sorry?' I say, digesting this news and wondering how she got hold of it.

'He rang from Leicester Forest services. Blinder of a headache. Poor thing had to stop driving,' she says, the voice of authority on my own dad. My flesh and blood. 'I told him to turn off his phone and try to have a sleep in the car before he sets off again.'

I feel a mixture of panic and betrayal – Dad doesn't get migraines and why would he phone Lorna before me?

'Does my grandma know?' I say, knowing that Grandma

will be kicking herself for deciding to stay at the farm and sit this one out whilst her son is ill on the edge of the M1.

'I called her.' She smiles. 'She's sending your uncle Peter to pick up your dad.'

How come I didn't know about any of this? Why is she invading my family with her whiter-than-white do-gooding? Standing there, all king-of-the-castle with that smug smile on her face, with her equally smug boyfriend. I bet they have horsy nicknames for each other. Boak. I'm mentally poking her eyes out when the #SaveOurDairy man trudges over. He assesses the contents of my bucket, pressing his glasses firmly onto the bridge of his nose to stop them falling into the pitiful few millilitres of remaining milk.

Lorna flashes me a smile. 'Never were much of a farm girl, were you?' She plucks a 'Prize Loser' rosette from the pile in her arms and I'm reminded of the times she used to make me play this horse-riding game on the bottom branch of the willow tree at the farm – she, always the winner, and me, always the loser, despite being three years her senior. She stands to face me. Her teeth are coated in black streaks and her breath smells of liquorice. My chest gets hotter as she fixes the rosette to my jacket, all fingers and thumbs, the pin pricking my skin.

Maria bustles over, arms full of coffee and shopping. 'I've lost Bev and Kat,' she says, fiddling with the hearing aid hidden under her Sweaty Betty ski headband, her eyes travelling to Lorna and Guy.

'Maria, meet Lorna and Guy,' I say, aware that country and city life are about to collide. 'Lorna's my dad's vet up in Derbyshire.' My hands sink deeper into my pockets. 'Lorna and Guy, this is Maria, my flatmate.'

'Pleased to meet you,' Lorna and Guy say in unison.

'Hi!' Maria takes a step forward, unsure whether to offer them the hand with the skinny cappuccino or the arm full of shopping.

The country–city collision intensifies when Bev and Kat wander over, Kat's eyes unable to leave the crotch bulge in Guy's jodhpurs, a look of horror etched on her face.

'These are my friends, Bev and Kat.' I yank Kat's arm, trying to break her gaze.

'Hello.' Guy offers them an assertive handshake, whilst Lorna's eyes drift down to my Converse and stay there a while.

'We like to show our support at these events,' Lorna says, though I'm not sure to whom. 'Were it not for dairy farmers like Billie's dad, we wouldn't be in business.' She looks up, her large grey eyes level with mine. 'How's the PhD going?'

'It isn't,' I say too quickly. 'I'm still working on securing a scholarship.'

'You've been working on that a while now, right?' she says. 'Three years?'

Maria's elbow digs into my ribcage, her eyes widening.

'Two years,' I say, one-upmanship suddenly vital.

'It must be longer than that because you had to miss your dad's sixtieth for a career fair,' Lorna says. 'We threw him a little party. You remember, Guy?'

'Great canapés!' Guy lights up his cigarette and blows smoke into my face.

Guilt curdles in my gut. Why does she never cease to make me feel inadequate, selfish and about three years old?

Her eyes run across the gold italic font of my 'Prize Loser' rosette. 'We can't tempt you back to the farm then?'

They all look to me, country folk and city girls. The roof of my mouth starts to itch. Even when I press my tongue against it, it won't go away. The whole reason for fleeing the country and coming to London was to get away from things like this: the stench of fresh manure, the wax jackets, the Lornas and Guys, 'salt of the earth' people driving 4x4 Porsches while others are beaten by the crushing misery of the failing dairy economy. Unleashing my inner city-girl was the best thing I ever did, and now here I am, in London's Covent Garden, surrounded by dairy farmers; at the very crux of everything I escaped from.

'No,' I say. 'Definitely not.'

# CHAPTER TWO

# CHEMISTRY

The first day back at work after an extended Christmas break is always a killer, but an inch of snow makes this one particularly unappealing. *Breakfast News*'s Maroon McGinnis says Britain is officially experiencing the 'Big Freeze', and she's always right because she's a weather goddess. Today should be about building snowmen and frolicking in chunky knitwear, not trudging to Queen's Research laboratories in leaky wellies and wet socks for a PhD fair.

The lab is icy cold. Its windows gape to release the vile stench of beta-mercaptoethanol; a blend of rotten eggs and burning rubber. Paper hats and cracker jokes remain strewn across my work-space along with the 'Young at Heart, Older in Other Places' calendar that Dave bought me in last year's Secret Santa. I flip the cover over to January and log on to my laptop to discover the PhD fair is – due to Queen's heating problems – now being hosted by our pharmaceutical sponsor, Klein Selby Gilet, in their new building over the road.

The KSG complex boasts award-winning architectural design and a biodiverse roof carpeted in turf, which today is lost in snow. Inside, a giant vase of purple orchids mirrors an identical arrangement at the other end of the reception desk. Blue-chip symmetry is key, which means the equidistantly spaced plasma screens on the back wall all show the same muted pharmaceutical news. The receptionist presents me with a tray of name badges. Looking through them, I can only imagine that I'm 'Billy Elliot'.

'So, what *is* your name?' she says between phone calls.

'Billie Oliver. Billie with an 'i.e.' Like Billie Jean King.'

She takes a thick black marker to the badge in an attempt to transform 'Elliot' into 'Oliver', which means I'll be answering to 'Billie Ollvot' for the rest of the day.

The auditorium is a few degrees too warm and packed to the rafters with students from all over the world. I love that about London – the cosmopolitanism, the diversity, the anonymity: three things you don't get on the rural Yorkshire/ Derbyshire border.

Sparkling water and freshly made coffee are the order of the day – a far cry from the festering ashtray of used teabags and polystyrene cups at Queen's events. The windows have made-to-measure blackout blinds, allowing display banners to gleam under strategically rigged spotlights. Life-size stock images show airbrushed models in pristine lab coats and immaculate surgical masks, their glistening pipettes poised over sparkling-clean test tubes. 'Healthier, Happier'. An energetic man with minty breath hands me a stress ball and asks if I've signed the 'Stronger for Longer' petition. I'm not sure whether he's campaigning against a new drug or lobbying for better toilet paper.

The agenda comprises a morning of presentations by PhD alumni, lunch, and then the post-grad fair itself. I take a seat and leaf through a 'Happy Pharma' pamphlet, and there he is, hogging the centre spread: Professor Williams, Ambassador of Eclampsia Research and holder of the PhD purse-strings. My throat tightens and my skin prickles. I need to nail my pitch today. His headshot suggests he's grown a beard since I last cyber-stalked him. As I reassess the audience for facial hair, the room falls silent for KSG's first speaker and PhD alumna, one Joely Chevalier.

It isn't the rhythmic tap of stiletto heels on parquet flooring as she strides to the lectern, or the caramel-sweet scent of jasmine and vanilla that lingers as she passes. It isn't her gentle hum, her aloof swagger, or the way she confidently leaves one hand in the pocket of her tailored navy curved-hem trousers. And it certainly isn't the intoxicatingly sexy French accent, as she hasn't yet spoken, but there's something about Joely Chevalier that robs me of my ability to swallow and has me hanging on her every movement.

She rolls back the cuffs of her crisp white shirt at the lectern, her eyes slowly skimming the room, before dipping her chin towards the microphone and huskily bidding everyone, '*Bonjour.*'

A surge of panic swells in my gut at the thought of having to be as good as her to bag a post-grad. She has no notes whatsoever, and is casually freestyling her way through slide after slide of ovarian statistics by geography, her hands gliding effortlessly over colour-coded maps like a seasoned weather girl. Her French lilt serves only to accentuate her command of the English language, referring to 'phenotypes', 'epidemiology' and 'complex pathophysiology' with ease. The pocket lining of my trousers feels really itchy, and my shirt feels too tight as Joely Chevalier singles me out and directs her speech at *me*. Our eyes lock. I daren't inhale, exhale, blink or swallow, lest it ruin the moment, which abruptly halts when I realize that she's actually looking at a distinguished, muscular guy behind me, who's encouraging her with nods, smiles and no doubt a raging hard-on.

She slips through the stage exit to rapturous applause and I feel my insides go all mushy in the same way they did when Beyoncé wore 'that leotard'.

By lunchtime, snow is whirling outside the floor-to-ceiling glass windows of the KSG restaurant, flakes falling thicker and faster. I wonder whether Dad and Grandma are snowed in at the farm. Snow rarely settles here, children making snowmen out of roadside slush, but back at the farm five-foot snowdrifts are commonplace and, as the nearest shop is two miles away, you can be cut off for days. Weeks even.

Around me, salads are being shunned for soups and attendees are starting to worry about their return journeys, several travel websites announcing cancelled trains. It takes half an hour of loitering next to the drinks machine before I spot my goddess over at the cold buffet table. She frowns at a salmon *amuse-bouche*, tilting it this way and that, as you might assess the authenticity of a diamond. I rearrange my fringe, grab a tray and meander over.

'Not a fan?' I say, in a way that hopefully suggests our paths have inadvertently crossed, as opposed to the choreography I have manufactured to reach her side.

She looks at me with dark chocolate eyes, her piano fingers sliding a silver bumblebee across a delicate chain under her chin.

'*Du café*, Joelle?' Christophe Concordel (according to his name badge, which could mean he is not Christophe Concordel at all), the handsome, sculpted guy from earlier, muscles in. He's taller and more chiselled than I remember; the sort that bench-presses his body weight before breakfast and owns a range of men's fragrances.

She takes the cup and saucer from him, their eyes meeting.

'Great presentation.' I cling to the role-play I've rehearsed, but Christophe has edged his way into our conversation and now the three of us are making small talk about food: French food in China, Chinese food in Britain, and British food in Iceland (the supermarket).

He reads my name badge. 'Billie Ollvot, Queen's Research.'

'It's actually "Oliver". Billie Oliver. Typo,' I say.

He rolls up the sleeves of his navy cashmere jumper to reveal monogrammed shirt cuffs, and spears a gherkin with a cocktail stick. 'You know, we could triple your salary at KSG?'

I glance at Joely before looking him in the eye and countering his gherkin by stabbing at a dried-up cheese croquette. 'That's not what motivates me,' I say, dropping the croquette into my mouth with paralleled nonchalance, but it's so freaking hot it's all I can do not to choke the whole fucking thing out into my serviette.

Joely's face becomes a frown as tears stream down my cheeks and Christophe's eyebrows rise, although whether as a result of my killer assertiveness or my laissez-faire attitude to food hotter than lava, I couldn't say.

'Let me show you the bathroom,' Joely says when it becomes clear I won't be speaking again any time soon.

Christophe turns away with a very Gallic shrug, and I try not to trip over my coat, which keeps slipping off my bag as she leads me through the crowd towards the expansive reception lobby.

'That was amazing!' Her dark chocolate eyes drink me in. 'The way you spoke to Christophe. Nobody ever speaks to him like that! He's the COO of Europe, so everyone just tells him what he wants to hear.'

Part of me wants to curl up and die. Have I just committed career suicide?

She adjusts her shirt collar, unleashing an exotic musk that messes with my pheromones, and I decide not to tell her I was oblivious to his rank. 'Are you here for PhD sponsorship?'

'Yes. Eclampsia Research.'

Her eyes shine. 'Hit me up with your pitch!'

The thought of having to pitch to this goddess is like being asked to take a dump in front of someone. I just can't. My nose crinkles with mortification.

'Go on!' she says.

'OK, I'm Billie Oliver.'

'Nice to meet you Billie Oliver.' She sparkles.

'And I'd like to . . .' Her eyes undress me. At least I think they do, though she could just be genuinely interested in biochemistry. 'I'd like to pitch for a place on your Eclampsia Research PhD course, Professor Williams.'

'Professor Williams?' Her brow puckers.

'I was just role-playing—'

'Professor Williams has cancelled because of the snow!

17

He's leaving now, to drive north before the trains are cancelled and everyone wants a lift.'

'He . . .' High-pitched ringing inhabits my ears. I've waited too long for this moment.

'If you're quick, you might catch him.' She gestures out of the window to a figure in a long coat, battling the elements with a shovel in the far corner of the car park.

I drag on my coat, wondering what sort of person drives into central London on one of the snowiest days of the year and pays the congestion charge for the privilege. 'It's really nice to meet you, but I need to talk to him!' I say, hurrying towards the rotating door.

'In the snow?' she calls after me.

It hurts to leave her, but it'll hurt more if I let this opportunity go. 'I'll be back!'

Wind howls across the car park. Snow turns to sleet. The sky is an apocalyptic charcoal grey. I hold down my swirling tornado of hair as flecks of ice whip around my ears. My cheeks sting. My shirt cuffs freeze. Squinting into the blizzard, I slip and slide towards the Citroën Berlingo that revs triumphantly next to a pile of discarded Christmas trees.

'Hello!' I shout pointlessly.

Professor Williams, the embodiment of a friendly wizard, clambers out of the driver's seat, his beard snow-dusted in patches. He holds a can of anti-freeze and a Eurythmics CD case featuring Annie Lennox sporting very short, very red hair.

'Sorry to bother you.' I extend my hand with rehearsed self-assurance. 'I'm Billie Oliver, from Queen's Eclampsia Research team.'

He shuns my handshake to squirt anti-freeze over the wind-screen, electric-blue gullies trickling through snow like old veins. As he reaches for the middle of the windscreen, his metal-framed spectacles make their way off his nose, clinking on wet glass.

'As you can see, I'm a little preoccupied.' His voice is gentle, and he enunciates every consonant with care, clearing the snow off his glasses.

'Here.' I hand them to him with numbing fingers, and he finishes scraping the window clear of snow.

He smiles, sleet stuck to his eyelashes, and climbs into the driver's seat. 'I'm heading past the tube station, if you need a lift.'

I don't need a lift. Hell, I don't even need the tube, but there's no way I'm turning down an opportunity to talk to him. His car smells of sweaty feet and fast food. The passenger footwell is littered with empty crisp packets and trampled polystyrene burger boxes, a dried gherkin stuck to his laptop case.

He turns on the lights and starts the engine, hot air blasting out of every ventilator. 'You wanted to talk?'

'Yes.' I squeeze my hands under my thighs. 'I'd love to do your Eclampsia Research PhD. I've been working in this field since my Bachelor's, and it's something I feel passionately about.'

'OK,' he says slowly, as we crawl across the car park.

'I've spent the last two years testing minerals and anti-hypertensive medication, which will eventually get packaged as a KSG drug, but without a PhD, I can only go so far.'

'Where do you want to go?' He keeps his eyes on the road.

I puff out my chest. 'I want to find a cure for eclampsia.'

He chuckles beneath his beard. 'Would you like to boil the ocean too?'

My chest compresses. 'I mean, I'd like to play a part in finding a cure for eclampsia.'

'Why is curing eclampsia important to you?' He negotiates his way out of a bus lane.

I pinch at my neck until it hurts. 'Because my mum died of eclampsia.'

'I'm sorry to hear that.'

'Giving birth to me,' I blurt.

He flinches and I'm not sure whether it's the profound impact I've had on him or whether it's in response to the double-decker that has just sprayed us with slush.

'Sorry,' I say. 'I didn't mean to make it personal.'

'No need to apologize. People sit up and listen when it comes from the heart.' As we pull up to some traffic lights, he engages the handbrake and tries to peel off his coat without undoing his seat belt, contorting into all sorts of shapes a human shouldn't be. 'Tell us what you lost. What your father lost. What your siblings lost, if you have any. Tell us how it happened and what we need to do to make sure it doesn't happen to anybody else.'

I contemplate this. 'I did write it up as a use-case. I've got all the stats. All the timings. All the—'

'It's not a use-case, Billie. It's a story. Your story.'

'OK,' I say, aware that we're already pulling into the bus stop outside Oval tube station and our conversation is about to draw to a close.

Professor Williams turns to face me, his intelligent eyes

twinkling. 'Billie.' He takes off his glasses and swabs each lens with his tie. 'Your research is strong. I like your spirit. I like your passion. I like the way you tracked me down in a blizzard. I like *you*. The one niggling doubt I have is more around depth of field.'

I nod, having no idea what he's talking about.

'In fact, you've got the depth, but maybe need to focus a little more on the breadth.'

'Ooookay,' I say slowly. Surely this would baffle Alan Turing.

He swivels round, encumbered by his waistcoat. 'We know how many women are reported to have had pre-eclampsia. We know a lot aren't diagnosed. You don't need to bombard us with statistics, you need to think outside the box. Bridge the gap between academia and real life. Get out of the lab and live your research. Make it stand out. You don't want to be another candidate dotting the Is and crossing the Ts, you want to be the one everyone remembers.'

I nod, unsure whether he has just revealed unto me the meaning of life, or handed me a shit sandwich. Just how exactly is one supposed to *live* eclampsia without getting it?

'Come back to me when you're ready,' he says, reaching for the handbrake.

My bones go brittle and my legs start to cramp. Can't he see that I'm ready now? I've been ready for ten fucking years! And yet he does this all so eloquently, with a serenity impossible to argue with, and in spite of myself and the fury that builds within me, I like him. I just hate the words coming out of his mouth.

'I feel like I'm ready *now*.' I force a smile.

His eyes remain faithful to the rear-view mirror. 'They all do.'

Reluctantly, I get out of his car; a run-of-the mill person, with run-of-the-mill dreams, and a run-of-the-mill chance of achieving them. I chew the inside of my cheek until it bleeds run-of-the-mill blood.

After a painfully cold trip back to KSG via my favourite boulangerie for melt-in-the-mouth brioche, the post-grad fair is cancelled. I check the canteen in the hope that Joely Goddess Chevalier is lingering, but the place is deserted. Pots chink and kitchen staff chatter behind closed metal shutters. I sit with my head in my hands and desperately will the reversal of time. There is only one person who can make me feel better, and that's Dad.

It's 2.30 p.m., which means he'll have finished all his chores after morning milking and will now be sitting in his paisley print armchair with his feet in a washing-up bowl of warm water. I picture him leafing through the *Dairy Farmer*, running his fingers through his mop of greying honey-blonde curls as Hallam FM broadcasts the weather forecast. He never misses the weather forecast. A rivulet of sweat will be trickling down his wind-chapped face, despite the house being deathly cold – he always overheats when he soaks his feet. In the hallway, next to that bloody awful stuffed partridge he and Grandma refuse to chuck away, there'll be an unopened bill with a list of chores scribbled on the back of the envelope. Somewhere on the list will be 'Phone Bilberry', but he appreciates it when it's *me* who calls *him*.

My sticky brioche fingers find 'Home' sandwiched between 'Bev' and 'Kat' among my phone Favourites.

'Brioche?' Dad says, having run me through a list of which cows are lame, which cows are pregnant, and how one of the cows has adopted her cousin's calf, as its mother has a bad case of mastitis. 'Very cosmopolitan.' I guess everything is cosmopolitan when you live on a five-hundred-acre dairy farm. 'Hang on, your grandma's saying something. Oh, she says she knows she's a bit late, but "Happy Queer Year!" Says she learned it from a lady at church.'

Bless Grandma: for someone who thinks pasta is exotic and motorway driving is for adrenaline junkies, raising a dyke granddaughter must be strange at times. Dad, on the other hand, always overcompensates, his enthusiasm effervescent. 'Met any nice girls of late?'

If only I liked nice girls. 'No.'

'It'll happen.' Speedo barks in the background. 'How old are you now, thirty-three?'

'Thirty-two.'

'I guess people don't get married until a lot older these days,' he says, insinuating that all is not lost, and that one day I will achieve my life potential – to be half of a couple. I could bite, but what's the point? He has my best interests at heart and is trying to fulfil the role of both mother and father. He clears his throat. 'Lorna left a rather eye-opening newspaper article for you about the perils of London being the gay capital of Europe.' He lowers his voice. 'Billie, you don't go to gay saunas, do you?'

I spend the next ten minutes reassuring him that he is worrying unnecessarily, and that I have never, and will never, have the urge for orgy in a Vauxhall dungeon. Bloody Lorna; she makes the *Daily Mail* look liberal. For a twenty-nine-year-old vet whose life revolves around the bovine ailments of one small village in Derbyshire, she's outlandishly opinionated and terribly homophobic.

'Any more migraines since last week?' I change the subject.

'No, it was just a one-off. It's very echoey. Where are you?'

'In an empty canteen. I just pitched to a professor from Sheffield University and—'

'Billie, that's amazing!'

'I kind of bombed.' I replay the journey of solid gold cringe in my mind's eye.

'I'm sure you didn't,' Dad says warmly. 'I'm sure you were great.'

'I really needed to impress him, and it all went pear-shaped.'

'You're too hard on yourself, Bilberry. If you were only half as good as your best, you'll have outstripped everyone there.'

'That's the thing, there was no one else there.'

'There you go then. You've won already.'

That's the thing about Dad. He always knows what to say and how to say it. Bolstering me in times of need. Guiding me over life's hurdles. He's been like it for ever: encouraging me from the poolside when I swam my first length, reassuring me that my teenage acne would disappear, setting my mind at rest that the odd failed spelling test really doesn't matter. Nothing's unsurmountable with Dad. He just has that natural ease about him.

'How's the milk situ?' I say, the restaurant staff now filing through to eat their lunch.

He lets out a cough. 'The Sheldons have gone bust. Third dairy farm in Derbyshire to go under this year. Fifty-three, no pension, no qualifications, nothing.'

My skin starts to itch. I've come to dread these conversations as there's nothing I can say or do to help. 'I'm sorry, Dad.'

'Still, the snow hasn't got to us yet, so we're OK. You did the right thing, becoming a scientist. Carry on doing what you're doing, and the world will be a better place.'

'Thanks, Dad.'

I know his twinkly blue eyes are smiling. I can hear it in his voice. There's no one else in the world that makes me feel as loved as Dad. By the time I hang up, I'm in an infinitely better place. I block out the PhD thing, and append various fictional endings to my encounter with Joely Chevalier, involving inevitable nudity and a much more gratifying form of chemistry.

# CHAPTER THREE

# FRIENDS

By the time we hit early February, the lab is still icy cold, and nobody has been in to look at the heating. Dave wanders over to my work-space just as I'm in the throes of measuring umbilical vein endothelial cells.

'How's it going, Shitbag?' His latex gloves twang as he launches them into the bin.

'Good, Dinosaur.' I try not to lose count. 'You?'

'Great.' He washes his hands in the sink next to me. 'Things are hotting up with Molly so—'

'Hang on a minute,' I say, pipette poised. 'She wasn't called Molly last week.'

He removes his tortoiseshell glasses from the bridge of his crooked nose, puffs hot air onto each lens, swabs them with a paper towel and drops them into the breast pocket of his lab coat. 'You're thinking of *Jenny*.'

In the four years that we've been lab mates, Dave has fallen for about fifty women. For a soft lad in his forties, he does rather well.

'It's the whole "single dad" thing. Girls love it.' He picks up a placental sample, squints at the label, takes his glasses back out of his pocket and holds a lens up to the text. 'You should try it.'

'Try what?'

'Online dating. Pummel's the best thing I ever did. There must be some good lesbian dating sites.' He takes his phone out of his back pocket and peruses a little too diligently. Dave lives in a fantasy where all lesbians look like airbrushed Hollywood actresses, have an insatiable sexual appetite, and engage in hot, heavy petting purely for the gratification of heterosexual male voyeurs.

'Did I tell you we got funding?' He flicks through photos of twenty-something girls.

'No!'

'KSG signed off a six-month extension yesterday. New person. Joely someone or other. French surname.'

I can't stop smiling. Joely Chevalier. Even her name sounds as if she should arrive draped from head to toe in pure white silk on a jet-black steed. As I return to my work, it occurs to me: she's now my Business Sponsor, so it's my responsibility to build a relationship with her. I intend to take these responsibilities very seriously . . .

**Subj: Obstetric Abnormalities Conference**

Dear Joely,

It was great to meet you at the conference. Sorry I had to rush off!

I'm very keen to follow up with a KSG/Queen's Research collaboration and work out how we could help each other. Maybe we could meet for a coffee sometime?

Best regards,
Billie Oliver
Senior Analyst, Queen's Research & Development

Joely Chevalier. *Billie Chevalier.*

The girls get in touch, requesting 'urgent brunch'. How can brunch be urgent? By its very nature, brunch is supposed to be late and slovenly.

Borough Market is buzzing, the smell of moules marinière mingling with slow-cooked beef bourguignon. I wander between carts of organic vegetables and piping-hot pans of Ethiopian goat curry. Past beef empanadas, salted brownies and cinnamon churros. Truffles and marinades, lobsters on ice, and beyond Charcuterie de Bretagne, where great hunks of cheese are piled one on top of another, the French flag pinned to the top of each tower. I'd love to show my dad all this. The only market he goes to is Bakewell cattle market, where you're lucky if they're not out of chips. Although the price of a bacon butty here would probably give him palpitations.

We meet in Vinopolis so that Kat can go cheese-mad in

anticipation of some Vin et Fromage corporate hospitality masterclass her work is launching. It's dark inside and feels refrigerated – hardly the place for brunch. My eyes take a moment to adjust before I can make out exposed brickwork, glass, stainless steel, and Kat sitting at a long oak table.

'Bill!' She throws her arms around me in the manner of an affected actress. Her hair has been dyed a deep burgundy and she's a swirl of autumnal colours and knee-high suede boots – the sort of outfit a novelist promoting her fourth book would wear, rather than a corporate accountant.

I squeeze her shoulders. 'How was Frankfurt? It was Frankfurt, right?'

'Good,' she says.

Bev appears from the washroom, smelling of geranium and orange handwash. Her Mohican is back to its trademark fluorescent pink. 'Buddy!' She claps her arms around me. 'How did the PhD fair go?'

'It got cancelled.' I can't bear to relive the horror. 'Just like our Christmas party.'

'You didn't have a Christmas party? No wonder you never get laid, Bill!' Kat says, gesturing for us to take a seat.

Bev sits down next to Kat and squeezes her knee. 'That, Kitty Kat, would imply you're guaranteed a shag at a Christmas party.'

'Aren't you?' Kat teases.

'Maybe at Ernst & Young, Katherine Mellor,' Bev says. 'But the annual Zoological Society of London's knees-up in the reptile house is not so accommodating.'

A lady in a white apron and a severe ponytail brings out a tray of diced cheese samples, a plate of crackers, a bottle of

Malbec and four glasses. Kat gets stuck in, commenting on the creamy consistency of the Beaufort Alpage, while Bev glances around the room, a strict vegan.

'Bev's just back from Doncaster,' Kat says, a blob of Soignon goat log dripping from her chin.

I pass her a serviette. 'Doncaster?'

'I had to transport a pair of Bactrian camels from Yorkshire Wildlife Park down to Whipsnade. Four hours in a lorry with the male stamping and bellowing,' Bev says.

'Was he OK?' I ask, not knowing what else to say. I know nothing about animals.

'Turns out he was in heat and trying to mount his lady friend,' Bev says.

Maria enters, laden with props. Her long dark hair cascades down the back of her fake mink fur coat. 'Hi, girls!' She takes off oversized sunglasses and air-circles her orange face with an orange finger. 'Meet Melania Trump!'

'What happened to you?' Kat's face scrunches in horror.

Maria unloads her bags onto the wooden bench, unaware that she's being eyeballed by a wine-tasting group for leaving the door open. 'The Lambeth LGBT players want me to audition for *Melania the Musical*.'

'Does it matter that you're not gay?' Kat wonders.

'To me?' Maria asks, adjusting her hearing aid.

'I think she means to the membership of the Lambeth LGBT theatre group,' I say.

Maria thinks about this for a moment before reaching into her red leather holdall and retrieving a tube of lip gloss. 'I don't see what difference it makes, do you?'

'Well, isn't it like joining a Christian canoe club and not

being a Christian?' I say, realizing this is an appalling comparison.

'That's the thing, though,' Maria says, dabbing at her bottom lip. 'You'd be going *canoeing* rather than *Christianing*. I'm sure they don't care.'

'The lesbians or the Christians?' I say, rummaging through my bag for my phone and finding it stuck to a sanitary towel.

'Either. A canoe is a canoe just as a performance is a performance. If they kick off about it, I'll just tell them they're being heterophobic,' Maria says.

A cursory glance at my phone tells me there's still no email response from Joely Chevalier – not that I'm checking every ten minutes or anything.

The waitress reappears with her touch-screen tablet and looks over our heads at the wine-tasting group, who are getting rowdier by the minute. 'I've been asked if the "gossip girls" can keep the noise down,' she says.

'Isn't that a bit hypocritical?' Kat snaps.

'No worries,' Bev says, taking Kat's hand in hers. 'I think we're ready to order.'

'Yes, sir, madam, sir?' The waitress looks Bev up and down.

Bev remains undeterred. 'Can we see your champagne list?' She taps her fingers on her thigh. 'We're celebrating.'

'Celebrating what?' Maria asks her.

'Gaaagh!' Kat screams, thrusting a diamond-adorned finger at us.

A girl from the wine-tasting group on the next table makes a point of slamming down her wine list.

'Congratulations!' I say, leaping up to hug Kat and then Bev.

Maria takes what feels like a million photos with her phone – Bev and Kat, their heads squished together in premarital bliss, appearing on social media within seconds.

'Have you set a date?' Maria says, when we finally settle back down.

Kat nods. 'December. Gives me time to plan. You know what I'm like with a spreadsheet.'

We do know what Kat's like with a spreadsheet. Whether it's comparing gym membership deals or planning someone's hen party (Kat's a popular 'matron of honour' choice), there's always a spreadsheet to hand. When Neve and I went our separate ways, Kat did me a Splitting-Up spreadsheet.

Bev runs her hands over her Mohican. 'So, how would you ladies feel about being best women?' Her eyes flit between Maria and me.

'It'd be an honour,' I say, as Maria squeals with delight.

We fill an hour discussing the dynamics of the wedding. Bev, having two mothers and no father, can't decide whether her mum or her mama should give her away. It's even more upsetting for Kat – her dad still hasn't come to terms with the fact that she's with a woman and is refusing to come to the wedding. We're talking venue options when my phone bleeps.

**Re: Obstetric Abnormalities Conference**

Dear Billie,

Sorry for my late reply. I'm working long days in Belgium. Next week, I return to London just for the weekend. Are you free on Sunday? It would be good to meet.

Best wishes,
Joely

I can barely breathe.

'So, who is she?' Bev looks at me.

I feel my cheeks flush. 'Is it that obvious?'

'Buddy, it'd be obvious even if I hadn't known you since sixth form,' she says.

'Is this the French girl?' Maria says, reaching for the Gruyère.

'Before you get all excited, she's probably straight,' I say, trying to decide whether my blue-cheese sample tastes a little or a lot like mould.

'That's the most Billie sentence I've ever heard,' Bev says.

'How do you mean?' I say.

Bev's eyes widen. 'Putting up the barriers before it's even taken off.'

'I do that?' I frown.

'Yes!' The three of them chorus.

They stare at me for longer than is comfortable, and I'm debating whether to leave them to their porn de fromage so I can obsess over a response to Joely in the Ladies' loo, when the waitress arrives with four flutes of champagne.

'Cheers!' Maria raises her glass. 'To the gossip girls!'

The wine-tasting group cast furtive glances.

'To the gossip girls!' We raise our glasses.

Maria glances at my phone. 'Bloody hell! She's asking you out on Valentine's Day?'

'Valentine's Day is on Sunday?' I feel a surge of panic, which refuses to disappear even after three large gulps of champagne. 'Shit, I bet she has no idea.'

'Or maybe she does?' Maria thumps me on the arm with encouragement.

'Does she know you're a raging homosexual?' Kat says.

'I have no idea,' I say, wondering if this is problematic.

Maria looks at me. 'Sometimes people need things spelled out.'

Shoehorning your sexual orientation into an email thread with a colleague/customer/sponsor is easier said than done. A couple of champagnes later, I finally settle on:

**Re: Obstetric Abnormalities Conference**

Hi Joely,

I've just realized Sunday is Valentine's Day and although I'm in the habit of dating women, you might not be ☺

Best,
Billie

In the sober light of the next day, I cringe at my email. I barely know the poor girl, who must be squirming with embarrassment. There's no way I'm drinking ever again. I consider a follow-up apology mail, but Dave grabs my feet and mimes sawing them off in homage to the obsessed woman from *Misery*. He reckons I should have assumed it was a date and 'that's what most blokes would have done.' I am not 'most blokes'.

My hangover isn't helped by my phone, which won't stop bleeping with text messages from Grandma. 'Are you prepared for the "Big Freeze Part 2"?' I'm not sure whether she's talking about a new Disney film or the weather. 'Have you heard Dad's changed his chocolate allegiance to Bournville?' Having been a Dairy Milk man for four decades, this is in fairness massive news. 'Did you know I've got a new phone? Can you do the FaceTime? Now?'

It takes standing in the Ladies' loo to get a strong enough signal to FaceTime, thanks to Tel-Useless-4U, which I would happily leave were I not tied into a ridiculously cheap two-year partner deal with Neve.

'Hello? Hello?' I say, tapping the screen in a futile attempt to remove a blurred face that is not my grandmother's.

'Hi, Billie!' A voice crackles as the horseshoe-shaped scar on Lorna Parsons' forehead comes into focus. Why is my dad's vet answering Grandma's phone? 'Your gran's busy making tea,' she says, as though reading my mind. 'Are you in a toilet?'

'No.' I angle myself away from the flush.

She pulls off a fingerless glove with her teeth and traces the line of her scar with a bitten fingernail. 'How's work going?'

'Good,' I say, determined to keep the conversation short. Her large owl eyes flicker around my surroundings. 'All OK with you?' I append out of obligation.

She winds a tendril of mousy hair around her finger. 'Yes, thanks. It's pretty steady at the moment. Of course, things will get silly again when we hit calving season.'

'I guess. Look, should I call back later?'

'No, it's lovely to chat. How's the love life?'

I may have known Lorna pretty much all my life, but we

35

haven't been friends since adolescence. At school she was three academic years my junior and, back then, unless you were acknowledged at assembly for a sporting achievement or a music accreditation, you were invisible to anyone outside your year group. The only reason I knew Lorna was because her father was my dad's vet and she used to turn up (with cheese and pickle sandwiches in neat, white triangles) at the farm on weekends to fawn over Andy Pickering, my dad's farm hand – Andy was the 'evil twin', whereas his brother Paul was the 'nice twin'; she seemed to have a thing for bad boys.

When we were little, we were friendly enough – we'd build dens down by the stream and used to pretend that we worked in a perfume factory. We'd crush fallen rose petals with a stick and mix them with rainwater in a bucket, coming up with names for each scent. 'Pearl water', 'Lemon drizzle', 'Eau de fart'. When we got bored, we'd go up to the old barn to do gymnastics, using hay bales as crash mats. We'd take it in turns to run the length of the barn and launch ourselves off an old trampette that Dad got when the village nursery were having a sort-out. Grandma used to say we'd end up in A&E with the amount of crash landings we had, but the most damage we did was to the barn door, which fell off its hinges after an overzealous handspring of mine. It was fine between us until adolescence got in the way and made everything awkward – handstands becoming a no-go, lest knickers get flashed and errant pubes put in an appearance. From then on in, I got into football, whilst she remained loyal to horses, and we simply grew apart.

As teenagers, we kept a firm distance. It was clear to both of us that we were becoming fundamentally different people. The biggest divide, though, was my sexual orientation, which

Lorna has never been able to come to terms with. I can still feel her eyes upon me, judging me, staring at me like you might try to fathom impossible self-assembly instructions. Shortly after, I went away to university, then she did, and by the time she graduated from Nottingham Trent and returned with Guy Bonneville a few years later, we were pretty much off each other's radar – until two years ago, when her father retired, and she became my dad's vet and formed Parsons-Bonneville Premier Vets with her boyfriend, Guy.

'Are you seeing anyone at the moment?' Her big owl eyes assess me from my phone screen.

Disclosing my non-existent love life to her over FaceTime from a draughty toilet feels about as natural as discussing bowel movements with the Queen. 'Nobody in particular,' I say, doubtless making her skin crawl at the thought of a lesbian pick-and-mix.

'You know I've a friend in publishing, lovely chap who—'

'Hi, Billie.' Grandma covers the screen with a burned oven glove. I'm saved. Her kind eyes smile under a tangle of wiry eyebrows. 'Are you in the work loos again?'

I stick my tongue out at her. 'How are you guys?'

'Not great. Your father had to dig through a four-foot snowdrift at an unearthly hour this morning to get the milk out, only for us to be completely cut off from the co-op. Gallons of the stuff – it's a wonder it's not frozen over. It's a good job Lorna has snow chains, otherwise we'd be in all sorts of bother. What we really need is one of those drones. Apparently, they're all the rage down your way. It's breaking your father. He struggles to do a jigsaw at the moment, and you know how he loves his jigsaws.'

'It's just a blip!' Dad shouts in the background. 'We've got through plenty of blips before.'

'A blip? It's more than a blip!' she hollers. 'Honestly, Billie, I don't know how he does it. You wouldn't catch our John up at four a.m.'

Grandma means Peter. John is my dad. You certainly wouldn't catch Uncle Pete up at 4 a.m. You may, however, catch him up the skirt of a teenage waitress in a burger joint, which my auntie June did a couple of years ago, and for which she is still trying to forgive, although *forgetting* is a totally different prospect, especially when alcohol is involved.

'Do you want me to come up at the weekend?' I say.

'You wouldn't be able to get here even if you wanted to,' Grandma says, before dropping her voice to a hushed whisper. 'I'm a bit worried about your dad.'

'Is this the Bournville thing?'

'It's not just the chocolate,' she says quietly. 'I think he's got a touch of the dementia.'

'Really?'

'He does get very forgetful, Billie.' She waves goodbye to Lorna, who lets herself out.

'About what sort of things?' I say.

She scratches her chin. 'I can't remember.'

I try not to smile. 'Maybe it'll come back to you.'

'He just gets ever so muddled, like that thing with the food bill the other day.'

'You got Dad to go out for a meal?' I say, aghast. Dad never eats out.

'Oh no, hang on, that was your uncle John.'

'Dad is John, Grandma. You mean Uncle Pete?'

'Yes. Like I said, ever so muddled.'

I swallow my laugh. 'I'll keep an eye out.'

Just as I hang up, my phone bleeps with incoming mail.

**Subj: Sunday?**

Hello Billie,

Are you OK for Sunday? See you 7 p.m. at the London Eye!

Joely

Sweet Jesus! Did she get my sexual-orientation-clarification message or did Tel-Useless-4U never send it? Maybe she feels obliged to meet me for fear of coming across as a homophobe if she doesn't. Maybe she doesn't give the slightest shit that I'm gay and this is all above-board bonhomie. Maybe she wants me! Any which way, fortune favours the brave, and as Grandma once said before blowing ten quid on a seashell cat ornament during a day trip to Skegness, 'Life is too short for pussyfooting around.'

# CHAPTER FOUR

# VALENTINE'S DAY

It's dark and the wind is arctic. I thrust my hands into the pockets of my leather jacket and poke a finger through the hole in the lining in an attempt to identify the small spherical object I've spent the last twenty minutes playing with but can't quite grasp. Jocly is officially twenty minutes late when it starts to hammer down with rain. The London Eye is closed due to severe weather conditions. Sandwich boards slam flat and leaves whirl in small tornados as litter gets wind-whipped along the South Bank. A group of tourists huddle beneath the bridge under inside-out umbrellas. People shelter in cafés, bookshops, theatre foyers; anywhere to get out of the driving rain.

I jitter, unwittingly squeezing the small metal ball between my thumb and forefinger into something flat, and realize I've crushed the hollow ball locket Neve bought me two years ago when we were going to buy a place together, but I freaked. Maybe I did push her away. Maybe there is something wrong with me. Maybe I'll never be able to let anyone in.

I leave the locket in the lining of my pocket as Joely Chevalier struts towards me in kitten heels and a black poncho, the wind blowing her sleek, dark hair across her face.

'*Bonsoir.*' I put on my best French accent.

'Hi!' She sweeps her hair out of her lip gloss with a leather-gloved hand.

I'm not sure whether to kiss her on the cheek or shake her hand. Thankfully, she takes matters into her own hands to *faire la bise.*

'You know some good places around here?' she shouts over the wind.

I feel under pressure to come up with somewhere cool but cosy; the sort of place that doesn't scream 'date' but allows intimacy. 'Yes,' I say, recalling a small vintage bar Maria and I used to hang out in when she was in a theatre club down the road.

I lead her along the river's edge, pointing out London landmarks she probably knows more about than I do. Big Ben, the Houses of Parliament. A gust of wind blows a tray of caramelized peanuts off a small trolley, which clatters and tumbles along the embankment, the cold air sickly sweet with crystallized sugar. We head further along the river and down the side of the neon-lit National Theatre, away from tourist hotspots laden with love hearts and rammed with romance to the Scooter Caffe.

Joely Chevalier's eyes dart around the dimly lit room. Couples huddle. Conversation thrums. Pink cupids hang from the ceiling. Heart-shaped confetti covers the table tops. 'When I Fall in Love,' blares out of the speakers, and I cringe inside as we make our way to the bar. The mirrored shelves on the

41

back wall boast a rainbow of heavy-duty spirits, from electric-blue Bombay Sapphire to blood-red Campari. I drum my fingers on the counter. The last time I felt this nervous I was having my uterine polyps removed.

'What would you like to drink?' I pray she opts for wine over coffee.

Her chocolate-brown eyes run across the row of liqueurs. 'A cocktail?' My heart leaps with hope, which I swear she sees. 'I always ignore Valentine's Day. It's just commercial bullshit.'

'Agreed.' My heart sinks firmly back into place. At least I know where I stand – I can drop my guard but not my knickers.

We head down a wrought-iron spiral staircase to a candlelit basement with our drinks. Her eyes shift around the room of happy couples. The only seat available is a wicker kissing-chair in the corner. With a heavy shrug of her shoulders, she acknowledges the funny side and sits down, pressing her bag against her stomach.

'How did it go with the professor?' she says.

'Badly.' I look at the floor. 'I've been trying to get on a PhD course for three years now and I'm still no closer.'

'Every path is different,' she says.

'I guess.' An awkward silence ensues, during which her eyes are drawn to a framed photo of the London Eye.

'Have you been on the big wheel?' she asks.

'Once. I took my grandma and her friend. They took their knitting with them.'

'Knitting?'

'You know.' I mime knitting needles. 'With wool to make jumpers.'

She throws her head back and laughs. 'I love this.'

My shoulders relax an inch. 'I'm not sure they even looked out of the window.'

We spend the next ten minutes listing London landmarks and establishing whether we've frequented them. The OXO Tower sounds ridiculously sexy in a French accent.

'My husband and I visited the Tower of London,' she says wistfully.

I feel like someone's just stuck a pin in me, the word 'husband' hanging out in my head, an unwanted guest. 'How long have you been married for?'

'We separated three years ago.' She twirls the stem of her martini glass between her thumb and forefinger.

I squeeze the broken locket through my jacket pocket lining and gaze around the room, trying to appear blasé. 'Whereabouts in France are you from?'

'Bordeaux. Though I was born in Versailles.'

'Nice.'

'It's like the countryside, though we didn't have pigs and cows in the house like Marie Antoinette. How about you?'

'I was born in Derbyshire. In a cowshed.' I try to say the words without thinking them through but it's already too late: I'm dying on the barn floor with Mum.

A montage of my mother plays out in my mind's eye, forged from home videos I've watched over and over. My mother sits on a threadbare turquoise sofa, heavily pregnant. Her face is kind and awash with freckles, her expression contemplative. The bottom of her floral smock top has ridden up showing an inch of mottled skin stretched across the bump that is *me*. Her wedding ring is a smaller version of the one that dangles

43

around Dad's neck, its yellow gold glinting in the light. The wallpaper behind her is the same one we have at the farm today, but the colours are more vibrant, the blues and greens popping with life.

'Is he kicking?' Dad says off camera.

She smiles, her teeth endearingly goofy. 'How do you know it's a *he*?' Her fingers rub the wings of a ladybird brooch pinned an inch or so below the neckline of her top.

'We're pretty screwed on names if it's a girl!' Dad says, his hand creeping into shot. 'The only name we can agree on is Billy.'

'What's wrong with Billy for a girl? Billie, like Billie Jean King,' she says, accidentally knocking the ladybird brooch, which makes its way onto the sofa. She picks it up and inspects it. 'I think it's a girl. The ladybird thinks it's a girl too.' She smiles directly into the camera.

'*Ça va?*' Joely Chevalier's eyes peer into mine.

I nod. My mum died, yet I got to live. And here I am, sitting in a pub with a stranger when I should really be doing something meaningful and . . .

'It's that bad, Derbyshire?'

I pull myself together. 'Sorry.'

It's not grief – I never knew my mum, so I don't miss her. It's not even sentimentality. It's more the overwhelming burden of feeling that I should achieve great things with my life. That pressure that sits on my chest, strangles my windpipe and haunts me at the most inopportune moments.

'Billie?'

Moments like this. I feel all spacey and disconnected, like I'm watching someone else on a date, that isn't a date.

'Maybe we should have met in the lab.' Joely glances around the room.

Air compresses in my lungs. 'No, no. It's good to have a drink!' I almost grab her thigh. 'Can I get you another?' I gesture to her empty glass.

She reaches for her poncho. 'I should probably get my train.'

'Hey!' I blurt. I want to kiss her. I want her to put her coat back and stay for another drink. I want to spend time with her. 'We should—'

She stands up. 'I've got an early start tomorrow.'

I can't seem to claw back the moment and, before I know it, she's stroking my arm in the way you might a frightened hamster and guiding me up the staircase. Desperate to reclaim the evening, I suggest the pub next door, but my voice gets lost in the blowback of a moped screeching down a side street, and we're now walking at pace back to Waterloo station in painful silence. She envelops her chest in her poncho, navigating bicycles and buses. I'm out of breath by the time we reach the concourse.

'Listen,' I say as she stands in front of me and reaches into her bag for her purse. 'I know I shouldn't say this, not with you being my business sponsor and me being your . . .'

She looks straight into my eyes, sending my ovaries on a rollercoaster journey of hope and uncertainty.

'But I really like you,' I say, determined not to let the moment slip away. 'I don't want to freak you out, but I like you a lot.'

She looks around and, just when I think I've made a monumental mistake, leans over and kisses me. I can barely breathe.

Joely Chevalier is kissing *me*. Our torsos are pressed against each other and we are actually kissing. She smells divine. And I'm there, in the moment, engaged in the longest, slowest, most stomach-flipping, hot French kiss of my life. A kiss I shall never forget.

It's been nigh on impossible to concentrate at work since locking lips yesterday with possibly the most beautiful woman in the world. I replay the kiss God knows how many times, she finally pulling away and conceding that she really must get her train, leaving me breathless on the concourse. I can't stop checking my phone either. We've had a couple of exchanges, which on the face of them are pretty straight-forward, but are loaded with suggestion. 'Look forward to building our relationship further.' 'It's important we meet regularly to align our synergies.' 'Should we meet again next week when you're back from Paris?' (Me to her.) 'Or sooner?' (Also me.) 'Tonight even?' (Me again.) 'I'm the only one in the lab today as everyone's at a client meeting.' (OK, I should probably stop now.)

At five o'clock, I'm about to leave when the lab door opens.

Joely Chevalier stands before me in a pencil skirt, high heels and a grey leather jacket with an upturned collar. The scent of fresh flowers lingers in the corridor. Her skin glows and her eyes shine. My stomach fizzes as we stand, face to face under the glow of the emergency light. She props her compact wheelie-case against the wall.

'Are we alone?' She runs her finger along my collarbone.

I nod, unable to breathe properly.

'I had to see you.' She pushes me gently against the wall,

the lab darkening as my shoulders press against the light switch. 'I'm going to Paris, but I had to see you first,' she says, kissing me on one cheek, her lips brushing mine before kissing the other cheek. Her breath tastes of peppermint. 'I can't stop thinking about you.' She peels off her leather jacket and tosses it onto her case.

I kiss her, slowly at first.

Her tongue finds my neck.

My fingers navigate the edge of her top and walk their way up her back, our eyes locking as I undo the top button of her shirt. She kisses me long and hard.

I undo the next button, my hands sliding over her hips.

Another button. Her stomach.

Another button. Her buttocks.

Another. Her back.

And another. Her breasts.

My tongue finds its way across her chest. My fingers disappear under her skirt. Her thighs are toned yet soft. Her eyes dart towards the door and, reassured we're alone, she reaches for the bottom of my sweater and pulls it over my head, our bare skin touching through her unbuttoned shirt.

I go to undo her bra, at which point she grabs my hand and leads me to the nearest work bench. She pushes me onto the work stool and kisses me from my neck to my stomach, her tongue making its way down to my hips and lingering until I gasp. Then, bringing her head in line with mine, she looks me in the eye and undoes the metal clasp on my trousers. Her fingertips slide beneath my knickers. 'I can?'

I kiss her urgently. 'Yes.'

My trousers fall to the floor as she tears off my underwear

and parts my legs. Gently, she touches me. I rip off her satin bra and press my chest against hers. Tingling all over, my hands move up her skirt, between her legs. Together, we're a blur of Anglo-Franco soft skin and a harmony of gasps and groans.

Joely Chevalier stares into my eyes. 'Paris can wait.'

# CHAPTER FIVE

# FRANGLAIS AT FERNBROOK FARM

The last five weeks have been a whirlwind – picnics in Regent's Park, cocktails in Soho, aperitifs at the top of the OXO Tower, several steamy sleepovers at her flat in Brentford (she has remote-controlled blinds and a Nespresso machine). We've shared stories, dreams, her bed, a toothbrush, so I figure I've invested enough wit and charm for Joely to come into contact with my avocado three-piece bathroom suite and schizophrenic shower. It may not quite be the perfect backdrop for fantasy girl-on-girl shower sex, but it's a lot more practical than an hour's train journey to Brentford after a night out in Soho.

We lie in my bed drinking coffee and flicking through her *Wallpaper* magazine, picking out high-end designer interiors we will never own. I feel a bit like Eliza Doolittle in her company: a 'farmer to pharma' gentrification project. I've never bought a *Wallpaper* magazine in my life and yet here I am now, oohing and aahing over voile curtains and onomatopoeic manga backdrops (Shazam! Kapow! Kerchang!); a veritable culture vulture.

'Can I ask you a question?' I whisper, trying to sound sultry but struggling with a bit of phlegm and sounding more like Gollum.

'Of course.' Her eyes consume 'bold florals on canvas'.

'Is this your first relationship with a woman?' I ask, and then cringe that I've somewhat jumped the gun in terms of our relationship status and want to swallow my fist.

She folds over the corner of her page and drops the magazine onto my Sainsbury's economy duvet cover. 'Twice.'

'It's just with you having been married to a guy, I thought maybe—'

'Bisexuality has its advantages,' she says matter-of-factly.

I prop up the boob that has crept under my armpit (mine, not hers). 'How do you mean?'

She lets out a slow exhalation of breath. 'My parents are not altogether normal.'

'Are anybody's?'

'They know about my boyfriends, but not the girls,' she says casually. 'They loved Christophe.'

'You and Christophe were a thing?'

'For three years.'

'Oh,' I say, trying to sound casual.

'It didn't work. He drove me crazy.'

The thought of Joely getting intimate with Christophe makes my skin crawl; although I want to ask a million questions, I know I can't handle the answers. 'You honestly have no preference between guys and girls?'

'Not at all.' She picks up her magazine, her attention

returning to damask wallpaper. 'Every relationship is different. My mother and father are the perfect example; they love each other but they both have their adventures. My father likes women younger than me and my mother is sleeping with the assistant manager of *Monsieur Bricolage*.'

I splutter on my coffee. Is adultery hereditary, and will I too find myself trapped in the deceptive embrace of a poly-amorous relationship?

'Do you have moisturizer?' She gets up to peruse the toiletries on my chest of drawers, which allows me to gawk at her long, toned legs, her womanly hips (mine are so boyish) and her small waist, until I become aware that she can see me in the reflection of my wardrobe mirror. She picks up Bev and Kat's wedding invitation, which is balanced against my lamp. '"Bill plus one"', she reads, raising an eyebrow. 'Who are you taking?'

'It's a way off yet.'

She turns to me, flashing a grin. 'I'm not doing anything on the eleventh of December.'

'You want to come?'

'Sure!' She studies the invite. 'It's in a cinema?'

'Yeah.' I slip into the silk kimono she persuaded me to buy and immediately feel so much more sophisticated, like I should be serving grapes on a silver platter rather than burned toast on a cracked Sainsbury's saucer.

She spreads her fingers over her sternum. 'I love the cinema. We should go this weekend.'

'Sorry.' I squeeze her to my chest. 'I promised I'd go back to the farm this weekend. My uncle's renewing his wedding vows.'

'Is that a British thing?'

I look at the carpet. 'It's an Uncle Pete thing. It normally means he's slept with someone.'

'For real?'

'Honestly, it's awful, but I've promised I'll go and they're having a bit of a party, so . . .'

She kisses me on the lips. 'I also love parties.'

I feel like I'm in a rollercoaster carriage, which has heaved its way slowly up an impossibly steep slope and is now poised at the top, ready to drop. Suspended somewhere between pleasure and pain, excitement and trepidation, my stomach somersaults backwards and forwards with the thrill and dread of letting go. What's the matter with me? The goddess that is Joely Chevalier is asking to come home with me and here I am, having one of my psycho-meltdowns.

The rollercoaster plummets. 'Would you like to join me?'

She smiles. 'I'd love to.'

I'm like a burst dam, feelings forcing their way out of every tiny crack until my defence mechanism crumbles, and a torrent of emotions I haven't felt for years gush forth – excitement, apprehension, joy, fear, love, lust. Man, was it worth the wait.

As our taxi winds its way up hill and down dale, I try to see the world through Joely's eyes: stone-faced buildings morph into stony-faced sheep huddled in fields, their backs to the unrelenting wind, coats blown into rosettes of knotted wool. Fields roll into weather-torn moorland, a horizon of grey, gold and purple. Bracken bows. Heather dances. A grouse squawks like a hooter from a lump of granite rock. The temperature dips. We bounce over potholes, and Kiss FM thankfully goes out of range.

On the final stretch, we get stuck behind a tractor, our journey peaking at the breakneck speed of fifteen miles an hour. A pheasant struts into the road, a flash of red around its eye, the shine of teal feathers blown against its copper breast. It dips into the hedgerow as half a dozen motorbikes roar up the hill towards us.

'Bikers love it up here,' I say to Joely.

She stares out of the window, hands clasped tightly over the bag in her lap, and says nothing.

The terrain changes as we climb higher, tufts of grass replaced by spongy blankets of sphagnum moss and sulphur-yellow spikes of bog asphodel. Cotton grass buffets in the strong wind. Swaledale sheep bleat at the roadside. Higher up still, small red dots become rock climbers on Baslow Edge, a vast gritstone escarpment, dramatic in both height and width, upon which Highland cattle rove freely.

'*Ça va?*' I ask, squeezing her hand.

'*Nerveuse.*'

'It'll be fine.' I run my thumb over hers, wondering whether it will be. The dynamics of my family are a minefield. Dad should be pretty straightforward, but Grandma probably won't allow herself to understand a word Joely says on account of her being 'foreign'. Joely, on the other hand, will probably perceive both of them as quaint *Jean de Florette*-type characters and read imagined depth into their simplicity, in a way that lightbulbs are regarded as award-winning installations at the Tate gallery.

A heavy stench of manure penetrates the windows as we

climb the hill out of Baslow. The little wooden sign welcoming us to 'Fernbrook Farm' is caked in bird poo. Our taxi rumbles up the dirt track to the farm, flanked by monochrome masses of muscle grazing on rich green grass. An enormous black face hangs over the stone wall, a single white spot centred on a broad hulk of forehead.

'Big Dot,' I say excitedly. 'No wait! Little Dot.'

'The cow?' Joely bites the inside of her cheek and inspects her nails.

I nod, explaining how Dad and I once rescued her from a deep bog, my anecdote a little more sprawling and a lot less humorous than I'd intended.

'I don't trust cows,' Joely says. 'Their noses are always wet.'

'That's because they sweat through their nose,' I say.

She holds onto her bag even tighter.

The meadow stretches out beyond; a place where we used to picnic on fresh strawberries, baguettes and homemade flapjack with the farm workers and their families back in the day when dairy was a thriving business with a community feel. The old treehouse Lorna and I used to play in has gone, and there's no trace of the old barn, where we used to do gymnastics, or the pillar outside we used as a third person to hold the elastic in French skipping – that plot of land now belongs to a sheep farmer, who never uses it. Gone are the days when truck after truck came and went and the five-hundred-strong herd took over the entire hillside. We must be down to a third of what we were, the cows scattered over just two fields.

We pull up at the far end of the yard next to Grandpa's rusty old Cropmaster tractor, which died long before he did;

a tangle of metal barely visible through the mass of unruly nettles and thick brambles that have grown over it, into it and around it, the cabin shell now home to a family of robins.

'This is it?' Joely looks up at the house, and frowns. 'The farm is enormous, but the house is tiny.'

I've never thought of it like that before. It's simply home.

Joely's long, bronzed legs swing out of the taxi, her cork wedge heels crunching on the gravel of the potholed yard. She rocks cut-off denim shorts and a cropped pop-art T-shirt with the print of a black-and-white distorted cow's face on the front, her red polka-dot Cath Kidston wheelie case bucking and rumbling over brick ends and hen feed.

Sun beats down on the corrugated-iron milking shed, a hive of activity at dawn yet now silent, save for the odd creak of expanding metal and scuffle of hen claws on concrete. Dust dances in shafts of sunlight streaming in through broken roof panels. There's no sign of Grandma. Instead, a scrap of paper torn off last year's RSPB British Birds calendar is taped to the porch door of the house, declaring, 'Back in 5, dinner's in the oven.'

Speedo barks. I push open the front door and he rushes full pelt towards us, his tail knocking Grandma's umbrella off the hallway table. Good old Speedo! He must be ten now. I pat him all over and ruffle his ears, which always feel colder and softer than I expect.

Joely ducks behind me. 'You have a dog?'

'Don't worry, he's friendly.' I grab his cracked leather collar and pull him back, muddy Rhodesian Ridgeback paw prints stamped all over my jeans.

Speedo squeaks, his tail thwacking against Joely's bare legs.

'He jumps?' she says, pinned to the wall.

'He's just excited!' I tickle his ears. 'He'll leave you alone in a bit.'

The smell of roast lamb and rosemary infuses the house. I hang Joely's coat in the cupboard under the stairs while she locks eyes with the stuffed partridge on the hallway chest.

'*Dégueulasse*,' she mutters, pulling a face akin to having discovered a shit in her shoe, and I feel like I did at primary school when I knew I'd taken Annabel Gallagher's denim jacket home instead of my own: complicit.

'It was my great-granddad's. No idea why they keep it.'

The porch door judders open. 'Where's my Billie Goat?' Grandma hands me a mesh shopping bag of vegetables. She hugs me tightly to her chest, her kind eyes smiling under a tangled brow. Her skin smells of cooking apples and talcum powder.

Joely stands at my side, her long arms dangling redundantly.

'Grandma, this is Joely. Joely, this is my grandma, Kathleen.'

Grandma smiles and, without a shred of subtlety, assesses Joely's cropped cow-print T-shirt. The arches of my feet curl.

Joely smiles awkwardly. 'Pleased to meet you.'

'All the way from Paris, hey?' Grandma chuckles.

'London,' I counter. 'She lives just outside London.'

A new painting catches my eye behind her head, hanging above the radiator in the hallway; a kaleidoscope of terracotta spirals and blue animal footprints. Grandma notes my slightly astonished look – we haven't had new things in here for as long as I can remember.

'Beatrice's grandson brought it back from Alice Springs.' Grandma shunts us into the kitchen with the *Radio Times*.

She takes three packets of Safeguard cattle wormer out of her enormous pockets and dumps them on the pine table. 'Says it's aboriginal, though I reckon it's a print.' She winks, the joke lost on Joely.

'Beatrice is a good friend of Grandma's,' I explain.

Joely nods. 'I remember you telling me in the sauna.'

Grandma's eyes widen. She fiddles with the mole behind her ear in the way that she does when she's anticipating the electricity bill.

'Fitness First is not *that* kind of sauna, Grandma,' I clarify.

Grandma jams two pyramid teabags into her country cottage teapot and waits for the kettle to boil.

Joely's eyes dart around the kitchen to a row of off-white thermals hanging from the ceiling airer. 'I'm sorry to be impolite, but do you have WiFi?'

Grandma opens the cutlery drawer and wipes flour off a laminated copy of the passcode with a wet dishcloth and hands it to Joely.

'Thank you,' Joely says.

I take Joely's case and show her upstairs. The house feels the same as ever, its stone floor cold underfoot, its exposed brickwork crumbly and scratchy. The landing wall, unevenly plastered by Dad ten years ago, displays several floor-to-ceiling forked cracks. *Money Box* blares from a pocket-sized radio in the bathroom and the whole upstairs stinks of lemon, though I'm not sure why.

My bedroom looks just the same as it did twenty years ago. The bed under the window is made up with the *Star Wars* duvet cover I chose from the Argos catalogue, aged twelve. The guest bed has my *Spiderman* one. Those were the glory days, when farming was lucrative, and Christmas presents were kick-ass. Now the carpet feels thin and scratchy, and the walls could do with a lick of paint.

Joely settles at the small desk my grandpa built for me when I was little; a desk on which I've written letters to Father Christmas and university applications. She takes out her shiny laptop and *hmms* and *mmms* until I agree I'll leave her to it. Really, it should be me putting in the extra work hours, what with my KSG funding meeting on Monday. The approval process has got tighter since Christophe Concordel identified me as risk, based on 'conflict of interest', and no longer allows Joely to approve our budget.

I wander back downstairs. Grandma stands in the yard with her yellow Marigolds pulled up to the elbows of her long-sleeved floral dress, a brood of Orpington chickens pecking at her wellies. Instinctively, I open the fridge door. Four tinned pears swim in a bowl of syrup alongside a lonesome sausage in a jacket of fat. I pluck a Babybel from a tangled red net wedged in the egg rack, read the sell-by date and chuck it in the bin. Home, sweet home.

'Bilberry!' Dad appears at the kitchen door, his freckled face speckled with mud.

I grab four chocolate digestives out of the Charles and Diana biscuit barrel, two for him, two for me, and plant my face into his chest like I'm seven again. His skin is cold and smells of sunshine. He ruffles my hair and presses me into the wedding band that hangs round his neck until I'm pretty sure it's left an imprint in my cheek. That's the thing about Dad's hugs; they're that comforting, you'd forgo a limb for them. I come up for air and study his face; his freckles, his tangle of honey-grey blonde curls, the laughter lines around his eyes, crusty with salt from wind-induced tears.

'Where's Jolene?' he says.

'*Joely*. She's upstairs, doing a bit of work.'

Grandma comes back in with a handful of fresh mint. She hands me a stash of reindeer serviettes we didn't get through at Christmas, and while Dad and I sort out the cutlery, launches into a monologue about the economic ruin of British dairy farming. 'I blame our sad state of affairs on my grandfather-in-law. If he hadn't become so obsessed with cows, none of this would have happened.'

Poor Grandma. Becoming a farmer's wife, a farmer's widow and then doing it all over again for the next generation is like marrying into the royal family without any of the perks. She's given up her whole life to dote on men devoted to dairy, and the sick twist is that she's lactose intolerant.

Dad has disappeared by the time Joely comes downstairs. Who can blame him? He's probably heard that monologue a hundred times by now.

'I thought it might be nice to eat outside,' Grandma says.

I lead Joely out of the back door, across the stepping stones to the small patio, where a wooden table sits in the sun next to a budding clematis. Grandma follows with an intricately engraved, silver condiments tray. I'm not sure why, because it's empty.

'I can't be faffing with spooning sauces into each little pot, but I thought it looked pretty,' she says, placing it in front of Joely, only to pull great honking plastic bottles of Co-op's own ketchup, brown sauce and French mustard out of her apron pockets. 'If you need to wash your hands . . .' She waves to a hard, cracked bar of soap on an upside-down bucket next to the outside tap. Joely favours a small bottle of hand sanitizer, which she drags out of the handbag that comes everywhere with her.

'Billie Goat, call your dad in, won't you?' Grandma rearranges the bottles so that the French mustard is directly in front of Joely.

Dad isn't in the yard or the field. He's not in the milking shed or the barn. This in itself doesn't worry me, it's more the fact that Joely has been left with the one-woman tornado that is my grandma for longer than is healthy. Eventually, I find Dad in his shed asleep on his workbench, his face stuck to May's edition of *Dairy Farmer*. The shed door creaks back and forth, fanning a cobweb attached to the loosely fitted window. A pair of hedge cutters dangle above his head, the air an aroma of wet grass and creosote.

'Dad?'

He lifts his head, confusion spread across his brow. 'I'm not supposed to be here, am I?'

I put my hand on his shoulder. 'What do you mean?'

'It's Wednesday. I'm supposed to visit the co-op on Wednesday.'

'It's Saturday, Dad. Saturday lunchtime, and I've come up with Joely for Uncle Pete's party tomorrow.'

'Of course!' he says, reddening a little. 'I'm never much good after a power nap.' He twists the ring on the chain around his neck. Round and round, it goes; thirteen years of marriage, conversations, laughs, dreams and arguments all wrapped up in a small gold band.

'Come on,' I say. 'Dinner's ready.'

He stands up and stumbles slightly, nudging the shears hanging above him, which swing back and forth on their hook. Steadying himself on the workbench, he reaches into his pocket for a foil wrap of aspirin. 'I've got a bit of a head-ache, Bilberry,' he says, emptying a couple of tablets into his hand and knocking them back with a mouthful of cold tea. Then, within seconds he's standing on a huge sack of topsoil, reaching over lawnmowers, plant pots and paint brushes to find 'a little something to celebrate'. He drags out a dusty bottle of ginger wine. I have trouble keeping up with him as he strides over to the patio.

'And this must be Mademoiselle Joely!' The crow's feet around his twinkly blue eyes deepen with delight.

'Nice to meet you,' she says, her body hardening as he leans in to hug her.

Grandma plonks roast lamb and veg down in front of us and gestures for us to help ourselves to gravy.

'So. How. Long. Have. You. Lived. In. England. For. Jocly?' Dad picks mud out of his fingernails with the corner of his debit card.

'Are we pronouncing it right, love?' Grandma breaks the seal on the dusty bottle of ginger wine. 'Joely. Joelee.'

'Perfect.' Joely's eyes follow each twist and turn of Grandma's parsnip as it journeys through gravy. 'Although I am baptized Joelle, which means "God will be willing".'

'Very nice,' Grandma says, studying Joely as if she's Renaissance art.

Joely smirks. 'Not really. God will be willing to do what exactly?'

'Exactly,' Grandma interjects at the wrong point.

'Anything? Nothing?' Joely pokes at a roast potato. 'It means nothing, so I prefer Joely. It's prettier.'

I start to feel a little bit like I did in my German GCSE oral exam, when I wasn't sure what topic of conversation would be next on the list, and whether I would conclude the hour without fainting.

Dad looks down at his lamb. 'What do you think of the north of England, Joely?'

'It's very nice,' Joely says, unconvincingly. 'It's a great pleasure to see the house of *ma petite Anglaise.*'

'*Ma* what?' Grandma says.

'*Ma petite Anglaise,*' Joely says. 'My little English girl.'

'Are we talking about a painting?' Grandma says.

Joely coughs into her serviette. 'Your granddaughter!'

'What about the Moulin Rouge?' Grandma volunteers out of nowhere.

'What about it?' I say, mortified.

'I've never been, but I imagine it's terrible,' Joely says, reading the label on the jar next to her, and making no attempt at concealing her disgust. 'Is this mustard?'

'French mustard,' Grandma says proudly.

'She's a firecracker, this one!' Dad laughs. I haven't seen him this excited since he won some luxury gardening gloves at my secondary school tombola.

'Little Dot's got big!' I say, trying to keep the conversation normal. 'We drove past her and I actually thought she was Big Dot for a minute.'

'Yes.' Dad chuckles.

'One of our friendliest cows,' Grandma explains to Joely.

'They all have a name?' Joely says.

'Of course,' Dad says. 'You can't be born into the family without a name.'

Joely looks at me. 'You know all of their names?'

'Most of them.' I sense that this, in Joely's eyes, is deeply unattractive, so I try to downplay my involvement without offending Dad.

It takes me two glasses of ginger wine to realize I haven't been breathing deeply enough and I've got a stress headache from shielding Joely from the inevitable parochial chitchat that comes with running a farm. It's pretty wearing digging us all out of conversational no man's land. The tense atmosphere only dissipates when Grandma announces she's going to drop some cheese round to Doreen in the village, and Dad takes this as a cue to muck out the henhouse.

'One day I hope to be a grandmother,' Joely says, her head in my lap as we lounge on the lawn.

'I'm sure you will,' I say, but can't imagine age ever creeping up on Joely. It's hard to imagine how anyone with such porcelain-smooth skin and glossy dark hair could ever get old. She's just not that kind of person.

Joely walks her fingers across my shoulder. 'I'm sorry I hid away with my work earlier.' She kisses me gently on the neck, making her way higher and higher until her tongue is in my ear. 'I was just nervous.'

'It's OK.'

The beech hedge rustles, causing us both to look round. There's nothing there. I look into the field beyond, where the cows graze silently, nipping at wood sorrel and celandines. My eyes are about to leave the field when I notice a ruddy-faced sweaty man staring at us over the fence, his skin covered in tattoos and his face full of piercings.

Dad appears with a bag of sawdust. 'I see you've met Nathan,' he says, waving to the hairy man over the hedge. 'He's from the agency. Does the odd day for me here and there. Nathan, this is my daughter, Billie.' Nathan stands up properly so we can see him over the hedge and pulls at the plaited tuft of hair sprouting from his chin. He stares at Joely.

'And her friend, Joely,' Dad adds.

I go to wave, but he looks away. What is it about farming staff and people skills? It's as if their love of animals is inversely proportional to their love of people. I've seen various people come and go. When the farm was bigger, Dad had a toothless operations manager called China, who found it impossible to look anyone in the eye, let alone talk to them, but he was brilliant with the herd and understood each and every one of them.

Joely hugs her knees to her chest. 'What time are we leaving tomorrow?'

If I can just get Joely through the next twenty-four hours, we should be OK.

Baslow Methodist Church is a tiny building on School Lane, no bigger than a cottage. It may not be a particularly grand piece of architecture, but it has played host to every religious event of my family for the last four generations on account of my great-great-grandfather's affinity for the vicar; I'm convinced, the source of my gay genetics.

I'm struggling in one of Joely's wrap dresses. It may be designed for 'any shape, any size' but definitely requires more chest than I've got for it to sit right. A sea of hats and suits mingle on the pavement opposite. Grandma has driven to Bakewell to pick up her friend, Beatrice, who's moved into a flat above The Bridle Shop and can no longer drive. Heads swivel towards Joely.

'Do I look OK?' Joely says, adjusting the tiny silver dragonflies in her ears.

'Perfect.' I nod hello to a couple I don't know.

'I should have worn the other earrings.' She examines her reflection in a small compact mirror.

'Joels, you look great.'

'Do you mind if we go back for the other earrings?'

'Trust me, the dragonflies look perfect.'

She snaps the compact mirror shut and exhales sharply.

A group from Auntie June's belly-dancing club make a beeline for us and are about to pounce, when one of them twists her ankle on the kerb, her pantaloons shedding gold sequins onto the pavement. Joely spots her escape and marches me towards the village shop.

'We need to buy confetti!' She flings me into the store, out of earshot and away from prying eyes.

Ginger, the three-legged village cat, wanders down the cereal aisle towards us.

'Everybody is staring!' Joely hisses behind the cornflakes.

'They're not,' I say, aware that Marjorie Pearce, the store owner, is openly staring at us right now from behind the till. Her snow-white hair has been chopped into a bob, which swings under her ears as she moves this way and that, trying to get a better look at us. She's bony thin these days and wouldn't look amiss on a broomstick.

65

'They are.' Joely shivers, her legs and arms covered in goose bumps.

'Well, fuck them!' I say, glaring at Marjorie, whose birdlike frame is now pivoting on tiptoes, neck craned, spying on us over the chewing-gum stand like an inquisitive meerkat. 'They've had plenty of years to get their head around it. They must be used to the idea by now.' As the words leave my mouth, I realize that, although that should be the case, it really isn't. Take Marjorie, for example.

Marjorie has known me since I was six. She has a boy a year older than me and a girl a year younger than me, and we were all at primary school together. She's given me lifts to gymnastics displays, trampolining competitions, book clubs and swimming lessons. And while she took me under her wing as a nipper, me being motherless and her being maternal, she dropped me like an illegitimate brick as soon as village rumours of me 'getting the bus the wrong way' morphed into concrete evidence, when her son caught me with my tongue down the throat of a fellow girl guide.

'Looking for anything in particular?' Marjorie bobs her head this way and that like an owl trying to get comfortable, white curtains of hair swaying at the sides of her pointy chin.

'We're good, thanks,' I say, grabbing Joely's hand and exiting the shop. We don't need confetti that badly.

'See you in a few moments at the party!' she shouts at our retreating backs.

Outside, the happy-once-again couple arrive in a shiny black trap pulled by a shiny black carthorse. Auntie June looks several shades darker than usual and is crammed into a segmented, cream satin dress that someone should have told her not to wear. Uncle Pete looks like he's dressed for golf.

A small crowd of people whoop and cheer as Auntie June clambers down, her full-length dress getting caught in the wheel. Someone behind me whistles 'Here Comes the Bride', prompting Uncle Pete to follow with Chopin's 'Death March'. Auntie June bends over to pick up her fallen bouquet of white roses and in doing so, falls out of her low-cut dress, giving everyone an eyeful.

Uncle Pete climbs down from the other side, a Canon camera clanking around his neck. 'Billie!' he says, singling me out. 'You're a dab hand at photography, aren't you?' He lifts the strap over his head and hands me the camera. 'Time to put that diploma to use!'

I don't have a photography diploma. He's probably thinking of the evening photography course I did eight years ago purely because I had a crush on a girl who was doing that module (Anne-Marie, willowy blonde, wore Gucci Rush), which I quit when Anne-Marie told me she had a boyfriend and our teacher congratulated me on an accidental shot of my bedroom carpet when I was playing with the settings. However, I sense by the lift in Joely's face that she is impressed that I *do* have a photography diploma and figure this is not a moment to disappoint.

'Sure,' I say. 'Uncle Pete, this is Joely.'

'*La belle Française!*' He bows in what he considers playful camaraderie but Joely interprets as mocking. 'Nice to meet you, Joely.'

She flashes a withering smile and I want the earth to swallow me up. It's not like Uncle Pete isn't a moron but, still, a little tolerance wouldn't go amiss.

Auntie June joins us. 'Thanks for stepping in, Billie.' She giggles as Uncle Pete helps himself to a handful of her bottom as they play out one of their demonstrably frisky phases that we have to endure biannually when Uncle Pete is dry and remorseful for sleeping with whoever he's slept with. Joely flashes me a look; although it's widely accepted that you can't pick your family, it's still pretty mortifying.

'Have you met Joely?' I try to get things back on track.

'Hi,' Joely says, admiring Auntie June's dress. 'You look beautiful.'

I can't tell whether Joely really does think my auntie looks beautiful or not, partly because of her poker face, and partly because Auntie June clearly looks like an enormous chrysalis.

'Your dad's not sure he can make it.' Grandma appears at my side in the sky-blue twinset she wears to every church occasion. 'Hoof crisis, apparently.' She drops her phone back into her navy handbag and tuts.

We both know Dad is skiving. He hates anything to do with weddings and public displays of affection.

Beatrice totters over in pleated lemon yellow, a cream handbag wedged in the crevice of her inner elbow. She's very shaky these days and has to walk with a stick.

'Have you introduced Joely to your auntie Bea?' Grandma says.

Auntie Beatrice is not a real aunt but is as good as. She and Grandma met at primary school in Hathersage and they've been thick as thieves from Girls' Brigade to the Women's Institute. Puberty, childbirth, the menopause and widowhood; they've been through everything together, their *womance* spanning nine decades.

'Who've we got here then?' Beatrice says, squinting at Joely.

'Beatrice, this is Joely,' I say.

Joely smiles. 'Nice to meet you.'

Beatrice turns to me. 'You know, the whole women-with-women thing wouldn't have been allowed back in our day.'

'I remember you saying,' I reply, raising an eyebrow at Joely, who glances round the car park. Beatrice has rolled this gem out a good few times over the years, but this is the first time she's opened Pandora's box in front of a new girl-friend.

I make up an excuse about needing the loo and usher Joely into the church garden.

'You OK?' I say.

'Your family are a little—'

'Embarrassing?' I suggest.

'They don't like me,' she says.

'Of course, they like you, they're just . . . Well, you know what families are like.'

Her phone rings, which she answers straight away, scuttling past Uncle Pete, who demonstrates his golf swing to a lady in leather. Resignedly, I pick up the camera.

Click. A troupe of semi-naked belly-dancers awaiting their moment under a floral pagoda. Click. Auntie June's original bridesmaids, who have tripled in size since their debut. Click. Marjorie, store keys jangling from her bony fingers, scavenging hyena-like for gossip. Click. Tazzy, local lollipop lady and Village Intelligence, named after the Tasmanian devil on account of her Australian ancestry, cuddly exterior and deadly-strong bite. Click. Doreen Peterson, a plump, cheery old soul with rosy cheeks and a whiskery face, who moved into the village from Cornwall a year ago when her son got a job up here. Rumour has it, she's bought out the butcher's to open a bakery, which the evil son persuaded her to call 'Buns & Baps', the pun completely lost on her. Click. Paul Pickering, ginger, always wears a waistcoat, not to be confused with his twin brother, Andy Pickering, my dad's ex-farmhand (also ginger), who recently got charged with sheep rustling. Click. Joely leaning against the entrance to the church, a faraway look in her eyes. Click. Uncle Pete, his hand down one of the bridesmaid's tops.

'Please replace divots!' a bald man with bad sunburn yells in a harsh Northern Irish accent as the belly dancers thunder across the lawn in preparation for their dance. Graham Pearce, Marjorie's husband and Dad's feed-provider, lurches towards me, his head a shiny lobster pink. 'Bell Ender!'

That's the thing about being called 'Belinda' when someone with a strong Northern Irish accent pronounces it.

I go to take his photo.

He frowns. 'Did you ask for consent?'

He's obviously joking. Or is he? I can't tell. I never could when I was little, either. It's weird to think that I was once sick on his carpet and used to help his children raid his record collection when he was out.

'Who's the lovely lady then?' He gestures to the car park with his can of Carlsberg, where Joely is immersed in her phone conversation.

'That's Joely,' I say proudly.

He lowers his voice. 'I think it's wonderful. Take no notice of what the others say.'

'Right,' I say, bracing myself for what's coming next but,

luckily, we're saved by the bell, which announces the start of belly dancing.

Tambourines jingle. Tassels swish. Sequins gleam and flesh undulates. Track number two from 'Sexy Sadie' sees Auntie June transforming into some sort of braying unicorn a bit too close to a bed of begonias, and I'm so bloody relieved that Joely misses the whole thing, frowning at her phone in the shade of a rhododendron bush.

'Everything OK?' I ask when she finally wanders back over.

'Just work.' She slips her phone into her bag.

For a company dedicated to improving the quality of human life by enabling people to 'do more, feel better, live longer', KSG seems hellbent on destroying the health of its employees. Still, I've got a pretty big meeting with KSG tomorrow and I've not checked my phone once. I know this party's not exactly her cup of tea, but she could surely fake it a bit. It's not like the 'Culture under Attack' installation exhibition she took me to was particularly my bag, but I still managed to nod and smile in the right places, because it's common decency not to piss on each other's bonfires.

We head into the church. I keep having to yank up the wrap dress and check I haven't exposed a nipple.

'I always feel strange when I visit a religious building,' Joely says. 'Like I haven't merited the right to enter.'

'Brace yourself. It's not exactly Notre Dame.' I smooth the dress down over my hips.

The church is draughty. Grandma helps Beatrice up the aisle and takes her place front right. I sit down next to her and look to Joely, who adjusts the clasp on the front of her dress, sending

71

a waft of hyacinth and cedar in my direction. She puts her hand on my knee and I ripple with pride. Perhaps I've been too harsh on Joely. Weddings are always difficult when you don't know anyone.

The order of service contains a flyer for 'Knit, Natter, Craft and Chatter'. Beneath the lyrics to 'All Things Bright and Beautiful', there's a blurry photo of Auntie June and Uncle Pete cutting the cake on their wedding day. She's all toothy and un-composed and his whole face is a grin.

The church organ starts up and a large lady in vicar's robes waddles to the front.

'Oh dear!' Grandma says loudly as the vicar takes to the pulpit only a few inches away from us. 'This one's rubbish!'

'I'm sure she'll be fine,' I whisper, bracing myself for an onslaught of *fattist* comments – anyone slightly paunchy and Grandma has them down as elephantine.

Grandma peers over her hymn book. 'Her hemline's all over the place!'

The vicar's eyes become slits and her voice rises a few decibels. She reads a poem pledging the fusion of hearts and minds, and the cultivation of compassion. Pews creak, bottoms fidget and bags rustle until Auntie June and Uncle Pete recite their vows, promising to love, honour and *trust* each other. Auntie June talks about embracing the joy of equanimity, and I can't be the only one wondering whether that means she has the right to sleep around too. Finally, he pushes a sapphire onto her finger (she's removed her previous eternity rings for the occasion). Grandma mutters her disgruntlement at the elaborateness of it all and Beatrice has fallen asleep. I'm beginning to wish I'd never subjected Joely to any of this, when she takes my hand and squeezes it under her shawl, and I don't want this weekend to end.

On the way out, Grandma introduces me to a group of tea-drinking, bourbon-dipping pensioners as 'the queer one'. A lady in beige trousers and a floral blouse asks us if we'd 'like to make friends with God' at next week's pizza night. I explain we're only up for the weekend, Joely clinging to my arm, her knuckles all white.

In the corner of the car park stand the horse and trap, and I drag Joely over to admire it slash escape the casual homophobia. She admires the vintage carriage, running her fingers over the gold-embossed Yorkshire rose on the back.

'I wouldn't. It's quite dirty,' a familiar voice says. Lorna Parsons appears from behind the horse, a deep frown etched on her forehead. She wears white jodhpurs and a herringbone blazer with a trim of navy velvet. Lorna Parsons, who is leaving newspaper cuttings about gay saunas with my dad. Lorna Parsons, who humiliated me at school and earned me the most abhorrent nickname a girl can get. I shudder at the memory, the words 'bull sperm' ringing in my ears. Lorna Parsons: my countryside nemesis.

'Hi,' I say. 'I thought these days Guy was the horsy one and you were all about cows?'

'We help each other out.' She busies herself with the bridle.

'It's beautiful.' Joely gestures to the trap, her face alight with wonder.

'My mum found it dumped behind some caravans at the back of the livery.' Lorna yanks at the bridle with impatience, the buckle not doing what it should. 'She decided to restore it.'

'Lorna, this is my girlfriend, Joely. Joely, this is Lorna, my dad's vet.'

'Nice to meet you,' Joely says. She turns to me. 'What's a livery?'

Lorna looks up and, I swear, does a double-take at my wrap dress and looks away again.

'It's a kind of farm where you stable horses,' I say.

Joely looks horrified.

'Stable,' I say. 'Not staple.'

'It's not really a farm,' Lorna says haughtily.

'OK, it's a place to keep horses.' I exhale sharply.

'It's a lot less interesting than a farm,' Lorna says, battling with the bridle. 'I should know, I grew up there.'

Joely zones out. 'Can we take a ride?'

Lorna rearranges her fringe over the scar on her forehead, her eyes glued to the problematic strap. 'I shouldn't really.'

'What about just to the end of the lane and back?' I say.

'OK, if we're quick,' Lorna says.

Joely hitches up her dress and climbs the side step. I go to follow but Lorna blocks my path with her arm. 'Other side,' she says. 'I need to be in the middle if I'm to steer.'

I walk round to the other side and clamber in. The seat cushion feels as though it's been stashed in a damp stable for decades and smells of mildew. Joely eyes the dog-hair-ridden blanket strewn over the back rest with suspicion. There isn't much leg space, something that doesn't bother a short-arse like me, but encumbers Joely, who is forced to dangle her legs out of the side.

'Come along!' Lorna loosens the reins and cajoles Lightning McQueen into a plod, and I'm reminded of the days she used to come up to the farm on weekends with her dad, and we went through a phase of playing horses. *Come along! Giddy up! Walk on!* I must have been about nine, which would make her six. One of the lower branches of the weeping willow lent itself to become a horse, saddled with an old blanket from the shed. We made stirrups out of an old piece of rope and reins out of one of dad's belts. She'd spend hours perfecting her rising trot on it, the tree creaking as it bounced her up and down. Every now and then I'd get on and she'd pretend to be my riding instructor, correcting my posture and critiquing my method of holding the reins. She told me back then she'd marry a rich man, qualify as a vet and ride a horse and trap. I guess some people just know what they want out of life.

'Is he your horse?' I say as we trundle past the church, a group of lads racing each other on mountain bikes, mounting the kerb as we pull out into the lane.

Lorna focuses straight ahead. 'Guy's.'

'Lorna and Guy are the Posh and Becks of Derbyshire,' I say to Joely.

'I'm not sure that's quite how I'd describe us!' Lorna says.

I laugh. 'They're the agricultural darlings of Derbyshire.'

Rosebay willowherb bows in the breeze at the roadside. Sunshine pinches at our skin. The sky is vast and blue. Church bells chime. Hooves clip and clop. The brook trickles melodically and I try not to get annoyed that Joely isn't looking at any of it and is instead checking her phone. I point out a blue tit, a vintage postbox, a wild rabbit darting through a muddy field. Nothing. She still stares at her screen.

We grind to a halt for our engine to evacuate his bowels over the road.

'How was the ceremony?' Lorna enquires as fresh dollops of manure thump onto the tarmac.

'Fine,' I say.

Lightning McQueen finishes his business and helps himself to a mouthful of roadside grass.

We plod on in silence until my phone rings, *Home* flashing up on the screen.

I pick up. 'Hi, Dad.'

'I think I've stopped being sick now,' he mumbles.

'Sick?'

'Your grandma's not answering her phone. Remind me where I'm supposed to be.'

'If you're being sick, you shouldn't be going anywhere. Go to bed and we'll be home in a couple of hours.'

'But I'm supposed to—'

'You're supposed to rest. You've missed the service anyway so go to bed and I'll come and check on you in a bit.'

'OK,' he says.

I slide my phone into my pocket, my head lolling from side to side. Within a few seconds I feel twice, maybe three times heavier than normal.

Clip, clop. Clip, clop.

*I'm a bit worried about your dad, Billie.*

Clip, clop. Clip, clop.

*He's getting ever so muddled.*

Clip, clop. Clip, clop.

*He won't do a jigsaw any more, Billie. You know how he loves his jigsaws.*

Clip, clop. Clip, clop.

*Beatrice thinks he's got a touch of the dementia.*

76

Clip, clop. Clip, clop.
*I've got a bit of a headache, Bilberry.*
Clip, clop. Clip, clop.
*Ever so muddled.*
Clip, clop. Clip, clop.
*I've got a bit of a headache.*
Clip, clop.
*A headache, Bilberry.*
Clip.
*A headache.*
Clop.

I slam my hands down onto my thighs. 'I need to get Dad to hospital!'

# CHAPTER SIX

# CHESTERFIELD ROYAL

Chesterfield Royal is a hospital set on several acres of undulating lawns with 'everything from cashpoint facilities to a Costa Coffee outlet', a hospital I wish I was not sitting in now, waiting for my grandma to walk out of *that room*.

My pound coin clinks through the slot of a Beverages-on-the-go vending machine. It whirrs and grinds until piping hot, watery coffee spatters against a beige plastic cup. If I hadn't been tasked with parking the car, I'd know first-hand what's happening. Instead, my mind races and spirals, lurching between migraines and brain aneurysms.

A baby animal calendar hangs on the staff noticeboard, featuring snow-fox cubs play-fighting on ice. It suggests we are still in February despite it being May. How come life always stands still at the wrong time?

I flick through a pile of tattered *Hello!* magazines, their centre-spreads littered with Dutch aristocrats and the latest divorces on the reality TV circuit. Seeing how many words I can make out of the letters spelling Nicole Scherzinger takes only about seven minutes. Dad would find eight times as many as me. Nobody can beat him at Scrabble. He knows every word beginning with Q that doesn't need a U, and all those ridiculous words that don't need any vowels. It doesn't matter that neither of us knows the meaning of any of them, because they're in the Scrabble dictionary, so 'sixty-three points, thank you very much, Bilberry.'

Sun beams through a small window, open as far as the safety lock will allow. When I pause the inner workings of my brain, I can hear birds singing and the click-click-click of a rotating sprinkler. A gentle spray showers the immaculate lawn. It seems wrong that it's a beautiful, sunny evening. It seems wrong that my uncle is celebrating while my dad awaits his fate. It seems wrong that Joely is on her way home without me. I understand that she has an important work gig first thing tomorrow, and she doesn't exactly know Dad, but it still feels wrong. Like mislaying a biscuit you've only part-eaten.

I try to anchor myself to something tangible by concentrating on everything I need to know for my KSG meeting tomorrow afternoon, but there are only so many metabolic microseconds of eclampsia I can juggle before my mind short-circuits back to Dad.

A stash of children's picture books sits in a toy wheelbarrow under the windowsill. I pick up *The Tiger Who Came to Tea* and stare at the cover, blocking out the huge orange beast to study the little girl in the purple pinafore and chequered tights. Sophie. Dad used to read this story to me when I was a little girl. I can hear his voice now, interchanging 'Mummy' for 'Grandma' to protect me, even though I didn't mind Sophie having a mum. Everyone else had a mum, so why not her? I was more in awe of Sophie having a tiger sitting at her kitchen table, glugging tea directly out of the teapot spout, and I particularly liked the page where Sophie's dad came home from work carrying a briefcase and wearing a suit. My dad never wore a suit or carried a briefcase, so the concept was fascinating. I leaf through the pages, reliving Dad's tiger's voice. He did a brilliant tiger's voice. And a brilliant Dad's voice. He's a brilliant dad.

The second hand of the big white clock on the wall ticks loudly. I piece together the lyrics of 'The Lightning Tree' in my head – a song Grandma used to sing to me whenever I felt like giving up; when I thought I'd never be able to tie my ninja belt, when I couldn't handspring over the vault in gymnastics, when I couldn't read music and didn't fit in with the recorder crowd. And just when I've remembered all of the lyrics, Grandma comes out of *that room* and I know by the look on her face that I'm not going to my KSG funding meeting tomorrow.

The consultation room is small and garishly illuminated by ceiling panels. The walls look greener than they probably are, and everyone's skin looks supernaturally white. Dad lies on the sort of half-bed, half-stretcher you have in the first-aid room at school, two nurses conferring over paperwork at the sink behind him. He looks small and bewildered.

'Dad?'

He balls a tissue in one fist, his eyes all swimmy. 'Sit down, Bilberry.'

Everything goes tight across my chest. There's nowhere for

me to sit, even if I wanted to. I don't know what I want to do, apart from wheel Dad's bed out of here and pretend none of this is happening.

'It's a brain tumour.' The pupils in his eyes are like tiny pinpricks. 'They don't know yet whether it's malignant or benign.'

My throat constricts and there isn't enough oxygen in the room. Dad is my solo parent, my mentor, my friend, my confidant. The axis on which my world spins. If I lose him, I lose part of myself. The skin on my face alternates between feeling too tight and then feeling patchy with numbness. A dichotomy of dread and hope.

'It'll be OK, Bilberry.' He takes my hand. My dad: the man who brought me up, changed my nappies, chose my clothes, taught me how to read, combed nits out of my hair, tended to my grazes, got me through school and into college. My dad, who has always believed in me and taught me to be true to myself. My rock. Without him, I wouldn't know who I was any more. Who would I ask for advice? Who would I go home to? And where would home be? There'd be no farm without Dad. No cows. No nothing.

Grandma leans against the door and stares at the ceiling as if she's pleading with the God she's not believed in for eight decades. My stomach churns like a diesel engine full of petrol, and all I can think about is Dad leaning over the old stone wall, watching over the herd whilst they graze in silence, Hyacinth plodding over to nuzzle his arm. It's not just me that can't live without him.

'Dad,' I squeak.

His hand feels dry and scratchy in mine and I don't know

whether my mind's playing tricks on me because we're in a hospital, but his face looks slightly lopsided, one eye pulled down slightly and the corner of his mouth a tiny bit droopy. He reminds me of Mr Spud, a King Edward potato that Dad drew facial features on and hid under my bed when I was seven in an attempt to cheer me up when I was lonely. An angled moustache made from a pipe cleaner. One eyeball too low, the other too high. A forerunner to Mr Potato Head. My dad did that for me. Created friends for me when I was lonely, knowing that in spite of the three of us being a self-sufficient ecosystem, it wasn't always healthy for a young girl to be so cut off.

Mr Spud even wrote me letters. They'd come hand delivered, but in a fully addressed envelope to 'Miss B. Oliver'. They made me feel important. Like somebody cared. He wrote to me about school. About choices. About it not mattering if I didn't want to do ballet. About trusting my gut and doing what my heart tells me. Mr Spud even wrote me a postcard about puberty and a girl's need for her mother at the time of becoming a woman. It was accompanied by a gift-wrapped 'first period kit', comprising sanitary towels, tampons, a discreet pink satin carry pouch, and an NHS pamphlet with a menstruation Q&A. There was nothing Mr Spud hadn't thought of.

'It's not supposed to be this way round.' Grandma dabs at her nose. 'I'm supposed to go before you are.'

Dad closes his eyes. 'I'm not going anywhere.'

A nurse in slip-slop Crocs comes in to take his blood pressure, the phut-phut-phut sound of the arm band inflating, followed by the hiss of its release, numbers flickering on the digital reader like those on a roulette wheel. *Every step of the way.*

Dad looks at me, his rough thumb skimming the back of my hand reassuringly. 'Can I ask one thing of you?'

If he talks about dying, I don't know what I'll do. I've never for once in my life considered a world without Dad and now here it is, a monster haunting this very room. I look at him through a blurry mess of tears, an invisible fist squeezing at my throat and I can't speak.

'Would you stay and look after the girls?' he asks softly. 'I can get Nathan in from the agency to help, but it needs someone hands-on to run it. You may not have done it for a while, but it'll all come flooding back.'

It's weird, all the things that go through your mind at moments like this. I want to say I haven't brought enough knickers. That I don't know how half the milking equipment works. That, although I'd love to help out, I've got a KSG meeting tomorrow. I can't quite catch up with the moment, so I just nod, my face a hot, bloated mess of snot and tears.

It's only when Grandma comes over and puts an arm around me, and he, in turn, puts an arm around us both, cradling us to his chest, that I realize how loudly I am crying. A family scrum, the three of us squashed together, like we have been for most of our lives; a small, symbiotic unit of three. A triangle of trust. But a triangle is no longer a triangle with only two sides. With only two sides, there's no centre, no core, no heart, nowhere for energy to anchor itself. Triangles are rigid. You construct buildings with triangles – roofs, pylons, braces – because they can't be twisted out of shape. Take one of its sides away and a triangle is useless. We can't function without Dad.

'Can you do that for me?' he says.

My dad. My lovely dad. It's like the world has slipped off its axis and the universe is spinning out of control.

'Of course.'

# PART TWO

# (WO)MANNING UP

# CHAPTER SEVEN

# DAIRY MILK

**From: Bev**
Hey buddy, hope this message doesn't wake you up.
Just on my way back from Soho. They've got this new
club called Esteem which does these bloody brilliant
cocktails. We'll go when you're back x

**From: Bev**
Auakgm;oiuqpyapnb,k aoufpoeiuf90uhirgjoijmfkl

**From: Bev**
Sorry. Butt text! Hammered!

It's been nearly two weeks now. The good news is, the tumour
is benign. The not-so-great news is that, despite the family
moment of crisis, Grandma is having to look after Beatrice at
her place since she had a nasty fall the day after Dad's diagnosis
and broke three ribs, so it's just me and Speedo on the farm.

I wake with the taste of Dad's baking-soda toothpaste on my lips. The room smells of lemon and it takes me a few seconds to associate it with the citrus pet-odour-exterminator that Grandma's insisted on ever since Speedo rolled in badger faeces and pressed it into the upstairs carpet. My phone is vibrating on the bedside table. Five a.m. Through bleary eyes, I piece together the Darth Vader duvet and matching beanbag.

The wooden slats of our staircase feel smooth against my toes. Speedo whines to be let out. I put on the kettle while he does his stuff, daydreaming of Joely fast asleep under her goose-feather duvet, making that contented snuffling noise that isn't quite a snore. My tea is several shades darker than usual and now contains a teaspoon of sugar. I stare into space, waiting for my body to start functioning. Twilight is a creature I associate with red-eye flights and changing time zones, and now here it is, oozing through the windows, a sepia hue pushing its way into my daily routine.

Ten minutes later, I'm in leggings and the ZSL T-shirt that Bev gave me at a Pygmy Hippo sponsorship event, stepping over my Converse and into Grandma's wellies. The yard is a patchwork of cowpats, hen droppings, mud and brick ends. My commute is all of fifty metres, past three wheelie bins, an old wishing well and a small herb garden, which used to be an enclosure for a Gloucester Old Spot that my dad looked after for his retired pig-farming friend. It now smells of rosemary and thyme.

I wander into the cowshed. Nathan, the Neanderthal dairy operations manager from the agency, stands in one of the pens, his wellingtons lost in deep straw. He's actually a lot more sociable than I gave him credit for and hasn't been loitering behind any bushes of late. He pours hot tea from a Thermos flask into a plastic cup and balances it on the breeze-block wall. 'Morning! Any news on your dad?'

'He's still waiting for the operation. It could be another week yet,' I say.

He nods, running his hands over the stomach of a pretty cow with long eyelashes, huge eyes and symmetrical markings; either Parsnip or Sally. He pats her lower right flank and thrusts his fist upwards against her abdomen in short, sharp bursts. Her ears flicker. She turns her head round to check me out and I know instantly it's Parsnip. She's always been curious, just like her mother, Jupiter – I remember going with Dad to pick up five cows from a smallholding in Whirlowdale. While the other cows were easily bribed into the back of the trailer with a rolled barley ration, Jupiter was far more interested in who we were, and where we were taking her to, staring us down with curious eyes.

'Ringworm.' Nathan gestures to the coin-sized bald patches around her eyes and lower legs. 'We thought it were lice at first, but three lots of Closamectin and not the blindest bit of difference.'

Heavy boots scrape across concrete and a skinny girl drifts into the cowshed, shoulders sagging with world-weariness. She wears black jodhpurs, a Nike hoody and a sloppy expression, somewhere between boredom and resentment. Her hair is shaven on one side and flops over to her shoulder on the other.

Nathan dips his hands into a bucket of water and wipes them down his thighs. 'This is my daughter, Rachel.'

Rachel looks at the ground and twiddles with the silver ring in her left eyebrow, all teenage embarrassment and awkwardness.

'Hi.' I go to shake her hand, but she plants it firmly in her sweatshirt pouch.

'Rachel's agreed to help out every other weekend,' Nathan says, taking a vape pen out of his pocket. 'Under my supervision, of course.'

It's only now I realize it's a Saturday, what with the days blending into each other and no clear definition of where one week ends and another one starts.

'Great.' I turn my attention to the cow. 'Is Parsnip OK?' I inject her name into conversation like I'm on first-name terms with the whole herd.

'We're just checking on the foetus.'

'She's pregnant?!'

'Five months.'

'But she's hardly showing!'

He looks at me and then at Rachel in a way that suggests they've already agreed I'm a moron. 'They quite often don't. You realize you've got seven that are expecting?'

'Right,' I say, inwardly hailing Mary.

'Your dad was experimenting with selling off calves, so you'll have a steady stream of births over the winter.' He lets go of Parsnip. 'Seems all right.'

'Seven pregnant, three lame and two sick,' Rachel corroborates. 'We've separated them off.'

'I'll look at them after milking,' I say, wondering when I can have another mug of tea.

Nathan puts down his bucket and raises an eyebrow. 'So,

you're going to roll your sleeves up and get stuck in, are you?'

I smile awkwardly. 'That's what I'm here for.'

I'd be lying if I said I didn't feel entirely over-faced by the enormity of what I've taken on. In spite of working on the farm during every school holiday, it's been fifteen years since I last helped out properly, and things have changed a fair bit: the technology, the machinery, nutritional advice; even the way that you identify and report on lameness. The amount of data you can get by implanting a tiny subcutaneous sensor is insane. Information at your fingertips: how much a cow eats, drinks, moves and sleeps. Her body temperature, her stress levels, acidity levels affecting rumination. Her heat cycle and responsiveness to a bull. Early detection of mastitis and disease. Analysis paralysis.

On balance, I can deal with the data, but it's the physical and medical aspects that I find intimidating. I haven't got a clue about the onset of lameness, Blackleg or Red Nose. Still, I can't let it get the better of me. I owe that to Dad.

Rachel opens the gate to the field and stands back as 150 cows buffet their way across the yard to the milking shed, led by Star as always. *Follow the star.* A cacophony of groans reverberates under the corrugated-iron roof. Machinery hisses. Gates rattle and clank. Monitors bleep. Pipes glug and cows grunt. We plug the cows into the milking machines, seventeen at a time. The vanilla smell of fresh milk mixes with cow dung and you can almost taste it on the back of your throat. What Nathan can do in twenty seconds takes me two minutes, and I'm painfully aware that by the end of morning milking, he has done 80 per cent of the grunt work, even after my days of practice.

'You want worker's hands.' Nathan watches me inspect the blisters that are forming beneath my fingers. 'Grow thicker skin and you'll be fine.'

I'm not sure I want thicker skin. I *am* sure I want a cup of tea and a bath. And a slice of Grandma's homemade bread. I miss her. I miss the lists she writes on the back of used envelopes and leaves strewn around the house. I miss the mouldy satsumas in the fruit bowl and tinned pears past their sell-by date. What I wouldn't give for the smell of cooking apples and lavender talcum powder to return and everything to be normal again.

Grandma is suffering. She hasn't eaten for days and won't stop making jam. She always makes jam in times of crisis. She was the same when Grandpa died. No wonder she's shattered, what with stirring huge vats of gooseberry jelly for hours on end and running between me, Beatrice and Dad, like we're some sort of love triangle. Poor Grandma, she can't function straight. I heard her whispering on the phone to Beatrice that it's only right she goes before him. But she won't talk about it with me. She finds it difficult to look me in the eye. Like I might ask scary questions she hasn't formulated answers to. She can't bear being at the farm without Dad, and winds up wandering from room to room looking at his stuff without saying anything. On reflection, it's actually fortunate that Beatrice needs her because when she is here, there's a huge tension between us. I can't put a mug down without her swiping it away a second later. We're both guilty of snapping at each other because we're exhausted, worried sick and don't know what's happening from one day to the next.

Wikipedia doesn't help. *A benign brain tumour can be as*

*dangerous to remove as a malignant one, depending on where in the brain it is.*

'You do think he'll be OK, Billie Goat?' Grandma whispers after each visiting hour, her eyes threatening to overspill with tears.

'Yes.' I hug her tightly, trying my hardest to convey rock-steady faith.

It's strange how family generations have an unspoken emotional hierarchy when it comes round to supporting each other through tough times. Grandma weeps on Dad, Dad weeps on me, I weep on Speedo and Speedo whimpers to himself. Together we are a set of emotionally dependent Russian dolls, one sheltering the next from a breakdown. The *Dairy Farmer* continues to plop through our letter box and nobody is reading it. As the backlog grows, so do our anxieties.

It takes ten minutes to hose everything down, but a further twenty to disinfect the equipment. The cows swagger out, hips sashaying, udders relieved. I head back to the house to sort the calf bottles and get sidetracked by looking at my phone: several emails from *Women's Health* promoting various Benjamin Button-style age-reversing miracle creams. A mail from a Nigerian head barrister, informing me that an inheritance from an unknown relative who moved to Africa in the 1970s is coming my way if I, 'kindly Mr Billie Oliver', send over my bank details. And a few mails from friends.

**Greetings from The Shard!**

Bill,

I'm writing to you from the 72nd floor of The Shard –
check out the photos! Everything's glassy and shiny and
you can see all the way out to the Thames estuary.
They have these state-of-the-art lifts with retina recogni-
tion and mood lighting – maybe you could install this
shit in your milking shed!

How's it going up there? Hopefully you'll be back soon.
Gotta dash else I'll be late to my next business breakfast.

Kat x

*

**Bev's Hen Party**

Hi-di-hi campers,

It's hen party time for Bev! Well, it will be in November.
How are you all fixed for the weekend of 20/21? Bev
wants to do something in London, so nobody gets bank-
rupted. Probably a meal and a shedload of drinks.
RSVP to me!

Maria x
(one half of the maids-of-honour ensemble – bless Billie,
she's up to her neck in cow dung!)

*

**Berlin, Baby! Save the date**

Doooooods!

Please save the date for 23/24 October for Kat's hen
party! Given that this is a once-in-a-lifetime thing, she'd
love us to all do something special and hit Berlin. Once
I've got numbers, I'll look into flights and accommoda-
tion.

RSVP to me!

Maria x

(one half of the maids-of-honour ensemble – bless Billie,
she's up to her neck in cow dung)

*

**Confession**

Shitbag,

How's it going? Are you dying on your ass up there in
God's Own country?

Hope you don't mind but I've nicked your locker. I've
taken up running and need somewhere to stash my
gear – your fail for not changing the default number on
your combi-lock.

When are you coming back?

Hugs and kisses,
Davo x

The microwave beeps. I don't know when I'm coming back. It feels like my former life has been frozen in time. I've unopened bills on my bed back in London. Clothes laid out for the KSG meeting I never attended. Uneaten food in the cupboards. Neglected PhD application forms. All hopes and dreams temporarily on hold and, meanwhile, my compassionate leave has run out – apparently compassion has an expiry date no matter what – and I've been forced to request an unpaid sabbatical.

**From: Maria**
Lesbian hen party conundrum: We can't have B&K's parties on the same date as that excludes their mutual friends, but now I've got people dropping out of both because they can't afford to go on two. And if they pick one, then that's like a bride v bride popularity contest. FFS!!!!

My face tingles as hot steam rises from each bottle as I fill them with formula.

Nathan pops his head through the window. 'What's keeping you?'

'Just sterilizing the bottles!' I hold them up as evidence.

'Why would you do that when they're licking God-knows-what all day?' He assesses the bottles. 'If they're for Carlie and

Mia, they'll need more than that! Ten per cent of their birth weight per day in milk, they'll need. I assume you know what you're doing?'

I clearly don't know how much the calves weighed when they were born, but I'm loath to ask him – even though he possesses every bit of information I need, I do have a smattering of pride. Instead, I make a mental note to go through their birth logs.

The calves at least fill me with hope. Carlie and Mia dance around the pen when they see me approach with milk, nuzzling at my waist in anticipation. They judder and twitch, nipping on the bottle teat and pulling as hard as they can, full of innocence and urgency. Carlie's delicate black legs skate Bambi-like on the concrete as she tugs at the bottle, her hooves slipping and sliding. She has panda-like markings around her eyes, the rest of her face pure white. When she's finished the bottle, she rubs her milk-stained curly moustache on my leg.

Rachel's face appears over the wall. Her breath smells of Cherry Coke.

'How old are they?' she smiles.

'Carlie's four weeks and Mia's six weeks.'

She lets herself into the pen. 'Can I help?

'Sure.' I hand her the bottle that Mia's attached herself to, which promptly flies out of her hand, sending an arc of milk spurting onto the straw bedding.

'It's easier if you hold it at an angle, like a pen,' I say, picking up the bottle. 'Air won't get trapped that way.' I repeat the advice Dad gave me as a teenager.

'They're really cute.' She tickles Mia's chin.

A couple of Orpington chickens strut into the pen, bushy leg feathers blowing in the breeze like baggy pantaloons.

'How's the GCSE prep going?' I say.

She pulls a face. 'OK. I'll definitely fail Maths, though – something else for Dad to go mental about!' Mia's tongue lollops down her sleeve. 'That tickles!' she squeals, dancing round in the straw.

'Rach?' Nathan hurries in, knocking over a broom, which clatters to the ground. 'Out!'

'But, Dad . . .?' she says.

'Time we got breakfast,' he says gruffly.

I stroke Carlie's soft ears. 'You can grab something here if you want?'

'No,' Nathan says sternly. 'Thank you.'

Rachel reluctantly hands me back the bottle. 'My dad, the asshole,' she mutters.

I head back inside to tackle the accounts. The blurry digits of the oven clock suggest it's only 8.30 a.m. Joely will be on her way to work now, her crisp white shirt scented with passionflower linen spray, a pencil skirt complementing the contours of her hips, her bare legs never-ending.

**To: Joely (future wife) Chevalier**
Up to my neck in cow dung, thinking of you xxx

The house feels eerily quiet without anyone here. Floorboards creak in places they didn't a week ago and my eye is drawn to detail I wouldn't normally notice: cobwebs drifting over the curtain poles, the flutter of moths in the cupboard under the stairs, speckles of mould on the bathroom ceiling. Night-time is worse. It brings out its own score of sound effects – the groan of contracting furniture, the sudden drip of built-up water in the showerhead onto the porcelain bath, foxes rutting, owls hooting. The flicker of bats in the barn. Everything feels colder without Dad and Grandma here.

I sit at the kitchen table, half-heartedly tapping at a hard-boiled egg with a teaspoon while working through spreadsheet upon spreadsheet of accounts. At first, it all just washes over me – cash-flow plans, SWOT analysis, herd health programmes. Dad's got a plan for everything: nutrient management, waste management, calf care, you name it, there's a spreadsheet for it. The figures in the columns stare back at me and I can't make head nor tail of it. It may as well be written in hiero-glyphics. It's only when my eye is drawn to the Grand Totals at the bottom of last month's profit-and-loss spreadsheet that it becomes glaringly obvious that we are running at a hefty loss. A huge loss. A loss I feel sick to the core about.

Flicking back through the previous months' accounts, it's the same story. Loss upon loss. The losses getting greater as time goes on. To think that my dad has been carrying this burden for months, perhaps years, the stress eating at him whilst I was merrily gadding about in London, oblivious. I push away my boiled egg and pick up the phone.

I'm supposed to be discussing the calves' feed blend with the nutritionist. Instead, I alternate between calling Joely and Grandma. Joely's voicemail kicks in after seven rings and Grandma's mobile phone is switched off. It's probably in a cupboard in this house. I can't get through on Beatrice's landline either. Every time I call, it's permanently engaged –

no doubt thanks to Auntie 'just checking on John but really want to yap about myself for hours' June.

**From: Joely (future wife) Chevalier**
In non-stop meetings, thinking of you xxx

I go back into the big barn to reclaim the packet of cherry Bakewells I've left in the wheelbarrow when I notice Nadia circling her pen restlessly. A heavy mucus discharge suggests this is the onset of labour. With Nathan having disappeared until later, I call Lorna.

'Has she expelled the water sac?' she asks.

My eyes skim the straw for a saggy blob of something. 'Remind me what a water sac looks like.'

'You'd know it if you saw it. Is she standing?'

'Sometimes.' I heave myself onto the second bar of the cold metal gate. 'Then she'll lie down and shuffle about a bit.'

'She may just be uncomfortable. It's a heavy load.'

Nadia gives me a filthy look. She doesn't want me there.

'So how will I know when she's about to give birth?' I say.

'You'll see the head and hooves come out,' Lorna says breezily. 'I personally think she's another week away.'

I don't understand how she can be that sure. I remember Parsnip arriving ten days before her due date when Jupiter gave birth to her under a hawthorn bush in somebody else's field. We had to walk miles to find her, Jupiter being a private, independent cow with not much time for humans. She'd managed to get over a stone wall that none of the others could jump, knowing that there was more wood sorrel and dandelion on the other side to dine on. Only the best for her girls.

She birthed Parsnip's twin sisters under the very same bush. They came early too, each of them with an almost heart-shaped white blotch on her forehead. Lady Love and Lady Lovely.

Nadia cranes her neck and lets out a deep grunt.

'I think you might need to come over,' I say.

'Any reason to believe it's going to be a difficult birth?' Lorna asks me.

I watch Nadia twist and turn in her pen. 'Aren't all births difficult?'

'They shouldn't be. She's very healthy.'

'Are you saying you don't need to come for a birth?'

'I'll be over tomorrow anyway, unless you think you need me now.'

Nadia lets out a haunting groan. 'I think I need you now.'

Forty minutes later, Lorna stands before me in running gear, cheeks flushed and hair damp. She holds a bottle of livestock wormer in one hand and a Dectomax drench gun in the other. I get a hot flash of the bull sperm incident: the taunts in the school corridors. *Cum again?* Her superiority. My humiliation.

'I've got Star and Mary down as having eye-worm,' she says. 'So, I thought I'd kill two birds with one stone.'

'Right,' I say, realizing those names correspond with the cows in the pen I have been ignorantly checking for lameness. 'Nadia's in the barn.'

We head into the cowshed, where Nadia groans from the second pen.

Lorna assesses her from ten feet away. 'Nope,' she says tersely. 'Not in labour.'

'She seems in quite a bit of pain,' I say, feeling inadequate, incompetent and about three years old.

Lorna opens the gate and lets herself into the enclosure. Nadia allows her to run her hands over her neck and withers, down further over her crops, around her brisket and down her leg towards her knee, raising her hoof compliantly. Considering Nadia doesn't even like me stepping into her pen, this in itself is a triumph.

Lorna studies her claws. 'That'll be the culprit!' she says, pointing out a red area of Nadia's cloven hoof. 'She's got a sole ulcer.'

I lean over the gate but can't really see what she's talking about and don't want to distress Nadia by coming closer.

'How's her diet?'

'Good,' I say. 'I mean, I think she's eating healthily.'

'You think?' She raises an eyebrow and picks up her iPad. 'Here we go. Alfalfa, haylage, barley and wheat grain. She's on commercial supplements. Any reason she doesn't have access to pasture?'

'I just thought . . . what with her calf coming and . . .'

'Her calf probably won't be here for at least another week,' she says. 'I appreciate you've got plenty of straw in here but it's patchy. The best thing you can do is get her out in the fields. She'll be missing the social aspect as much as anything. I'll trim the horn down once I've seen to the other two ladies.'

She picks up the bottle of wormer she's left on the breeze-block wall and we wander over to Star and Mary, who have never been that keen on each other. It's not that they out-and-out hate each other, and they're certainly not vicious, but in a natural environment, they would probably choose to ignore each other, a bit like Lorna and I.

Lorna pulls on latex gloves and loads the drench gun, which spews out orange-brown goo. I try not to think about bull sperm – the sticky eyebrows, the humiliation – but it's too late, I can't hold it back.

I was fifteen, which means Lorna would have been twelve. It was summer up on the farm and the air was honeysuckle warm. I'd just come back from a run and noticed that Dad had sectioned off around ten cows for insemination, a process I still to this day find traumatic for a number of reasons. Bertha and Hyacinth knew what was coming and were antsy – a lot of tail swishing and hoof grinding was going on. A few moments later, Lorna's dad arrived with all the gear. He was dressed in khaki shorts – which he wore whatever the weather – and carried a heavy tank of liquid nitrogen, containing bull sperm in individual straws, which he parked next to the cowshed entrance. As soon as he removed the lid, gas smoked out like something out of a sci-fi movie. With a long pair of tweezers, he extracted a single straw of semen and had just plopped it into a pot of warm water when Lorna came running in with his phone. I remember she was wearing denim shorts and a butterfly T-shirt. 'Mum's on the line. Says it's urgent.'

Her dad peeled off his rubber gloves to take the call. No sooner was he out of sight, than Andy Pickering, my dad's farm hand, appeared from the barn with this smirk on his face. He always had a glint in his eye, but it was clear he was up to something. At first, he just started dicking around with this joint that he'd rolled and asking if, like humans, cows can get stoned. Lorna laughed along with him – she had a bit of a thing for Andy and used to follow him around like a lost puppy, God knows why, because he was a grade-A moron. Then he made his way over to the straws of bull sperm.

'Here, Billie, fancy some spunk?' he said, peering into the canister.

I looked away, repulsed. The sight, smell and texture of semen has to be the singularly most revolting thing in the world.

He picked up the box of disposable gloves and pulled on a pair.

'What are you doing?' I said.

'Cum again?' He laughed, reaching for the thawed straw of semen.

'Leave that alone,' I said, looking around for Dad.

Lorna giggled. She always giggled when he was being a dick.

'Make me!' Andy said, lifting the straw out and waggling it at me.

Again, I looked around for Dad, but then remembered that he'd driven off to get fencing supplies. 'Andy, put it back! It's not funny. Do you know how much that stuff costs?'

He held it up to study its form. 'What is it, golden jizz?'

'Just put it back!'

'Royal jizz? Here, has anyone given you a pearl necklace before?' He held the straw above my head. 'Maybe a pearl crown?'

I ran away with a yelp, but only as far as the barn door.

'It's OK,' Lorna shouted. 'It won't come out unless you cut the end off.'

Andy turned back to her. 'Scissors?'

Lorna's eyes travelled to a large pair of secateurs on the hay bale in front of her. She looked at him, wide-eyed. 'You wouldn't.'

He snatched them up. 'Wanna bet?'

'Honestly, Andy. You can't.' I was getting really worried. 'My dad'll go mental. Lorna's dad'll go mental and one of the cows won't calve if you waste it.'

I tried to grapple them off him, but he spun his body around like a shield, twisting this way and that. I grabbed at his arm but it was the wrong one and, within a split second, he'd managed to snip the straw. Before I could react, he'd flicked it at me, and there I was with warm, gloopy bull sperm sliding down my face.

'Bull's eye!' he shouted, laughing at me as semen slid through my hair, its rancid pulp clinging to my eyelashes and spattering my lips.

'You fucking idiot!' I screamed, then turned tail and ran into the house, repulsed and humiliated.

That moment, right there, when I was dripping with seed and standing in the shower fully clothed, should be 'the bull sperm' incident, but it didn't end here. Instead, news travelled to the school gates and got twisted and contorted along the grapevine until it became public knowledge that Billie Oliver let a boy from Gosforth Comprehensive spunk all over her at her farm for a tenner. If you didn't believe it, you only had to ask Lorna Parsons.

It was no use trying to explain what really happened. Nobody was interested in the truth. They just wanted pornographic gore, and the more spunk the better; animal, human, who cared? I wish I hadn't. Puberty is hard enough

105

without abhorrent nicknames. 'Spunk girl', 'Jizabell' and, worst of all, 'Cum stain Belinda'.

Lorna peers at me now, clearly unbothered by memories of our past. 'Any news on your dad?'

'No.' I look at my shoes as hot tears surface out of nowhere and I'm unsure whether it's the mortification of the past or the hopelessness of the present that is getting to me the most. And then I feel guilty for allowing myself to obsess over a ridiculous incident that happened years ago whilst there are hugely more important things at stake. 'Sorry, I'm fine until I have to talk about it. And then I'm not.'

She sucks her top lip in contemplation. 'Why don't you take twenty minutes out?'

That's the thing about Lorna, she's pathologically unempathetic. She can't just sling her arm around you and give you a hug. I remember when I was nineteen and had come back from university for Christmas, she and her friend, Jessica, were mucking about on the tractor and I cut my hands on this hoof-trimming equipment her dad had left out. I can still feel the pain now. There was blood everywhere and I felt so faint I had to sit down and put my head between my legs. When I came around, Jessica had my hand wrapped in a towel whilst Lorna just stood there staring.

I miss Joely. I miss my friends. I miss human contact. I miss waking up in my own bed, in the shoebox Maria and I call home, and trudging to work in wet socks. I miss my life.

I leave Lorna to it and head indoors.

**To: Joely (future wife) Chevalier**
Are you still coming up next weekend? xxx

Three little bubbles appear on my phone screen beneath her forthcoming message, which vanish without materializing into a text. A few seconds later, they reappear and then vanish again. Five minutes later my phone bleeps.

**From: Joely (future wife) Chevalier**
I'm trying to make it happen, ma petite Anglaise.
Christophe wants me to go to Belgium with him on
Sunday, but I've told him I cannot travel until Monday
morning xxx

The thought of Joely gallivanting around a foreign country accompanied by a man with the looks of James Bond and the pay packet of James Goldsmith makes me shudder. I want to ask her if she's still attracted to him and enjoys his company. Whether they hang out in the evenings when they're away on business. Whether they order each other's drinks and share breakfast in hotel restaurants. Whether he would tuck in her label or tell her she has lipstick on her teeth. I want to ask all these things, but I don't want the answers.

**To: Joely (future wife) Chevalier**
Thanks. Miss you xxx

**From: Joely (future wife) Chevalier**
Miss you more xxx

No sooner than her text appears, a black van with swirly italic silver lettering appears in the yard and a lady with a severe fringe gets out holding a large bouquet of pink peonies. I feel all warm inside knowing Joely has remembered my favourite flowers. She hands me the bouquet, through the window. The soft petals tickle my nose as I inhale their fragrance. I open the small, pink card wedged between the stems.

Hang in there, buddy! Call us if you need us. Don't forget you're brilliant.
Love Maria, Kat and Bear xxx

Peonies. Friends. Love. Kisses. I dissolve into tears at the kitchen sink. A friend-set is like a toolset. You need different tools for different occasions: Maria for entertainment, Kat for career advice, Bev for loyalty and Joely for love.

Stuck up here on my own, I don't have the right tools for the job.

## CHAPTER EIGHT

# JELLY BABiES AND PYJAMAS

**From: Maria**
Lesbian hen party conundrum #17. Most of the hens are
couples so it's hardly going to be 'girls let off the leash
having unbridled fun', is it? Should I invite guys? Also,
what's the deal with vagina earrings?

Dad lies in one of the eight hundred and fifty beds at Sheffield's
Royal Hallamshire Hospital. He's been transferred here for
brain surgery. I wander through the west wing with his freshly
washed pyjamas and a bag of Jelly Babies, wondering what
he'll be like this time. Bloated or haggard? Alert or subdued?
Asleep or awake? The hospital is a monolithic twenty-one
storey maze of corridors, makeshift waiting rooms and wards
you can't quite get to. I find 'Neurosurgery' colour-coded
green on the map and head up in the lift.

When I eventually identify N1, he's not there, and I panic
that he's gone into theatre, anaesthetized and alone.

'John Oliver?' The nurse repeats, squeezing a Hello Kitty toy under her chin, which squeaks each time she releases its furry pink stomach.

She leans over the monitor of her computer and informs me that he's been moved to Magnolia on N2. My lungs expand with relief.

I follow the smell of detergent down the corridor, the soles of my trainers sticking to the freshly mopped floor. Left through the double doors, past a waiting room of sombre grey faces. Left again at the next set of doors, and sharp right. I see him before he sees me. He's sandwiched between a heavy-breathing lady surrounded by visitors and a tiny woman who's fast asleep. His head is shaved in preparation for surgery, and a circle has been drawn onto his scalp with black marker. I try to conceal my shock, but it's difficult – Dad doesn't look like Dad without his mop of honey-blonde and grey curls. The twinkle in his eyes has gone and his skin is white-grey. I tell myself it's just temporary and that he'll be back to normal soon. Still, my stomach feels queasy looking at him.

'How are you?' I say, giving him a gentle hug and sitting down in the asylum-green plastic chair at his bedside. 'How was the journey over? Did they put you in an ambulance?'

'Ambulance car.' He puts his hand on mine. 'What are you doing coming to visit me again? I keep telling you, you've a farm to run!'

'And I keep telling you, you can't get rid of me that easily.' I pluck the larger of the two greetings cards off his bedside table. It features an orange robot spewing a speech bubble that says: 'Since laughter is the best medicine, you should tell yourself some jokes,' and is signed 'with love from Pete and June'.

'It's good to see you,' he says, 'but promise me one thing . . .'

'Go on.' I put the card back.

'Put the cows before me. Don't come rushing to my bedside if the ladies need you. I've got onsite medical staff, they haven't. They're more in need than I am. Have you got a pen?'

I tap at my pockets and shake my head.

'Maybe you could make notes on your phone then. Daisy needs to cut down on TMR, she's getting a bit hefty and the extra weight plays havoc with her arthritis. Julia's been lame on and off all winter, so you need to keep an eye on her. Nadia must be due any day, and Louise and Allie can't be that far behind.'

Is there a bovine organization chart I'm unaware of? 'Which one is Julia?'

'Large, bossy, always first to the milking shed. Hangs out with Mildred. You know, the one with what looks like a black maple leaf on her neck.'

'Wow.'

'Hates Pandora. God knows why.'

'Here,' I say, reaching into my pocket and pulling out a squashed Ginsters pork pie.

'I take that back.' Dad chuckles. 'You can visit whenever you want.' He fingers the wrapper. 'You won't tell your grandma?'

'I'm sure your cholesterol can take a back seat just this once.'

His eyelids start to droop but he presses on regardless. 'There's a kink in one of the hosepipes, which could probably do with being straightened out.'

'Dad?'

111

'Not the blue one, the yellow one.'

'Dad?'

His eyes shift to mine and he nods for me to speak.

'I love you.'

He inhales deeply. 'I love you too.'

The ward is stripped of colour. Starched white sheets. Watery blue blankets. Pale green vertical blinds. Cream flooring. Even the daffodils on the neighbouring bedside table have lost their yellow to the garishly bright ceiling lights. Everything is rinsed of its vibrancy.

'How's little Carlie getting on?' Dad says.

'She's fine. Loves her milk. Won't be too long until she's on solids.'

'There you go! Sounding like a pro already.'

I pick at the blister at the base of my inner middle finger. 'The accounts are a bit worrying.'

Dad looks at his feet.

I open the packet of Jelly Babies I've bought him. 'I knew business was bad but . . .'

He rummages for a red one. 'We were doing all right until . . .' The expression of frustration on his face evaporates and a curtain of uncertainty closes over him. 'Where are we?'

'We're at Sheffield Hallamshire.'

'The hospital?' he whispers.

I reach for his hand. The cannula in his forearm is bandaged tightly, a neat plastic valve protruding from one end. 'It's OK.'

He stares ahead and then with complete clarity says, 'Nobody cares, Bilberry. It all went belly up when milk prices dropped another sixty-two pence per litre. All of the big

112

supermarkets, all wanting to be the cheapest, no matter the consequences. As long as milk's affordable, everyone will pour it over their cereal. It doesn't matter that dairy farmers can't make a profit any more.' He takes a slug of water. 'Truth be told, we'd be better off selling the herd, selling the equipment and renting the farm out as a B&B.'

'You'd do that?' I plunge my hand into the bag of Jelly Babies and pull out a green one, yanking its head away from its body, until its gelatine neck spews out emerald gunk.

He laughs. 'Run a bed and breakfast? I'd be bloody useless!'

I want to ask him about selling up, but no matter how I shape the question in my head, it feels wrong. The farm is part of his life and I don't want him to think I've written him off. It's bad, though. No matter which way you spin it, we're in financial shit; cow feed, labour, vet fees and depreciation are killing us each month.

I form the words clearly in my head. *Would you consider selling up?* But each time I twist my tongue around them, the words get jumbled in my throat. Second-guessing Dad's reaction reminds me of gearing myself up to coming out to Grandma. The memory is so vivid, it could be yesterday.

I was seventeen and sitting on the kitchen worktop, raiding the first-aid box for a plaster as I'd cut my knee falling over on the way back from a run. Grandma came in cradling a huge bread bowl covered with a gingham tea towel. She asked me if I'd like to show Beatrice's grandson around Sheffield. 'Take him to see a film or something,' she said.

'As long as this isn't a set-up.' I pressed the only plaster I could find, a *Star Wars* one featuring a wide-eyed Yoda flashing a green light sabre, against my kneecap. 'I'm not interested in anything romantic.'

I remember bread dough plopping against the floured surface of the kitchen table as Grandma's knuckles pounded the yeasty putty, her sapphire engagement ring swivelled around her finger into the palm of her hand. 'You'll have to get romantic at some point, Billie Goat. Happens to everyone.'

My knee stung, but not as much as the words on my tongue. I had rehearsed this moment for ever. I'd role-played it in my head hundreds of times; out loud in my bedroom, in the cowshed, in the fields, in God knows how many public toilets, so I knew how it would play out my end, but was still unsure how she would react, despite thinking through every possible connotation of a reaction. I'd role-played against her scooping me up in her arms and telling me she always had her suspicions and loves me just the way I am. Unconditionally. I'd role-played another version where she was too shocked to speak and had to go for a walk over the fields to digest what I'd said, returning tight-lipped and unsure. In another, she called my dad in and asked him to have a word with me until I 'see sense'. There was even one incarnation where anger frothed at her mouth and she wanted nothing to do with me. Though, in this version, I could never fully create the image in my mind's eye so I knew it would never happen. It was time to roll the dice.

'Romance may overcome everyone at some point,' I said. 'But it might happen in a slightly different way for me.'

Grandma dolloped the dough into a bread tin, pressing it firmly into each corner. 'How do you mean?'

I lowered myself down from the worktop and leaned on

the back of the nearest kitchen chair. 'Grandma, you might want to sit down.'

She opened the oven door, a rush of heat invading the room. 'Are you going to tell me you're attracted to women?' Her eyes remained faithful to the bread tins.

My words caught in my throat. 'Yes.'

The oven door clinked shut and her wet dishcloth swished backwards and forwards over the table until every last trace of flour disappeared.

'You're choosing a difficult path, Billie Goat,' she said eventually. 'It'd be a hell of a lot easier if you found yourself a man.'

'For who?' I squeezed the back of the chair. 'For you?'

She moved to the sink and ran the hot tap. 'For you.'

I hovered at her side. 'I don't have a choice, Grandma. I can't help it. I'm genetically gay.'

'That's a thing, is it?' She wrung out the dishcloth under hot water.

'Yes.'

'Since when?'

'Since for ever. It's just not always been acknowledged.'

'Well, Billie Goat, your dad and I love you, no matter what you decide.'

We didn't hug. We didn't retreat to our corners. We didn't do anything other than carry on as normal, and I couldn't for the life of me work out whether it had gone seamlessly well or dreadfully badly. It was as if I'd chosen a profession she didn't value; something random I'd arrived at in a moment of madness. It didn't feel conclusive, or like it was a weight off my shoulders. If anything, I felt more confused than ever.

And it was at this moment I realized that there is no monumental coming-out moment, moreover a succession of coming-out moments, which last a lifetime: coming out to your grandmother, your father, your friends at school, your team-mates at football, your dad's farm staff, the ladies at Grandma's bridge club, your sixth-form mates, your colleagues, your professor. What is it they say? It's not the destination, it's the journey.

'Your grandma will come round,' I remember Dad saying that evening.

I'm not sure there ever was a turning point where Grandma did 'come round', more of a gradual, unspoken acceptance. It wasn't until my auntie June took her and Beatrice to see *La Cage aux Folles* at the Sheffield Lyceum that Grandma had full-blown gay pride for me and made a point of triumphantly humming 'I Am What I Am' whilst doing the washing up.

It was different coming out to Dad. It just spilled out when he ordered a BLT at a Hathersage teashop and made some crap pun about it being one letter short of LGBT. I told him it was a shit joke and then told him I was gay. He hugged me, likened me to a 'Jersey cow rather than a common Friesian', and then we both finished our sandwiches. I felt the glow of satisfaction for days after that, weeks even. As if the pair of us inhabited this warm, cosy bubble that nobody else had access to. Our own little secret. It definitely made us closer. Stronger too.

I form a different set of difficult words in my head now: although they should be simple, they're far from it.

'Dad?' I cross and uncross my legs. 'Do you think you'll stay on the farm for ever?'

Dad presses at the edges of the translucent plaster securing the cannula in his arm. He smooths the blanket down over his chest. 'Ideally we'd downsize. Get a small plot of land for five cows or so. Somewhere a bit closer to town, not so cut off from everything.'

I feel my shoulders relax. 'That's what you'd do?'

He pulls at the neck of his pyjamas. 'I would if I could.'

'So, what's stopping you?' I say.

'Wolfgang Huxley-Lipyeat.'

'Who?'

'The Wolf,' he clarifies.

It takes me a few seconds to recognize the name. 'Our landlord?'

He nods. 'Nobody will buy me out unless I top up the leasehold, and he wants £120,000 for it. That, or it's £300,000 to buy the freehold.'

'Three hundred thousand? How can he make those sorts of demands?'

Dad looks lost. Not in a confused way, but in a defeated way – like life itself has gobbled up the very essence of who he is and spat him back out again, upside down and inside out. His eyelids close.

I sit for a while, not knowing what to do, the clock at the end of the ward ticking so much louder than before, Dad's gentle snoring almost drowned out. I take the clean pyjamas off my lap, put them on the bed next to Dad's feet and straighten out the collar and cuffs in the way a chambermaid might prepare the presentation of loo roll, like it somehow matters. I squander another Jelly Baby and pick up the smaller card on the bedside table. It's handmade, bumpy in texture and features a pencil sketch of a Friesian standing in a grassy field. Inside, a lady called Pat wishes him a speedy recovery and looks forward to seeing him back on the bowling circuit. Judging by the pyramid of kisses beneath her signature, she seems to be quite fond of him.

I study Dad. His egg-like head. The absence of his mop of curls. The circle they've drawn on his scalp. The faded smattering of freckles across his nose. The way his chest gently rises and falls under his cotton pyjamas, his wedding ring, hanging from his neck, glinting in the light with every inhalation. Hair sprouts from his earlobes. I wriggle my hand into his and feel the weight of his palm in mine.

Forty minutes later, a skinny nurse with the bedside manner of an SS officer declares visiting time is over. Reluctantly, I peel Dad's fingers away from mine, kiss them and place them by his side.

Everything hurts.

**From: Maria**
Bilbo! I've only gone and got cast as the main ovum in *Menstruation the Musical*!!! I'm stoked. Thought I'd be tampon chorus for sure. How's it going up there? Do you reckon you'll be able to make *Alternative Eurovision* on Friday? I got you a ticket. Love ya, M x

**From: Dave Work**
Hey Shitbag, quick reminder that the Newcastle postgrad fair is next week. There are two courses that are your bag. Just thought being up north, you could pop over.

P.S. Met your French girl the other day at a meeting.
H.O.T. Mother-fucker!

Does life not have the decency to stand still for just one second when the shit hits the fan? If only *popping over* to Newcastle was an option right now. Not only do I feel a sense of frustration, but a sense of guilt. Guilt that I should be driving my career right now, the agent of my own destiny. Forging a path to greatness and bagging a PhD. And then I feel guilty about feeling guilty. I shouldn't be thinking about myself and what I'm missing out on. I should be concentrating on Dad. Besides, how could I possibly prepare for a PhD fair in Newcastle right now? It's all I can do to get through the days at the moment. The treadmill of farm and hospital. Farm and hospital. Farm and hospital. It's like one of those dreams where your legs are lead-heavy and, no matter how hard you try to forge forward, you can't move.

As soon as I'm out of the lifts, I subscribe to *Science Matters* in a bid to 'stay at the cutting-edge of science matters, because science does matter'. I'm so busy scrolling through articles that I promise myself I'll read later that I've wandered into the hospital gift shop and have no idea why.

Why are hospital gift shops so random? Rather than selling bed socks and headphones or anything that might be of practical help to someone who is bedridden, the Royal Hallamshire gift shop is stocked with African face masks, Indonesian jewellery and Balinese cookery books. A row of wooden bird boxes sits below a display of catchphrases carved into shabby-chic nautical driftwood, should anyone fancy giving their garden an overhaul after being discharged. *Live. Love. Laugh.*

God only knows why I've wandered into this Aladdin's cave, but just as I'm about to leave, I spot a piece of treasure in a glass cabinet next to the till: a silver ladybird pendant just like my mum's brooch in the home video. Its wings are delicate and striking in equal measure; the craftsmanship that has gone into its intricately sculpted antennae, the raised spots, the segmented legs is insane. That such a precious thing can be found nested in a hellhole of death, disease and decay surely means there's hope. A lucky ladybird, just like my mum's. With Joely's birthday coming up soon, it almost feels like fate that I should buy it for her. It's too perfect not to.

The lady behind the counter, all incense sticks and tie dye, apologizes that they're out of pendant boxes and will a ring box do? I say that's fine and she explains that the ladybird symbolizes the essence and embodiment of the divine feminine and a profound connection of two souls, emerging to journey to freedom together. As well as unearthing treasure, it seems I've hit the aesthetic and spiritual jackpot. I pay up, write 'Goddess Joely' on the tag with a novelty Eiffel Tower pen at the till, and leave with a handful of gift-wrapped hope. *A profound connection of two souls.* Everything slots into place: I bloody well love Joely and it's about time I told her so. And what better way than with this ladybird?

A few laps of the ambulance bay and I've got her birthday all planned out: I'll take the early train down after milking and meet her for brunch on the South Bank before heading to the Tate Modern where we'll cavort between the acrylics and oils of 'The Ladybird and I', an exhibition of 'LOVE – arts meet amour'.

'Happy Birthday!' I'll say, carefully fastening the ladybird pendant around her neck. We'll stroll on to the second exhibition, 'Curiosity: Art and the Pleasures of Knowing', where I'll reflect about curiosity being 'an ambiguous passion: the virtuous impulse behind the search for knowledge and at the same time a disreputable desire for novelty and strangeness', because it says so on the internet. She, at this point, will be in awe of my appreciation of the intellectual and aesthetic freedom of this artform and will beg me to go home with her.

Without consciously thinking about it, I video-call Joely from the hospital entrance.

'Billie!' Her face appears, doing a 180° in the KSG corridor. 'It's so good to see you.'

'You too!' I say, feeling travel-sick as her phone tilts left then right, as she strides between two walls lined with KSG catchphrases in block print. SYNERGY. EQUALITY. STRAIGHT-FORWARDNESS. TRUST.

'Are you in the hospital?' she says.

'Yeah. Just seen Dad.'

'Is he OK?'

'Kind of. It's pretty difficult,' I say.

'I can only imagine,' she says. 'I miss you! I miss your face.'

I smile. 'I've just bought your birthday present.' My hand reaches for the small gift-wrapped box in my pocket, the soft ribbon running between my fingers. 'If I can get Nathan to cover, I thought I could come down to London and take you out.'

'I'm so sorry, *ma petite Anglaise*, I'll be in South Korea for my birthday. Did you get the link I sent you?'

It's only when she says it that I recall a text she sent a

couple of days ago with quite a few links that I promised I'd check out later and then completely forgot about.

'It's OK,' she says. 'I know how busy it is on the farm.'

'I'm sorry, Joels.'

She presses her nose playfully with her forefinger and smiles. 'Don't worry about it. Did I tell you I miss you?'

'Did I tell you I miss you too?' A fuzzy feeling fills my stomach and I'm dying to tell her I love her but want to save it for when we're face to face. 'So, tell me about South Korea!'

'KSG have an Obstetrics event in Seoul and want me to deliver the presentation I did in London. It got some good feedback, so . . .' She acknowledges a man in a suit passing her in the corridor with a bow of the head.

'That's brilliant, Joels!' I feel bad. We're both so busy fighting our own fires that we're not aware of each other's. 'Amazing.'

'Yes.' She grins.

'Well, when you get back, we should celebrate. I thought you might like to see "The Ladybird and I" exhibition at the Tate.'

'What is it?'

'An exhibition of love. *Art meets amour*, told through ladybirds.'

Her grin dissolves into a frown. 'Can I be honest?'

'Of course.'

'I hate ladybirds. They are essentially flying beetles.'

'Right,' I say, shoving her present back into my pocket, a metallic taste in my mouth.

'Their legs are like sticks and they carry sexually transmitted infections.' She all but balks. 'I'm sorry, Billie. I'm moody because I miss you. I miss you too much, and this fucking job . . .' She scrunches up her face. 'I know Seoul is a great opportunity, but I'd prefer to be with you. And I have a stupid award ceremony this weekend before I go, and I just want to spend time with you.' She stares into the camera, her forehead locked in concentration. 'Can I show you something?'

A few seconds later, a link to a duck-egg-blue silk dress by Oliver Bonas appears on my screen. 'You think this is OK for collecting the award?'

'You didn't tell me you've won an award!' I give the dress a cursory glance.

'Not me directly, but with Christophe. For the successful trial of the EPE drug.'

I feel as if I've been freeze-dried in a vacuum. Like the air has been sucked out of me and I am held expressionless against my will. This is the drug made from the biochemicals *I* have spent the best part of two years testing and retesting. The drug whose effects *I* have prodded and probed under a microscope. The drug whose qualities *I* have assessed and reassessed. And now I'm having it explained to me like I'm an outsider. Like I never played a part in its journey.

'Congratulations,' I say, my mouth drying.

'Christophe is really happy. He wants the entire KSG team behind him at the awards ceremony.'

'Right,' I say. His name alone makes my blood run cold, but as Kat always says, *Negative energy is a waste of emotion.* 'Joels, it's a beautiful dress. Let me get it for your birthday. The thing I've got you probably isn't . . . I was struggling to know what to get you, to be honest.'

Her eyes widen. 'No, it's too expensive!'

'It's fine. You'll look amazing in it. It's a brilliant achieve-ment, which deserves something special.'

'Thank you.' She clip-clops down the corridor. 'I'll come up as soon as I'm not working these eighteen-hour days, I promise.' She stops in front of a framed poster promoting work/life balance. 'I've got to go.'

'OK.'

'*Ciao*.'

'*Ciao*.' I sound ridiculous saying *ciao*.

I ache to see her. To feel her soft skin against mine. The smell of her hair as she leans into me. The outline of her shoulder blades as I lie next to her. The gentle tch-tch-tch sound she makes when my leg's been wrapped over hers for too long and cramp's setting in. We fit, Joely and I; an Anglo-French jigsaw of yin and yang.

I buy her the dress – so what if I have to sell a kidney next month.

# CHAPTER NINE

# RANCiDiTY

Two weeks later

**From: Maria**
Lesbian hen party conundrum #67. BERLIN IS
CANCELLED!
Kat and Bear have decided to combine parties so that
people don't have to shell out twice! What's the fucking
point in having a hen do if the person you're going to
marry is on it?!

**From: Dad**
Just a reminder that Heather is allergic to goose grass
so you may want to keep her out of the bottom field.

**To: Joely (future wife) Chevalier**
Happy Birthday to you! Happy Birthday to you! Happy
Birthday, Goddess Joely! Happy Birthday to you! Hip,

hip, hooray! Hope you have a cracking day and sorry I
can't be with you xxx

**@SCIENCE MATTERS**
Don't become a dinosaur! Why keeping current is critical
in scientific research.

**From: Wincanton Co-operative**
Your milk tanker has arrived. Please dispatch within the
hour.

A shiny silver milk tanker rumbles up the hill, hissing and
juddering as the driver performs what must be a nine-point
turn before managing to reverse into the dirt track. The tail
of the tanker swings around in the yard, missing the bulk-
milk-tank outhouse by only a few millimetres. A tall man in
a faded red boiler suit jumps down from the cabin. His lips
are unusually red and the hair on his chin is soft and fluffy.
I'd put him at around thirty-five, though it's difficult to pin
an age on him, his baby face contradicting his greying hair.

'Is the boss around?' he says, clanking open the double
doors to the outhouse, his heavy boots clomping across the
wooden crates we use to protect the floor.

'My dad's ill, so I'm the boss at the moment.' I retie my
hair in a ponytail.

He lowers his head so as not to whack it on the low ceiling
and presses the agitation button. The room comes alive, pipes
juddering as milk rushes and gurgles. His long, spidery fingers
find their way into latex gloves and rip open a small sachet
containing a disinfectant wipe. He scribbles 'Fernbrook Farm,

tank ID 2591, 02 June' onto a label and sticks it to his plastic sample pot, then measures the temperature of the milk. 'Man's job really, farming.'

'What makes you say that?' I say, recategorizing him as older.

'Requires a lot of strength.' He makes a point of handing me the ladle that dangles just out of my reach, giving it to me in a way that suggests he has just saved me from the jaws of a shark.

'Thanks,' I say reluctantly, wondering whether he's going to call me 'lil' lady'.

I lift the metal lid from the stainless-steel tank. Milk gushes and whirls hypnotically in the vat below. I plunge the ladle into the deep well and pour its contents into the small paper container he's holding out.

He takes a sniff. 'What I'm looking for here is—'

'A good odour?' I suggest. 'Not too bitter, soapy or cowy.'

He clears his throat, lifting his chin to make himself taller. 'Very good, but has anyone taught you about rancidity?'

'Spontaneous rancidity or induced rancidity?' I hand him the lid to his pot.

He studies his sample dipper. 'Someone's been busy learning.'

'Someone grew up here!'

He retreats to the tanker, tapping numbers into his phone, and studies a dial in the back of the vehicle. Happy with the results, he affixes the pipe, turns on the pump and sends the milk chugging into the tanker. The motor hums loudly, the pipe pulsing in fits and bursts.

He turns to me, his face open and friendly. 'Sorry if I came across as mansplaining.'

I smile. 'Sorry if I came across as a know-it-all.'

He unscrews the pipe, milk froth spewing out onto the concrete floor. 'I'm Charlie.' He extends his hand.

'Billie.'

'Billie? Bit of a tomboy, are we?' He heads to the back of the lorry to read the meter. The last drops of milk drain from the tank and a sharp blast of hot water fizzes and spatters against the steel drum as my thumb hits the wash button. 'Here.' He takes the Biro from behind his ear and leans on the dashboard to scribble on the back of the print-out. 'If ever you need anything . . .' He hands me the small piece of paper with his phone number scrawled in large digits. '. . . or want me to take you out.' He jumps into the cabin. 'There's a place in Bakewell that does great burgers.'

'Thanks,' I say, wondering at what point I should tell him I don't like *burgers*.

The tanker chugs and grinds its way across the yard towards the lane, and I'm left struggling with my thoughts. I should feel insulted by the objectification implicit in Charlie's offer to 'take me out'. Kat would be outraged, spewing bile on feminist forums. *Like I'm not capable of taking myself out?* I should have told him I'm gay and that women don't need to get 'taken out', they just go out. I should be annoyed, but if I'm honest, it's comforting that someone wants to spend time with me.

I miss Joely. I want to hold her in my arms and wish her a happy birthday. I wonder what she's up to. I miss the way she makes a tray of coffee and brings it up to bed with an eggcup of daisies freshly plucked from the grass verge outside her flat. I miss the way her anecdotes don't quite conclude and are left hanging in the air, for me to draw my own conclusion. I miss her barking inappropriate English colloquialisms she's learned from her teenage nephew at trailer-trash TV, which sound both ridiculous and amusing coming out of the mouth of a grown woman. 'Snatched!' 'Straight fire!' 'Skurt, man!' I want to curl up on her leather sofa, her head under my chin as we shoot the shit, dissecting the day as a Netflix documentary unfolds in front of us. 'Sick!' 'She's after your cheddar!' 'Nice rides!' It's all yin and no yang without her, dualism broken, our opposing but complementary forces doing their own thing. Don't get me wrong, I understand that revolutionary medical milestones take precedent over visiting dairy farms, but I just need to see her. That, and I feel like a bit of a loser if I'm honest – there she is, saving the human race, and here I am, stagnating on a farm with unshaven legs.

In an attempt to clear my head, I jog to the top of Baslow Edge with Speedo. The hill up from the dirt track is a killer at an incline of 30 per cent, but it's worth it for the view alone. A patchwork of greens and golds unfolds beneath us; a network of valleys cradled in the bosom of surrounding hills, stone villages nesting in their crevices. Fields lighten and darken in moving patches as cotton-wool clouds roll across the sky. It's blustery, my cheeks pummelled like plasticine with each gust of wind. I hop from rock to rock, Speedo lolloping alongside me, his tongue streaming out like a windsock. We scramble over an isolated gritstone outcrop resembling a stack of giant pancakes, one rock piled on top of another, and over to the sheltered gully created by two boulders standing only a foot apart. Mum's ashes were sprinkled here. I should feel something spiritual, but I don't. I was in an incubator at the time and, the way Dad tells it, the whole thing didn't really go to plan, what with the blowback of the ashes in the wind and Grandma spraining her ankle on the way back down.

I settle down on the stones in the gully, gazing first out at the view and then at Speedo, who is lapping water from a sinkhole eroded by rain in the granite rock. As his tail wags from side to side, my eye is drawn to a ladybird, which crawls beneath a neighbouring bilberry bush. I try to manoeuvre it onto my hand, but it takes flight, buffeted by the wind. I toy with talking out loud to Mum, asking her for advice. How did she manage to live on the farm for so long? Did she actually enjoy it up here? Would she have had more children after me? Does she think Grandma would forgive me if I threw away the stuffed partridge in the hallway? But I know that there's no point in getting emotional. The scientist in me knows that philosophizing, hypothesizing and romanticizing is a waste of time. Time that could be spent on practical, tangible things, like getting Speedo down from the ledge he's about to blow off, getting my ass home and formulating a game plan to get myself off the farm, reintegrated into society, and back in the lab, where I belong.

I make all sorts of resolutions on the way back down. Firstly, to increase Nathan's hours so I stand a chance of extricating myself from daily farm life. Secondly, to make more of an effort to keep in synch with Joely – I've been sucked into a routine of self-preservation and it's important I understand what's happening in her world too. Thirdly, to enjoy the countryside more and treat it as a creature of beauty rather than a beast of constraint. To live in the present and not in the future or past. And fourthly, to pick up bread on my way home.

*

Down in the village, Baslow Scarecrow Festival is under way – straw men hanging from trees, straw women perched on stone walls, their eyes made of everything from dried satsumas to painted golf balls. Football heads, straw heads, heads made out of stuffed pillowcases. Stitched mouths, felt-tipped mouths, mouths made out of paper plates. Friendly scarecrows. Spooky scarecrows. Arty scarecrows. Scarecrow hybrids – Superman meets Worzel Gummidge. SpongeBob meets the Scarecrow from *The Wizard of Oz*. Grinning turnips in old tuxedos. Haunted faces with giant mouths. They're everywhere – in people's front gardens, on shop walls, the village green. Dangling from road signs accompanied by cardboard crows painted black.

The scarecrow festival has certainly got bigger and better since I was a child. I remember going when I was six. I'd made my own scarecrow, who used to tell me stories about the farm through her handstitched mouth. Her head was a football shoved into an old stocking. Her cheeks were scribbled pink. She had button eyes, straw hair and an old felt hat Dad used to recycle each year. I dressed her in Mum's old clothes from the bag in the bottom of Dad's wardrobe – a floral shirt and some faded dungarees. Grandma helped jam her legs into a pair of old wellingtons and prop her upright on a piece of broken fencing. I used to have tea parties with her, sharing doll's cups and saucers and filling them with water from the muddy stream. She used to plait my hair with her straw fingers and help pick out my clothes. She'd call me in when my tea was ready and hold my hand on the way to make-believe school.

When I showed her to Dad, he cried. I wasn't sure whether it was because she wasn't pretty enough.

131

'What's her name?' he said.

'She hasn't really got one,' I said. 'She's sometimes a teacher but most times she's a mummy.'

I remember him looking away at this point and that's when I knew my scarecrow wasn't good enough. That I'd have to make a better one next year. Still, we took her to the festival in the back of the truck that Dad drove back then and propped her up in the village square alongside half a dozen other scarecrows. Mrs Headley, Baslow village chairwoman at the time, strolled around with a clipboard, awarding points for design, strength and scariness.

'What's her name?' she said, admiring the string of plastic beads around my scarecrow's neck.

I looked at Dad and knew he'd be upset with me if I called it Mum. 'Mrs Headley,' I said.

'Flattery will get you nowhere,' Mrs Headley said, raising an eyebrow.

I think I came fifth.

Now, though, the village is rammed with visitors in their hundreds. Fifties feel-good music blares from speakers outside the village hall. Small children dance under fluttering bunting, and thirty or so primary school pupils line up next to a cart of tomatoes, all of them dressed as crows.

Tazzy accosts me. She looks a lot smaller without her lollipop overcoat on. 'Gone back to France, has she?'

'Sorry?' I say.

'Your lady-friend.'

'She lives in London,' I say, Speedo pulling me in the direction of bacon rolls.

'Caused a bit of a stir, apparently.' She lowers her voice

conspiratorially. 'Marjorie mentioned she might be moving into the village?'

'I don't know what gave Marjorie that impression.' I look around in the hope of a coffee van.

'You know Paul Pickering has a new partner?' She glances over to Paul, who is stooped over a barrel of cider, which has leaked all over his chequered waistcoat and is now flooding the boot of his car, a sulphurous smell invading the car park. 'From Wales, apparently,' she continues. 'Brought her to the Sportsfield Trust car-boot the other day and she snaffled the lot. Stone bird baths, folding chairs, a toaster. Nesting. Looks like she's here to stay.'

'Right,' I say, patting Speedo.

'You couldn't do us a favour, could you?' she says, pointing to a stall further up the green. 'Doreen's manning the tombola but needs raffle tickets from the store.'

'Sure.'

I wander down the road. Speedo goes nuts at Ginger, who sits on the mat outside the store licking his balls. I guess one of the advantages of having three legs is that it's easier to access your scrotum. It's easier to take Speedo in with me than chain him outside next to the cat. The door slides open, emitting the smell of fresh pizza. I make my way over to the till. Marjorie looks at Speedo and then at me.

'Not with Joelle today?' she chirrups from behind the counter, licking margherita sauce off her bony fingers.

'Joely? No.'

'She was very glamorous.'

'Yes,' I say. 'I've been sent to get raffle tickets for the tombola.'

'Italian?' She slides a book of raffle tickets over the counter rather than putting it into my outstretched hand.

'French.'

'French, hey. Well, our Graham certainly thought she'd got that "*Je ne sais quoi.*" See you soon then, Billie,' she says, and for a split second I think she's going to call me 'Billie love' in the way she did when I was a girl, when life was simple and preconceptions didn't flutter in the breeze along with your washing. I'm almost nostalgic for it. 'Seat belt on, Billie love.' 'How was your day, Billie love?' 'Your mum would be proud, Billie love.' How ridiculous that I should crave it from someone like her.

I'm about to nod goodbye when, out of the corner of my eye, I catch sight of a milkmaid fridge magnet behind the counter and get a burst of inspiration. 'Marjorie, how would you feel about me bringing one of the cows down here on the weekend and milking her outside the shop as a bit of a "Save Our Dairy" publicity stunt?'

'One of *your* cows?'

'Yes.'

'And you'd be milking by hand?' she says squeamishly.

'Yes.'

She wipes down the bit of counter I've just leant on. 'I'm not sure there's enough space.'

She eyeballs me until I take the raffle tickets and leave. The bread can wait.

At only thirty pence a cup, the cider is going down well on the village green, and the donation bucket is getting fuller, what with 'Guess the name of the scarecrow', 'Pin the crow on the scarecrow', 'Adopt a scarecrow'. I make my way over to the tombola.

'Billie!' Doreen smiles.

134

'How's it going?'

'Good, thanks.'

'Bakery going well?'

'Not bad,' she says. 'It was definitely the right thing, moving here.'

'We're a friendly bunch,' I say, and then have an out-of-body experience as I become aware that I've included myself as a member of the village and made her the outsider, which is not a fair representation of how things are at all.

'I'm a bit worried about my son, though.' She runs her fingers over her whiskery chin. 'He's ever such a nice lad but he doesn't have much luck with girls.'

I can't work out whether this is the beginning of a coming-out story for her son and that I, as the only gay in the village, am the natural audience, or whether she wants me to hook up her son with some of my single and straight girlfriends, of which I have zero up here.

'I did wonder whether *you* might take him out sometime,' she says, her arms wobbling as she folds up the raffle tickets. 'Lovely girl like you.'

It takes me a few seconds to compute what she's saying, the concept is so alien to me. 'I'm not sure I'm entirely—'

'Bell Ender!' Graham Pearce, Marjorie's husband, wanders over, devouring pizza. He's less sunburned than the last time I saw him, though his head still looks like it's been buffed with a polish cloth. 'You couldn't do us a favour? Only the Baslow Primary kids have made an effort to come dressed as crows, and they are eager to chase a scarecrow out of the village.'

'Right,' I say, wondering where I fit into all this.

'And the only scarecrow costume they've got is an age-thirteen boy's one.'

'Right.'

'And the only adult that will fit in it is probably you.'

'Sure,' I say, thinking it sounds quite fun. 'Although shouldn't it be the scarecrow scaring away the crows?'

He licks his moustache. 'Only if you want social services involved.'

He hands me a nylon outfit that clings to my running tights with static electricity when I put it on behind the bacon-butty van. If this is an age-thirteen outfit, it's definitely shrunk in the wash. The hat, on the other hand, is massive, and falls over my eyes. In the reflection of the van door, I can see I've got full-on camel toe and am everything horror movies are made of. Still, I guess that's the point.

Graham adds a clump of straw to my hair. 'Where's the French girl?'

'Joely?' I say. 'She's back in London.'

'Lovely legs,' he says, knocking the arm off a straw *Star Wars* C-3PO as he manoeuvres a newly acquired slice of pepperoni stuffed crust into his mouth, gazing into the distance. At what point is it socially acceptable for people to openly perv over your girlfriend? I'm about to turn my back on him and re-engage with Doreen when he appends, 'What a waste!'

I raise an eyebrow. 'Sorry?'

He shakes his head. 'Beautiful girl like that.'

'A waste?' I say, frowning with feigned confusion.

'I just meant what with—'

'I know what you meant,' I say, as around fifty ten-year-olds

136

flock around me in crow outfits and a voice booms over the loudspeaker introducing 'the moment we've all been waiting for: The Scarecrow Massacre.' To my horror, the school kids descend on the cart, pushing and fighting to grab as many tomatoes as they can.

I look to Doreen, who offers up a shrug and takes Speedo. Before you know it, I'm being strong-armed into a field vacated by two piebald carthorses and told to 'run!'

'Kill the scarecrow!' one boy shouts, lobbing a tomato at my head.

'Kill him!' another one echoes, throwing a whole handful.

I run through the field, trying not to twist my ankle on the muddy divots as tomatoes splatter against my back, my arms, my legs, pulpy seedy juice running down my neck. The children are fucking huge, their crow costumes making them seem even bigger. One of them knocks my hat off. A couple of the older boys are taller than me and come thundering down the hill, chasing me with open beaks, wings made out of old kites, faces masked by feathers. They hurl tomatoes like cricket balls.

'Kill the scarecrow!' they chorus.

I manage to dodge and weave to the other side of the field, plastic beaks pecking at my shoulders.

'Kill the scarecrow!'

They chase me over the stile, which at least buys me a few seconds as crow wings get stuck on the wooden frame. Tomato juice drips down my sock.

'Kill the scarecrow!'

Up the lane I run, looping back to the village green, where I collapse, hands on knees, panting.

'You can't stop there! You're supposed to run out of the village!' Tazzy shouts. 'You're the evil scarecrow, remember!'

A murder of crows mobs me. They pile into me, flapping and flailing. Pecking and punching. Their wings blocking out daylight.

'This was definitely not in the job description!' I shout.

'Come on, Bell Ender. Let them run you out of the village,' Graham yells.

I manage to scramble to my feet and grab Speedo. We run off up the hill, back to the farm and don't look back.

I'm not sure they are such a friendly bunch. And I'm still very much the outsider.

Nathan stands at the gate, holding a stopwatch as we arrive back. He does a double take when he sees me, and I forget for a second that I'm a tomato-drenched scarecrow. It's not until Rachel comes sprinting around the corner in shorts and running vest that I appreciate they're doing some sort of exercise drill.

'Nice top!' I say, pulling the scarecrow costume off my shoulder to show her that I'm also wearing a Nike breathable Dri-FIT Academy running vest, though mine is in navy. 'What are you training for?'

Rachel stops, out of breath, hands on hips. 'Half-marathon. How's your dad?'

'OK,' I say. 'Still waiting for the op.'

'Yeah.' Rachel pants. 'Dad said.'

Nathan tilts his head towards her sweatshirt, which hangs on the gate post.

'What?' Rachel says, still breathing hard.

He frowns. 'Cover up.'

'I thought I'd got another round?' she says.

'Tomorrow,' he says hastily. 'You'll catch a cold dressed like that.'

Her face creases with confusion. 'But—'

'Now,' he says with finality.

She raises an eyebrow at me before dragging her sweatshirt off the post.

Realizing that I'm playing piggy-in-the-middle, I head inside and pour myself a glass of water. From the kitchen window, I can see them bickering, Nathan all folded arms and furrowed forehead, Rachel all frenzy and fury. Watching them reminds me of squabbling with Dad as a teenager; of being a teenager and trapped on the farm while my school friends had started hanging out in town. I was a fifteen-year-old who knew everything there is to know about the fauna and flora of the Peak District, but nothing about live music, new cinema releases or getting fingered round the back of Itsu. I was deeply uncool and I knew it. There was a whole world out there and yet there I was, confined to acres and acres of hillside. I vowed back then that I'd escape.

Nathan taps on the kitchen window and gestures for me to open it, which I do, knocking Grandma's begonia off its saucer, soil spilling onto the draining board.

He leans forward. 'Rachel won't be coming to the farm any more.'

I reposition the begonia. 'Is she OK?'

'She's fine.'

My eyes travel to the passenger seat of his car where Rachel sits biting her nails. 'If boredom's the issue, she can—'

'Boredom is not the issue.' He tucks his T-shirt into his belt and looks behind him, like you might check your blind spot before overtaking on the motorway. 'She needs to focus on her GCSEs.'

He looks down at the car key in his hand and walks back to the car. It's a shame. Rachel was good and seemed to enjoy it here.

**To: Joely (future wife) Chevalier**
Hope your birthday has been well and truly smashing! I've just been dressed as a scarecrow and had the village throw tomatoes at me! Sorry I can't be with you today. Miss you xxx

I rummage through the cupboards in pursuit of lunch, since I forwent bread from Doreen's, but the only food in the house is cereal, tinned fruit and shrivelled, root-sprouting potatoes. Our postcode is beyond the delivery catchment of all take-away food establishments, and if I want fish and chips that badly, I've got to drive four miles to get them. How the hell have my folks done this for so many decades?

There's no way I'm martyring myself to microwaving an old potato and smearing it with cake-making margarine, so I peel off the costume, grab a shower (I have tomato seeds inside my bra), grab the car keys and set off to the nearest McDonald's Drive-Thru.

The radio blares with a Dolly Parton classic, a blur of grey, gold and purple swooshing by on either side. I tap out the tune of 'My Tennessee Mountain Home' on the steering wheel and, in another stratosphere, Dolly and I are taking a drive together. I sing from the bottom of my lungs, as the country road snakes around boulders and open moorland. Golds and purples become greens and yellows. A forest of evergreens carpets the valley, eventually opening into a limestone quarry. I head over the Sheepwash Bridge and up the hill to Marlow's lookout, singing my way through clusters of villages, stone walls and red pillar boxes, until we're on the road to Chesterfield.

McDonald's is every bit as dirty as I want it to be. I've never been mad-keen on junk food but never has a spicy chicken burger tasted so good. It also feels good to be able to wander round shops, walk alongside people and feel part of the human race. I potter into Waterstones and am leafing through Caitlin Moran's latest paperback when Maria calls.

'Bilbo!'

'Hello, stranger!' I say. God knows why as I hate it when people address me like that.

'How are you getting on up there?'

'Good,' I say, putting the book back on the shelf. 'Well, good if you discount tired, worried and sore.'

'How long do you think you'll be up there for?'

My whole body tightens, as if it's been asked to shrink a dress size. 'Who knows,' I say, short of breath. 'He hasn't even had the operation yet.'

'Sorry, Bilbo,' she says softly.

'Don't be nice to me,' I say, making my way over to non-fiction. 'I'll cry if you're nice to me.'

'OK,' she says, her voice sharpening. 'I'll be nothing short of a heartless cunt.'

'Perfect,' I say. Another celebrity cookbook.

'I hope you don't mind, but a guy from my theatre group is staying in your room just for a few weeks while you're away. You know, to pay the rent.'

'OK.'

'I thought it might help both of us out.'

I know it makes sense, but it still feels a little bit like I've been evicted, not only from my home but also from my own life. From my friends, from my flat, from my job, from gaily gadding about Soho in the company of kindred spirits to Peak District purgatory.

'Sure,' I say. 'As long as he doesn't smoke and has control of his bladder.'

'He's nice.' She sounds coy and evasive, neither of which is in keeping with her personality.

'What sort of nice?' I say, moving over to the Lifestyle section, where several bookshelves are dedicated to Agriculture. I move swiftly onto Music.

'Just *nice*.'

I recognize this tone of hers. 'You've slept with him, haven't you?'

'How did you know?' she says quickly.

'I have known you for six years, Maz! So, what's he like?'

'He's called Darius and he's a swimwear model.' Do swimwear models called Darius exist outside of Jilly Cooper books? 'You'd like him, Bilbo. He's really down to earth.'

She lists the various things Darius has going for him and I make a mental note to disinfect everything when I get my room back. If I get my room back.

On my way out of Waterstones, I get a message from Joely.

It stings – Joely spending her birthday on the other side of the world with her ex-boyfriend, who is clearly still besotted with her. *The best time ever.* My stomach flops over itself. I open the attachments: Joely in a Power Ranger-type suit, helmet under arm, about to step into a souped-up go-kart against a backdrop of skyscrapers. Joely sitting in a go-kart giving the thumbs up. Joely and Christophe Concordel, arms around each other's waists in matching outfits. His, a masculine steel grey. Hers, hot pink. Can't he just fuck off to one of his yachts and get shipwrecked?

Surely, she must know this would hurt me. Were the shoe on the other foot, I certainly wouldn't be sending her photos of me and Neve, all pally the other side of the world. I know he's her boss but still, an ex is an ex and, to him, she'll always be the one that got away. I bristle at the thought of their bodies touching. Her hand on his shoulder. His arm around her waist. It's the little things that hurt.

# CHAPTER TEN

# MADEMOISELLE

**From: Maria**
Lesbian hen party conundrum #121. One of the girls
mailed me saying she's got pulsating vulva straws and
vulva ice-cube moulds. PULSATING VULVA STRAWS,
Bilbo!!!! Please tell me that's not a thing. How fucking
hideous!!

**@SCIENCE MATTERS**
DNA. The Internet. Antibiotics. Medical Imaging. Artificial
Intelligence. What will be YOUR scientific discovery?

**From: Dad**
Loved the photo of you and Speedo but he does look
like he's porked up a bit. Go easy on the dog biscuits
and make sure the pair of you do the village on foot!

**From: Rachel Fletcher**
Hi Billie. Sorry my dad won't let me help on the farm ☹

I'll still do the pantomime race with you though. C U @
Ridgecroft @ 12 ☺

Ridgecroft is an immaculate patchwork of unframed fields
maintained by roving Swaledale sheep. I drive up to the west
wing of the sort of country mansion you'd find in a high-
budget British period drama, Grandma attempting the cryptic
crossword in the passenger seat as the Land Rover vibrates
over cattle grids. Inside the grounds, a large man trussed up
in tweed directs us to the overspill car park, where row upon
row of four-by-fours unleash families, buggies, picnic blankets,
wheelchairs, West Highland white terriers in tartan coats and
Chihuahuas in waterproof onesies; every man and his dog.

Grandma rummages in the boot, glass tinkling as she rearranges homemade jam into a large Tupperware box. 'I thought
I'd try and offload some gooseberry jelly,' she says, wiping her
hands down her coat. 'God knows, we could do with an extra
bob or two.'

We join the procession, Speedo snuffling at a pile of banana
skins overflowing from a bin that hasn't been emptied since
yesterday's show. A bugle honks over the hillside and a 1960s
BBC-type voice booms over the loudspeaker announcing the
arrival of the former Cressbrookdale Master of Foxhounds,
here to sell off the remainder of his retired pack of dogs. A
man in a pristine red felt blazer with shiny gold buttons
appears on horseback, surrounded by a dozen or so high-
energy, sniffing, yelping beagles. On the other side of the car
park, a ragtag bunch of students brandish posters of half-dead
foxes.

'For fox sake, keep the ban!' they chant.

Country pomp is my idea of hell, but there's no way out of it; I've become part of the mass influx of visitors heading towards the Grand Ring. We drop Grandma's gooseberry jelly off with two ladies sitting at a table with their legs too wide apart, moaning about having no change. A 'rodent race' is about to start next to them, involving a man in a turquoise tracksuit shoving a ferret down a transparent tube, while a weasel sits licking his balls. Grandma sidles up to me just as a rat is being bribed into another pipe with a Cadbury's Brunch Bar.

'They're asking if it's organic!' she harrumphs.

'The Cadbury's Brunch Bar?' I say.

'The jam!' She shuffles to the next stall to rummage through bric-a-brac.

Speedo follows the scent of roast duck to a catering van. We've got a whole two hours to kill until the pantomime cow race, which is due to follow a medieval jousting display in the Grand Ring, and I'm already hungry.

'Fancy a butty?' I shout over the scream of jets as the Red Arrows fly overhead in triangle formation.

Grandma lifts her foot away from a ferret on a lead. 'Not if it's on cheer-whatsit!'

'Ciabatta?' I say.

'Full of holes and plays havoc with your fillings.' She squints at the fluffy blue vapour trails blotting the sky.

The rodent race is declared a draw and money is refunded as none of the animals makes it to the finishing line. Grandma gets sucked into a conversation about mint sauce with one of the jam ladies, so I wander over to the AGA Rangemaster cookery theatre marquee, where a girl in leather trousers is handing out organic plain puffed-rice samples.

'Were they roasted in an Aga?' I say, Speedo yanking me in the opposite direction.

'No.' She avoids eye contact and fiddles with her apron.

'OK.' I conclude our conversational cul-de-sac and make to leave, but then see Lorna and Guy, hovering at the entrance to the marquee in matching Parsons-Bonneville polo shirts.

I attempt to resuscitate the culinary chat with the Aga girl. 'I'll take a packet!'

'Billie!' Lorna waves a packet of smoked ostrich biltong at me.

My chest feels hot and grainy. It's one thing having to interact with Lorna at the farm on matters strictly veterinarian, but it's an altogether different proposition when it's out of hours and Guy is involved. I crouch down to feign interest in a bottle of flaxseed oil until Lorna's elongated shadow looms over me, the peak of her baseball cap disproportionately large, her arms as long as ladders, her fingers like those of Edward Scissorhands.

'Hi, Billie!' she beams, all freckles and chapped lips.

I put the flaxseed oil back and look up. Guy's cheeks are smothered in fluorescent pink sunblock, despite it being not quite warm enough for a T-shirt. He smells of the sort of aftershave you'd win in a tombola, and wears zip-off-leg trousers converted to knee-length shorts.

'How do?' he says.

'Not bad.' I can't stop staring at their matching polo shirts.

Guy lights up a cigarette and is immediately asked to move outside.

'Any news on your dad's operation?' Lorna pulls her cap down over her forehead.

'Not yet,' I say, raking my top teeth over my bottom lip.

It's been four weeks, but it feels as if we've been waiting forever for this operation. God knows what it must feel like for Dad, especially having been told twice that it's going to happen, only to be gazumped by patients in more urgent need.

She reaches for my knee and then thinks better of it, placing her hand safely back in her pocket.

A loud whirr above the marquee becomes a deafening thump, thump, thump and the people around me hang onto their hats, bags and hair as an enormous gust of wind lifts the sides of the marquee, sending organic plain puffed rice flying. It feels like we're about to take off, people clutching their belongings, hands pressed over ears as they make their way outside. Anoraks inflate, leaflets dance, and grass is swept to one side by the force of the wind as a giant set of gleaming propeller blades slice through the air. A shiny blue helicopter with the words 'Huxley-Lipyeat' emblazoned across the side hovers over the Grand Ring. Speedo squeaks, burying his nose into my legs. A huge man pours out of the helicopter, shirt billowing. Wolfgang Huxley-Lipyeat has landed.

'I'd better say hello!' Guy straightens his shirt collar and accelerates in the direction of the Distinctly British Elite tent.

'The Wolf!' Lorna pops a small strip of biltong into her mouth.

I nod. 'My dad's landlord.'

'Though I think all the foofaraw today is about Mademoiselle,' she says, mistaking my private analysis of the word 'foofaraw' for a look of intrigue. 'Come on, she'll be with him. You have to meet her.'

My gut instinct is to pretend I need the loo, buy myself a large slab of chocolate-coated flapjack, and hide under a tree until I have to do the pantomime cow race, but I need to check out this brute who is holding my dad's future to ransom with the freehold.

I follow her into a crowded marquee, where a proud man in a brown suit pins a winner's rosette to a Tamworth pig alongside a line-up of British saddlebacks. Sheep bleat and shears buzz as a lesson in wool-weaving gets underway in the corner. At the back, a group of people hang around a make-shift stage.

'There she is!' Lorna points to a nervy woman in ribbed tights, who leads a cow into the marquee. 'A thoroughbred Holstein Friesian worth just shy of a million.'

'Mademoiselle is the *cow*?' I say.

'Not any old cow. The most perfectly proportioned cow on earth. Perfect udder size, perfect teats, perfect genes.'

I roll my eyes. 'I didn't know they did Miss World for cows.'

The energy in the room changes when a huge man blusters through the crowd, the medals pinned to his enormous chest clinking against each other like miniature cymbals. He has a chocolate Labrador at his heel and smiles and nods as he makes his way to the stage, shaking hands and patting shoulders.

Lorna leans towards me, her breath oaky with hickory. 'The Wolf!'

He takes to the stage, the microphone lost in his chubby fingers. His smile is open and friendly, his cheeks rosy and his hair is a mess of white curls; he'd make a great Father Christmas, if he wasn't holding farmers and their farms to ransom. 'Ladies and gentlemen,' he addresses the room. 'May I introduce the World Dairy Exposition's Supreme Grand Champion of All Breeds! I give you: Mademoiselle.'

A steady ripple of applause fills the marquee.

'Farmers are bidding thousands for her embryos.' Lorna folds her arms over her chest conspiratorially. 'He makes hundreds of thousands each time she calves.'

I weigh him up, this mountain of a man. He must be thirty stone. Pound for pound, I'm probably the weight of one of his legs. The microphone zings and crackles. Out of breath and huffing through his chins, the Wolf taps at it with frustration. 'Lovely to see so many of you here today! I love hosting the Country Show. It's one of the best events of the year. Be happy, be merry, have fun!' He salutes everyone before handing Mademoiselle and the microphone back to the lady in the green tights and joining his friends for a pint of locally brewed cider.

I pull at my eyebrow, bristling with unease. This is the man who has got my family over a barrel with the freehold and who owns most of the land around here. He has too much authority, telling people what they can and can't do, and yet he seems perfectly approachable. Now is a good a time as any, I decide.

I wander over and introduce myself. 'Hi!'

'Hello.' He gives me his full attention.

'I'm Billie Oliver, John Oliver's daughter.'

'Who?' He shakes my hand and studies my face like he's trying to recall it.

'My dad owns Fernbrook Farm.'

'Aha.'

'It would be great to talk about the freehold sometime,' I blurt.

A group of middle-aged men in wax jackets approach him

with a huge silver trophy and lots of handshakes. He turns back to me. 'You should talk to my lawyer, love. Here.' He hands me a card and turns away again.

Slowly I retreat, feeling like I did when I was five and Auntie June slapped my hand hard for trying to pinch a marzipan robin off the Christmas cake before it had been cut.

Lorna looks at me, eyes wide.

'I'd better get off to the cow race,' I say.

'Me too,' Lorna says. 'I'm judging you!'

Is this legal? I've spent the best part of my life being judged by Lorna Parsons.

**To: Rachel Fletcher**
Hi Rach. Not seen you here yet so I'll meet you at the paddock in 10 ☺

It's raining heavily by the time the pantomime cow race is due to start. Everyone's either fucked off home or scarpered under the tarpaulin canopies of burger vans the other side of the car park. Half a dozen die-hard OAPs from Grandma's bridge club crowd around a flask of coffee with outstretched hands, wielding polystyrene cups, but that's it in the way of an audience. The paddock is set up with dog-eventing obstacles that we, as two-man cows, are supposedly going to jump, swerve, tilt, push and rotate over and around before crossing the finishing line, which has been washed away by the rain. The earth is churned up with ankle-breaking divots from the jousting. According to the betting stakes board, I am tipped to win 3–1, though God knows why. I look around for Rachel.

151

The cow-print costume smells stale and musty. I pull it over my ankles and zip myself into the back end, Grandma giving me gyp for getting the tail all wonky. What is it about me and dressing up at the moment? The material is thick and itchy.

Three 'cows' line up: two brown and one white. I am 'Cow Pat', one of two Holstein Friesians, the other making its way out of the gents' Portaloo.

'Ready?' Lorna shouts over a megaphone from the other side of the paddock.

'No!' I shout, my waist lost in baggy stomach chamber. 'I'm one man down!'

Three pantomime cows become four as the other Holstein Friesian squelches through the mud into the Grand Ring. From the look of it, Lorna and Guy are having a ding-dong, handing the megaphone back and forth to each other. Eventually, Guy takes the megaphone and steps onto the winner's podium whilst Lorna strides through the muddy paddock towards me. I assume she's going to reprimand me, until she gestures for the cow's head.

'Are you sure?' I say, scanning the field for Rachel.

Silently, she steps into the front of the cow costume. Unlike the hind legs, the front legs are elasticated at the ankle. No matter how hard she tries, she can't get them over her wellingtons, so she's forced to remove each boot, one at a time, leaning first on Grandma and then on me for support. Awkwardly, her hands grasp my shoulders, the cow's body twisted back on itself in almost a figure of eight. She then becomes aware that she's touching my bra strap through my T-shirt and shuffles her hands out wide but doesn't have enough shoulder to grip onto and promptly loses balance, her socked foot plunging into the mud. Her face looks like Maria's did when she got into the unheated lido in February; a kind of wide-eyed, wide-mouthed plasticine face of horror.

'You OK?' I say, stifling a laugh.

She nods, grimacing as she lowers her muddy foot into her wellington.

Once we're both in the costume, I obviously have to bend over and hold her waist. It's only uncomfortable because I know that she's uncomfortable with it, and I don't want to weird her out, so instead of properly grabbing onto her waist, I grasp her polo shirt on either side. Grandma fastens us together with Velcro and leads us to the start line. We haven't yet started, and I feel like I'm going to pass out. It's not so much the damp smell or the non-breathable velour. It's not even the bending forward while digesting roast duck; it's the fact that no matter how many of these awareness campaigns we manage, nothing ever changes. People still drink milk. Supermarkets still undercut each other. Dairy profits continue to plummet. A pantomime cow race witnessed by those who have planned it and a couple of hangers-on won't make a scrap of difference.

'All right back there?' Lorna says brightly.

'Yes,' I say, trying not to faint.

The starter pistol fires and Lorna lurches forward, my fingers losing their grip and sliding down her hips, which causes her to stop abruptly, my head slamming into her buttocks. She stumbles forward, her hands trying to locate my hands through the costume, which after grabbing my right shoulder and my left breast, she finally finds and places firmly on her waist.

'Hold on tight this time!' she commands.

Pain shoots down my back as we jolt this way and that, the cow suit feeling snugger and snugger. I've never considered myself claustrophobic, but I've not felt this boxed-in panic since getting stuck, aged eight, in the Alton Towers adventure tunnel, where I had to be escorted out by first-aiders.

'First jump coming up!' she alerts me before bounding into the air.

I follow, the sound of Guy's booming voice awarding points for cadence, traversing, tempo and *schwung*, whatever the fuck that is.

'And another!' she shouts.

I tighten my grasp around her small waist. She doesn't have an inch of fat on her.

'Coming up to the seesaw!' she says. 'Ready?'

I can't speak. I'm too busy clinging on for dear life.

'Toe, heel. Toe, heel!' She shuffles along.

The ramp tilts beneath me and it's all I can do not to catapult forward and crush her.

'And back down again. Heel, toe. Heel, toe!'

Sweat trickles down my face and pools in the bottom of my spine.

'Coming up to the slalom,' she announces. 'Six high poles. Ready to zigzag?'

I try to catch my breath but there's not enough oxygen in this suit.

'And zig, and zag.'

'Lorna?' I say, trying to get her to stop for a second.

'And zig and zag.'

'Lorna?' I've no idea whether I'm zigging or zagging. I just need air.

'And zig and zag.'

'Lorn—'

'Approaching the beam.' She drags me upwards. 'OK and sashay, sashay, sashay, stop! Sashay, stop! Sashay, stop!'

I swear this is worse than step aerobics.

'Sashay, sashay, sashay, stop! Sashay, stop! Sashay, stop!'

'Lorn—'

'Hold it!'

'I need to—'

'Go!'

'I need to stop!'

'Go, go, go! As fast as we can!'

Thwack! My shin hits something hard and I fall backwards. A moment later, Lorna is lying on top of me, her buttocks in my face, and I'm pinned to the ground, cold mud seeping through the velour into my hair, skin and ear. One of the underwires has escaped from my bra and is spearing me in the sternum. I can barely breathe so have no choice but to push her arse out of my face, which entails grabbing her buttocks, one in each hand, and thrusting them away as you might a medicine ball mid-squat. She squirms, trying to leverage herself off me but, in doing so, the costume gets twisted at the waist, which only serves to slingshot her back on top of me.

This time, we're stomach to stomach, though I can't see her face and she can't see mine. It's like being stuck inside a duvet cover, both of us scrambling in different directions for the opening. This time I really do feel short on oxygen and have no choice but to roll her off me, but not knowing which way is up, I only go and roll on top of her. Now, I'm lying on her chest, our breasts squashed together until she wriggles sideways, sending something crashing onto my knee. Pain screams throughout my leg. Instinctively, I go to curl up in a ball but can't. It's like trying to make a cup of tea in a straitjacket.

'Are you OK, love?' Grandma's voice accompanies the squelching of footsteps.

A moment later, I hear the sound of Velcro ripping above my head. Bright light. The smack of fresh air against my face. Rain on my cheeks. I can breathe again.

Lorna rips off her cow head and throws it to Guy, then looks down at me, hands on hips. 'What were you doing back there?' she laughs.

'I've no idea!' My hair is matted with mud and the taste of soil lingers in my mouth, my teeth and tongue gritty, but it somehow feels quite cathartic; momentary respite from the burden of responsibility. Lying in the mud, I pluck the sopping cow-print velour away from my thighs. 'Do you think we raised any awareness?'

Lorna looks over at Guy, who is frantically crossing his arms in the air above his head. 'I think we've been disqualified.'

He flips our score to zero on the chalkboard.

'Boo!' Lorna shouts at Guy, giving him the double thumbs down.

'Rules are rules!' he shouts.

She helps me up and for a moment, it feels like we're on the same team. Like she's not judging me for being inadequate or incompetent. Like the bull sperm incident never happened. Like we just shared a small, surreal moment in a muddy field in Derbyshire. A barrier removed.

'Joely's been trying to get hold of you!' Grandma says, handing me my phone as Guy trudges over with a packet of homemade fudge.

'Better luck next time!' he says.

I scroll through the list of missed calls and text messages, all from Joely.

'There won't be a next time.' Lorna peels off the rest of the cow costume, holding onto Guy as she manoeuvres herself out of her wellies. She thrusts the sopping, muddy suit into my hands, gives me a snooty look and disappears with Guy. Just like that, it's as if our 'moment' had never happened. What is it with her?

'I'm heading off, too.' Grandma hugs me goodbye. 'My knees are playing up and we've been out in the drizzle for long enough.' The truth is, it's got nothing to do with her knees or the rain and everything to do with her gooseberry jelly not selling. 'You'd better call her back.'

'Lorna?' I say, watching the Parsons-Bonneville duo retreat to a hot-dog van.

'No, you daft apeth. Joely. She's been very persistent.'

I wipe raindrops off my phone screen and mentally prepare myself to be all zen about Christophe. As Kat would say, he is a risk I can't mitigate, and jealousy is wasted emotional energy.

'*Ma petite Anglaise!*' A pair of chocolate-brown sparkly eyes come into focus as FaceTime loads.

'How are you?' I feel giddy looking at her. Like I've just

been hooked up to some battery charger, my body alive with electricity.

A small crease forms above her nose. 'What happened to your face and your hair? It's . . .'

'Like I've been rolling around a muddy field in a cow costume?'

'Sorry?' she says. 'I think the line must be bad.'

She holds her phone further away, presumably to gauge how strong her signal is, and in doing so reveals a neon-lit pedestrianized shopping street, bursting with life. Steaming pans of dumplings. A pyramid of what look to be doughnut balls piled high under low-slung bunting. The fluttering of flags from all around the world. Trays of exotic vegetables, fresh fruit, a flower stall. Roll upon roll of vibrant silk every colour of the rainbow – from gold-embroidered fuchsia to plain pastel blue.

'Wow, it looks amazing there!' I drink it all in.

'We went here this morning.' She holds up a postcard featuring ornate pavilions and sun-soaked lotus ponds. *Life and Seoul.* It's a far cry from the muddy paddock I have just been lying in.

'You and Christophe?' I say too quickly.

'No. He's sightseeing with his girlfriend,' she says, matter-of-factly.

Christophe has a girlfriend! This is music to my ears. Chocolate to my taste buds. Silk to my touch. This shouldn't make a difference, but it somehow does.

Her face lights up. 'How did your cow race go?'

'Good!' I chuckle. 'Messy but good.'

'Great. I'm sending you a big kiss.' She smacks her lips

against the glossy *Life and Seoul* postcard. 'Well, once I've worked out the word for "stamp"!'

We may be on the other side of the world from each other, but we're in synch again. I'm just taking time out and I'll be back soon, better and stronger. This is just a temporary diversion. It's not so much that I believe that true love conquers all. It's more about finding your equal and knowing that, with the right person, you'll get through things together. Joely and I complement each other. I feel indestructible knowing that we're a team. Her yin to my yang; a counterbalancing partnership. A partnership I'm proud to be part of. Two strong females allowing each other their independence. The way things should be. She's perfect. Intelligent, thoughtful, beautiful. Driven, determined, divine.

'I love you,' I blurt.

Her face freezes and, for a moment, I think I've lost my internet connection, until I notice her top teeth raking her bottom lip.

My emotions feel like the milk in our outhouse tank once the agitation button's been pressed – a swirling, gurgling, tempestuous torrent gushing out. I just need the world to stand still for a moment. For my nerves to shut the fuck up and calm the hell down. I want to hold my breath underwater until the only thing I can hear is my heart.

'I love you,' I say again. This time it's clear, considered and unquestionable.

And in letting go, I feel free. Light. Indestructible. Like I have birthed a newer, better me. The new me. And I'm ready for anything.

# CHAPTER ELEVEN

# BULLSHiT

**From: Maria**
Lesbian hen party conundrum #129. Is a 'Yay! Same vagina forever!' T-shirt too much?

**From: Dad**
You might want to try Florence with aloe vera as well as the antibiotics. Very good for mastitis.

Rachel is waiting in the yard when I get back from the Country Show. Her legs are splattered in mud and her face is red and blotchy. I look around for Nathan's Mondeo but it's not in its usual spot.

'Are you with your dad?' I say, knowing that she lives seven miles away.

She shakes her head. 'I'm sorry I let you down at the show. Dad wouldn't give me a lift.'

'How did you get here?' I open the porch door.

She nods at a muddy mountain bike leaning against the wall and follows me into the kitchen. I throw the car keys into the fruit bowl and put on the kettle.

She sits down at the big pine table, looking lost and unsure. 'It's about my dad.'

'Does he know you're here?'

She shakes her head. 'You won't tell him, will you?'

'Not if you don't want me to.' I offer her a custard cream from the Charles and Diana biscuit tin, which she dismisses with a shake of her head.

'I just . . .' She dips her chin and bites on her tracksuit zip. 'I really want to carry on working on the farm, but my dad says I can't.' She lifts her head and looks me in the eye. 'In case you crack on to me.'

Time slows. Blurred digits on the kitchen clock pulse. My heart beats louder and louder even though it feels as though I've stopped breathing. I dig my fingernails into the palms of my hands in the hope of diverting the pain, but how does anything else stand a chance of hurting when you've just been punched in the guts like that? White-hot anger builds in my glands.

'I'm a lesbian, not a paedophile,' I say quietly.

'I know!' she says. 'And I like working here. It's the only thing I really love at the moment, and he won't let me do it. He thinks you'll put ideas in my head.'

I bite angrily into my custard cream, the biscuit splintering in my mouth. I feel poisoned.

Desperation pools in her eyes. 'You won't tell my dad I told you, will you?'

I chew at a raggedy piece of skin next to my thumbnail. 'No.'

'Only he's right screwed up. Ever since my mum left him for—'

The porch judders, Rachel's eyes darting to the hallway in trepidation. Floorboards creak, the door bangs back on itself and, a moment later, Nathan is standing in our kitchen, hands on hips like some sort of wronged Hobbit, here to reclaim his lost ring.

'I thought I'd find you here.' His eyes bore into Rachel before turning to me. 'Listen, I can just about put up with it, but I don't want you going anywhere near my daughter.'

'Sorry?' I reach for the back of my chair, feeling the urgent need to hold onto something solid and reassuring.

'You may not have done anything yet, but it's what you're thinking of doing.' He tugs on the leather toolbelt strapped around his waist.

'Nathan, I'm a gay woman, not a fucking paedophile.'

'Call it what you want. I find it offensive.'

My face burns with shame and fury. Buried moments come flooding back. Painful memories I've locked away. I think about the names I got called at school, after I'd come out and everyone had moved on from the now unlikely sounding jizz story. 'Carpet muncher.' 'Rug rat.' 'Muff diver.' The casual homophobia at sixth-form college. 'Getting on the bus the wrong way.' 'Licking the wrong side of the stamp.' Having to wait until the other girls finished their showers and got changed before I could take mine, to avoid the humiliation of everyone fleeing upon my arrival lest I see them naked and want to shag them all. I think about Graham and his 'what a waste' comment. I think about Andy Pickering and his interpretation of lesbianism, thinking he's got the all-clear to tell me tit jokes. I think about the documentary that Joely and I watched about violent, knife-slashing, head-smashing homophobia in Russia, until I'm practically vibrating with rage, my teeth aching from being clamped together so tightly.

I want to explode into tiny pieces. And then I remember something Bev once said at sixth-form college and, suddenly, I'm sixteen all over again.

I remember the smell of sweat and cheap deodorant lingering in the corridor outside the sports changing rooms. I'd just finished playing football and was feeling quite good about the final winning goal I'd scored. Further down the corridor, Rebecca Needham, Claire Reading and Fiona Cobb were huddled next to the window. Whispers. Sideways glances. Fake laughter. I didn't need to hear them to know that they were bitching about me.

When I reached my locker, there was something not quite right. The key wouldn't turn in the lock. Upon closer inspection, the lock was bunged up with bubble gum and the locker itself was actually open and had just been wedged shut with one of my notebooks. I removed the book, the door swinging open, and there it was in thick, black marker:

DIRTY LEZZA. On the inside of the door.

DIRTY LEZZA. On my bag.

DIRTY LEZZA. On my textbooks.

DIRTY LEZZA. On my coat.

DIRTY LEZZA. On my ring binders.

DIRTY LEZZA. On my pencil case.

DIRTY LEZZA. DIRTY LEZZA. DIRTY LEZZA. They may just as well have written it on me. Taken the pen and vandalized me.

'It wasn't us!' Claire shouted from the safe sanctuary of their mini clique.

I closed the locker, my belongings sullied with shame. It creaked open again. And no matter how many times I tried to wedge it shut, it was intent on gaping wide enough for everyone to see that Belinda Oliver was a DIRTY LEZZA.

I wanted to die. It felt like I'd swallowed a razor blade and my throat was being slashed to ribbons.

I turned to the girls. It's not like I didn't know them – I sat next to them in biology twice a week. 'Do you know who did this?'

Their eyes darted between each other, Claire taking a step forward and, for a moment, I thought she was going to ask me if I was OK. Sling an arm around me in an act of sisterly solidarity. Offer to get me a sweet tea. Tell me I'm not a 'dirty lezza' and that nobody deserves to be treated like this. And that I, who have been nothing but friendly to everyone, will rise above all of this like a phoenix from the ashes, and that justice will be served.

'I'd prefer not to take sides,' she said.

It felt like the razor blade was making its descent down my windpipe, slicing through the lining of my trachea and splicing through my lungs. Breathing normally was like trying to blow up a burst balloon.

'Fiona?' I said, hopefully – I'd let her copy my phototropism notes the previous week so she kind of owed me.

'I'm sorry, Billie. I don't know,' she said.

'Me neither.' Rebecca shrugged.

And it was at that moment in time that I lost faith in mankind. To not have an opinion on something so disgusting.

To not take sides between 'right' and 'wrong'. To have no backbone. No moral compass. No sense of sisterhood. Happy to sit back and be the reader of a script that desperately needs writing. To not reach out and help a fellow human being in case you lose a few street credibility points. Everything in my head went black until Bev appeared down the corridor.

'Hey, buddy!' she shouted. 'Coffee on the way home?'

I couldn't speak. It was all I could do not to cry. I had that pins-and-needles feeling in my nose and the tears were already on their way.

'Here, do you reckon I could pull off a Mohican?' Bev brushed the sides of her hair into a shark's fin with the palms of her hands, her expression transforming into a look of concern. 'Billie?' She walked up to me, the other girls scuttling off. 'Holy fuck!' she said, assessing the damage, DIRTY LEZZA screaming at us. She wrapped her big bear arms around me. 'OK, Billie, we've got this.' It was the way she said 'we', adopting the problem as hers as well as mine. Making me feel like I had a team behind me. Removing the feeling of being ostracized. 'Firstly, I've been here. I know what it's like and you are not alone.'

Hot tears plopped down my face as she took my chin in her hands. I wiped them away with the heel of my hands.

'Secondly . . . Look at me, Billie.' It's not that I didn't want to look at her, I just didn't want anyone to look at me. Not like that. All damaged and mangled. 'Secondly, repeat after me, "I am a strong lesbian woman and I refuse to feel devalued by the ignorance of others."'

I slid down the lockers until I was crouched, head in hands. 'Come on. We can't let them win.' She too slid down to level with me. 'Repeat after me, "I am a strong lesbian woman and I refuse to feel devalued by the ignorance of others."'

'I am a strong . . .' The words felt pointless.

She wiped my tears away with the cuff of her fluffy jumper and I remember thinking how nice it smelled and how soft but strong it felt.

'We're not going until you say it all the way through,' she said.

I inhaled deeply. 'I am a strong lesbian woman.'

'Again!'

'I am a strong lesbian woman.'

'And?'

'And I refuse to feel devalued by the ignorance of others.' I smiled involuntarily.

She dragged me to my feet. 'From the top!'

I stood up, allowing more air into my lungs. 'I am a strong lesbian woman. And I refuse to feel devalued by the ignorance of others.'

She stood opposite me, taking my hands in hers. 'One more time.'

This time, we said it together, our voices filling the corridor. Like we meant the words more than anything in the world. Like sisters. Like brothers. Lesbi-friends.

'We are strong lesbian women, and we refuse to feel devalued by the ignorance of others.'

She smiled at me. 'You realize these pricks would fold if you confronted them and told them how they make you feel?'

'You reckon?'

'Hell, yeah, buddy. They'll be clueless. Trust me, they'll walk out feeling worse about this than you will. Bullies always fold if you stand up to them.'

I reached into my locker for my books.

'What are you doing?' she said.

'It may be vandalized but it's still my stuff.'

'No,' she said. 'No, it isn't. All of that's going in the bin, including the locker. This is the first day of your new life as a strong lesbian woman, who refuses to feel devalued by the ignorance of others. And from now on in, you will not be shamed. You will not be sullied. Leave the past behind.'

I looked into her kind eyes and knew that the friend in front of me was going to be a friend for life. 'You know, I think a Mohican would suit you.'

Now, I take a deep breath, and I look at Nathan. 'Have you ever stopped to consider that your hatred and judgement might be considered offensive? That your bigoted, homophobic views are hurtful and cruel? That you're just frightened because it's something you don't understand? I'm a person with feelings like every other person, and just because I'm not attracted to men, doesn't mean I'm a sex pest towards women and girls.'

He pulls a face. 'Someone's got her period!'

Rachel looks away, embarrassed.

'No,' I say matter-of-factly. 'I'm just a strong, lesbian woman, who refuses to feel devalued by the ignorance of others. One day, you'll wake up and realize how unacceptable your behaviour is. Who knows, one day you might even apologize. But in the meantime, you're fired.'

His face looks a little bit like my childhood hamster did when he ran into the patio window. 'Come on, Rachel.' He stretches an arm out to her, which she ignores. 'You heard them.' He bundles her out of the door. 'They're firing us.'

'*I'm* firing *you*,' I say.

They walk out, Rachel retaining eye contact with the floor.

I stand at the kitchen window and watch Nathan manhandle Rachel's mountain bike into the boot of his car. The engine starts up. Rachel holds the palm of her hand up to me apologetically and slips into the passenger seat. The car revs dramatically. As I watch it bounce and jolt down the lane, my fingers trace the indentations of the matchstick mother I carved into the edge of the sink unit when I was ten and Dad wouldn't let me have the pet rabbit I knew Mum would have authorized had she been around. It makes me wonder how she'd have dealt with all this. Whether she'd have been the sort of mother who would wrap me up in cotton wool to shield me from cruelty and pain, keeping me off school and letting me have too many biscuits. Whether she'd be strong and indestructible, beating her chest with mantras promoting positive self-talk, trailblazing her way through life and forging a road for me and all other warrior women to follow. Or whether she'd be somewhere between the two: a nice mum with a kind heart, who just wanted her daughter to be treated the same as anybody else's. Although I'll never know, my gut tells me she'd be a mix of all three.

Britain is experiencing a heatwave. Flesh is on display on every tiny triangle of grass in London. Even Camberwell Green, a place normally associated with needles and drug addicts, is awash with scantily clad girls frolicking in the sun.

I spot her from afar. She floats through a mass of sunburned bodies, wearing a floppy straw hat, a vintage turquoise dress and heeled strappy sandals. I wave but she doesn't notice me. A group of teenagers choreograph a street dance routine on the bald, dry grass. The chime of an ice-cream van. The bark of a dog. She sees me, propping her sunglasses on top of her head and smiling. As she gets nearer, she pulls her headphones out of her ears and flicks back her hair, which now sits in a blonde bob. An involuntary chemical reaction stirs in my core. I want her.

'*Bonsoir*,' she says, kissing me fleetingly on each cheek.

When does *jour* cease and *soir* begin?

She looks me up and down. 'Why are you wearing pyjamas? You've got a PhD meeting with Christophe in ten minutes.'

'I . . .' I look down to discover I am indeed wearing pyjamas. They're not even my pyjamas. They're Dad's.

Everyone is laughing and pointing, staring and shouting. I'm flanked by cows. Hundreds of them bellowing and stamping. A huge flash of light suggests we're on a film set and then it starts pouring with rain.

Gasping for air, I sit bolt upright. Awake again. Back on the farm. A flash of lightning illuminates my bedroom for a second or two. It's 2 a.m. I'm not in Dad's pyjamas. I'm not trying to hustle for a PhD. And Joely Chevalier is not at my side. Instead, I'm running a dairy farm, solo.

I pluck my sweat-drenched T-shirt away from my chest and take a sip of water. Torrential rain hammers on the conservatory roof below. I want to settle back to sleep, but know I should really bring the cows in, out of the field. Speedo whimpers outside my door. He hates storms so I let him in. He plops down onto the duvet and wedges his nose under my pillow. Once he's settled, I venture downstairs and grab the cold metal torch from the cupboard under the stairs to assess the damage. Rain drums against the porch glass. Window boxes smash on the ground. A cable from the overhead telegraph pole whips in the wind. I step clumsily onto the bristles of our hedgehog boot brush before finding the left and right of Grandma's wellingtons – I'm going to have to brave the elements and bring the cows into the barn.

Speedo squeaks and trembles at the top of the stairs, his ears flat against his head. Outside, the storm is raging, an angry sky bubbling with dark cloud. I slip on Dad's anorak, pull the hood tightly over my head, and step into the yard. The wind forces me back against the porch door and it's a struggle to stand still, let alone forge forward. Another crack of lightning forks across the sky, irradiating the yard like a television studio set before the farm is suffocated once more by darkness. The rain is deafening, like a military shelling, and the yard a battle zone. Buckets clatter, bamboo canes crack, a wheelbarrow is blown upside down, metal scraping against concrete. Head down, I stagger towards the field, two steps forward, one step back, wrapping Dad's flapping, billowing waterproofs around me.

Thunder rumbles around the hillside, a cauldron of fury. I stumble and slide through mud-filled gullies, the grass conspiratorially slippery, the pathways unlit. The gate is reluctant to open, the rain pounding heavier. The wet, wooden frame finally swings over my feet. A blurry mass of darkness moves around the bottom of the field, changing shape before becoming a stampede led by Star, who bolts towards the opening, her knees buckling in deep mud.

'Come on, girls!' I yell at the undulating blur of dark bodies, wondering how the fuck I'm going to do this without being able to see properly. Ten, eleven. 'Inside!'

Their hooves pummel the ground, slipping and sliding through thick sludge. Twenty-nine, thirty. They push and shove at the open gate, three cows wide. Survival of the fittest. Thirty-eight. They stumble and roar, bewildered and drenched. 'Come on!' Forty-two, forty-three. I lurch ahead of them to the barn, my pyjama shorts stuck to my skin.

The herd batters and barges against the barn door. Fifty, fifty-one, heavily pregnant Parsnip. I squeeze my way through them, shifting them into pens, ten at a time. Sixty, seventy. Sally, Antonia. Ninety, one hundred. Loretta, Thea. One hundred and twenty. They buck with anguish in the yard until they can find a way in. One hundred and forty. One hundred and forty-five, or was it four? I don't know why I'm counting. I could count them a million times over and get a different total every time. I grab Dad's old hay-splintered jumper from a hook next to the pitchforks and shove it on under his anorak. Teeth chattering, heart pounding, I head back out to the field.

'Come on, girls!' I trip over a fallen branch, dropping my torch in the cold mud and crawling into the hedge to avoid being stampeded.

'Inside!' I shout from the scratchy claws of the hawthorn bush, peeling my hair off my face and wiping the torch down with my sleeve. The field empties, mud sloshing, hooves thumping. I can do this. I can do this. I can do this. Nearly there. 'Hello?' I manage to pull myself up, the wind forcing me back into the hedge, hawthorn tearing my face. A second attempt and I'm up and staggering around the perimeter of the field, shining the torch inwards at head height. 'Anyone left?'

Thankfully, I've got them all.

I did it. The warm glow of satisfaction pinches at my cheeks and swells in my core. I take a shower and sit in bed drinking tea with Speedo's nose in my lap. I'm too wired to go back to sleep, and it feels good to be tucked up safe and warm, knowing that the cows are too, the storm raging outside. Listening to the rain pounding on the conservatory roof below, my thoughts return to Joely.

The Pelican Pharmaceutical Market Excellence Awards are splashed all over the internet. Four clicks in and there's a photo of Christophe Concordel holding a crystal star trophy, all bleached white teeth and glowing tan. The lapel of his tuxedo puckers over his pectorals. Two more clicks and his tuxedo has been removed in favour of a wing-collared pleated- front shirt. Another click, and he's centre stage, his arm around Joely, who poses like a Hollywood A-lister in the duck-egg-blue dress I bought her for her birthday. They look like a couple, award-winning smiles and eyes dazzling with pharmaceutical stardom. Another photo and he's pulled her into his chest, her hand spread over his washboard stomach. There is no sign of the 'entire KSG team behind him'. Or his girlfriend, for that matter.

A few hours later, and it's the sort of summer's day you dream of mid-winter. Sunshine floods the land, the sky an eternal blanket of blue. Goldfinches tweet. Crickets tick. A blackbird hops onto the top branch of a silver birch, his yellow beak opening to let out flute-like song. A cowslip bends with the weight of a bumblebee and I can even hear the sound of frogs croaking down on Baslow pond.

I'm two hours late milking, having fallen asleep with Speedo. The cows let me know it, their chorus of grunts reverberating across the barn. Bodies writhe and squirm against each other, their hot wet coats steaming. They heave and harrumph, restless and uneasy, a haunting anxiety to their groans. Creatures of routine, they're thrown out of whack. I've seen them late for milking before, both when Dad was too busy rescuing a goldcrest that had flown into the shed window and when Grandma broke her collarbone falling out of the tractor, but I don't remember them kicking off like this.

They barge through the gate when I open it, udders swollen like balloons, jostling for position to relieve the discomfort. Despite being on my own, milking goes like clockwork. I juggle seventeen cows simultaneously: an average of five minutes thirty seconds per cow. Cleaning teats, checking milk quality, attaching milkers, assessing pedometer readings. I'm a couple of readings short and about to double-check, but first need to sort out Speedo, who's going bat-shit crazy at the gate to the field, barking and growling. My fingers fumble for the latch to let the cows back in, but Speedo snaps at me, and then at the cows.

'Cool it, Speed!' I open the gate, expecting the herd to bustle in, but they stand motionless in the yard. Parsnip makes a strange bleating noise, craning her neck to the sky. I try to lead her into the field, but she refuses to budge, hooves anchored to the ground. Willow and Cobweb join her, aping

173

the noise she's making, which is somewhere between a whimper and a bellow; an eerie, guttural bleat.

'Come on, ladies.' I shout. 'We need to get a moooove on!'

Speedo shoots past me, making a beeline for the oak tree at the top of the field. The grassy bank is slippery from last night's mud-slide. He doubles back to get my attention, leading me towards the circular bail feeder surrounding the old oak, and there, in broad daylight, the brutal reality of last night hits in high definition. Three great slabs of beast, black and white, silent and stiff, lie flat on their backs on a plush carpet of luscious green grass, their hooves pointing up at the heaven that killed them. Stacked like fallen dominos, legs outstretched like the plastic cows I had on my farm playset as a child, glossy coats gleaming in the sun.

My ears go hot, and high-pitched ringing fills my head. They bear no marks, no whiplash wounds, no visible sign of death; nothing. Had I found them in the midst of the apocalyptic storm, it would have looked like what it is: mass murder under angry skies. Now, it just looks plain wrong; the country-side too idyllic, the peace and quiet too comforting. Like murder in a cake shop. Speedo trots between the bodies and sniffs each one. The leaves of the old oak tree rustle in the breeze, its branches snapped, its bark savaged. I crouch down next to the largest one. She's predominantly black with what looks like the outline of a planet in blurred, white fur on her neck: Jupiter. I look away, bile rising in my throat. Jupiter, the gentle, doting mother. The giver of life and protector of children, who would always go the extra mile for her girls: jumping walls for fresher dandelion; knocking down fences for melancholy thistle leaves. Only the best for her girls. Steering them out of danger. Away from machinery. Away from humans. Finding them shelter, away from the storm.

I force myself to face her, my stomach sliding over itself as my eyes travel to Lady Love and Lady Lovely, who lie next to her; sisters in synch as they were in the womb, their lives starting together and ending together. Heart-shaped white blotches of fur on their foreheads blow in the breeze. I reach out to touch Lady Lovely's neck. Her skin is warm and wet. Hope is merciless. It has me holding my hand under her nostrils, waiting to feel her hot breath.

I cup my hand around my mouth and retch. I can't look at them any more, but I can't leave them either. How the fuck can this have happened? It's not until I hear hooves slopping through mud and feel hot breath on the back of my neck that I realize I'm not alone. Parsnip is at my side. She cranes her neck towards the sky and lets out a guttural groan, which reverberates through the ground. Her head swings around; huge black eyes ask why I'm not doing anything about it, why I'm not helping up her mother and twin sisters. Her ears flicker. Her tail swishes. The whites of her eyes show.

I wrap my arms around her neck. 'Here, here.' I stroke her cheek.

She lets out another haunting groan.

'Come here.' I snivel.

She rests her chin on my shoulder and lets me stroke her face. It feels like tattered silk. We stay huddled together for a while – I need her as much as she needs me – until Fizz calls her and the cow-hug is over. I watch her slowly walk away, head bowed, like someone leaving a grave.

The cows understand what's happened; witnesses to the

whole cruel affair. They watched the lightning strike and know who's missing. Parsnip was obviously trying to tell me earlier. My stomach heaves. I've lost Parsnip her mother and her two little sisters. I've lost Parsnip's unborn calf her rocksteady, wise grandma. Matilda and Dalia have lost an auntie and two cousins. All of them have lost lifelong friends. Part of the sisterhood has died, and things will never be the same again.

I slide down onto the ground and pound my fist into the mud again and again, and still wretchedness curdles in my gut. Cold mud seeps through my running tights. I can't do this any more. I slam my heels into the ground and fling mud as far as I can, cold grit cathartic between my fingers. I want to fling it to Seoul. I want to throw it at Christophe Cocking Concordel and soil his gleaming white teeth. Fuck. This. Shit.

I'm done. I didn't choose to be here. I didn't choose any of it. My life belongs in London, curled up in bed with Joely Chevalier, choosing aspirational wallpaper and daydreaming about living together. If I hadn't had to take on the farm, none of this would have happened. The cows wouldn't have died and, who knows, Joely and I might have been living together by now. Shared bedroom. Shared toothbrush holder. Shared dreams. Free from the crushing misery of dairy life. Free from the bone-stinging nausea of fatigue and hopelessness. Free from this hellhole.

It feels like every single cell in my body has had the oxygen sucked out of it. What's the point any more? To think that I actually thought I could do this. To think that I actually thought I could help. It's nonsensical. I don't have a clue what

I'm doing. I don't have the experience, the knowledge or the desire. And now I've let down Dad.

I give up.

I peel off my clothes and take the longest shower of my life, trying to wash away death. Speedo follows me down to the kitchen, where I sit in Grandma's dressing gown, my fingers wrapped around a mug of black coffee. The house is silent save for the ticking of the grandfather clock in the hallway. The number for a local fallen stock collection company is listed at the back of Dad's red lever-arch file amongst a register of preferred suppliers. I dial the number for Take Stock.

An unusually jolly man answers the phone and promises to come over ASAP. He lightens the heavy conversation with 'okey dokes' and 'easy peasies', which doesn't feel appropriate given the circumstances.

'Don't worry,' he says brightly. 'We've a state-of-the-art processing facility over in Bradford, so they'll be well looked after.'

I close the file.

An hour later, a dirty Blue Group lorry rumbles down the lane and hits the old henhouse, flattening its wire coop. A young guy with acne and a wisp of upper lip hair jumps down from the cabin. 'Is your husband here?' He rolls up the sleeves of his overalls.

'No.'

He glances around the yard. 'Your dad?'

'No.' I want to rip his head off and shove it up his arse.

'Well, if you could just point me in the direction of the

farmer,' he says, reaching into his pocket and pulling out latex gloves.

'You're looking at her.'

He walks back over to his lorry, climbs onto the passenger side step and raps on the window. 'Rob? I think we might need reinforcements.'

We trudge through the field, sun gleaming through the branches of the oak tree. Today should be a day for dog-walking through sun-drenched fields, picnicking amongst buttercups and daisies, building treehouses, paddling in streams, not a day to be calling a rendering and incineration company to remove three beautiful beasts. We stand in front of the carcasses, Rob offering his 'reinforcement' services in the form of crunching prawn-cocktail-flavoured crisps and licking his fingers.

'Part and parcel of the circle of life, I'm afraid.' He pulls the corners of his crisp packet apart and tilts the last crumbs into his mouth.

'Shall we get it over with?' I say.

'Okey dokey.' He strolls back down the hill, hands in pockets, whistling.

The lorry backs up until it's only a few metres away, releasing a heavy-duty rope attached to the vehicle's tow bar. I study my feet as they wrap the other end of the rope around Jupiter's ankles, binding her front legs together.

The engine starts, wheels spinning and whirring as wet mud flies in all directions and Jupiter's bulk slides through the grime, thick snot flying from her nostrils as she's dragged across the ground. The buzz of the lorry's hydraulic lift being lowered to the ground bulldozes birdsong. I make the mistake of taking one last glance and wish I hadn't. Jupiter's twisted neck disappears over the mangled body of a dead horse.

'Lovely,' the main guy exclaims. 'Just the other two now.'

They repeat the process, rebolt the back of the van. 'Everything shipshape.'

Acid burns in my throat and I'm throwing up in the hedge when Lorna's Parsons-Bonneville Premier Vets SUV parks up. She gets out of the car, looks into the back of the Blue Group lorry and quickly turns away, slamming the car door shut. Shielding sun from her eyes with her hand, she scans the horizon until she spots me in the field.

'Billie?' She trudges up the hill, pulling the cuffs of her long-sleeved dri-FIT top over her hands.

I stare at the yard.

'Are you OK?'

Side by side, we stand in silence, watching the lorry rumble up the lane and drive off into the distance.

'How many did you lose?' she says quietly.

'Three.'

She nods slowly, a small dimple forming in her chin. Clunkily, she squeezes me into her collarbone. 'Let me make you a coffee.'

We walk back to the house.

'Firstly,' she says, rummaging through our kitchen cupboards for sugar. 'You may have lost three cows, but you saved one hundred and forty-seven.' The bottom of our broken cutlery drawer falls out and a shower of teaspoons clatter on the pans below. 'Secondly, you singlehandedly sorted it all out, without even missing milking.' She takes a jug of fresh milk out of the fridge. 'And thirdly . . .' The postman appears at the front of the house and hands Lorna a postcard through the open window. She glances at it. '*Ma petite Anglaise.* I guess this is for you.' She hands it to me, my heart skipping a beat. 'And thirdly . . . I can't remember what the third thing was.'

I look down at the postcard. *Life and Seoul.* A picture-perfect lotus pond. A gold-adorned pavilion. A moonlit cityscape of neon-pink skyscrapers. I rub my thumb over the area I know Joely has kissed. Her handwriting is elegant and evenly spaced, the tops of her l's curling over like a crest of a wave. I'll save it for when I'm alone.

'Very romantic!' Lorna sits down opposite me and tucks her mousy-blonde hair behind her ears. 'I can't remember the last time I got anything handwritten.'

I toy with a smile.

She looks at me, all chapped lips and freckles. 'There is nothing more that you could have done, Billie. You're in shock. You've just been through something horrific. The most horrific thing you'll probably ever go through.'

A light breeze comes in through the window, Grandma's bird calendar flapping against the wall and fluttering through months at a time. The room darkens as the sun dips behind the clouds and, for a moment, all I can hear is the tick of crickets. Lorna fiddles with the *I* ♥ *London* salt and pepper pots I bought Grandma years ago as a joke. Her fingernails are bitten right down to the pink bits and the backs of her hands are rough and weathered. The salt and pepper pots clink against each other as she moves them to the centre of the table, her gaze momentarily diverted to the gift-wrapped ring box containing the pendant addressed to 'Goddess Joely' in the fruit bowl.

'You're doing a fantastic job,' she says.

I run my bare feet over the wooden frame of the table. The silvery pink scar on her forehead looks softer than usual; no longer a blemish, rather a feature that's become part of her face. Part of her. It's not until she flattens her fringe down over it that I realize I've been staring. 'Thank you,' I say quietly.

She dabs her finger on the flecks of pepper that have escaped onto the table. 'You know, I've always—' Her phone bleeps. 'Shit!' She jumps up and pours the remains of her coffee down the sink. 'I'm late for my next appointment and I haven't even looked at Nadia. Are you going to be OK?'

I nod mechanically.

'I'll come back first thing tomorrow and check Nadia out, then I can check in on you too.'

'Sure.'

'Promise you'll call me if there's anything you need.' She reaches across and gives my arm a squeeze. Her hands are small and rough.

'Thanks.'

The door clicks shut behind her.

The postcard sits on my knee. I'm about to read it when I see a mail come in from Joely on my phone, so I go to that first, wondering whether the 'I love you' I blurted out on the phone is going to reciprocated.

Dear Billie,

I'm sorry that it's so difficult on the farm and that nobody is available to help you. It's crazy how much your life has changed in a month, isn't it?

I've reflected a lot recently and, although it's difficult to say this, I think our relationship is probably not the best thing for either of us any more. You're so busy with the farm and my roadshow has been extended so I don't know when I can see you at all. I tried to contact you yesterday to talk it through, but you didn't pick up again. You never pick up.

Sadly, I think it's better if we separate. You can focus on the farm and I can concentrate on my work projects.

You are special, Billie. You are funny, kind and intelligent. I am sure you will succeed, whatever you choose in life. A relationship will not help you at the moment.

I will miss you.

Bisous,
Joely

At first, I read it as a cry for help, our relationship redeemable if I can lavish her with attention. But each time I call her, voicemail kicks in, and instead of kicking in after its usual ten rings, I'm being cut off at two, three and four. It can't all fall apart like this. It just can't. I was committed. I am committed. The farm thing is just temporary, and we can overcome this. Surely, she can see this. Maybe she was drunk when she wrote it. Maybe she just felt neglected. Maybe she should answer her fucking phone. Why is it so much easier to communicate with animals than humans? And I don't mean in the reductive 'I'm hungry' or 'I'm in pain' sense. Cows are great communicators. Their body language will tell you if they're having a good day or not. If they're feeling unloved or pushed out. Confused or unsure. Jealous or angry. A tail flick of annoyance. A moo of intrigue. A bellow of disgruntlement. A limb-locked stillness of fear. It's all obvious without words. Words just seem to complicate things.

I don't know whether I'm coming or going. Am I the old or the new me? Am I moving forwards or backwards, or simply treading water and moving around in circles? All I know is that I'm torn between two worlds, an outsider to them both. Even my clothes don't seem to fit: the ones I brought with me and the ones I've borrowed up here. Nothing fits any more.

I pick up the postcard.

Dear Billie,

Greetings from South Korea! Comment vas-tu, ma petite Anglaise? There are people everywhere and everything is mirrored which makes it look twice as busy.

The roadshow is going well. My presentation is like an autopilot now and I bore myself with the same words every day.

I miss you like crazy. I can't wait to see your face again. Let's go travelling before we settle down and have babies!

Bisous,
Joely

Airmail is a cruel mistress. If you're going to express your feelings in a postcard, then bloody well make sure you're still going to feel the same way by the time it's delivered – the simple things, for fuck's sake.

I stamp and scream, screwing myself up into a ball of fury. Speedo retreats upstairs, his ears flat against his head. I can't lose her. I just can't.

Two minutes later, I find myself rummaging in the drawer underneath the television until I have it in my hands: Kay Oliver RIP. Thank God Dad had the old tapes digitized before they wore out completely.

I open the plastic case and slide the disc into the DVD player slot. A few seconds later, my mother's twenty-something face appears on the screen. She wears a black felt mortar board and clutches a degree scroll. Her hair is chopped short and dyed a rusty red. She grins mischievously, a hotchpotch of eyeshadow shades running from her eyelids over her eyebrows. The sort of person you'd describe as 'kooky'.

'Two-one, two-one!' She jumps up and down. 'To world domination!'

She has more freckles than I remember. I pause the DVD here, otherwise she'll go on to talk about her future and she'll do this little air-punch thing, which I can't cope with right now. It's only when I've been staring at her face for about two minutes that I notice a tiny mole beneath her nose that I've never spotted before. Considering I've watched this video hundreds of times, this in itself is revolutionary – but what's even more uncanny is that I have the same mole – same size, same colour, same place. I raise my fingers to it and feel a sense of belonging. Sated, even. Like she kept that discovery in the bag for me and knew to release it only when I really needed it. The only thing is, it makes me miss Dad even more, in the capacity of a parent. Someone to lean on, look up to, be guided by. Someone to cry on. I want Dad back.

I turn off the television and head outside, allowing a cocktail of anger, sadness and guilt to pour out in the form of hysterical sobs. Who cares? There's nobody here to see me.

I stumble across the yard, looking up at the low-hanging sky through a blur of tears. The long dirt track stretches out in front, separating me from the rest of the world. I snap a twig from a hazel tree and crush a cluster of hornbeam catkins into a gritty lime-green powder in the palm of my hand before running as fast as I can down the lane, my lungs full of air. Then I stop and scream as loudly as I can. A flock of starlings takes flight from a nearby silver birch. Wings flap, cows bellow, squirrels scatter but nothing changes.

I kick a stone, only to stub my toe, and trip over, my hands pebble-dashed with blood, dirt and tattered skin. My knees are grazed, and my leggings torn. I want to be scooped up and cradled into the maternal bosom of my grandma. I want Dad to ruffle my hair and tell me everything's OK. I want a set of giant curtains to open, revealing an applauding audience, my life a hoax; Billie at her most broken on reality TV. I want to go to bed and stay asleep until this whole episode is over. God, I'm pathetic.

Then, once I've indulged the moment for long enough to accept that nobody is going to come to my rescue and that I have to (wo)man up, I peel my body off the ground and cower in the shelter of the dry-stone wall. Dull, matte bracken fronds dip hypnotically in the wind. A ring ouzel keeps watch from an abandoned millstone, and a smudge of dark cloud hangs low over the moorland horizon. A centipede crawls across my boot, her body snaking its way into the grooves of my sole. I dig my fingernails into a clump of soft, damp moss and stare at the gnarly old oak tree at the top of the field.

My phone signal flickers between two and three bars. I call Grandma, who this time picks up.

'How is he?' I feel detached from my voice, like it isn't my own.

'Tired.'

I rub my thumb over the rough granite wall and am about to confess about the storm, when a soft tickling makes me look down. A ladybird has found its way onto my finger, crawling across my knuckles like it hasn't a care in the world. I look at my hands. They don't look or feel like mine any more. Muck and grime emphasize the cracks and crevices. My skin is dry and ragged. Then I realize that I'm not supposed to be looking at my hands. I'm supposed to be looking at the ladybird. The ladybird who has visited me throughout my life in various forms. Yes, ladybirds appear on memorabilia. Yes, ladybirds land on people. But do they really visit everyone else at their ebb low? I'm not spiritual, but is the ladybird my mum?

'Billie? Are you OK?' Grandma's voice crackles.

And while half of me thinks I may have become one of those madwomen unaware that birds are living in her hair, the other half finds comfort in the idea. I don't have to tell anyone about this. I can just keep it to myself. Keep *her* to myself. Part of my armour. So, I'm actually not alone. I'm not actually running this farm on my own.

'Yes, Grandma. I'm fine.'

# CHAPTER TWELVE

# PRiDE

**From: Bev**
Sorry, B. Think of it as a relationship sabbatical. You
can always give her a shout once you're back in
London. I see this all the time with our flamingos on the
ZSL breeding programme. One bird gives the other the
cold shoulder for a couple of months, but they always
seem to get together in the end. Any chance you can
come down for Pride? Hang in there, buddy x

**From: Dad**
If Florence's teats still look red raw, she might need
something stronger. Could you ask Lorna?

**From: Kat Mellor**
Bill, honey. It may sting like a mother-fucker but trust me
it's better that it happens now. How's about you come
down to Pride for a 'fuck it sambuca' and take your

mind off Joely? Every time you get the urge to call her, call me instead. Chin up, chest out and fuck her. Love you x

**From: Dad**
That photo you sent of Lady Penelope eating dandelions is actually Bessy!

**From: Bev**
P.S. Titania and Theodore had a six-month cooling off period and now their third egg has hatched so, there you go. Living proof!

**From: Maria**
That's shit, Bilbo. I'm really sorry. Can I be honest? I know you won't want to hear this right now, but I don't think Joely's right for you anyway. You need a girl who'll roll her sleeves up. Someone who loves you for being you, and that includes the farm girl part of you. Darius found a bunch of *Wallpaper* magazines in your bedroom. That is SO NOT YOU, Billie! Joely's flaky and vapid. She's not good enough for you. Love you lots and lots and lots xxx

**From: Dave Work**
Send her a tit pic.

**From: Maria**
P.S. So clearly, you'll get back together, and I'll look like a dick for saying all this, but you're my best friend and I

owe you the truth. So, if you do get back together and I
tell you I didn't mean what I said and that I'm sure
Joely's neither flaky nor vapid really, I'll be bullshitting.
There you go, Bilbo. On the line. Love you xxx

**From: Maria**
P.P.S. Pride next weekend. Sure you can't come?

**From: Dave Work**
P.S. Any chance you can post me your pass, so I can
use your credit at the canteen?

**From: Lorna Parsons**
Keep forgetting to mention, your Land Rover's left brake
light doesn't work. Hope you're feeling better about
things. Remember, it wasn't your fault. Let me know if
you'd like me to pop over.

**Subj: Parsnip**

Hi Lorna,

Hope all's well with you.

I'm worried about Parsnip. I checked her stats and she's
not eating nearly as much as she should, especially as
she's in calf. Each time I go into the field, she's standing
under the oak tree in the exact spot Jupiter died. She's

189

lost a lot of confidence and has dropped towards the back of the line on journeys to and from the cowshed. When I call her, she'll come to me and rest her head on my shoulder, but she's not interested in socializing with the rest of the herd.

Yesterday, she wouldn't even take an apple off me and I know how she loves her apples.

Any ideas how I could help her?

Thanks,
Billie

Two days later, Dad has the operation to remove his brain tumour. Craniotomy. Funny how medical terms can legitimize anything, like bludgeoning your head open and poking at your brains. It certainly puts getting dumped back into perspective. After milking, I try to immerse myself in 'Fly Genetics: What fruit flies can tell us about our immune system', but it's difficult to concentrate knowing that he'll be gowning up to go into theatre.

When I realize I'm never going to be able to concentrate, I call Grandma, who also doesn't seem to know what to do with herself, and we meet for lunch at the Derbyshire Craft Centre; a gift shop and café on the edge of Curbar, where middle-aged women in clunky wooden jewellery buy cat ornaments and out-of-season Christmas decorations. The onsite deli smells of fresh coffee and old lady's perfume. Minestrone soup and broccoli quiche are up on the specials board and the cake counter is bursting with homemade patisserie. Banana bread. Mango meringue. Oreo cheesecake. Victoria sponge. Pineapple turnover. Coffee and Kahlúa chocolate ganache. None of it looks real.

'Beatrice had her assessment yesterday.' Grandma skirts around the elephantine lump in the room that is Dad. He should be anaesthetized now, floating in a private bubble of virtual reality, the neurosurgeons hovering with scalpels and medical instruments. Every gleaming metallic blade will have a name. Bone chisels, clamps, retractors, distractors. Anything and everything to get anywhere and everywhere.

I try to focus my attention on the list of hot beverages chalked up on the blackboard, but I can't take anything in. I should be in the lab now, holding some of those medical instruments. Experimenting with life-changing possibilities. Protecting and future-proofing mankind. Or at least a very small subset. Making sure pregnant women don't die of eclampsia. At the helm of scientific discovery. The words of the menu bend and blur. Dad would choose tea. English Breakfast with milk. Never without milk. Fucking milk. I should tell her about the storm, but it doesn't feel like the right moment.

Grandma helps herself to a tray and eyes up the walnut coffee cake. 'It'll be three weeks before they decide whether she's eligible for care, by which time she should be back on her feet. It's a bloody nonsense.' She eyeballs the waitress, a large girl in a skimpy top who makes a sloppy job of pouring semi-skimmed milk into a tiny jug.

'Can we stop talking about Beatrice's hip?' I snip.

She shuffles her cup of black coffee into the cradle of its saucer and orders two slices of Bakewell tart.

'Sorry,' I add. 'I'm just stressed.'

The tearoom behind is alive with the clinking of cutlery and chinking of china. We make our way over to a table that looks out onto a small, overgrown garden. Grandma undoes the buttons of her camel coat and moves the vase of synthetic carnations off the table, placing them on the windowsill with a loud tut.

I stare at the slice of Bakewell tart in front of me. It just looks plastic. 'Joely's called it off.'

Grandma fiddles with the mole behind her ear. 'I'm sorry, Billie Goat.'

I stir my tea. 'I'm not sure she likes me as a farmer.'

'I'm not sure I like her being so unsupportive.' She lowers her plate to the table, her slice of Bakewell tart tilting to one side. 'Her tops were too skimpy anyway. All that midriff hanging out.'

A smile creeps into the corners of my mouth and dissolves almost instantaneously, tears springing to my eyes. I really wanted Joely and me to work. We belong to the same professional world and understand each other's dreams. We fit together. Her yin to my yang. We could go places. Adventure together, spend summers in our Paris pied-à-terre, romancing on the banks of the river Seine, our over-achieving bilingual children skipping around a gingham picnic blanket of eclectic cheeses and fresh baguette. I'm so much stronger with Joely than without her. Together, we're indestructible.

'I was thinking,' Grandma mumbles through pastry. 'Once your dad gets better, we should plan a few things.'

I stare at my slab of Bakewell tart. 'What kind of things?

It's not like Dad will want to go whale-watching in South America or snorkelling on the Great Barrier Reef.'

'He does have an adventurous streak, Billie. He just hasn't exercised it for a long time.' She dabs her finger over a line of pastry crumbs.

We brainstorm a bucket list without wanting to call it that. Achievable dreams without needing a passport – taking a flask of tea to the rocks at Robin Hood's Bay, enjoying a pub lunch in the Lake District and eating fish & chips on Filey beach. Once we've exhausted ideas, we stare at our plates and wonder if we'll do any of the things on the list, both of us silently choking on worry, neither of us daring to voice our fears lest it be a betrayal of Dad and his fighting spirit.

I gather some coins together for a tip while Grandma spends what feels like hours extolling the virtues of Sky TV and Beatrice's power-shower.

'Did you know Mary Berry has her own show on Sky Living?' she enthuses.

I understand she's not really being a heartless bitch and it's just her way of blocking out reality, but still. The surgeons should be stitching his head back together now.

Grandma hugs me in the gift shop for longer than is comfortable and I worry that she doesn't smell of *Grandma* any more. Gone is the lingering scent of lavender talcum powder and the smell of cooking apples. It's not that she smells of Beatrice's flat either; she's just lost her scent. She could be anyone.

**RE: Parsnip**
Dear Billie,

193

Guy once had a session with an animal bereavement counsellor in Sheffield and said it was really useful. Let me know if you want his details and I can bring them over.

Lorna

*

**Re: Parsnip**

Dear Lorna,
Thanks for the animal bereavement contact, though it's Parsnip I'm more worried about than me. Although she's eaten a bit more the last couple of days, she won't leave the oak tree and stands there bellowing for hours. She's definitely missing her sisters too as she's taken to following Hazel and Holly around like they're her surrogate twin sisters. Is this normal cow behaviour?

B

Three hours later and I'm making my way through the corridors of Sheffield Royal Hallamshire Hospital while Grandma drives round the block to find a free parking space. Dad is a lot better than I expected. His head is heavily bandaged, but he wears fresh pyjamas and seems more alert. He pulls out his headphones when he sees me.

'How's the English patient?' I kiss him on his stubbly cheek.

'Podcasts and steroids are wonderful inventions.' He smiles. 'How's my Bilberry?'

I've promised myself I won't mention Joely. That it's all about Dad and putting on a brave face. He needs positivity and it's entirely the wrong moment for me to whine about my misfortunes, which are relatively trivial at the end of the day.

'Joely's ended it,' I blurt. What the fuck is the matter with me?

Dad smooths the crisp white sheet over the top of his blanket. 'If it's any consolation, your mother gave me the run-around for a good six months before we started going steady.' It's no consolation at all. 'You're a good egg, Bilberry. If she can't see that, then she's not right for you.'

I'm not sure how I feel about being a 'good egg'. It wouldn't bother me so much if it was written by my PE teacher on an end-of-year school report in relation to some sort of sports day episode where I'd volunteered to do the long jump because no one else would, but it's not exactly something I'd acclaim in a dating profile. People neither aspire to be good eggs nor do they aspire to snare a good egg. Good eggs are those that get left behind. Dad's normally a lot better at this sort of thing. Then again, he has just had a major brain operation and I should get the fuck over myself.

Grandma appears, all flustered after an altercation with a traffic warden. She slams her handbag down on Dad's shins and takes out a bundle of brandy snaps wrapped in clingfilm.

'How are the girls?' Dad says.

My throat tightens, slabs of dead cow appearing in my mind's eye. Their glossy coats. Their glassy eyes.

'Billie's doing a great job by the looks of things,' Grandma says, dividing up the brandy snaps and handing them out like lollipops. 'Did I tell you Betty at Knit, Natter, Craft and Chatter says we should convert the farm into an Outdoor Survival retreat?'

'A what?' Dad says.

'You'd be surprised what people will pay to sleep in a potato-sack hammock at minus three. Although I'm not sure about having to install a heater in the barn.'

'The barn? Aren't they supposed to hand-weave their own wigwams?' Dad says.

The moment to tell them about the cows has gone.

'It depends,' Grandma says.

I should have told Grandma at the Derbyshire Craft Centre.

'On what?' Dad picks bits of brandy snap off his blanket.

'Whether you've ticked "deluxe" or not,' Grandma says. 'They'll pay extra for a fry-up.'

I can't tell them now.

Dad rolls his eyes. 'Isn't the whole point of an Outdoor Survival course that they're supposed to be self-sufficient?'

'Strictly speaking, but Milli Vanilli didn't sing their own songs, did they?' Grandma concludes.

Dad looks at me as I'm typing Milli Vanilli into Google. 'Any calves yet?'

'No.' I almost adopt the brace position you get shown in the event of a plane emergency landing and wait for pain to rain, but it doesn't come. Dad is on form, Grandma is too, and Milli Vanilli is a disgraced R&B duo from Munich, infamous for miming to somebody else's vocals in the early 1990s. Charlatans of the pop industry. Faking it as a profession. And I kind of feel for them.

The next day, it's difficult to concentrate on milk yield knowing that my friends are living *la vida loca* at Gay Pride. Maria has taken it upon herself to send videos from London with the intention of making me feel part of it, which is both good and bad. I stare at the video thumbnail on my phone. If ever there was a square inch that oozed the spirit of Pride, this is it: three grinning girls, smacked with verve and splashed with colour, standing next to a glittery Polly Darton float. I press *play*.

London is a sea of feather boas, baby-pink cowboy hats, inflatables, scantily dressed beaux in hot pants, sweaty pleather-clad dykes and swathes of giggling lipstick lesbians, gay for a day. Transvestites strut in bridal gowns, their lace trains held by a fleet of children in rainbow T-shirts. Gay men in rubber, lace, bubble wrap and clingfilm. Gay men in glitter, blusher, wigs and wings. Gay men in mascara, lipstick, tiaras and heels. Pride may be a celebration of freedom of expression for all of us, but it's a sky's-the-limit carnival of colour for the extrovert gay man. And man, are they beautiful.

'Hey, Bill!' Kat's rainbow-painted cheeks loom into the camera. 'Thought we'd share a bit of Pride with you.'

Bev pops up alongside her, waving into the camera. 'Happy Pride, buddy!' She wears a T-shirt with two proud peacocks, beak to beak across her chest.

Maria slings her arm around Bev's neck. 'Today is about being outrageously G-A-Y and using the word "fabulous" in abundance, whether you're on a dairy farm or on the parade,' she says theatrically.

The camera pans along Marylebone's maze of chintzy teashops and upholstered antiques. A 'Come out, come out, wherever you are!' banner hangs at the entrance to Harley Street. I can almost taste the atmosphere from muscle memory – a blend of hot dogs, candyfloss, tobacco and lip gloss.

Maria twirls in circles, showing off her rainbow-striped mini-dress. 'Stolen from the Lambeth LGBT *Josephine and the Technicolour Dreamboat* wardrobe.'

The camera lurches as a Trioga Montara motorhome, spray-painted gold with 'Gay Team' emblazoned across the bonnet, swings into shot, hooting its novelty horn and farting diesel. I can just about make out Bev's mothers at the helm, waving ketchup-laced hot dogs.

'Love, not hate!' a group of off-screen female voices scream fiercely.

Bev leans into the camera. 'Mum's and Mama's LGBT pastry-making course mates!' Her eyebrows dance before the camera tracks up to the roof, which has been ripped off to provide a small stage to a group of middle-aged women wearing heart-print aprons embroidered with 'We're Here, We're Queer'. They drum on cake tins with wooden spoons. 'Love, not hate!'

The camera jiggles and jolts as the girls climb on board, a close-up of Kat's hand grasping at the thin metal handrail leading upstairs, tiny rainbows painted on her fingernails.

'Love, not hate!' the ladies bang and boom.

The camera tilts to show swathes of people lining the streets below, all high on life: street performers, musicians, dancers, singers, old lesbians, young lesbians, tall lesbians, short lesbians, fat lesbians, thin lesbians, butch lesbians, femme lesbians, lesbians of every nationality you can think of; and for every lesbian of every shape and size, there are twice as many gay guys with ten times the amount of invention. A group of oiled muscle men in tiny red Speedos promote 'Gay Watch', waving fervently from a silver open-top bus. The next float along hosts an array of sequined drag queens, all tight bottoms in silk gowns.

Maria's head emerges. 'Billabong!' she squeals. 'Don't go to bed early as we want to bring you a bit of Soho, live! Stay tuned for part two!'

Bev's giant thumb looms into shot and the video ends.

I look around the kitchen. The smell of freshly made coffee fills the air. Sun beams through the open window. Birdsong carries on the summer breeze and I have never felt so fucking lonely. I miss Joely. I miss London. I miss my friends.

Durham University's alumni newsletter drops into my inbox. My chest tightens as page after page of glossy photos capture award-winning graduates on makeshift stages, eco-friendly architectural wonders designed and constructed by 'our very own'. Year after year of postgraduate success, my classmates namechecked in print for early career achievements, outstanding contributions to international development, humanitarian relief, AIDS awareness, Ebola treatment and every other selfless, heroic cause imaginable. And meanwhile, I'm shovelling shit for a dying industry; an unremarkable cog in the insignificant wheel of an underfunded dairy farm going nowhere.

Even Julia Spears, infamous for plagiarizing my essays and doing more speed than a Formula One driver, has secured government funding to trial her breast cancer breakthrough drug. On the next page I see Andrew Colman, a lad from my biochemistry class, has become Scientist of the Year, his hands wrapped around a gleaming trophy. I couldn't possibly feel any more cut off from the world of science if I tried.

Grandma appears at the kitchen door holding a can of polish and a yellow duster.

'Thought I'd better get everything shipshape for his lordship's return.' She stops to look at me. 'What's the matter with you? You've hardly said a word all day.'

'Nothing.' I stare at the thumbnail of the girls on their Pride float. 'Life is peachy. I've been dumped by my girlfriend. I've taken six months' unpaid leave from a job that I love. I've given up my flat, my life and my friends to run a dairy farm, which is obviously everything I ever wanted because it's *so* enriching, *so* career advancing, *so* sociable, *so* culturally diverse. Not to mention profitable!' I know I'm being a dick and have overstepped the mark, but I can't stop myself. 'The highlight was being accused of paedophilia.'

'You know the agency laid him off?' Grandma says, duster on hip.

'Nathan?'

'Yes, can't get a job now for love nor money.'

'And I'm supposed to feel sorry for him?'

'Not at all. I just mean he got his comeuppance.'

'And meanwhile, I'm supposed to be *living my lab findings* to get a PhD, which, of course, is so very easy on a dairy farm in the middle of nowhere. There are literally hundreds of women struggling with eclampsia out in the hills of rural Derbyshire.'

'Anything else?' She rubs the duster vigorously over Dad's silver 'Dairy Innovator of the Year' trophy.

'Yes!' I smash my fists on the table. 'It's Pride!'

'What is?' Her arms wobble as she polishes.

'Today is.'

She stands the trophy on the draining board and admires it. 'You've lost me.'

'Gay Pride. The parade in London. All my friends are there, and I'm stuck—'

'Here with me?' She sneezes on polish fumes.

'Grandma, missing Pride is like missing Christmas.' I drop my head into my hands and sprawl theatrically across the table.

She plucks the dry, curled-up teabag off my saucer and drops it into the compost bin. 'I wish things were different too, Billie, but they're not. If there's one thing I've learned over the years, it's that life can wrongfoot you at any moment. It can cut a chunk out of you at the blink of an eye. We are all at the mercy of Mother Nature at the end of the day, and that's why you've got to enjoy life while it's yours to enjoy.'

'Which is precisely why I want to be at Pride!' I interject, but Grandma is on a trajectory all of her own.

'I understand what it's like to run the farm, Billie. I ran it for years and it was a lot bigger back then. Not just when your grandpa got sick either. He lost his nerve years before when we lost eighty cattle to tuberculosis. He was never quite the same after that.'

'*Eighty?*' I say. 'You never told me about that.'

She nods. 'It's too upsetting, that's why. It broke him. Still, it kept me busy.' She runs her duster over the kitchen tap. 'If I could still do it now, I would, but my back doesn't bend in the way it used to.'

Water drips from the tap and everything slows. A rhythmic

plip, plip. Dad's pillowcases hang from the ceiling airer and the pages of a discarded *Dairy Farmer* flicker in the breeze.

'Three cows died in the storm,' I say quietly.

'Oh, my good God.' Grandma slams down the polish. 'Are you OK?'

I nod slowly.

She walks over to me and cradles me to her bosom. 'You poor, poor thing.'

'I'm sorry. I didn't mean what I said earlier.'

She clasps her arms around my neck. 'You're doing a great job, Billie Goat.' Her skin is conker-smooth and dappled with freckles. A soft pinch of skin hangs at her elbows. I look into her face. A face which has never worn make-up or pretended to be anything that it isn't. A face that has never lied or betrayed. A face that understands on every level. 'Beatrice has had me for long enough,' she says. 'I'll get my things this evening.' An honest face that smells of cooking apples and talcum powder.

Grandma is back.

### Re: Parsnip

Sadly, it's totally normal cow behaviour. I dare say she's probably depressed. Cows are deeply emotional animals and it'll take her a while to accept her loss. Maybe take a bag of apples up to her. The important thing is to keep an eye on her weight and food intake, which you are. Try not to worry and she should gradually come around. How's about I pop over tomorrow and take a look?

L

At 7 p.m., my phone jingles, with the girls coming to me live from Pride. 'Keep Calm and Come Out' is projected onto the walls of Whitehall Place, in rainbow font just like it was last year, the same silver raindrops and magenta umbrella icons cascading across the screen. Below, a crowd of thousands await The Weather Girls, who are headlining for a second year running. Watching it on screen feels like déjà vu; a re-enactment of last year's event, only at arm's length.

While I'm sure the atmosphere is electric there in the flesh, seeing it on video is like peering into a sweet shop when you're penniless. It kind of hurts. The Two Tonnes O'Fun take the stage, one in a blood-orange tunic and another in a hot pink sundress. I frown. Surely budgets haven't been slashed so much that they have to wear the same outfits as last year. This is Pride, after all.

The rainbow face-paint on Kat's cheeks has rubbed off and she looks worse for wear, her eyes sunken with inebriation. Maria's forehead lunges into the foreground. Her hair has been cut since this morning, back to the bob with a heavy fringe she'd had last year until the maintenance got too much. God knows how or why she got that done during Pride, but that's Maria for you. She's the only person I know who can nip to the shops for milk and come back in a whole new outfit including accessories. '*Hi.*' She snaps her head to one side. 'Help me out here, Bilbo!'

I suffer an out-of-body experience when *my head* pops up on screen. '*Ah-huh.*' I'm wearing a cowboy hat with 'Closets are for Clothes' written on a ribbon running around it. It takes me a few seconds to realize this is the video Kat took at last year's Pride. Although it's only twelve months ago, I look significantly younger: my skin fresher; the lines around my eyes not so gully-deep.

My heads snaps up as a knock on the door brings me back to the here and now. Back to the primrose-yellow-painted kitchen, the rough oak table and the smell of furniture polish, Speedo barking frenziedly.

'One sec!' I press *pause*, grab him by the collar and open the door.

Standing before me is a lilac mermaid shimmering from head to tail in sequins. Long red locks cascade in ringlets to her waist, her chest is strapped into two Hawaiian coconut shells held together with string, her lips are silver and her eyelashes pink.

'Surprise!' She thrusts a bunch of pink carnations at me. 'Sorry, they're the only thing I could find at the petrol station.'

'Maria!' I shriek, tearing her off the doorstep and squeezing her so tightly that sequins flutter to the ground. It feels so good to see her in 3D and feel the warm hulk of a friend.

Speedo is more interested in barking at the hire car. Maria holds on to her red nylon wig and shuffles backwards. 'Well, we thought if Muhammad won't come to the mountain . . .'

'*We?*'

'Surprise!' Kat and Bev jump out from behind the car and run towards me, smeared in face-paint and joie de vivre. Speedo seems to understand and adopts the barking whine he reserves for chasing rabbits.

I'm rooted to the spot. 'What about Pride?'

Kat pulls the knot out of her T-shirt and flattens the creased cotton over her lipstick-daubed stomach. She passes me a chilly bottle of Pol Roger Brut Vintage champagne and a bag of Marks & Spencer's sea salt and cider vinegar kettle chips. 'We couldn't have Pride without you, Bill!' She studies me. 'Look at you! You look so . . .'

'Frazzled? Grubby? Unkempt?' I laugh.

'Tiny,' she says. 'There's nothing of you.'

'Good to see you, buddy.' Bev gives me a bear hug. Her Mohican is festooned with glitter, which has made its way across the two peacocks on her chest. 'I hope we've not come at a bad time?'

'You've come at a bloody brilliant time!' I squeak.

'Sorry about the outfit.' Maria jumps across the yard to get her handbag. 'I did a costume swap with a girl in Piccadilly and can't get the bloody thing off!'

Two hours later, after I've given them a guided tour of the yard, the milking shed, the various barns and our crooked little farmhouse, we're strewn over the lounge floor drinking champagne and playing Boggle, the salt making its descent through the egg-timer.

'How's the hen party planning coming along?' I say, topping up our drinks.

Kat and Bev share a steely glare.

'It wasn't my idea!' Maria holds her hands up.

'I don't mind a bit of glitter, but I draw the line at pussy whistles,' Kat says.

'It's Coleen from the meerkat enclosure at work,' Bev explains. 'It's her first lesbian hen party and she gets a bit excitable.'

'I don't want her at my hen party,' Kat snarls.

'She's harmless,' Bev says. 'You're always going to get someone bringing tat on a hen do.'

'Not on my hen do, you don't. If anyone turns up wearing plastic boob earrings, they can fuck off home!'

Maria's eyes widen at me in a 'see what it's been like?' way. 'I thought we agreed not to talk about the hen party this weekend?'

'Deal!' Kat throws down her pen and opens the kettle chips. 'So, what happened with Joely, Bill?'

Just hearing Joely's name is like having a pin pressed into my skin. I jot down 'bit, bait, bat, tab'. 'She lost interest the moment I became a dairy farmer.'

Bev rotates the Boggle grid. 'Shame.'

'Not really.' Maria frowns. 'Billie can do better.'

I put down my glass, my head heavy. 'I can't begin to tell you how difficult it's been.'

'Forget her, Bill. She's not worth it,' Kat rants. 'You're fabulous. She isn't. You're the real deal. She's a fucking control freak. You're . . .'

'Not Joely,' I say. 'The farm.'

'Right,' Kat recalibrates.

'The price of milk is at an all-time low.' I know I sound like Grandma, but I can't stop myself. 'We make half the profit we did seven years ago.' As I'm saying the words, I'm also thinking about Joely and whether all my friends think she's a control freak. 'And I feel guilty.' I lurch between streams of consciousness. 'I feel guilty for not trying enough on the PhD front.'

'I think you've got enough on your plate,' Bev says.

'And then I feel guilty for feeling guilty, because obviously Dad is the priority right now,' I continue. 'And I miss Joely.'

206

'Shit,' Kat says. 'We really need to get you out.' She looks to Maria.

Maria wears this gawky grin. 'Billabong Oliver, would you care to step this way?'

Joely's not a control freak. Far from it. She's just an independent lady, who knows what she wants and how she wants it.

I follow Maria into the hallway, out of the front door and across the yard to the dilapidated old barn, where my Dad's Ford New Holland 8340 Turbo usually stands caked in dry mud, next to a defunct hoof-trimming machine, but is now decorated with streamers, feather boas, tinsel and feathers, masquerading as a carnival float. A giant inflatable rainbow-coloured cow buffets in the breeze, its hooves anchored by string to the tractor cabin.

'Your Pride chariot awaits!' Kat says, the three of them grinning from ear to ear and curtseying in a row.

'So that's why you were so interested in the tractor earlier!' I say.

'Can you start her up?' Bev dangles the keys in front of me.

I grab at the cold, rusty handrail and clamber in, the smell of wet dog and cattle wormer infusing the cabin. Sponge prolapses from the upholstery, and grains of chicken feed have made their way into every groove, cavity and crack. Speedo bounds in with a heavy thud. He licks my face, thwacking his tail against a small metal butter churn. Maria and Kat stand on the ledge on one side, whilst Bev balances on the other. I turn on the headlights, illuminating the blurry cowshed, and can't work out whether bats are swooping and diving in my peripheral vision or whether I'm just too drunk.

'Where are we heading?' I say.

'Nowhere. Anywhere.' Kat removes tinsel from the gearstick. 'We just wanted you to get a taste of Pride.'

It takes three or four goes before the tractor comes to life, engine shuddering and bonnet rattling. My legs are barely long enough to reach the pedals, so I'm forced to perch on the edge of the springy seat to peer over the steering wheel as the tractor inches forward. We bounce over the yard, the girls wobbling and whooping. My arms judder as the pull of 20,000 pounds of metalwork ripples through my core. It's like trying to hold back the tide: I'm standing on the pedals trying to counterbalance the weight of the tractor as the bonnet swings around more slowly than I'd bargained for and under-shoots the lane. Elderberry branches crackle and snap as we lurch forward, holly clawing at the paintwork and the front wheels planting themselves and Maria in the hedgerow.

'Way to go, Bill!' Kat cries as Bev pulls Maria out of the undergrowth minus the wig and minus one of the Hawaiian mermaid coconut-shell cups.

I hear laughter and it takes me a few moments to realize it is mine.

A loud guttural moo makes me jump as Buttercup's colossal head swings over the hedge. She looks at us like we're aliens and calls her family over. Within seconds, four Holstein Friesians are staring at us. Fizz grunts loudly, nostrils flaring, her maternal instinct inciting her to shield Holly and Hazel from this enormous metal beast and all its roaring.

I manage to reverse the tractor out of the hedge and embark on a three-point turn, which results in Bev having to open the gate to the field of cows to give me more space and the tractor somehow free-wheeling into a ditch. Fizz stands and stares. Bev wipes mud out of a cracked coconut shell with her sleeve and hands it to Maria, who is groping under the hedgerow for her earring, cupping one bare breast in her hand.

Buttercup lets out another deep, guttural groan. Her head pivots around as a Land Rover approaches along the lane, sloshing and crunching through puddles and grit, Grandma at the wheel. My heart sinks. I'm reminded of the time I drove Grandma's Mini Cooper to Graves Park aged seventeen, and naively drained the car battery listening to The White Stripes with Bev. Dad had to come out in his pyjamas with a pair of jump-leads to rescue us. It was pretty cringeworthy. Only this time, I feel more humiliated because it's Grandma and she will not find the fact that I've driven the tractor amusing in the slightest.

Kat grabs the dog blanket from the seat and wraps Maria in it.

Grandma gets out of the Land Rover, looking like she's been stung in the bits by a bee. 'Keys?'

'They're in the ignition,' I say.

'Sorry, Mrs O,' Bev says. 'It was our fault.'

'I'll need the four of you to push.' Grandma gets into the tractor and slides the gearstick into reverse.

Fizz, Holly and Hazel stare at the four of us as we enter their field and line up against the bonnet, Maria rearranging the blanket every few seconds. When Grandma signals, we push with all our might but can't get the tractor over the lip of the ditch, it's so damned heavy.

Grandma turns off the engine at which point Fizz wanders over, followed by Buttercup. They stare at the tractor a while.

209

Fizz looks at me and moos. It's like she wants to help me.

'Stand back a sec,' I say to the girls. 'Grandma, can you take the handbrake off?'

For a moment, I delude myself into thinking I'm some sort of cow-whisperer and that I can coax Fizz and Buttercup into pushing the tractor out by adopting a husky yet sympathetic tone akin to that of David Attenborough. My on-the-job understanding of bovine psychology can overcome practical obstacles, such as the weight of a nigh-on nine-tonne tractor, and as long as I talk to them softly and mimic their body language, mind will prevail over matter. They'll simply comply, backing their haunches into the bonnet with synchronized precision and lever it out like some sort of *cow*dozer.

Instead, Fizz and Buttercup stand there staring me down as if I'm insane. Neither of them blinks. Neither of them moves a muscle. A Friesian jury silenced by curiosity. It reminds me of the time they first came face to face with a horse when the equestrian centre down the road had problems with their fencing. The whole herd stood statue-still, like cardboard cut-outs, heads angled to get a better view of this braying intruder. They may have a foreboding presence but, being prey animals, cows will retreat if attacked, despite it being their pasture, their home, their territory, and I know Fizz is contemplating bolting right now.

Grandma sticks her head out of the tractor. 'For Pete's sake, what are you faffing about at?'

An hour later, the five of us have filled the ditch with pieces of wood and levered out the tractor. As I'm reversing, I can see that Parsnip is lying next to Hyacinth and Petunia, part of the herd again, and I feel all warm inside.

Grandma retires to bed muttering something about girl power. Determined not to give up on their idea of a Pride float, the girls reattach the inflatable cow to a wheelbarrow, throw me into it and charge around the yard singing the lyrics to 'It's a Sin', as the Pet Shop Boys blare out of Kat's iPhone, including a moo intermission by Buttercup. We don't even get to the end of the song before the three of them are out of puff and I feel like throwing up. Like a child's first home-made birthday card to their parent, it's both shit and awesome. This is our Pride, and I wouldn't change it for the world.

Who needs romance when you've got friends? You can look online for love. You can trawl bars for sex. But friendship is a damned sight harder to recruit. How often in life do you find an enduring, rock-steady, die-on-the-sword faithful friend who makes you laugh your arse off and isn't afraid to call you out for being a dick? I'm so lucky to have three of them. A team of friends. For life.

# CHAPTER THIRTEEN

# THE WOLF

**From: Maria**
Lesbian hen party conundrum #189. You would not
believe the shit that's out there, Bilbo. One girl has
ordered Spot the Pussy, lesbi-hen tiaras and something
that looks like roadkill but may be a prosthetic lady
garden. I can't bring myself to ask what you're supposed
to do with it.

**To: Lorna Parsons**
Parsnip update: she's socializing again. Boom!

**From: Lorna Parsons**
Great! I know she's not due for another few weeks, but
we'll move her into the barn soon so we can keep a
close eye – she's only a heifer.

The girls went back on Sunday night: Bev and Kat for work, and Maria for an Olivia Twist audition in which she's hoping to play Fagana. Despite the eerie silence, a sense of warmth remains the next day. Laughter has permeated the cracked walls. It has seeped into old beams and floorboards, cupboards and furniture, the whole house reinvigorated and topped up with love. Kat's perfume lingers in the bathroom, Bev's chocolate sits in the fridge, Maria's carnations hang out in the hallway like old friends: the world is an infinitely better place.

After morning milking, I catch Grandma squinting at a fragment of coconut shell next to the ditch where the tractor got stuck and I can't stop laughing. Buoyed by the frivolity of the weekend, the four of us trying on jumpsuits in one cubicle in Sheffield's Topshop, Maria reprising her Melania Trump role and teaching us the lyrics to 'Fake Schmooze', Bev and Kat squabbling over the details of their hen parties, I at least feel stronger when Dad's scan results come back.

According to the surgeon's report, they have succeeded in removing 90 per cent of the tumour and now need to blast the remaining 10 per cent using radiotherapy. He starts a six-week course next week as an outpatient and can come home today.

At half past two, we go to pick him up, only for a nurse we've not met before to tell us that his infection is too severe for him to be discharged. I panic until a few minutes later a different nurse confirms that he doesn't have an infection and that his notes got mixed up with the lady in the next bed.

By four o'clock, Dad's back in his armchair staring out at the empty fields. I haven't let any of the cows into the upper field today. I don't want them anywhere near that oak.

'It's good to be back.' He stretches his legs out in front of him, a lopsided grin on his face, which hopefully doesn't hurt, but looks like it might. His head is still bandaged and the area beneath his collarbone is dotted with circular plasters previously responsible for attaching tubes, cannulas and God knows what. He props himself up with a 'Home Sweet Home' pink patchwork cushion that Grandma won at a Farming Association raffle and declared 'nauseatingly twee' but hasn't yet taken to the charity shop.

'Tea?' I say.

'That'd be wonderful.' He tries to get comfortable. 'The tea was like piss in hospital.'

I potter into the kitchen, smiling. It feels so good to make his rancid brew again: 'Strong, builder's, like treacle so you can stand your spoon up in it.' I bury my hand in the Charles and Diana biscuit barrel, which is full again, and drag out four chocolate digestives. Two each. It's good to have him home. I grab a couple of back copies of the *Dairy Farmer* and stick them on the tray next to his tea.

Dad is standing, nose pressed against the window, when I get back.

'How many did we lose?' he says, taking a biscuit and waggling it at the field opposite.

My stomach drops hard and fast. 'How did you know?'

'The cows are all inside despite it being sunny, and the field is like a mud slide where things have been dragged across it.'

'I'm so sorry.' I fling my arms around his neck and dissolve into the little girl who spilt milk all over his antique mahogany desk at the age of seven. 'It was the oak tree and there was an electrical storm and the cows had gone to shelter and the water soaked into the tree roots and I've read that sap coursing through trees makes a good conductor and . . . Three.' My chin wobbles. 'We lost three cows. I'm so sorry, Dad.'

He cuddles me into his armpit and kisses the top of my head. 'I'm sorry you had to go through that.' He stares out of the window for what feels like an age. 'And how did you . . .?' He waves his chocolate digestive in a circle.

'I found a fallen stock collection company in your notes.'

He pulls me to his chest, his wedding band digging into my cheek. 'I'll be back in the driving seat soon, Bilberry. I promise.'

I close my eyes and wish it were true.

Dad and I spend the next hour on the sofa, Speedo lying across our laps like a duvet. On the television, an LGBT literary agent is being interviewed in the Channel 4 studios.

'There's a common misconception that straight people don't want to watch, listen or read about gay or trans characters,' he says. 'It's about time we put that right. Gay heroes are part of everyday life. Surely, they should be celebrated by everyone, and not simply shoehorned into an LGBT category?'

The programme then cuts away to footage of last week's London Pride, thousands marching through the streets of Piccadilly.

I look at Dad, my brain ticking over. 'What if we did a march?'

'A march?' he says.

'Marches make headlines. What's stopping us marching for better milk profit margins?'

Dad blows his nose, the smell of eucalyptus wafting across

the lounge. 'We're not exactly an eye-catching demographic like the LGBT lot, though, are we?' he says.

I look at the television screen, which screams colour, invention and vibrancy. He has a point.

'Unless we took the cows with us?' I say. 'Cows are eye-catching. The government would have to sit up and take notice if a herd of cattle marched on Downing Street.'

Grandma comes in with a washing basket of dried whites. 'Iris Wiggins' granddaughter tried all that and look where it got her: a broken femur and a night in the cells! The moment it's Downing Street, you've got the London Metropolitan Police to deal with on top of all the others.'

'Unless,' I say, looking to Dad. 'Unless we start with Sheffield town hall?'

Dad drums his fingers on the wooden arm of the sofa. 'You'd have to convince Wolfgang Huxley-Lipyeat.'

'Our freeholder?' I say.

'He's not just our freeholder,' Dad says. 'He runs both the local and national Dairy Farming Advisory Committee, which you'd have to go through to get the vote.'

'Two words of advice,' Grandma says, partnering socks and throwing them onto the sofa. 'Good. Luck.'

The Wolf didn't seem too bad at the Country Fair. I resolve to roll up my sleeves and put it to the man himself.

**From: Maria**
Good luck at the committee meeting! Public speaking tips I learned at drama school: Project from your stomach. Use two mirrored hands to show roundness of character. Think less, feel more. You'll kill it, Bilbo!

Wolfgang Huxley-Lipyeat's refusal to reply to either emails or telephone calls means that I'm forced to attend the monthly Dairy Farming Advisory Committee in Bakewell. The venue is a draughty community hall smelling of mildew. A broken piano sits on the stage, the corners of the room are littered with toys from an earlier playgroup session. Eight rows of seats are set up across a badminton court, divided by a narrow aisle, yet there must be only fifteen of us here, including the Wolf.

He is even more gargantuan than I remember and, despite his wealth, a piece of rope is holding up his trousers. He sits at the table of paperwork perched on a stage usually reserved for the Bakewell Players' bi-monthly performances of Jacobean tragedies, and ploughs through a plate of Jammie Dodgers, an overweight Labrador at his heel.

'Two minutes before we make a start.' He touches his mop of snow-white curly hair and consequently decorates the shoulders of his navy blazer with specks of dandruff. 'Agendas are on your seats. Minutes of the previous meeting stapled to the back.'

A purple caterpillar blurts out, 'A is for apple. B is for bee. Let's have fun as we learn our ABC', as I take a seat next to a large man, who sits with his legs set so wide apart, there's a suggestion he needs two hefty lads and a wheelbarrow to transport his testicles. His manspreading forces me to swivel my hips and dangle my legs into the aisle.

'One minute!' the Wolf announces.

I help myself to an agenda.

**Dairy Farming Advisory Committee: Public meeting no. 17**

Agenda

1. Call to order and opening remarks.
2. Farmers in crisis: Market prices and Supply Chain Management.
3. Dairy Product Price Support Programme.
4. Any other business.

I glance around the room and realize I'm the only woman, which doesn't seem representative of farming, given the many women involved these days, and the various Women in Agriculture committees and support groups that I know Grandma is signed up to. I recognize a few faces. Paul Pickering sits on the front row. Today his waistcoat is brown suede. According to the minutes, he's the inventor of the Paddock Poo-Picker, a wheelbarrow attachment revolutionizing the removal of manure using a double-scoop, multi-pronged pitchfork mechanism. The things you learn! I spot Graham 'what a waste' Pearce's shiny head next to Tommy Marshall, a dairy farmer Dad went to school with.

I nod hello to Graham and wonder whether he remembers that I used to sit in the boot of his Ford Cortina estate and play 'truth or dare' with his kids. It goes through my head that I should introduce myself to my well-endowed neighbour, but he's immersed in conversation with a clean-cut chap who sits the other side, so I idly flick through the minutes from the previous meetings.

Two things strike me. Firstly, there's not a single reference to a woman in the pages and pages of minutes. Aside from the minutes-taker, it's all *mister this* and *master that*. Secondly, every suggestion put forward by the committee has rejected written next to it.

'Gentlemen,' the Wolf addresses the room, removing his wristwatch and positioning it alongside the plate of biscuit crumbs. He rolls up his sleeves and peers over half-moon glasses at his papers. 'Thank you all for coming here today. I'll cut to the chase with an opening remark about solidarity. You'll have seen the articles in the press this week around Farmers in Crisis and I'm sure you'll agree that a crisis is indeed upon us. Since we launched the #SaveOurDairy campaign, we've had a number of minor successes but nothing getting us over the hurdles we need to jump. I'd like to hear your thoughts on how we pull together as a community to protect our revenue stream and our lifeblood: milk. Let me open up the floor to suggestions.'

Paul stands up, tugging his waistcoat down. 'Global exports. Asia are importing more and more milk, year on year. We should be looking at foreign trade as well as domestic deals, so not just beyond Britain's borders but beyond Europe's.'

'Very good,' the Wolf says. 'Can we get somebody to minute that?' He turns to the room, eyes skimming the front row over his half-moon glasses, and stopping when they reach me. 'Great. I see we've got a new secretary?'

'Hi,' I say. A radiator on the far wall starts to glug and for a moment I think it's my stomach. 'We met at the Country Show. I'm Billie. John Oliver's daughter from Fernbrook Farm over in Baslow.'

'Any good at shorthand, Billie?' the Wolf says, clearly having no memory whatsoever of our encounter.

'Pretty rubbish,' I say.

His eyes shift across his paperwork. 'You're not here to take minutes then? Bob's wife normally comes but—'

'No. I'm here as Dad. Well, as me but as Dad too. I'm running the farm for him.'

'She's the one that got me fired from the agency,' a latecomer booms from the back of the hall.

The room stills. Dust dances around the air vents and the evening sun shines through a stained-glass window, leaving a distorted kaleidoscope pattern in the tramlines of the badminton court. Nathan Fletcher, all motorbike leathers and padded trousers, sits himself down on a chair at the back of the hall and stretches his legs out over a shiny, grey helmet covered in Hell's Angels stickers. My cheeks burn, the hairs on the back of my neck stand up and all I want to do is leave.

'Any ideas from anyone else?' the Wolf says, as the room fidgets and coughs with unease.

I can feel Nathan's eyes boring into the back of me. *I am a strong lesbian woman, who refuses to feel devalued by the ignorance of others.* I wish Dad was here. He'd know what to do. I try to focus on the meeting, a man smelling of Lynx deodorant now holding court. He has bleached-blonde hair, a skinny tie, and wouldn't look out of place presenting a celebrity quiz show.

'Hamish Eccles from Ladybower,' he says to me before addressing the room. 'How about corporate sponsorship?'

The Wolf frowns. 'From who?'

Hamish Eccles from Ladybower holds his ground. 'Some of the big banks might be interested in sponsoring British Milk. It'd be good for their brand. Good for their reputation. You know, having their name associated with a worthy cause and a familiar product.'

'We don't want to come across as a charity, though, do we?' the Wolf says. 'Back in the glory days, we were the sponsor. Remember the Milk Cup? The Milk Marketing Board sponsored the football league for four years, for Pete's sake. Let's not forget we're a business. Let's not forget our consumers. Let's not put ourselves down.' He slams his fist on the table. 'Unless you have a contact at one of the big banks?'

'No, but—'

'Fat lot of good that is then!' the Wolf says. 'Case closed. Can somebody minute that?' He glances around the room. 'Come on, help me out here. We have a Farmers for Milk brand that is priced fairly; it would enable farmers to make a modest profit, but supermarkets aren't stocking it and so consumers aren't buying it. How do we get the message out there?'

My arms hang limply at my sides. I want to stick my hand up, but I can't. Not with Nathan here. He'll only shoot me down in flames and make me look ridiculous. I cross and uncross my legs. *From now on in, you will not be shamed. You will not be sullied. You will not be silenced.* I clear my throat and straighten my back. *Think less, feel more.* My eye is drawn to the doodle of a pig with an oversized snout, which has taken up residence in the left-hand margin of Buster Gonad's agenda and I can't think straight.

'Nobody? Anybody?' the Wolf looks around the room. 'On to the next agenda item then.'

My hand finds its way up into the air. Fuck it, and fuck Nathan.

Wolfgang Huxley-Lipyeat removes his glasses and points them at me. 'The farmer's daughter.' The gold nib of his fountain pen glints with each rotation between his chubby fingers.

'Maybe we could hold a dairy farmers' march?' I say, trying to take Maria's public speaking tips on board and project from the stomach.

Nathan's laugh rumbles from the back of the room, aided by acoustics.

'To gain publicity and spread awareness.' I try using two mirrored hands but become aware it just looks like I'm massaging various sized breasts. *Think less, feel more.* 'You know, get in the papers, get on the news and reach out to the public. Tell them that we can't allow Premier Milk to drop the price of milk any further. And ask them to buy our Milk for Farmers brand.'

The Wolf's chair scrapes across the stage as he pushes it backwards to give himself legroom to turn and face me. 'Do you really think anyone would be interested in a ragtag bunch of farmers in wellies and waxed jackets marching for justice?'

The arches of my foot start to itch. 'No.' I clear my throat. 'But they might if we unleash a hundred cows through the city centre.'

A murmur spreads across the hall and the energy changes, repressed silence evolving into animated whispers.

'It'd certainly bring traffic to a standstill,' Tommy Marshall says.

'It'd get people talking,' the guy next to him agrees.

'With *your* cows?' Graham shouts over to me, the suggestion being that *my* cows are in some way inferior to everyone else's.

'Ours and others,' I clarify.

'Do you have any idea how much planning goes into these

things?' Huxley-Lipyeat clicks his neck from side to side, crunching cartilage. 'Where did you say you've relocated from?'

'London.'

'And were you a dairy farmer in London?' He fingers his executive fountain pen.

'A biochemist.' My mouth goes dry.

'Which qualifies you in what way exactly?'

'No way whatsoever!' Nathan heckles.

Ignoring Nathan, I address Huxley-Lipyeat. 'Look, I may be new to all this, but I figure with a bit of common sense and a lot of hard work, we could pull this off. If it's any consolation, Margaret Thatcher started off as a research chemist and she ended up running the country!'

'Into the ground!' Buster Gonad shouts over a din of anti-Thatcher sentiment, the room coming to life in ardent disgruntlement. 'Maggie Thatcher, school milk snatcher.'

I loosen my collar. 'OK, OK, I appreciate she wasn't popular.'

'Bit of a sore point around here, lassie,' Huxley-Lipyeat snorts.

'Careful if you sign up,' Nathan hollers from the back. 'She'll probably sack you!'

The room falls silent.

I try to remain calm. 'For the record, I think you're a brilliant herdsman, Nathan, I just can't tolerate your hatred of homosexuals. At the end of the day, I am a person, too.'

The room fidgets uncomfortably. Throats are cleared. Chairs groan. Nathan picks up his helmet and stomps off, the door swinging behind him.

The Wolf looks at me. 'Tell you what, Bobby—'

'Billie.'

'Billie. You plan it, square it off with the police, agree it with the mayor, sort out warrants, insurance, transportation, marketing, social media, networking, press releases and whatnot and report back to this committee once you've got a date.'

'OK,' I say, glancing around the room. 'Can somebody minute that?'

# CHAPTER FOURTEEN

## GOING AGILE

**From: Maria**
Lesbian hen party conundrum #213. Bev's mothers have contacted me saying they want to come on the hen party, but to keep it a surprise. Bev will lynch me! She's still not forgiven them for flashing their tits in a Wolverhampton Burger King.

**From: Dave (work)**
They've recruited this Russian dude to cover your research. Billie Oliver he ain't. Miss you x

**@SCIENCEMATTERS**
Youngest ever Pfizer Award winner – Bradford's Meredith Little scoops gold, aged 25.

Oh, piss off, Meredith Little. I bet you're not running a 500-acre dairy farm.

I vow to get back on the science wagon and at least read up on stuff, but every time I open my laptop, I find myself trawling the internet for Joely. I can't help myself. It's the same when I'm planning the farmers' march. It's like sitting next to freshly baked cake – the temptation is too great. It starts off with me looking at her Twitter profile. @MlleChevalier. Her profile picture has a dramatic warm filter, showing her wearing a feathered mask and studying herself in an antique hallway mirror. The contours of her shoulders catch the light. She appears to be attaching a pearl droplet earring. I've been following her on Twitter ever since we met, but she has never followed me back.

'The fact that she has over a thousand followers but only follows ten people says it all!' Kat rages over the phone.

The concept of phoning Kat every time I'm tempted to phone Joely almost works. On the one hand, she's so vehemently anti-Joely, it soon quashes any amorous feelings I have towards her. On the flip side, she's that brutal, it almost makes me rush to Joely's defence.

'What do you mean?' I say, scrolling through Joely's Instagram page and obsessing over each photo.

'Having people follow you without following them back is like saying "you can be friends with me, but I won't be friends with you." It's a control thing, Bill.'

'Is it?'

'Of course it is.'

'What about Maroon McGinnis?' I ask.

'The weather girl?'

'She's got forty thousand followers and only follows ninety-nine.'

'She's famous. Celebrities don't count.' Her voice is loaded with annoyance. Kat and patience are not natural bedfellows. 'Failed relationships are a sunken emotional cost, Bill. You're tempted to throw more time and energy at it because "better the devil you know", and all that bullshit. Plus, you want a return from your investment, but it will never pay the dividends. Quit while you're ahead.'

'I'm not sure I am ahead,' I say on the exhale.

'What are you doing online anyway? I thought you'd be up to your eyeballs scooping up manure or whatever it is you do up there?'

'I'm planning a farmers' march. You should see me, Kat. I'm drowning in spreadsheets.'

'Spreadsheets?' she says, her voice brightening.

'One for transportation. One for managing the Press. One for marketing. One for—'

'Send them over. You know I love a spreadsheet.'

Within an hour, Kat has whipped my plans into one master spreadsheet with pivot table summaries on the front sheet and is calling me back.

'When did you say the march is taking place?' she says.

'Thirtieth of October,' I say.

'This year or next? Only I've forecasted a timeline for you and, given the various milestones on the critical path, the lead time needed to get people involved, and the hours available to you with a farm to run, your "go live" date is August next year.'

'That's not an option.'

'I thought you might say that,' she says. 'In which case, we have to implement Plan B.'

'Which is?'

'We go Agile,' she says decisively. 'Small manageable chunks. Lots of parallel working. Forget the traditional waterfall methodology and just farm it out to small teams.'

'Oh yes, because I've got hundreds of small teams available to me,' I harrumph.

'You may not have hundreds, but you've got one, which just so happens to be a dream team.'

'I have?'

'OK, so you make Bev the lead on anything to do with the animals. Insurance, transportation. She's got contacts through ZSL who'll probably do you a discount. If she can transport Mongolian camels down the motorway, what's a few cows across town?'

'Good point,' I say, wishing I'd thought of this earlier.

'I'll take over planning,' she says. 'No offence, Bill, but your spreadsheets suck. I'll project manage the lot for you. I'll be the task-master and make sure everything runs to plan, which leaves Maria, arguably the most prolific person on social media in the world, doing your PR. You know what she's like for all that shit. We may be a bunch of "gossip girls", Bill, but between us, we might just have the magic ingredients.'

We end the conversation, agreeing to have a daily conference call on Kat's bridge. It's my job to carry on running the farm, attend committee meetings and get the farming community signed up. I allow myself a cheese toastie, a cuddle with Parsnip and a sob of happiness. Thank God I called Kat and not Joely.

**From: Lorna Parsons**
Paul (Pickering, not the lad from the chippy) said you're
organizing a Save Our Dairy march. Guy and I would
love to help x

I don't know whether I'm more blown away by the offer of
help, the kiss at the end of the text or the suggestion that
there's a local chippy. I figure I should strike while the iron's
hot.

**From: Lorna Parsons**
☺ Also, let me know if you want me to hook you up
with Guy's lovely friend, who has his own textiles
company.

I should have known there'd be some sort of agenda.

**To: Lorna Parsons**
Urm. Sorry but I'm not that Into guys or textIles!

**From: Lorna Parsons**
I don't mean like that! I mean for printing banners. He'd
do them for free. His dad was a lamb farmer, so he
understands how difficult things are.

**To: Lorna Parsons**
Ah. Sorry. Yes, please ☺

Je suis une veritable knobhead.

*

Our conference calls become the highlight of my day. Just hearing the girls chattering away makes me feel closer to them. The idea was to run the meetings in the evening, but this only resulted in a virtual drinking session, talking shit and gossiping about the hen party. There's talk of Neve coming on the hen-do and would I mind? And I say, 'Of course not', even though it's a bit like swallowing a knife. Ex-girlfriends don't mix with the present tense as far as I'm concerned, and I'm not the type who can do the whole dinner-party thing with the ex. Not that I'm a dinner-party type anyway. Neve's not in my life any more, and although I never thought I'd say this when she ran off with Nic a couple of years ago, I'd prefer to keep it that way. The whole thing's cringe. It wouldn't be so bad if I hadn't spent a year in denial, phoning her, texting her, throwing a *pain au chocolat* at her head in a Starbucks on the Holloway Road.

'Does that mean Nic's coming too?' I say, plucking at my eyebrow with my thumb and forefinger. I can handle my friends still being friends with Neve – that in itself is OK – but I can't bear the thought of having to hang out with her and Nic as a couple, everyone observing me observing them. It'll overshadow the whole event.

'You don't mind, do you, Bill?' Kat says.

'No.'

God knows why I care this much. I haven't even thought about Neve in months.

In the end, we reschedule our daily 'scrums' for 7.30 a.m. This suits Bev and Kat as we're done in time for them to get to work and suits me as I've finished early milking by then. It does not, however, suit Maria, who is a nocturnal animal at the best of times but is finding it almost impossible to get out of bed before 10 a.m. since her swimwear model boyfriend has moved in and works only one day in twenty.

'It's approved!' Kat yells out of a window on my laptop screen.

'Can you not shout?' Maria pulls out her hearing aid in another window.

'Sheffield City council have signed the paperwork.' She holds up an envelope. 'Can you believe they're still paper-based?'

'The T-shirts have arrived!' Maria stands up, #SaveOurDairy emblazoned across her chest. 'They're not too bad. Bit too polyester, but with a bit of customization, they'll be fine.'

Another window pops up and Guy Bonneville's sweaty face comes into view. He wipes it with a flannel, which somehow makes it look even sweatier.

Kat cocks her head like a disgruntled peahen. 'Whoever's just joined the call, I'm afraid this is a private conference.'

'Hi!' Lorna's head appears next to Guy's. 'Sorry we're a couple of minutes late. Guy's just delivered a foal!'

'Bill?' Kat frowns.

'You remember Lorna and Guy? They're heading up operations,' I say.

'What does that mean exactly?' Kat squints.

'Deploying the troops on the day and mobilizing people, cows and kit,' Guy says with confidence. 'Though I'm not sure how much good the march will actually do.'

Lorna looks at him. 'Why do you say that?'

'It's the bureaucrats and politicians you've got to convince. Not the general public of Sheffield,' he says.

'Hi, I'm Bev.' Bev waves. 'Isn't it about educating the general public and persuading them to pay an extra ten pence for the Milk for Farmers brand?'

'Educating them, Ben?'

'It's *Bev*,' Lorna says firmly.

'You can take a horse to the water, Ben. You can take a horse to the water,' Guy continues, oblivious. 'You know the average IQ of a Sheffield dweller is lower than the average IQ of a horse?'

'Just ignore him,' Lorna says.

'Never underestimate the brain under the mane,' he goes on. 'It's all there on my equine intelligence blog, Lorn.' He nudges her with his elbow. 'The one you've still not got around to reading!'

'Surely IQ is irrelevant?' Kat says. 'Everyone drinks milk whether they're thick as a brick or not.'

'*Thuck* as a *bruck!* Isn't that wonderful?' Guy says. 'God love the Aussies!'

'She's a Kiwi,' Lorna snaps.

'Moving swiftly on.' Kat raises an eyebrow.

'*Swuftly!*' Guy mimics. 'Wonderful!'

Lorna swivels her back towards him. 'I do apologize.'

The Romeo and Juliet of farming sit in silence while the four of us brainstorm slogans. 'Moo-ve over for dairy'; 'They're Friesian our salaries'; 'We are not a-moo-sed!'; 'Seen but not herd!'; 'Udderly ridiculous!'; 'Milked dry!'; 'Déjà Moo'? We go full circle and back to the existing slogan, #SaveOurDairy.

'What the fuck?' Maria shrieks as soon as Lorna and Guy drop off the call. 'I thought you hated them, Bilbo?'

'Beggars can't be choosers,' I say, hearing the rumble and beep of the Wincanton milk tanker backing into the yard.

Kat looks at her watch. 'OK. South Yorkshire Police notice forms are done. Cattle transportation and animal insurance policies are done. The Press release, I'm working on. You'll have that close of play today.'

'Close of play, Kathryn Mellor?' Bev teases her.

Just as I'm scribbling down my 'follow-on action items', Charlie sticks his head through the kitchen window.

'You look like you're in the middle of something important,' he says.

'Planning meeting for the farmers' march,' I say. 'Ladies, this is Charlie from the co-operative.' I turn my laptop round until his face looms into view.

'Hi, Charlie from the co-operative,' Kat says. 'Do you drive?'

'I most certainly do.' He grins. 'If Billie here turns her screen around, you should be able to see my tanker in the yard.'

'Excellent,' Kat says. 'How do you fancy transporting twelve cattle in a . . . what's it called again, Bev?'

'Cattle Cruiser,' Bev says, running the palms of her hand over the bristles of her Mohican. 'It's coming to you for eight a.m. the day of the march so you've got plenty of time to load it with straw, get some hay nets up and make it comfy.'

'Happy to help,' Charlie says, leaning on the windowsill.

A Mediterranean-looking man walks behind Maria in nothing but a towel. He opens the kitchen cupboard and helps himself to my Shreddies and I feel nostalgic for London. I want my bedroom back; I want Maria's singing, Dolly Parton on the record player and dreams of a PhD.

Kat glances at the agenda. 'Great. I've got to shoot to work now. Same again tomorrow, ladies. Nice to meet you, Charlie.'

'You too.' Charlie waves from the window.

Bev and Kat's windows disappear, and I'm left staring at my flat as Maria has tottered into the kitchen. *Where'd You Go, Bernadette*, a paperback I bought myself last Christmas, lies open on the coffee table next to a plate of toast, half-read by somebody else. Steam rises from my KSG 'Healthier, Happier' campaign mug. The fairy lights that Maria and I bought from the Khao San road on our backpacking trip around Thailand surround the window. The rectangular bottle of Disaronno sits on the shelf behind the sofa, a lot emptier than it was when I last held it. A window to my former life. I leave the chat.

'Seem like a very nice group of young ladies.' Charlie appears beside me in the kitchen.

'They're the best,' I say.

'I was wondering . . .' He strokes the soft fluff on his chin. 'If you fancied going out for some breakfast?'

I'm desperate for breakfast but I want to be able to wear my fleece-lined jogging bottoms and watch shit TV in the lounge with a plate of scrambled egg on toast, Speedo at my side. I don't want company, but I owe him the courtesy. 'I've got plenty in if you fancy staying for something?'

Ten minutes later and the whole house smells of burned pork and sage. The smoke alarm wails as I pluck charred sausages from under the grill, Charlie heroically stretching up to press the 'stop' button to quiet the siren.

A dopey smile spreads across his face. 'Not much of a domestic goddess, are we?'

'Nope,' I concur. 'Though in fairness, it's never been an ambition of mine.'

He raises an eyebrow. 'How's about I give you a hand while you go and freshen up?'

Cheeky fucker – I've already 'freshened up' and, if I hadn't, I wouldn't be 'freshening up' for him. And what exactly does he expect? Am I to reappear all fluffed and buffed, waxed and exfoliated in some sort of pristine white doily?

'I'm fresh enough, thank you,' I say, grabbing a bowl and cracking eggs into it with aggression.

'Right you are,' he says.

We sit side by side at the kitchen table and make our way through scrambled eggs, neither of us speaking for a while.

'Makes a change to be having breakfast with an attractive young lady,' he eventually says.

I grab the peppermill and grind cracked peppercorns over the remainder of my egg with more force than is necessary. 'Charlie, I don't want you to get the wrong impression about me,' I say, running amok with ketchup.

'In what way?'

'No offence, but I'm probably not your type.'

'You most definitely are!' He puts a hand on my thigh.

'Let me rephrase that.' I remove his hand and place it back on his own leg. 'No offence, but you're not my type.'

'You haven't given me a chance yet,' he says, picking eggshell out of his teeth. 'I'm a decent guy. I know how to cook. I know how to—'

'I'm attracted to women rather than men.'

He holds a forkful of breakfast mid-air and looks at me. 'Are you sure?'

'Quite sure, thanks.'

He straightens himself out and looks at me as though I've just transformed into a chicken.

'So, if you're going to help out, it needs to be for the right reasons,' I say.

'I should probably make a move.' He pushes his plate away, gets up and heads for the door. 'Thanks for breakfast.'

The porch door clunks behind him and I'm left feeling amused, annoyed, but most of all relieved that I can slip into my fleece-lined jogging bottoms and grab the remote control. Fuck him. Speedo jumps onto the sofa beside me and, for the first time since I've been up here, I actually feel content. Surely, this is the start of a slippery slope to spinsterhood and can only result in me living here solo, hair unbrushed, surrounded by animals.

Onboarding cows is not easy. It's not like you can just pop them in the back of your car at the last minute; it requires a shedload of planning and isn't cheap. Don't get me wrong, Bev has sorted out a brilliant deal with a Cattle Cruiser company who'll go out to any farm across England, Scotland or Wales, but farmers are understandably reluctant.

I've got two hundred cows committed so far and, although this was my target, Kat is insistent that I hit a 'stretch target' of two hundred and fifty. This has pretty much involved a road-trip between milking each day, to visit dairy farms and recruit support. According to the Royal Association of British Dairy Farmers, the final dairy farm on my list, Birchover Hall Farm, is owned by a Mr Craggs. It takes me a good while to find the farm as the entrance is hidden behind a pub. When I do eventually spot it, a rodent-like man totters out, looking as though he's spent the last decade living in a field, the outdoor elements whipping and pinching at his skin.

'Hi,' I say. 'I'm after Mr Craggs.'

He holds a bony finger up to me. 'I've got it ready some-where. One tick.'

Legs bowed, he hobbles slowly across the yard to an outhouse and backs out, pulling something heavy.

'Here you go!' he says.

A dead sheep lies in his wheelbarrow, flies invading its eyes, its woollen coat matted and soiled.

'I think you might have mixed me up with someone,' I say, trying not to vomit. 'I'm here about the dairy farmers' march.'

He scrunches up his face. 'I were expecting a lad. Billy, they called him.'

'I'm Billie,' I say. 'A female Billie.'

He looks at me like I'm an undiscovered species. A spirited Border collie comes flying round the corner, growling at me, teeth bared. I'm willing to compromise a lot of things for this campaign, but losing a leg is not one of them.

'Sorry,' Mr Craggs says. 'He's doesn't see many women. He's a man's man, aren't you, Jack?'

Jack's bark becomes a whine. He pants excitedly then clam-bers up my leg, his red-raw lipstick popping out like a finger puppet. I try to shake him off, but his front paws are now welded around my kneecap as he vigorously humps me.

The farmer chuckles. 'Told you he were a man's man!'

'I should probably get going.' I try to peel myself away.

Mr Craggs clears his throat. 'I can bring fifty if that helps.'

'Fifty cows?'

'I'll not have the manpower to handle more than fifty.'

'Fifty's great.'

I may have effectively prostituted my leg, but I have hit my stretch target.

**From: Kat**
Hey Bill, we've cancelled the hen party as Bev was getting totally unreasonable about everything and the whole thing became one big ball of stress x

**From: Bev**
Kat's cancelled the hen party. Quite relieved TBH. She was getting way too Bridezilla about it x

**From: Maria**
Lesbian hen party conundrum #999 HALLELUJAH! THE HEN PARTY IS CANCELLED. What am I going to do with my life now?

**@SCIENCEMATTERS**
Biochemist, Brian Dywer, wins The Edinburgh Excellence in Science Award for his contribution towards eclampsia research in spite of losing both arms earlier this year.

Enough. I delete the Twitter app.

Although I've written to the Wolf to confirm that we're all set for the #SaveOurDairy march, he doesn't reply, so I have no choice but to track him down at the next committee meeting. The prospect is about as appealing as injecting heroin into my eyeballs but, as my namesake, Billie Jean King, once said, 'Pressure is a privilege.'

I pull on the cheap polyester #SaveOurDairy T-shirt that's arrived in the post and drive over to the Bakewell Community

Centre, expecting the committee meeting to be a similar affair to the previous one. When I get there, the car park is full, and every side road is lined with cars parked bumper to bumper. By the time I've found a space half a mile away, I'm five minutes late and caught up in a mass of bodies trying to get in at the main door. I check that I've got the right date and haven't inadvertently turned up to a popular Zumba class, but am reassured when an agenda gets thrust into my hand.

**Dairy Farming Advisory Committee: Public meeting no. 18**

Agenda

1. Call to order and opening remarks.
2. #SaveOurDairy march.
3. Baslow to Curbar thoroughfare proposal.
4. Any other business.

Inside, every chair is occupied. There must be another fifty or so people standing around the sides and up the back, plus the backlog in the foyer. I can't see Nathan, but I'm sure he's here somewhere.

'Quiet, please!' the Wolf orders. 'We'll make a start once everybody's in. We're out of printed agendas, so latecomers will have to share.' He's flanked by a grubby-looking man and a small woman, who I recognize as the lady in bottle-green tights from the Ridgecroft Country Fair. Tonight, she favours burgundy.

'I hereby declare the meeting open,' the Wolf says. 'With me I have our secretary, my wife, Mrs Penelope Huxley-Lipyeat and our treasurer, Mr Andrew Lane. Tonight, you'll notice that we have an increased attendance, which I can only assume is on account of the interest in our proposed thoroughfare, facilitating transportation of livestock and agricultural equipment from Baslow to Curbar and vice versa.'

He runs through a list of action items. Square footage of a proposed disabled loo for the Agricultural Society hall. A donated second-hand carpet that might fit the play barn. Do we have any volunteers for selling tickets to the Agricultural Society Campfire Christmas Carol Concert? A footpath closure on Manor Farm's Ringinglow estate. 'Which brings me on to our next follow-on action item: the somewhat naive notion of a #SaveOurDairy march, campaigning for a fair price for milk. Is John Oliver's daughter here with an update?'

'Yes,' I say, stepping forward.

His eyes dart around the room.

'Over here!' I wave.

'No,' he concludes. 'In which case we'll move on to—' His wife nudges him and points me out with her tortoiseshell glasses.

'I've got a date!' I shout.

His piggy eyes single me out. 'What's he like? Tall, dark, handsome?'

A ripple of laughter.

'Saturday the thirtieth of October. #SaveOurDairy farmers march through Sheffield,' I say, thinking less and feeling more until I become conscious that I'm thinking less, which only makes me think more. 'It's been approved by Sheffield City Council, South Yorkshire Police, the mayor of Sheffield, the syndicate of agricul—'

'The farmer's daughter's been busy,' the Wolf remarks, folding his arms over his chest and tucking his sausage fingers under his armpits. 'But without the support . . . Wasn't the plan to have a hundred dairy cows on parade?'

'That was the plan, but—'

'Let me guess, too difficult?' he says.

'I—'

'The cows were the selling point in all of this. You needed to make an impact. You needed to turn heads.'

'There'll be cows,' I say. 'Only it won't be a hundred. It'll be more like three hundred.'

The room murmurs.

A lady in a linen jacket and long skirt raises her hand. 'We'd like to join.'

A twenty-something lad in a T-shirt declaring 'Jesus is coming, look busy!' stands up. 'We would too.' He gestures to the band of brothers he has brought along.

'Where do we sign up?' an elderly man with a Yorkshire terrier trapped under his arm bellows from the back.

Within five minutes, fifty or so people have registered their interest, sending Wolfgang Huxley-Lipyeat into a flap as they migrate across the room towards me, pushing past chairs and tripping over bags. 'Order!' he shouts. 'May I suggest those wanting to sign up for the march make their way to the foyer so that we keep disruption to a minimum.'

I fight my way through the crowd to the back of the room, but there are too many of us to fit in the foyer. Glancing back into the hall, there look to be only a dozen or so people left, including the Wolf and his wife, who are both slowly turning a shade of purple. Even 'what a waste' Graham is folding up his camping chair and heading for the door. I stumble out into the car park, soothed by fresh air.

'Hi,' I say, my voice lost in the hubbub. 'Hello, everyone!'

'Why did you let Nathan go?' a lady in a denim skirt and silver eyeliner shouts. His wife? His sister? 'You know he lost his job at the agency because of you!'

'He was aggressively homophobic,' I mutter under my breath as I clamber up onto the gatepost. *Project from the stomach. Two mirrored hands. Think less, feel more.* 'Hi, everyone. The #SaveOurDairy march will be on Saturday the thirtieth of October!' I shout but my voice goes high and raspy.

'Nobody can hear you,' the same lady heckles. 'Let one of the men do it!'

'No.' A tall man in black lends me his support. 'It needs to come from Billie.' It takes me a few seconds to realize it's Charlie from the co-operative. He looks totally different without his boiler suit on. 'I'm sorry I was a dick. I don't take rejection well.'

'It's OK.' I pull myself up straight.

'Now, go for gold!' he says.

I fill my lungs with cold, Derbyshire air, stick my fingers in my mouth and wolf-whistle with all my might. 'Saturday the thirtieth of October!' I project from the pit of my stomach, gesturing with mirrored hands. 'Dairy farmers' march in Sheffield. We'll be meeting at the bottom of The Moor at ten thirty a.m. Bring your friends, bring your family, bring anyone and everyone you can think of.' The hand thing is somehow working. 'And if you really want to make a difference, bring your cows!'

'Is there a petition that we're supposed to sign?' somebody yells.

'Yes!' I shout. 'Save our dairy dot com.'

'What are we actually asking for?' someone else shouts.

'We're asking Premier Milk to stop dropping "A" milk prices. We're asking supermarkets to sell our Milk for Farmers brand, and we're asking consumers to buy it.'

'What about the press?' someone shouts.

'The local and national press have been contacted and there will be a Sheffield town hall press photoshoot at noon.' I can't get the words out fast enough. People are actually listening to *me*. My voice is getting heard. I feel high on adrenaline. 'More details at Save our dairy dot com.'

Phones come out of pockets.

'How do we get one of those?' A teenager in motorbike leathers points at my T-shirt.

'Save our dairy dot com!'

The car park spins. Bodies swirl beneath me. My hearing goes all funny and everyone sounds distant. I'm no natural public speaker and now a sea of people are listening to my every word and the moment starts to feel too big for me. The gatepost starts to feel quite high and the jump down to the ground a considerable drop. I can see Charlie mouthing something at me and reaching for me with his hand.

'You OK?' He helps me down.

'Yes.' I take a sip from my water bottle, my senses returning.

I hand out the leaflets we've had made up and spend the next hour fielding questions.

Charlie hovers as I pick up my belongings. 'Look, I know I was a complete tool the other day, but I'd love to help.'

'Thanks,' I say.

'Seriously, I'll bring a shovel and a wheelbarrow.' He practically walks on top of me.

'Great.'

He grins. 'Like I say, I'll be there with cowbells and thistles.'

I do worry for Charlie, though I guess there's someone for everyone.

As soon as I've driven out of view, I pull the car into a layby, open the driver's door and throw up onto the tarmac. I don't think I've ever been under this amount of pressure. Not where hundreds of people are relying on me. I guess there was the time I got cast as Mary in my Year Three Nativity, but that was over within an hour and didn't require having to manage anyone other than a Tiny Tears doll. It's pretty overwhelming, but I've started something now and it's time to put my money where my mouth is.

# CHAPTER FIFTEEN

# THE CALF

**From: Lorna Parsons**
Might be an idea to move Parsnip into the barn for her to calf this week. She was carrying breach last time I checked.

Dad's radiotherapy appointments are at Weston Park Hospital in Sheffield. Three hospitals in ten weeks; a hat-trick none of us was prepared for. Weston Park itself is well kept and grassy, alive with chrysanthemums, herbaceous borders and university students playing tennis. The hospital, however, is a decaying seven-storey concrete block on the A57 with a nicotine-infused ambulance bay taking delivery of people who have seen better days.

The waiting room hums with grunts, groans and the ticking brains of the stoically silent. Dad and I make our way into the radiology waiting area – a windowless corridor stinking of industrial-strength detergent, where eight plastic chairs sit against a wall. As we take a seat, it feels a little like joining Death Row. The 'Radiation On' sign light ups and everything goes quiet.

'Bilberry?' Dad says softly. 'If anything goes wrong, promise you'll do the march without me.'

My heart gallops. 'Dad, there isn't a *without you*. Even if you have to sit it out at home, you'll be there in spirit.' I stare at the hospital notice board, holding back tears. I know he doesn't mean 'without him' in terms of sitting it out at home, but I can't face the alternative. I stare at an advert for kitchen porters. A polite notice requesting that wheelchairs are not to be removed from the hospital site. A 'Learn languages while you recover' flyer.

He turns to look at me. 'You look bloody knackered!'

I grin. 'You may be ill, but that doesn't mean I can't punch you.'

The 'Radiation On' sign extinguishes and a small lady in a large wheelchair comes out, everyone in the waiting area silently grading their health against hers.

'John Oliver?' the nurse calls.

The radiation room is about the same size as our bathroom and is shrouded in darkness. Illuminated red and green buttons light up a dashboard of dials, levers and switches, like something from a spaceship. A cockpit of doom. I don't want to let him go.

He's in there for fifteen minutes. It should be two. I pace up and down the corridor, the 'Radiation On' light eventually extinguishing and Dad reappearing on the arm of a nurse.

'How was it?' I say.

His face looks ashen. 'Could you get a wheelchair?'

Everything inside me sinks. He thinks he's going to be marching through Sheffield in six weeks, yet he can't make it a few metres to the car. His fragility rattles my foundations. He's been unshakeable all his life – getting up at 5 a.m. every day for the last forty years. Lifting, shifting, moving machinery, cropping, milking, digging himself out of snowdrifts, herding hundreds of cattle, working the land. And now here he is, reduced to a wheelchair, asleep within seconds of getting in the car.

The drive back from hospital always stimulates thought. Today is no exception. I daydream about what I'd be working on now, were I in the laboratory kicking PhD-ass. I miss the lab. I miss the smell of latex gloves when you pull them out of the box. I miss the clink of metal instruments on glass beakers. I miss that feeling when you press a coverslip onto a cell sample and it magically glides across the glass slide if it's too fluid. I miss the inky smudge of iodine. Hell, I even miss gagging on beta-mercaptoethanol. But it's not so much the 'missing the lab' thing, it's missing the thrill of decoding the mysteries of Mother Nature. The satisfaction of feeling like you've cracked something, the exhilaration of sitting in the driving seat on a journey to find a cure; a journey that scientists around the world are on right now to help out people like Dad.

I glance at his moonlit face and wonder if he'll ever be strong enough to run the farm again.

A week later, Dad's physiotherapist, Derek Taylor, a small man with a shaven head, arrives on his moped. He takes off his helmet and balances it on the wall. His tracksuit has a cheap feel about it and looks as if it might go up in flames on a sunny day. He follows me in, recoiling at the stuffed partridge in the hallway. As we make our way upstairs, he complains of a bad back and tight hamstrings. The irony is not lost on Grandma, who takes me to one side while his lavender-infused beanbags heat in the microwave and loudly compares it to a barber with a bad mullet.

Before he goes into Dad's room, I corner him on the landing. 'Once you've done your stuff, will you let me know if you think Dad will be strong enough to attend a march in five weeks' time?'

'What sort of a march?'

'A dairy farming protest.' I hand him a leaflet.

Dad lies in bed like an injured wildebeest picked off from the herd, the three of us flapping around him like mother hens, propping his neck up with cushions and muttering clichéd phrases of encouragement. 'Onwards and upwards.' 'Patience is a virtue.' 'One step at a time.' Derek sits on the edge of the bed and rolls the left leg of Dad's pyjamas up to his knee. Dad's calves look shrivelled and pathetic; his previously strong, muscular legs replaced by dry, emaciated ones, after two months in nightwear.

Dad looks at Derek. 'Could you give us a second?'

Derek glances at Grandma and then at me before absenting himself.

Dad waits until the bedroom door has clicked shut. His eyes flicker from me to Grandma. 'I will be doing the march come what may. Whether I'm up to it or not has nothing to do with it. I *will* be doing the march.'

'Not if it kills you, you won't,' Grandma says.

'I damned well will,' Dad says, his hands balling into fists.

Grandma pulls hair out of the dog brush. 'I'd rather have your ego wounded than you drop dead from overdoing it.'

'*And*,' Dad continues, 'there's nothing wrong with my hearing, so there's no point whispering behind my back about whether I'm up to it or not!'

'OK,' I say slowly.

'I know it's your march, Billie, and I can't thank you enough for getting it off the ground, but it's my march too and it's important to me that I play a role in it. I want to put my voice to it, see my cows at it and contribute towards getting heard. I've been a dairy farmer for over forty years. It's my battle and nobody's going to take that away from me.'

I know not to say anything. This illness means the very essence of who he is has been pierced. This march is to Dad what the EPE drug launch was to me: the birth of something he has gestated. All that work behind the scenes leading to one final moment of truth: the launch of a drug; the marching of cows. Years of blood, sweat and toil, be it in fields, milking sheds, meeting rooms or laboratories. I just hope he doesn't think I'm trying to steal his glory just as Christophe stole mine. This is Dad's march. He doesn't want to be cut into the deal or cut out of it. The deal is his.

Grandma fiddles with the brooch on her collar. 'That may be so, John, but—'

Dad's chest rises. 'If I drop dead on the march, it'll be for a worthy cause.'

Her fingers work faster, like galloping centipede legs. 'I just worry about you.'

'Trust me, you'll need to worry more if I'm kept away from it. I don't think I could live with myself if I didn't go.'

Dad looks to me for affirmation and it feels all wrong. Like our roles have reversed and that I'm the parent and he's the child. Somehow, I hold the power and he awaits permission. I feel all discombobulated, my limbs disconnected from the rest of my body, my thoughts disjointed.

'Of course, Dad,' I say, wanting everything to go back to normal and for him to tell me off for bringing mud into the house.

'You can come in now, Derek!' Dad shouts.

A few seconds later, Derek reappears. 'Wonderful view you've got here.' He looks up at the mouldy patch in the corner of the ceiling.

'Hardly the Sistine Chapel, but it works for us,' Grandma says.

'I meant outside.'

'Outside it's bleak as buggery.' Grandma gives the window-sill a wipe with her sleeve.

'The moors, they're—'

'Where people get murdered?' she says.

His eyes widen as he rummages in his rucksack.

'Sorry.' Grandma clears her throat. 'But if you could just get on with it, we'd be very grateful.'

Derek slathers bergamot oil over the palms of his hands and presses them against Dad's leg. 'Thumbs to the centre.' He demonstrates his massage technique. 'Move in a circular motion and it'll get more oxygen to the muscles and really get the circulation going.'

'You want to put a bit of elbow grease into it,' Grandma says. 'He'll not feel a thing if you pansy around like that!'

Derek grabs hold of the bottle of oil before Grandma can

get involved. 'The idea is to invigorate rather than flood the bloodstream with toxins.'

'Take it from a woman who's made bread all her life, you need to give it some welly,' Grandma says.

Dad has a faraway look in his eyes. 'How many days until the march, Bilberry?'

'Five weeks,' I say, glancing at Derek's face for a reaction.

'I don't recommend pushing yourself too hard,' Derek says. 'You don't want to set yourself back.'

'I'll be going.' Dad grimaces. 'Whether it's in a wheelchair or on a flaming cow.'

Derek steps back. 'Very well.' He rummages in his North Face rucksack and brings out a leaflet showing a matchstick man doing various exercises. 'Build up to some of these in your first week, and I'll come back to assess you next week.'

Dad evaluates the exercises. 'Two days,' he says.

'Sorry?' Derek says, packing up his stuff.

'I'll be ready for assessment in two days.' Dad looks to me and then to Grandma. 'Cinderella is going to the ball.'

By the afternoon, Dad is dressed, downstairs, and listening to the weather forecast.

'Will you do me a favour?' I say.

'What's that?' he says.

'Stop putting pressure on yourself. If you can't walk it, we can always take the wheelchair.'

He looks at me like I've killed a small animal. 'There'll be no wheelchair, Bilberry.'

Shifting his weight to the edge of his armchair, he leans forward and hauls himself up with his NHS aluminium

251

walking stick. He straightens his back, holds onto the bookcase and edges his way around the room. Then, leaning the walking stick against the wall, he takes a few paces without it.

'I don't think you're supposed to be doing that yet,' I say, hovering behind him.

'What?' he says, full of annoyance.

'Walking without a stick. You're not supposed to be doing that until week four.'

'Come on!' he says. 'We're going for a walk!'

'Dad?' I shadow him into the hallway.

He shuffles over to the porch.

'Dad?'

He navigates the step.

'Can't we sit down and talk about which cows we take on the march?' I hold up my list out of desperation.

'Bring it with you.' He takes a step into the yard, and I know I have no choice but to follow him.

'Hit me up,' he says, hobbling towards the fir trees that mark the start of the lane and, just when I think he's going to stop to catch his breath, he speeds up.

Parsnip's head swings over the wall. I hold my hand out to her, which she sniffs through wet nostrils and then decides to lick. It feels like being exfoliated with sandpaper. I pat her goodbye.

'I'd take Parsnip if she wasn't pregnant,' I say, hurrying after Dad and passing him the list of cows I've identified based on three prerequisites. Firstly, they must be healthy. Secondly, they mustn't be pregnant. Thirdly, they must be easy to handle.

'I think you may have overlooked a few things,' he says, handing the list back to me and soldiering on.

'Like what?' I say, trying not to get annoyed.

'Firstly, you can't take Nigella or Florence because they both get travel-sick.'

'Really? Is that a thing?'

'Of course it's a thing. Cattle are not designed to stand in moving vehicles. And like humans, cows can get travel-sick too.'

'OK.'

'Secondly, you can't take Loretta and Mildred on the same trip as they despise each other.'

'Do they?'

'Mildred's really jealous of Loretta because she's really good friends with Betsy. And Betsy, being Betsy, plays them off against each other. You can't put them in close proximity else it might get physical.'

'Right.'

'And thirdly, you can't take Sally without taking Louise. She won't go anywhere without Louise. They come as a pair.'

We're halfway down the lane and I'm sensing that Dad's getting tired, but he refuses to stop. We walk the rest of the lane in silence, save for the sound of the wind, the rustle of leaves and the pete-pete-peta-peta of a nearby grouse. Sunshine pierces the clouds. Bracken sways back and forth. A partridge treads carefully around a patch of dark peat to shelter between moss-coated rocks. Dad presses on. Past elderberries and field maple, blackthorn and dog rose. Past ripe red rosehips and furry buds of pussy willow. The lane has never felt so long.

He takes a moment to catch his breath, leaning on the lichen-splotched stone wall and drinking in the view. Cows pepper the luscious green land. A hawk hovers overhead, tilting its wings periodically to maintain balance. Yellow gorse marks the border between pastureland and moorland, the terrain shifting from green to purple, great hulks of glittering granite emerging from a pink haze of heather. On the other side of the lane, a large speckled toad plops from a higgledy-piggledy stone in the wall into roadside grass, his warty skin camouflaged by undergrowth as he crawls into the ditch. My fingers find a snotty hanky and a squashed packet of Opal Fruits in Grandma's pocket.

Dad takes an Opal Fruit. 'I won't need a wheelchair, Billie.'

I wrap an arm around his waist. 'You've made your point.'

He runs his hand over the fuzz of hair growing back on his head. 'If the march is to be a success, you need to take Louise.' He stares at the horizon. 'She's good natured and consistent. If you've only got one pick, you'd pick Louise. Then it goes without saying, Sally will want to go with her.' He picks a fluff-ball of sheep's wool off the barbed wire running above the wall. 'Then there's Rosie.'

'Too feisty,' I say.

'She's spirited, I'll give you that, but she's also travelled sixty miles in the back of a lorry and didn't kick off once.'

'OK.'

'Beryl, likewise. You've got to take Beryl.' He chews his Opal Fruit. 'Did you have Patty on the list?'

'No.'

'You might want to add her. She's stubborn but you can bribe her anywhere with an apple.'

This is insightful, but it's also like covering someone's job during their maternity leave, only for them to come back and point out everything you're doing wrong.

I decide to let it go. It's his gig really. 'OK, that's five so far.'

'Fizz, Holly and Hazel make eight.'

'What about Buttercup?' I say.

'Is she still lame?'

'Yes.'

'Can't take her if she's lame. Roz?'

'Which one's Roz again?'

'Introspective, considered. White sock markings.'

'Heather's sister?'

'That's the one. Take Heather too. She's trustworthy. How many are we up to?'

'Ten. We need two more. What about Little Dot?'

'Too anxious.'

'She doesn't seem that anxious.'

'You haven't seen her in confined spaces,' he says. 'Thea. She's low maintenance, adapts well to change.'

'OK.'

'And if you're going to take Thea, you may as well take Bruschetta.'

'There you go, that's twelve,' I say, making a mental note to study the psychology of the herd next time I'm milking.

Dad's eyes travel back up the lane to the farm. 'Any chance of a piggyback?' He throws his head back and laughs. It feels so good to hear his laugh again. It feels like we're getting him back.

By the evening, I've gone stir crazy with cabin fever. I've got to go out. If I don't get some sort of social hit soon, I'll end up a madwoman. Local socializing options consist of 'Making friends with Jesus' at St Anne's Methodist Musical Medley;

watching a subtitled, three-hour Iranian art-house film in the village hall; joining a Darts and Knitting club 'for him and her' at the crown bowling club; or celebrating living art by singing candlelit ballads around Baslow's well dressing.

After an hour of shilly-shallying on the interweb (to appropriate Grandma's term), I decide to drive into Sheffield for an LGBT Singles Night at the City Hall. I pull on a pair of jeans and a top that hasn't got mud on it. In all honesty, I don't really care what I look like – I'm looking for friendship rather than sex. I apply utility eyeliner and mascara in the rear-view mirror of the Land Rover, and get as far as the end of the lane before realizing I've only gone and left the bloody house keys in the milking shed. I double back.

Parsnip's guttural groans echo around the barn. I peep over the gate. She's straining, whites of her eyes rolling like a cue ball. Her tail thrashes against the breezeblock wall as she lets out another roar, kicking away straw to grind her hooves against the concrete floor.

I open the gate and walk towards her, but she buffets my arm away with her wet nose.

'Hey,' I whisper, holding my hand out to her. Slowly, I edge around her to see two black hooves jutting out of the back of her like stone tulips. 'Good girl!' I stroke her neck, wondering whether I'm supposed to intervene. Ordinarily, I'd ask Dad, but he's asleep and Grandma's out playing bridge. I can't leave her like this.

The birthing assistance instructions on my calving app suggest that the cow will pretty much do it herself and that nature will run its course. It's only when I'm faced with photos of 'normal' and 'breech' that I go back for another look and realize the calf's hooves are pointing upwards as opposed to dangling downwards and therefore belong to its hind legs, bringing about a whole raft of complications. I've seen Dad pull out calves with his bare hands, but *he* knew what he was doing. There's stuff on the breech birth website about ratchets and all sorts of equipment I'm not sure we own, so I call Lorna, who says she'll come right away.

Parsnip stamps and bellows. Allie, her long-legged pregnant neighbour, grunts in solidarity from the next pen. I shove on Dad's overalls, mentally plotting Lorna's whereabouts on the road from Totley to Baslow, and debating whether to wake Dad. My attempts at fluffing the straw with a pitchfork to soften the calf's landing are fruitless as Parsnip does her best to kick it all out of the way. She stands, back legs slightly astride, and strains to release a further two inches of the calf's ankles, only for an inch to sink back in again as the contraction passes. Her big dark eyes look up at me pleadingly.

'It's OK, darling.' I try to stroke her neck, but she doesn't want me to touch her. Desperate to help in some way, I fill her water bucket, which she pointedly angles her head at and tips over my feet.

Lorna arrives in running shorts and a peach-coloured yoga sweatshirt, the damp patch around the neck suggesting she's freshly aborted a workout. She opens the gate and sets down her vet's bag, throwing me a pair of latex gloves. 'How long has she been like this?'

'Forty minutes.' I have the gloves on within seconds, their rubbery smell and soapy touch reminding me of the lab and the life I've left behind. 'Will she be OK?'

Lorna walks her hands around Parsnip's rump, pressing here and there. 'We don't know if it's a girl or a boy yet.'

'I mean Parsnip.'

Lorna holds her ear against Parsnip's stomach and listens for a heartbeat, which I'm guessing is inaudible as she cocks her head and repeats the process on the other side, her default expression one of concentration. She steps back, legs astride, hands on hips, leans forward and scrutinizes Parsnip's rump with the intensity of a Wimbledon line umpire. 'I'll do my best.'

It's clear that this is not your run-of-the-mill birth, but I'm in the dark as to what sort of birth it actually is. And as I'm trying to work out whether there is cause for concern, I think of my mother lying here, on the floor of this very barn, her swollen ankles splayed, her fate unwritten. She pushes me out. Me. Her. The placenta. A tangled mess of life and death. I think of Parsnip, sniffing her dead mother's ears. I think of Lady Love and Lady Lovely. And it's at this moment that I realize how important this birth is for all of us.

'The good news is . . .' Lorna grimaces as she pushes her hand inside, '. . . the legs have made it through the birth canal.' She twists at the waist, frowning at the roof, her hand still inside Parsnip. 'The bad news is . . . Damn, I thought I had it then.' She bites down on her lip.

Parsnip swings her head violently from side to side, twisting in circles.

'I'm going to have to give her pain relief,' Lorna says, ripping a sterilized needle out of a clinical packet with her teeth.

She jabs the needle into Parsnip's hindquarters and, a few

seconds later, Parsnip stands still, straining as a new section of her calf's legs appear. My instincts tell me that this is a good thing; that more of the calf is out, so we're one step closer to birth. Lorna's frown tells me otherwise.

'Should I pull?' I say.

She screws up her face with concentration. 'Can you get a bucket of warm water and a sponge?'

I locate a plastic bucket easily enough. It just happens to have a crack, though, which leaks a third of its contents by the time I've got it back to her. 'Here you go. I couldn't find a sponge.'

Without a second's thought, Lorna takes off her pastel peach yoga sweatshirt, dunks it in the bucket, wrings it out and uses it to gently pat Parsnip around her vagina. 'There, there, girl,' she says gently. Her fitted grey sports top clings to her sculpted frame, tiny droplets of sweat dampening the material between her breasts. 'I need your help.' She manoeuvres her hands around Parsnip's soft belly, checking and double-checking. 'When I say pull, I want you to gently pull the legs backwards and downwards.'

'OK,' I say. The calf's legs feel clammy and warm.

Parsnip contracts.

'Pull!' Lorna cries.

I pull tentatively, not wanting to snap the calf's fragile legs.

Lorna looks at me. 'Not that gently!'

I'm terrified. 'OK.'

Parsnip contracts again.

'Pull!' Lorna cries. 'Gentle but firm.'

I have no benchmark for the kind of 'gentle but firm' that's required of me. No experience of pulling hind legs out of cows' vaginas. No fucking clue. I pull in the only way I know, but nothing happens.

Lorna sticks her hand inside Parsnip again. 'I just need . . .' she whispers with muted panic, 'to make sure the calf's bottom doesn't rupture the . . .' She twists and frowns. 'Don't want to tear the . . .' She takes her hand back out and delves into her vet bag, pulling out all sorts of medical equipment until she locates a metal chain, which she affixes to the calf's hooves.

I close my eyes. The last time I saw a cow's hooves being tethered, Parsnip's mother was being towed away to be incinerated. I can't let anything else happen to her.

Lorna holds the end of the chain and pulls. 'Bloody hell! This one's stubborn.' She skids across the concrete on the heels of her trainers. 'You're going to have to give me a hand.'

She takes one chain handle and hands me the other. It's long. Three metres at the very least. We pad backwards until the chain is taut.

'OK, on the count of three,' she says. 'One, two, three!'

We pull, our hips crashing into each other like tandem water-skiers. As the chain cuts into the palm of my hand, the calf's knees and thighs appear, covered in blood and slime.

'Keep going,' Lorna shouts, the calf's rump now visible. We pull again, colliding into each other once more. 'And again.' We grit our teeth, arms straining, stomachs tight, toes rammed up against the ends of our trainers; the pair of us, spattered in blood, mucus and sweat. Finally, a limp, blue body hangs out.

'One last pull!' Lorna cries.

We wrap our fingers around the chain, heaving with all our might as a blue-black calf slides to the ground and bounces against the straw like a rubber toy. And that's when the enormity of the moment hits me; the calf's glassy eye looking at nothing, its lifeless body distended.

Parsnip stamps her hooves in torment, nostrils flaring.

'No!' I smell death but refuse to taste it.

Lorna kneels by the body, her bare knees matted in straw and cow dung. She squeezes her hand underneath its chest. 'No heartbeat.' Her voice trembles.

I crouch beside her, touching the calf's torso.

'Fuck!' Lorna yells, thumping the ground angrily. She grabs a piece of straw, discarding it for a bigger piece and sticks it up the calf's nostril. 'Come on!' she cries, desperately searching for a reaction that doesn't happen.

'What is it supposed to do?' I say quietly.

'Fuck!' she roars.

Rain tinkles musically against the metal roof. Parsnip circles the calf. She bucks and grunts; a tortured soul. I try to comfort her, but she won't let me near her. Her friends in the nearby pens grunt anxiously. And as I kneel in blood and slime, staring at the wet blue body in front of me, I realize that this moment isn't just important, it's everything. This calf cannot die. For Parsnip, for Dad, for the herd.

Lorna stands up, puts her hands on her hips and inhales deeply. 'Right,' she puffs, trying to regain control. She bends down, levers her hands under the calf and manoeuvres its small, limp body onto one side. Wiping mucus from the calf's nose with the bottom of her sports top, she slides her hand over its mouth and plugs one of the nostrils with the fingers of her other hand, while blowing gently into the other nostril. The calf's chest rises.

'What can I do?'

'Pray?' she says, between puffs.

Parsnip looks on in horror, nuzzling the limp body of her young as Lorna repeats the process again and again, blowing air into one nostril, rotating her head to listen for a breath, blowing and listening again. Her mousy-blonde hair is matted with mucus. Her freckled face is mud-spattered and bloody. Her grey sports top is soiled with slime. She doesn't look at me. She doesn't speak. She remains totally focused.

I dab the sticky coating from the calf's unconscious body with Lorna's sweatshirt, but it's totally unresponsive.

After five long minutes, Lorna sits back in the straw, hugs her legs to her chest and buries her face in her knees. Her face is blotchy and tear-stained. 'I'm sorry, Billie.'

I kick the bucket, startling Parsnip, who throws back her head and bellows.

'Let me try,' I say.

The calf's head feels heavy and damp in the palms of my hands, its fur sticky and warm. I dip my mouth to her nostril. Her nose is cold, wet and smells of congealed blood. I blow, unsure as to how much air I'm supposed to impart in one go, then listen. Nothing. I try again and again. Still nothing.

'I'm really sorry,' Lorna says, running her hands over the calf's bedraggled coat.

Parsnip turns her back on us and the world. She'll kick if I try to go near.

We lean against each other in the straw and sob, Lorna and I, lost and guilty. To be that close and then have life ripped away from you. Mother Nature is a cunt at times. I figure we should name her anyway. She was going to be Jupiter II, but that doesn't feel like a particularly noble idea any more. Maybe something poetic like Hero. Dying before she even knew life. Dying for a cause I'm not yet aware of. I'm not sure what we're to do with the body. Whether we bury her or whether she's considered fallen stock. I don't know how I'm going to tell Dad.

'This is the shit part of the job,' Lorna says.

We sit and watch as Parsnip licks her stillborn calf, her tongue methodically making its way around her head. A mother's unconditional love.

And I tell myself I'm seeing things when the calf's ears twitch.

Lorna slams her hand on my knee and leans forward. She opens the calf's mouth and my heart leaps in my chest as the calf suddenly jerks, splutters and shakes.

'She's alive?' I lean forward.

'She's a-fucking-live!' Lorna hurriedly unties the chain from the hooves.

Parsnip buries her head against her calf, her tongue lolloping over its delicate little face until it heaves out a tiny, miraculous grunt. This beautiful little creature. This pure black precious new life. She gets to her feet. *Jupiter II.* Parsnip drifts over to me and rests her chin on my shoulder. I stroke her damp, furry face.

'Well done,' I say. 'You're going to be a brilliant mother.'

She drops her head to nuzzle her calf.

'You OK?' Lorna says, shaking the hair out of her eyes.

'We did it?' I wring my hands together and look back and forth between Lorna and the calf. 'We did it!' I squeal.

'I know!' Lorna catches my excitement, hopping from one

foot to the other, then flinging her arms around me, her body boiling hot, but covered in goose bumps.

'Thank you, thank you, thank you!' I squeeze her, tears rolling down my face.

Euphoric, emotional, fragile, we are glued to each other and can't let go. I can feel her hot skin against mine. And that's when I kiss her. I kiss Lorna Parsons right on the lips. Not a grateful peck. A proper, deeply connected, undeniable kiss.

# CHAPTER SIXTEEN

## COVENTRY

Kissing your flatmate is like playing with fire, but kissing your vet is like throwing yourself to the flames. You can always find a new flatmate, but finding a new vet . . . and a good one at that? Especially when you've got four pregnant cows?

It's the next day and I keep reliving the cringe moment of suddenly becoming aware of Guy standing at the entrance to the cowshed, motionless, car keys in hand, watching, his face frozen. Us, mid-kiss, our bodies stuck together, my fingers tracing the valley between her back muscles. I expected Lorna to be shy, but she wasn't. She cradled my head in her hands and pressed her groin against mine, gently pushing me backwards until I was pinned against the breezeblock wall, her hands running all over me, her big grey eyes like pools of water. She smiled and kissed me again, and then over her shoulder I saw a figure in the doorway.

Guy shuffled his feet in the gravel to emphasize his arrival. Endorphins evaporated, replaced by cast-iron guilt.

'Now I feel like a dick,' I said under my breath, as Lorna turned to see Guy.

Her smile disappeared but her hands were still draped around my neck and I wondered whether she was going to try to style it out by pretending she was tying my hair back or something, but she didn't. Instead her big grey eyes fixed me with a steely stare I didn't understand. Like she was questioning me. And all the time, Guy was waiting.

I can still hear Lorna's steps across the yard, the passenger door of their Subaru-whatever-it-is clunking shut and tyres crunching through gravel. I can still see the reflection of her eyes seeking me out in the wing mirror.

**From: Lorna Parsons**
For the record, I am not without a conscience and know what we did was wrong.

I'm not sure how to reply, so I don't.

It's been five days now. Five days of Lorna coincidentally timing her mother-and-calf visits for when I'm out. Five days of Lorna avoiding coming into the house. Five days of feeling on edge.

'I haven't spoken to Lorna for a while,' Grandma says over breakfast.

'No.' I maintain eye contact with my Rice Krispies.

'It's not like her.'

I shrug my shoulders. 'She's very busy.'

'And what have you been playing at with Charlie?' She holds her bowl under the running tap, chiselling off stubborn cornflakes with a teaspoon.

'Charlie?'

'Charlie from the co-operative. I hear he asked you out.'

Nothing gets past Grandma. She's like a human firewall. I haven't told a soul, so God knows how she knows. 'Who told you?'

'His mother.' She turns off the tap and flicks water off her fingertips into the sink.

'Who's his mother?' I say.

'Doreen from Buns and Baps.'

'Charlie is Doreen Peterson's son?'

Grandma nods.

All of this is noise. What really matters is whether I'll be cited as a third-party adulterer in the disintegration of Lorna and Guy's common-law partnership, and whether Lorna'll ever show up again. And if she does, what I'll actually say to her and, more to the point, what I'll say to Guy.

It's all gone sneaky glances and double-takes down in the village, and I feel like a scarlet woman. It's got to the point where I'm driving seven miles to get toothpaste from a petrol station to avoid sly comments or a cross-examination. Where's the soothing, carefree anonymity of London when you need it?

'Hi!' I open the door to Buns & Baps, the bell tinkling.

Doreen Peterson stands behind a counter of sticky tarts and cream cakes and says nothing. The room smells of fresh bread and warm croissants; the sort of smell you want to bottle and dispense when things aren't going your way. A small black cat jumps down from the windowsill and winds its way around my legs.

'A large rye cob, please, Doreen.' She must be preoccupied with something as she's usually so chirpy.

'We're out of bread.' She folds her arms under her no-nonsense bosom, which is emblazoned with Buns & Baps, courtesy of the apron she's had made.

'What about the loaves behind you?' I point out.

'Reserved.'

I look to the basket of pastries under the counter. 'What about a croissant?'

'We've closed the kitchen now and all of these are taken.' The cat purrs.

'Well,' I say, shoving my wallet back into my pocket. 'Glad business is thriving.'

The bell tinkles as I leave, despite it not being a tinkly moment, and I've half a mind to go back in there and tell her what I think, a monologue of fury and injustice building in me – Charlie's a grown adult, for fuck's sake. And then I get a better idea.

'Hi again,' I say, reopening the door. 'Just to let you know that Buns and Baps are both a reference to *tits*.'

She looks at me blankly whilst feeding a wholemeal bloomer through her slicer.

'Tits,' I repeat, pointing to each of my breasts.

She continues to stare at me.

'It doesn't matter,' I say, closing the door again and at least getting a proper *dong* out of her visitor bell.

All of this because I won't go out with her son.

A package from Maria awaits me in the hall. I tear open the box to find a 'first-aid kit' containing macaroons, a bottle of

Disaronno, a satin eye mask and three copies of *Vogue* in order that 'you don't let yourself go.' Boutique catwalk fashion is at the forefront of my mind right now. Underneath the cardboard flap is a Starbucks loyalty card and Dolly Parton CD. I feel like I'm surviving a world war on modern-day rations.

She accepts my Skype call, eyes completely covered by an eye mask identical to the one she sent me, a plate of steaming pasta in front of her.

'What are you doing?' I say.

'Training my body to exhibit the behaviour of a barn owl.'

'Right.'

'It's part of the "Unleash the Inner Beast" animal theatre workshop I'm doing.' She grapples around the table for the pepper mill.

'It's right in front of your beak!' Frustration gets the better of me. 'Surely they've got to give you eye-holes?'

'It's not the mask, Billie. Owls are far-sighted and wouldn't be able to see an object that close up. I need to feel for it.'

'Feel for it?'

'With my filoplumes,' she says, sniffing around the table.

'Are you taking the piss?'

'There's no point in doing it half-heartedly. I'm supposed to be living truthfully under given imaginary circumstances.'

'What if the given imaginary circumstance was your flat-mate hanging up on you?'

She peels off the mask, feathers from the trim floating into her spaghetti. 'What's up with you?'

I blow my breath out at the ceiling. 'I kissed Lorna and now she's avoiding me.'

Her voice goes all high-pitched. 'Isn't she straight?'

'Definitely not.'

'Isn't she married?'

'As good as.'

'Isn't she your vet?'

'All very valid points.' I open a packet of Maltesers, which shower all over my lap.

'I didn't think you even liked her!'

I think about this. 'I didn't, but I do now.'

'Bloody hell.'

'And now she's avoiding me. It was lonely enough before, but now I'm getting treated like a leper by half the village. Like I'm some sort of wanton harlot.'

'Maybe you should feign mental illness and wander the streets in a lace nightgown in the style of *Marie Celeste*. Go loopy on them. Wield a shotgun and demand bread.'

'Wasn't *Marie Celeste* a ship?' I say, confused.

'Was it?'

'I think so.'

'But it must have been named after a real person called Marie Celeste in the first place. And anyone called Marie Celeste would definitely wander the streets in a floaty lace nightgown with a shotgun. Write to her.'

'To Marie Celeste?'

'Lorna! Write to her. Tell her how you feel.'

'I don't think I can. Not while I know she's in a relationship.'

She strokes the edges of her mask in the way a man might his beard. 'You need a distraction. Something to take your mind off things. How about internet dating?'

Ten minutes later, I receive an email thanking me for my

subscription to Licker, 'a unique online dating site dedicated to finding like-minded, educated women.'

Since when have licking and education been natural bedfellows?

The rural Derbyshire/South Yorkshire border appears to be a lesbian blind spot. A lazy trawl through cyberspace for 'like-minded, educated women' suggests that the nearest mutually compatible Lick is seven miles away. Once proximity is overcome, it appears that the entire Licker population is 'a perfect match'. This could be something to do with the dating profile Maria has created for me, in which I 'love travel, film, theatre, books, art, history, animals, sports and the great outdoors. I go to the gym three to five times a week. I work to live rather than live to work. I'm a non-smoker, an occasional drinker, a home owner, a dog lover, a museum regular, a DIY enthusiast and a positive thinker.' I'm a maximal minimalist and a minimal maximalist. I have that many characteristics that I have no distinguishable character. I love everything and hate nothing in a transparent attempt to have something in common with everyone; an insipid, generic, unremarkable void of nothingness. I am so inoffensive that I am offensive.

Three messages await me from a Polish acrobat who loves fire-eating, ghost-hunting, cryptozoology and fetish clubs, and is therefore a perfect match. I am about to send her a 'Hey, how's it going' mail when I realize she has deactivated her account now that she is in a relationship with the ghost of her ex-landlady.

I miss Joely. We were right for each other, whereas this just feels like going through the motions for the sake of it.

I half-heartedly plump for Lucy from Chesterfield, who likes gardening, Go-Karting, geocaching and is online.

'Hi, Lucy.'

'Hi.'

'Thank God someone else from round here is on this thing!'

'Did you read my profile?'

'Briefly!' (I lie, having just seen her photo.)

'Can you be discreet?'

A quick glance at her profile suggests she is married but looking to 'meet and cheat'. Delete.

People's interests are wide ranging. There are girls on this site into toy voyaging, car tattooing and dyeing their pets. I find myself signing up to Angels & Devils, a bimonthly singles night in Sheffield. The next event is a masked ball in the city-centre Winter Gardens. Do I really want to pay twenty quid to flirt with desperados in a giant greenhouse? Hell, yes.

I sign up and am allocated the name Angel6.

Angel3, fellow attendee of Licker's Angels & Devils Masked Ball, wants to connect.

'Hi, Angel6, any idea how to remove the shit angel icon?'

'Hi, Angel3,' I reply. 'Sadly not.'

'How's your day going?' Hmm. American, or just well mannered?

'Not too bad,' I type. 'Could bore you with the mechanics of my day job, which is turning out to be a day and night job, but you'd probably fall asleep.'

'What line of work are you in?'

I'm about to type 'biochemist' but then realize I am – to all intents and purposes – a farmer. Putting it out there doesn't feel right, though. Not without an explanation. It all feels too permanent.

'Wait, don't answer that,' she types, saving me from my indecision.

'Why not?'

'It was shop talk and nobody gets laid talking shop, right?' Definitely American.

'Sorry,' I type, almost blushing.

'No more shop talk, promise?' A girl who likes the driving seat. I like it.

'I promise. Have you been to one of these singles nights before?' I ask, aware of my inability to inject any sort of personality into my online persona.

'Last year's Halloween ball was pretty awesome. God, that makes me sound tragic, doesn't it?'

'Does it?'

'You know, like I've been on the shelf *forever*, annually turning up to some masked ball in the hope of snaring someone.'

'So how long have you been single for?' I type.

'Do you know nothing about phishing?'

'Phishing?'

'Extracting information from internet chat.'

'I guess not,' I concede.

'Rule number one, never talk shop on your first chat.'

'OK, hand slapped.'

'Rule number two, never ask a lady how old she is.'

'I didn't.'

'Just in case you do, because Angel6, between you and me, you don't seem massively tech savvy.' Has to be a fiery redhead.

'No offence taken!'

'Rule number three, never ask a lady how long she's been single for.'

'Is it rude?'

'It's a bit like asking someone how long they haven't washed for.'

'Really?'

'Not really, but everyone knows to lie about how long they've been single for, as they'll be judged on the answer.'

'Will they?'

'OK, let's role-play. I've been single for a year (I haven't, by the way). Does that make me look good, or bad?'

'Neither.'

'If you were a judgemental person, as I am – but you've probably realized that by now – you'd probably think a year is acceptable. A year shows that someone can be on their own; anything longer suggests you're undatable.'

'How about three months?'

'Rebound,' she types. 'Actually, it depends on whether you got dumped or did the dumping?'

'Are you asking me?'

'Of course not, that would violate rule number four. I was merely talking hypothetically.'

'Do you have a degree in internet dating?'

'Thankfully not, though it'd be more vocational than the American Fine Art course I'm currently on.'

'So, you're an artist?'

'Of sorts. I could wow you with renaissances and revolutions, but that would be almost as bad as talking shop. Shit, it's late and I've an early start tomorrow. Must sign off. Nice chatting, Angel6.'

'Ditto.'

I feel mentally invigorated for the first time in months. It's refreshing to meet someone with a bit of fire in their belly. That said, Angel3 could be a three-metre-cubed alcoholic called Kevin.

It's two weeks since I kissed Lorna. She continues to avoid me and the farm, and I'm now thinking the whole thing is ridiculous and blown out of all proportion. We are adults, and this is all just so childish, and maybe I should just apologize so we can move on. After all, I did kind of initiate it, despite her being in a committed relationship. I vow to pick up the phone and call her. After all, it was just a stupid, heat-of-the-moment mistake. Or was it? Perhaps I will not call Lorna.

'Billie!' Grandma shouts through the kitchen window. I turn round to see her grinning over the dishevelled window boxes. 'Allie's in labour.'

I glove up and rush out with a bucket of warm water.

Allie paces around her pen. The moment anyone so much as dares to put their hand on the gate, she roars. It all looks to be pretty straightforward, but what the fuck do I know? I decide to get Dad. He has a special relationship with her in the way that Thatcher had with Reagan. I find him in the conservatory, his eyes half shut and the television blaring.

'Dad?'

He rubs his eyes. 'I wish you wouldn't sneak up on me.'

'Allie's in labour.'

He shuffles his feet into his carpet slippers. 'Well, what are we waiting for?'

Refusing to stop for either his stick or his coat, Dad powers through the house to the back door, gingerly navigates the porch step and makes a beeline to the cowshed.

Allie lowers her head, her doleful eyes looking up at Dad as he opens the gate to her pen, maintaining a respectful distance. She cranes her neck, the rest of her body seemingly still while peristalsis enables her calf to slide out. Mother Nature does her stuff. There's no drama. No tears. Not even much sound.

The little calf stands up almost immediately and shakes her ears.

'Well done,' Dad says, stroking Allie's neck, his face alight with wonder. 'A beautiful baby girl.'

We call her Lydia, after one of Dad's nurses.

Lydia gives me a solid-gold reason to phone Lorna. I go to the bathroom, wash the gunk off my fingers and role-play what I'm about to say, training my voice to sound light and breezy.

'Hi, Lorna, it's Billie.' I don't sound in the slightest bit breezy when it's for real.

There's a small pause. 'Hello.'

'I've had another delivery,' I blurt.

'Flowers again?' Her voice cracks.

'Flowers?' I'm confused. 'I mean arrival. I mean we've had another calf.'

'Congratulations,' she says flatly.

'Thanks.' You'd think she'd be a tiny bit happy for me. I

mean, it's not like I've phoned the bin man. She is my vet, after all.

Silence ensues. I'm just building up to saying 'sorry' but can't quite grasp the appropriate words. Should I refer to kissing her? Or snogging her? Or . . .

'And sorry I made you feel like "a dick". That wasn't my intention,' she says almost aggressively, the inference being that *I* was more out of order for saying I felt like a dick than she was for cheating on Guy!

And now I don't want to say sorry – not now she's being mega-arsy about it. Besides, 'sorry' would suggest I regretted it and, truth be told, I don't regret it at all – it felt amazing. She can pretend all she wants that it never happened, but I've banked the memory, and nothing can erase it. One thing's for sure, though: the ice queen has frozen over again, and a repeat thaw is entirely out of the question.

'I'm guessing you need to check out the calf?' I gibber. 'Not that I'm forcing you to come and check her out against your will, I just thought '

'I'll send someone over.'

Someone? Is it really that bad that she can't see me?

Lorna only goes and sends Guy! I hide in the milking shed and let Grandma deal with him. I watch them chat in the barn. Guy gives Allie and her calf a quick once-over, glancing across the yard every now and again, presumably for me, in order to launch something at my head.

I wish I could turn back time. Not so we didn't kiss, just so that Guy didn't turn up.

An hour later, I'm in the cereal aisle of the village store

grabbing bread when Guy appears. This time, I have nowhere to hide. He has orange zinc sun block plastered across his nose, the *Daily Telegraph* under one arm and a bottle of Badoit in the other. I keep my eyes fixed on the shelf of Kellogg's miniature multipacks, the clacking of his cycling shoes on the floor tiles getting louder as he advances, counting out change.

'Belinda!' He's all elbows and bluster, knocking a string of freeze-dried beef stroganoff packets to the ground.

With no other option available to me, I slowly avert my gaze from the friendly faces of Snap, Crackle and Pop to meet his glare. Though when I do, he's actually beaming at me, chest puffed out in a garish lime-green cycling top with shouty logos.

'I was hoping I might bump into you,' he says, ignoring the rock climbers grouped up behind him, their harnesses jangling with metal carabiners and fluorescent ropes.

'Guy,' I murmur, glancing around the shop with unease.

'I've been wanting to ask you about your straw supplier, but thought we both might feel a little awkward, given the last time we met you had your tongue down Lorn's throat!'

Heat travels to my neck, my face, my ears. 'Guy, I'm sorry, I—'

'On the contrary, any time!' he says, letting out a belly laugh. 'Quite got off on it, truth be told!'

'LMT Supplies! Very reliable,' I say, scuttling out of the shop and retrieving Speedo, who is sniffing the wheels of Guy's Parsons-Bonneville hybrid bike and contemplating which spoke to piss on.

I walk home at pace, trying to digest the fact that Lorna and Guy are swingers. They say it all goes on in small villages, and indeed it does! Thank God for Maria keeping me on the straight and narrow with online dating. Life is so much easier behind a screen.

Later, I log onto Licker for a bit of escapism and see that Angel3 is online. Is it normal to be this excited about talking to someone I've never met?

'Hi Angel3.'

'Hi Angel6. Ready for Saturday?'

'The ball?' I type. 'I guess so.'

'Do you have a mask?'

'Not yet, but I remember learning how to make one out of papier-mâché at school.'

'I look forward to that. Are you arty?'

'Definitely not.'

'I look forward to it even more then.'

'I'm guessing you probably are arty, what with your studies, and will have hand-sculpted a postmodern facial masterpiece for the occasion?'

'I'll be more likely wearing my flatmate's Darth Vader mask.'

'At least I'll be able to recognize you!'

'How will I recognize you?'

'I'll probably have cowpat in my hair from working on the farm all day.'

*Angel3 is typing. Angel3 is deleting. Angel3 is typing. Angel3 is deleting.*

'But I'll be wearing Issey Miyake,' I add, trying to sound alluring and sophisticated.

'Back in a sec. My flatmate has set the smoke alarm off!'

*Angel3 is offline.*

Farming: an aphrodisiac's antidote.

I take her abrupt departure as an omen that I should be listening to Professor Carmody's podcast on 'Toxaemia Prevention in Pregnancy.' The first three minutes are excellent, but I'm asleep by the fourth.

# PART THREE

# COWGIRLS AND ANGELS

# CHAPTER SEVENTEEN

# #COWGiRL

## Dairy farmers march on Sheffield

*Milk! Milk! They're milking our Milk!*

The British Dairy Farming Association will hold a *#SaveOurDairy* demonstration on Saturday 30 October where farmers will march their herds in their largest campaign to date.

The march is a protest against the decision by co-operative giant, Premier Milk, to drop its 'A' milk prices for producers across Northern England due to increased pressure from super-markets. Milk producers in South Yorkshire and Derbyshire will see milk prices fall by 0.62p/litre. The dairy farming sector has seen profits fall by 50 per cent over recent years and is on the brink of collapse.

'My family has been in the dairy business for ninety-three years and we've never known things so bleak,' says Billie Oliver, a local Derbyshire dairy farmer. 'Further cuts in profit mean it's impossible to make a living.'

Supporters joining the march at the bottom of The Moor and making their way to Sheffield Peace Gardens are urged to do so responsibly and use public transport where possible.

On the morning of the march, Dad is downstairs at 5 a.m. This is the first time he's been up early since he got out of hospital. He stands at the window and threads Grandma's soft leather tape measure through his fingers. In spite of it being October, it's so misty outside you can barely see the cowshed.

'Let's hope it doesn't affect their milk supply,' I say, reaching for the kettle.

He puts down the tape measure. 'Milk them before you go, and they'll be fine. It's hardly the end of the world if they're a few minutes late back.'

I hand him a mug of tea, aware of our role reversal. He puts his arm around my shoulder, and we stand like that for a while, enveloped in nervous tension.

Three days before, Dad had his fourth round of radio-therapy. At the end of the session, he walked out of the treatment room without the aid of a stick. Neither of us spoke. I knew he felt sick – his skin was the same pebble grey it was every time he left that room and he was sucking on his cheeks to combat the nausea.

He made it all the way to the car and climbed into the passenger seat rather than collapsing into it. 'I've got this, Bilberry,' he said, to himself as much as to me.

We drove home listening to his Queen CD. The evening sky was the same metallic rose as Maria's Reeboks. He tapped his thigh to 'Radio Gaga' and I knew he was going to be all right. The nurse called him a 'legend' that morning and, at the time, I thought that Dad is not the sort of man you'd describe as a legend. Sporting heroes are legends. Space crusaders are legends. Men who derive more satisfaction from growing beetroots than driving Ferraris and are not swayed by charisma, influence or power, tend not to be legends. But as he tapped to the beat, silently battling radiotherapeutic waves of nausea, Dad was nothing short of a legend.

By 8 a.m., an enormous Cattle Cruiser beeps and flashes through the mist, its monstrous engine rumbling. A demonic energy spreads across the yard. Hydraulic floors lower and a metal ramp slides out, scraping across the gravel. Charlie jumps down from the driver's cabin wearing a box-fresh #SaveOurDairy T-shirt.

The cows squirm in the makeshift pen I've set up in the yard, pushing and shoving against each other with apprehension. Hot breath streams out of wide nostrils, hitting the cold, damp air to create clouds of steam, which hang, drift and dissipate. Patty, a stubborn heifer with stumpy legs, pushes her nose through the bars and tries to dislodge her head harness.

I fill the truck with hay while Charlie plays with the temperature control panel. Satisfied that everything is as it should be, he helps me cajole seven tons of cow out of the pen and up the ramp. Hooves slip and slide as the cows scramble up the metal slope, grunting and bellowing with uncertainty. Heather falls to her knees and drags herself back up again. Inside the trailer, they jostle for position, all vying for space next to the window, where they can slide their noses between the open bars and sniff fresh air. Those not so quick off the mark huddle in the middle, resting their chins on each other, whites of eyes showing as the gate clangs shut.

Dad appears in his #SaveOurDairy T-shirt and eyes the steep steps to the Cattle Cruiser cabin.

'Shouldn't you come in the car?' I say.

'Not on your nelly. I want to be with my girls!' he says, hoisting himself onto the first step, his arm trembling.

Charlie helps him into the cabin whilst I lug the rest of the stuff into the Land Rover.

I run back upstairs to get the rest of the T-shirts, which are dumped in a box at the bottom of Dad's wardrobe. Above the box, hanging between a shirt and a scratchy old tuxedo, is the black halter-neck dress that belonged to Mum, which Dad can't bear to chuck out on account of having the best night of his life with her at an agricultural gala where I suspect I was conceived. Go Dad! (And Mum!) Although I'm in a rush, I can't help but touch the soft silk of Mum's dress. It smells overpoweringly of mothballs. I run my fingers over the brittle lace around the neckline, pricking my finger on the pin of a brooch attached to the bust, lost in the folds of the dress. Bloody thing! I unclip it, and there in the palm of my hand is an ornate glass ladybird the size of a ten-pence piece, its red wings symmetrically dotted; the very same ladybird Mum was wearing in the home video. Truth be told, I'm a bit freaked out. I've been telling myself I made that shit up to give myself comfort; a set of simple, explicable coincidences. Carefully, I attach it to my T-shirt, grab the box and head downstairs.

Grandma sits in the passenger seat, studying a 'Milk for Farmers' leaflet. She wears a utility flannelette frock with a #SaveOurDairy T-shirt pulled over the top.

'Nice brooch.'

I run my fingers over it. 'It was my mum's.'

'I know. Her mother gave it to her. She used to call it her lucky ladybird.'

I smile, but before I can get too caught in the moment, I need to send Maria a quick message to tell her we're on our way. The girls must be somewhere between Chesterfield and Sheffield on the train by now.

The fog is thick and dense. I start up the engine and follow the blurry rear lights of the Cattle Cruiser through the mist, along narrow village lanes and up the steep, windy road to Sheffield. It takes a few minutes to get used to driving the Land Rover, having been at the helm of the tractor for the best part of a week. The windscreen wipers seem to turn on every time I want to indicate, and third gear is sticky. Grandma chatters away. All about the goings-on in Bakewell and the woman in the pie shop who wears too much pink. I can't join in. I'm too nervous. Every time I glance in the rear-view mirror, I catch a glimpse of the handle of the wheelchair I've put in the back for Dad, should it all get too much.

Fifty minutes later, we're in Sheffield city centre. The Cattle Cruiser pulls into a parking bay dotted with policemen and -women awaiting our arrival. Three other cattle lorries are already parked up, so I make a left turn into the Pay and Display at the bottom of The Moor and trudge over.

Charlie opens the back of the Cattle Cruiser and lowers the ramp. Rain drums on the tin roof. The cows are reluctant to leave the dry trailer, their hooves planted firmly on the hay-padded floor. I heave out Patty, who slides out on locked limbs, refusing to comply. It takes all my strength to pull her into the layby, the rope burning the palms of my hands. She bucks and kicks, sending a litter bin flying.

The police want the cows herded into a pen they've created with flimsy barriers used to control marathon crowds. Within seconds, the barriers have been kicked to the kerb and scattered over the pavement, cows pulling in different directions. Rosie, a small feisty heifer with a mind of her own, heads for a patch of dandelions on the grass verge, trampling traffic cones and knocking over a bicycle.

Farmers, families and friends mingle, trying to keep order as more and more cows are unleashed. We're causing quite a stir, what with herdsmen barking orders over groaning cattle and manure splattering onto the tarmac of the A61. A cow from a different herd has backed into a police car and dented its boot. Another has bolted into the central reservation and the police have had to stop traffic while three lads lure her back with hay.

Maria, Kat and Bev arrive. They've really gone for it – Bev has sprayed her Mohican in black and white stripes and looks more like a skunk than a Friesian. She and Kat wear cow-print onesies and Maria is dressed in a sequined version of the #SaveOurDairy T-shirt, complementing it with a mini-skirt and stiletto ankle boots.

'Really?' I laugh, gesturing at her apparel.

She squeezes me into her earring. 'You never know when you might find yourself on a podium, Bilbo!'

I swear Maria is a gay man trapped inside the body of a heterosexual female.

'Nobody told me it was fancy dress,' Grandma says, giving Bev's Mohican the once-over.

'Hi, Mrs O.' Bev gives Grandma a hug.

'Nice to see you again, Beverley.'

'You remember Kat, my girlfriend?' Bev says, gesturing for Kat to come over.

'Fiancée,' Kat counters.

Rosie takes a dislike to Maria's Chanel glazed hobo satchel and buffets at it with her nose. Maria looks up at Rosie. 'Bloody hell, I didn't realize cows were that big!'

Beatrice joins us with a placard asking people to support our 'Diary Framers'. She's been in firm denial of dyslexia for a good few decades now. Today, she wears a cow-print raincoat and black gumboots.

'Everyone, this is my good friend, Beatrice.' Grandma introduces her to the girls.

Beatrice smiles. 'Are they all lesbians?'

'Everyone but me,' Maria says heartily. 'I'm the queer one.'

'Very well,' Beatrice says, stopping short of her usual diatribe.

I assign each person a cow, offsetting temperaments and matching personalities in the way an online dating algorithm might work. Maria takes Louise, the most easy-going and least likely to trample her ankle boots. I give Sally to Kat, knowing that she'll follow Louise. Bev, a pro with animals, can handle Beryl while I take Rosie.

Dad clambers down from the cabin. He looks fragile and hollow, and a few years older than he looked a couple of months ago. Like a plaster cast of my dad without the blood, guts and everything that makes him *him*. I offer him the wheelchair, which he pooh-poohs with a shake of the head.

Several farmers amble over, bombarding me with questions.

Will there be hay and water at the destination? Do the trucks need a permit to pull up next to the cathedral? Will the press be at the town hall? Will there be a photoshoot? I feel very responsible and a little bit sick. I run my fingers over my mum's glass ladybird, reattach the rope to Rosie's head harness and take a step forward.

'Milk! Milk! They're milking our milk!' I chant, hoping that everyone will join in.

Thankfully they do.

Maria picks up her phone.

**@MilkforFarmers**
And we're off! Heifer great day. #SaveOurDairy

We must be about six hundred people and three hundred cows by the time we reach our official starting point at the bottom of The Moor. Mr Craggs from Birchover Hall Farm has kept his promise. The one thing I realize I failed to specify is that there should be a 1:1 cow-to-handler ratio. He, however, has single-handedly brought fifty, which are running amok, ploughing down everything in their path: market stalls, litter bins, signage. And even though there are hundreds of people here to support us, it appears that not many of them are hands-on when it comes to managing cows. Three heifers charge towards a cosmetics market stall. Lipsticks skitter across paving slabs and tubes of mascara roll into the gutter. Shop assistants pop their heads out of doors to see what the commotion is all about. An ice-cream van removes itself from our path, and a man selling knock-off designer sunglasses reassembles his Bay-Rans on the other side of the walkway.

'*Milk! Milk! They're milking our milk!*'

Saturday shoppers flee into Argos for shelter. A West Highland terrier chained to a post outside Costa Coffee barks and growls. Charlie's not only pushing a wheelbarrow of manure up The Moor, which is getting heavier by the minute, he's also tethered to a cow. Marjorie and Graham have agreed to each lead three of Mr Craggs's cows.

**@MilkforFarmers**
On the mooooove. Udder chaos! #SaveOurDairy

There must be about a thousand of us at Poundland, and our numbers have doubled by the time we reach Poundstretcher, thanks to the insurgence of farmers from Lancashire, North Yorkshire, Cheshire and Nottinghamshire, who have all joined forces thanks to social media.

'*Milk! Milk! They're milking our milk!*'

We pass an amusement arcade, where a toddler is having a screaming fit in a ride-on fire engine. Lights flash. Gunshots fire. Psychedelic music plays over the monstrous glare of computer screens whilst finger-sized aliens zap and zoom. Sally bolts in the opposite direction, dragging Kat into Dorothy Perkins and setting off the anti-theft alarm. Shoppers depart as Sally heads straight for a bargain rail of '£20 and under' clothing. Gold-flecked jumper dresses and black sequined halter-necks fall to the floor, a sparkly cardigan getting caught over Sally's hoof.

'Bill!' Kat yells, Sally's rump appearing in the shop window alongside a faceless mannequin dressed in autumnal burgundy.

I hand Rosie to Bev and head in after them. Sally refuses

to budge at first, her haunches backing further into the window display and threatening to knock over a genderless mannequin crouching in corduroy next to a cart of plastic apples. I pull a carrot out of my pocket and wave it at her. She ignores it at first but then, as I bring it nearer, she plods over, allowing me to grab her harness and walk her out.

'Sorry,' Kat apologizes to the bemused security guard.

Outside, Rosie pisses all over the cinema entrance, a river of hot yellow urine splashing against paving slabs and flowing down the pedestrianized shopping street. It feels like the longest cow wee in history.

'Don't worry, Bilbo!' Maria says. 'All publicity is good publicity.'

**@MilkforFarmers**
It's Friesian in @DorothyPerkins! #SaveOurDairy

More supporters congregate outside the parade of high-street shops with banners and cow bells. Paul Pickering emerges from the crowd in a #SaveOurDairy waistcoat he's had made up. He has a team of helpers, each with an award-winning Paddock Poo-Picker, clogs of cow dung removed from the streets with revolutionary efficiency, much to Charlie's relief.

He mobilizes the crowd behind him, chanting with gusto. *'Milk! Milk! They're milking our milk!'*

The fog starts to clear as our following swells, the first glimmer of sunlight piercing thick cloud. A pantomime cow trundles along beside me with some very enthusiastic inhabitants, judging by the moos. Our chants get louder, our voices bigger.

*'Milk! Milk! They're milking our milk!'*

We reach the main road, where a dual carriageway of heavy traffic blocks the way to our destination. Grandma attempts to negotiate with a bus, which ploughs through a puddle, spraying her with muddy water. The whole procession comes to a standstill.

'Hang on!' Tazzy charges through the masses in her road-safe fluorescent overcoat, lollipop held high. 'I'm not having anyone die on my watch, whether it's cows or humans.' Undeterred by beeping lorries and irate drivers, she plants herself in the centre of the road, a modern-day Moses parting a sea of traffic, and doesn't leave until every last one of us is over.

Faces peer out of tower blocks. Passengers stare from the top deck of buses. A hen party of girls dressed as Wonder Woman join us, recruiting shoppers and passers-by.

*'Milk! Milk! They're milking our milk!'*

As we reach the Peace Gardens, Rosie bolts towards a balloon seller, a dozen helium-filled silver Tyrannosaurus Rexes floating into the sky.

'Sorry!' I shout.

'You ignorant prick!' the balloon seller yells, holding a paper cup of tea in one hand and a bunch of inflatable dinosaurs in the other.

'I'm really sorry,' I say again, holding onto Rosie for dear life.

'You will be!' He launches his cup at me; hot tea drips from my eyelashes and runs down my cheeks. I wipe my face with my elbow, suffused with shock. 'What the fuck do you think you're doing, letting cows shit all over the place?' He sticks his neck out at me. 'Hey? Hey?' he shouts aggressively.

'That's enough!' The pantomime cow next to me rips off its head to reveal none other than Nathan, hair plastered to his forehead, his face red and sweaty. 'Did you have soy milk in that tea, lad?' He jabs his finger at the paper cup, which rolls across the pedestrianized street.

The balloon seller stares at him as if he's speaking a foreign language.

'Was that soy milk in your tea?' Nathan persists.

'It was just normal milk.'

'Well, if you want to carry on drinking normal milk in your tea, you'd better join in!' Nathan delves in his pockets and pulls out a ten-pound note. 'Here, sorry about your balloons,' he says, handing it to the guy.

'*Milk! Milk! They're milking our milk!*'

The balloon seller takes the money and storms off.

'You OK?' Nathan says to me.

I nod, dumbfounded.

'I'm sorry,' he says. 'Some of the things I said were unforgivable.'

For me, it's not what Nathan said, it's what he didn't say. If he's prepared to go all out with paedophilia accusations and tell me to my face that I'm offensive, who knows what deeper, darker homophobia lies beneath the surface. Call it paranoia, but I think I have a healthy wariness. I find myself unable to reply and am about to turn away when he puts his hoof on my arm.

'I'm ashamed of myself,' he says.

So there I am, in the middle of the march, surfing that fine line I'm quite familiar with now; the line between sweep-it-under-the-carpet, 'let's forget about it, it's all in the past now' forgiveness and allowing the conversation to breathe, as painful as it is, and make sure everything is properly dealt with and it's not going to rear its ugly head again.

'Where did the change of heart come from?' I say, acknowledging Grandma's *Are you OK?* look with one saying, *Yeah, I'm fine.*

'Rachel,' he says.

'Hi!' Her head appears from the back of their costume. 'I don't know how you did an assault course in this thing. I can hardly breathe!'

'You've been in the back of that all this way?' I say.

She looks at Nathan just as we arrive at the gardens next to Sheffield's town hall. 'I didn't want to be seen with Dad!'

Nathan shuffles me over to a bed of begonias and clears his throat. 'I'm sorry. Rachel gave me a good talking-to after that last committee meeting. Said I had to get with the "real world" and accept people for who they are.'

'Right,' I say as the crowd sweeps past us.

'He is sorry.' Rachel grabs my arm. 'He knows he's been a dick, don't you, Dad?'

Nathan mumbles something incoherent as the town hall's clock tower clangs to strike the hour.

I turn to him. 'Look, it's not that I'm terribly uninterested, it's just that we're in the middle of the biggest dairy farming march in history.'

'Sure,' he says. 'I just . . . I'm sorry. I'm going to be a better person. Not just for Rachel, but for you, because you didn't deserve that.'

'Apology noted,' I breathe. 'Now, I've really got to go.'

Nathan shrugs his shoulders and smiles.

'*Milk! Milk! They're milking our milk!*'

I catch sight of Dad through the crowds; he's flagging. His march has become a shuffle and he's stopping at every other lamppost to catch his breath. I reach him. His face looks a translucent white.

'Can't you sit down for a bit?' I say, gesturing to the wheelchair Grandma is pushing.

'No!' he says with fervent determination and stomps on.

**@MilkforFarmers**
Never *herd* of us? Check out our moooovement
#SaveOurDairy

Dad is just about done for by the time we've pushed our way to the front. He sits down heavily on a bench next to a lady surrounded by shopping bags and takes a swig of Lucozade. There are now thousands of us spilling out into the town hall's Peace Gardens. Children point and giggle from their fathers' shoulders as Friesians lap from water fountains. I look around for someone who might look like a journalist, but it's impossible to tell who's who, what with all the different groups congregating. Cows grunt. Farmers chant. Picket board slogans bob up and down in the air. *Keep calm and hug a heifer. Milk a cow, not a farmer. Talk is cheap, milk shouldn't be. Keep Britain farming.*

'Here!' Maria digs her hand into her satchel and holds up a cow-print bikini. 'Outfits for the photoshoot! I've got mine on already.' She twangs the black elastic around her neck.

'What on earth's that?' Grandma squints.

'It's a bikini,' Maria says.

Grandma holds it up. 'Where in God's name do you put your chest?'

'In the triangles, Grandma.' I demonstrate with a fist.

'We need to draw maximum attention,' Maria says, reaching into her bag and pulling out another three.

'You'll be doing more than that,' Grandma says gruffly. 'You'll have someone's eye out!'

I look at the bikinis and then at the crowd. 'I think that might draw the wrong sort of attention, Maz.'

Maria looks at me. 'What was I saying earlier? All publicity's good publicity.'

We all look at each other.

'Nobody wants to see me in a bikini.' Bev plants her hands in her pockets.

'I do,' Kat protests.

'Bilbo?' Maria flings a bikini at me.

The only place I would wear a bikini is on the beach and, even then, I wouldn't be comfortable. I shove it in my pocket as Maria points out the arrival of the press. Several newspapers have sent photographers as well as reporters. They set up just out of reach of the spray of the fountains.

I weave my way through the crowd to Dad just as someone from BBC *Look North* is thrusting a microphone in front of him, a cameraman hovering. He's back on his feet and surrounded by farmers and friends of all shapes and sizes – young, trim men in designer jeans, girls who could just as easily be off the perfume counter at John Lewis, and those who fulfil the farmer stereotype in wax jackets and wellies.

'What do I make of it or from it?' Dad says crossly. 'Not

enough, and that's the problem. British dairy farmers are running at a loss. As things are, it's unsustainable, unethical and unworkable.'

'Hear, hear!' Paul puts down his Poo-Picker and twists the buttons on his waistcoat.

I look around and I'm surrounded by so many familiar faces from the village. Tazzy, Doreen, Marjorie and Graham. Hamish Eccles from Ladybower. Roger Craggs from Birchover Hall Farm. Rachel, Nathan. The locksmith, the blacksmith, the co-operative staff.

'We're not asking for a lot. We just want *enough*,' Dad says into the microphone. 'Enough.' He autopilots like a battery-operated toy jammed on the wrong setting. 'Enough.' Bewilderment spreads across his face. He looks like a cat in water, panicked and bedraggled.

I take hold of his arm. 'Dad?'

'Enough,' he repeats as I twist my way into his armpit.

'He's not well,' I say to the BBC *Look North* guy, whilst propping Dad up.

'Sorry,' Dad says. 'It's taken it out of me.'

I'm not sure what to do. Or what I'm supposed to say. A sharp pain jabs at my chest. I should never have started this. I should have made Dad sit down earlier. Another sharp jab. I look down and realize Mum's ladybird brooch is stabbing me with its pin.

I grab the microphone. 'We need Premier Milk to stop dropping milk prices. We need the supermarkets to stock our Milk for Farmers brand and we need the people of Great Britain to buy it,' I tell the microphone. 'Not next year, not next month, but today! Five British farmers quit every week.

Five! In the last ten years, a quarter of British dairy farms have vanished. We're an endangered species under threat of extinction.' *Project from your stomach. Two mirrored hands.* 'This is my dad. He's been a dairy farmer all his life.' *This is not a use-case. This is a real story.* I think of Professor Williams and my failed PhD pitch. Me, blathering on about Mum dying. *Tell us what your father lost. Tell us how it happened and what we need to do to make sure it doesn't happen to anybody else.* 'He's sixty-three and, like so many other farmers, can't afford to retire. He's been working fifteen-hour days most of his life, seven days a week. He's lost equity. He's lost profits. He's lost a lot of the herd. And most recently he lost his health.'

'Go, Bilbo!' Maria shouts.

'Hear, hear!' Hamish Eccles shouts, which encourages swathes of people to grunt in solidarity.

Applause ripples across the Peace Gardens and I feel a huge surge of pride.

'People can help by buying Milk for Farmers branded milk. Look out for the "Fair for Farmers" guarantee label. For the sake of a few pence—'

'Thank you, Miss, erm . . .'

'Billie. Billie Oliver and my dad, John Oliver.' I look up at Dad, who is gazing into the distance.

'Thank you, Billie and Oliver. Back to you in the studio, Gary.'

As soon as the cameraman cuts, I help Dad into the wheelchair. He's already asleep by the time Rachel has worked out how to put the brakes on.

'Here, young man?' Beatrice nudges a photographer from the *Sheffield Telegraph.* 'Will we make the front page?'

'Page twenty-eight under the horoscope's more likely,' he says, turning to see what all the whooping and squealing over by the fountains is about.

'Come on, girls!' Maria yells, dancing through arcs of water in her cow-print bikini. 'I thought we were in this together?'

'To think of everything the suffragettes did for women's rights!' Beatrice scoffs.

'There are more of you?' The photographer loads a new memory card into his camera.

'You bloody bet!' Maria shouts. 'Billie?'

The photographer looks at us. 'Three of you dressed like that and I can't see how you *wouldn't* make the front page!'

'Hear, hear!' Charlie mutters.

'Billie! Billie!' the girls chant, as the cowpat-splattered earth fails to swallow me up. The angel and devil dance in my head, both of them wearing cow-print bikinis, neither of them distinguishable from each other. What would Billie Jean King do at a time like this? Would she compromise her feminist values for a headline-grabbing bikini shot? I feel like a groom on a stag do being forced into drinking a pint of vodka, tequila and rum: it will hurt both now and in the sober light of tomorrow when the photos are unleashed.

'I'll do it if you will!' a voice shouts.

The crowd parts to reveal Lorna Parsons, who stands before me in a trilby hat, a #SaveOurDairy T-shirt, cut-off denim shorts and cowboy boots. She offers me her hand.

I'm struck by a warm fuzzy sensation.

'I didn't even know you were here!' I say.

'Come on,' she says, friendly but reserved.

She tucks her long, mousy-blonde hair behind one ear,

grabs a bikini from Maria and takes my arm. 'I know this is your idea of hell, Billie, and trust me, it's not my idea of fun either.' She marches me across the gardens. 'But it clearly works.'

I find her presence comforting, in spite of the tense atmosphere. This is the first time I've seen her since our kiss and here we are, standing at the foot of the town hall steps, pretending nothing ever happened. I feel utterly confused. On the one hand, I've known her for decades and shared part of my childhood with her. Tree houses, holly-bush dens, French skipping, farm worker picnics, bull sperm. On the other hand, I don't know her at all.

I look at her. 'I've been wondering how you were.'

'We haven't got time for all that now.' She marches up the steps, eyes firmly on the big wooden door to the town hall.

I try to slow her down. 'Don't we need to talk about—'

'I think it's better that we don't,' she says, holding the door open.

Inside, wedding guests are tumbling out of a wood-panelled room.

'From memory, the toilets are down here,' she says, leading me down a corridor and, true to her word, depositing us at the Ladies'.

I follow her in, expecting it to be a washroom with a few cubicles, but it's just the one toilet.

'Sorry,' I say, backing out.

She grabs my arm and pulls me back inside. 'There's no time for you to wait.'

She locks the door, turns her back to me and starts fastening her bikini under her T-shirt. Next thing I know, she's whipping off her bra and shimmying out of her jeans. I'm still playing

301

catch-up. The last time we saw each other, we had our hands on each other's breasts and our tongues in each other's mouths and now we're to undress in front of each other and pretend the whole thing never happened?

'Come on, this might just get us on the front page.' She pulls on the bikini bottoms and removes her T-shirt. 'Well?' she says, hurling my bikini at me. 'What are you waiting for?'

'I . . .' She looks so fucking hot it's ridiculous.

'It's up to you, Billie!' she says. 'You can either die on the sword for your principles and we're some postage-stamp-sized entry on page thirty-seven of some shitty newspaper nobody ever reads, or you can swallow your pride and go for the front page of the broadsheets.'

Aside from Grandma, nobody has spoken to me like this since my Home Economics teacher at secondary school.

'I . . .' Are we going to pretend that we never kissed?

She stands, arms folded, leaning against the wall, one leg cocked, and I want to kiss her. I want to put my hands around her waist. I want to feel the heat of her skin. I want all of these things, but she clearly doesn't. I exhale heavily and reluctantly pull on the bikini, deciding that Billie Jean King probably *would* do it. She did, after all, agree to be carried into Houston Astrodome on a gold throne by a bunch of bare-chested hunky men in the name of feminism.

We make our way over the grass in bikinis and raincoats, back to the photographers. All I can think about is kissing Lorna in the cowshed. Her hot skin. Her groin pressed against mine. Our eyes having a conversation of their own.

The crowd has got bigger since we got changed and the demonstration is now under the surveillance of the mounted police, whose horses are being admired by a huge man in a cream linen suit that only serves to accentuate his girth, creases forming where the material strains over each bulge: the Wolf.

I throw a 'Hi' in his direction, but he ignores me. His thick neck turns towards a photographer from the *Yorkshire Post*. 'Where do you want me?' he says gruffly.

'Not you, her!' The photographer nods at me. 'The Cow Girl.'

His words hang in the air like bunting, celebratory and proud. *Cow Girl*. They buffet in the breeze, gathering force and momentum like a kite. *Cow Girl*. It makes me sound like some kind of Jane Austen heroine of the hills, which I'm clearly not, but it certainly has a ring to it. I try the name on for size, and whilst I'm dogged by imposter syndrome, I can't deny that it feels good.

'I can get the cows in as a backdrop if you two ladies join your friend in the fountains.' He gestures to Maria, who is dancing under the spray of a water feature.

'This is meant to be a dairy farming campaign!' the Wolf howls. 'Not something from the Folies bleeding Bergères.'

'It is.' Lorna drops her coat. 'But there's no point in having some fuddy-duddy civil servant scrutinize the paperwork behind closed doors. We need the Great British Public to buy our Milk for Farmers milk.' She throws her arm around me and yells, 'Milk, milk, they're milking our milk!'

I throw my coat at Bev, my body jerking with cold.

'Great!' the photographer says. 'And if the three of you could link arms. Fantastic. That's it! All say *moooo!*'

'Moooo!' we scream through gritted teeth – the water is bone-stingingly freezing.

'You're a disgrace!' the Wolf yells. 'You should be a-bleeding-shamed of yourself.'

Click, click, click. We sell our souls for the price of milk.

The Wolf snatches the petition and stomps towards the town hall offices.

'Take no notice of him, Billie Goat. You've done great.' Grandma wraps me back in my coat and hugs me to her chest, and I feel safe and soothed against her soft, dappled skin, chlorinated water drying in the folds between us.

'Well done, Bell Ender.' Graham holds his hand out for me to shake. 'Never thought I'd say it, but that was an absolute triumph.'

'Fantastic!' Tazzy wants a hug.

'Good work!' Hamish Eccles shakes my hand.

People are flocking around me and I can't tell who's who any more.

'All hail the Cow Girl!'

A sense of satisfaction builds within me. I feel a mixture of relief and hope, pride and elation. I watch Lorna disappear into the crowd, her trilby getting smaller and smaller.

'*Cow – Girl – Cow – Girl – Cow – Girl!*' they chant.

Marjorie waddles over with tears in her eyes. She reaches out and adjusts the lucky ladybird brooch on my chest. 'Well done, Billie love. Your mother would've been proud.'

Words stick in my throat and my eyes fill with tears. Marjorie Pearce has called me 'Billie love' for the first time in eighteen years. Lorna is talking to me. The march has been a success. I allow myself the satisfaction of feeling content in Marjorie's embrace until I realize there's one thing missing.

'Where's Dad?' I say.

'*Cow – Girl – Cow – Girl – Cow – Girl!*'

'Where's Dad?'

'*Cow – Girl – Cow – Girl – Cow – Girl!*'

'I need my dad!' I shout.

The crowd parts as Grandma pushes Dad towards me in the wheelchair. His body trembles as the wheels judder over uneven grass.

'Dad!'

He's awake, just. His left cheek bears the imprint of the wheelchair frame. His fingers are interlocked, as they always are when he's asleep, the sleeves of his jumper trailing from his lap. His eyes light up when he sees me and, for a second, I think he's going to leap out of the wheelchair and dance with exhilaration; but even if he could, Dad's never been a showman. Instead he holds out his arms. 'You did it, Bilberry! You did it!'

I grasp his hands in mine. '*We* did it!'

# CHAPTER EIGHTEEN

# THE MASKED BALL

**From: Rachel Fletcher**
Thanks for hearing my dad out. He's genuinely mortified.

**To: Rachel Fletcher**
Don't worry, he'll come around! Failing that, take him to see *La Cage aux Folles*. It worked for my grandma.

The next day, Lorna, Maria and I are plastered over the front page of three of the main broadsheets. Within the space of a week, one big supermarket chain has already signed up to our Milk for Farmers scheme and the marketing people are in discussions with two more. It's about time. Premier Milk has committed to increase milk prices by 1p per litre; although it's only a small win, it's a step in the right direction. There remains, however, the small matter of negotiating the farm's freehold – something of a challenge considering that Huxley-Lipyeat hasn't yet forgiven me for the bikini stunt.

A week after the march, we sit opposite each other in the Bakewell community centre's otherwise empty hall. For the first time, I'm actually on the stage with him at the big table.

'*Cow Girl*, the papers are calling you.' He looks at me through piggy eyes. '*Cow Girl*, my arse. What sort of person takes a cheap shot with a bikini?'

The faint buzz of a wasp comes and goes despite it being November.

'It got us on the front cover of every paper,' I say, taking a sip of water from my Evian bottle. 'Including the broadsheets.'

'It got *you* on the front cover of every paper. Not *us*.' He rearranges his belt, bloated flesh overhanging his waistband.

The smell of sweat hangs in the air. Aside from an abandoned badminton net lying on the side of a court previously hosting mixed doubles, it's just me and him. And a wasp.

'I admit the written articles could have been better, but that's not why I wanted to meet. I need to talk to you about Fernbrook's freehold.' He looks at me like I'm a parasite.

'My dad's been through a lot and . . .' I look up at the corner of the ceiling and there's the wasp, looping and burring, its legs dangling lethargically behind. 'The farm's too much for him. He wants to sell up. Downsize. Look after a couple of cows and experiment with cheese.' The Wolf rolls a blunt pencil between his chipolata fingers. 'Of course, we can't sell without topping up the lease or buying the freehold.'

The Wolf clears his throat, dislodging phlegm. 'I think you'll find we've been through all this before.' The wasp lands on his pencil and crawls towards his thumbnail. 'I've quoted your father a fair price and he wasn't interested.'

'You quoted him three hundred thousand for the freehold.'

He bats the wasp away with a slab of hand. 'Which is more than fair for five hundred acres. He also has the option of paying less to top the lease up to ninety-nine years.'

The wasp hovers above his head before landing in his thick white curls.

'Careful!' I gesture to the wasp. 'It's in your . . .'

He swats at it again, dandruff showering onto his shoulders. It'll be a miracle if neither of us gets stung.

I lean back. 'You quoted one hundred and twenty grand to top up the lease, which puts us in a bit of a pickle as we can't afford either option.' The wasp climbs into his empty glass. 'I was hoping we might negotiate.' His chubby fingers grab the base of the glass, flip it over and capture the wasp in one fell swoop. The wasp crawls slowly up the inside of the glass. 'My dad's an ill man. I'm not sure he'll be able to go back to full-time farming.'

'I'm sure you'll find a way. You seem to be quite good at looking out for yourself.'

Oxygen-deprived, the wasp starts to tire, its antennae desperately seeking a way out.

The Wolf shuffles his paperwork. 'Meeting dismissed.'


Sheffield's Winter Gardens stand in the city centre, sandwiched between the Millennium Galleries and the Peace Gardens. A huge temperate glasshouse filled with hundreds of plants from all over the world, it's the sort of place you *ooh* and *aah* over a begonia rather than attend a singles night. I smooth Mum's halter-neck dress over my hips, catching the faint musk of what must have been her. The dress is so *not me*. It feels as if I should sing twee songs to woodland animals dressed in little felt jackets in the manner of Snow White. Or kiss a man in a raincoat. I never did get the chance to make a headdress and can't decide whether the satin sleeping mask that Maria sent me looks OK with eye-holes cut into it, or whether I look like roadkill. I run my fingers over the ladybird brooch for reassurance.

'Better the Devil You Know' plays through speakers carefully camouflaged by lustrous ferns. A waitress in an ostrich-feathered headdress checks me in on her iPad, her acrylic nails tapping on the screen. She hands me a sticker that reads 'Angel6'.

'You couldn't tell me if Angel3 is already here, could you?' I say, trying to suppress the desperation in my voice.

'Not yet,' she says, moving her phosphorescent beaded nail tips down the screen. 'We always get plenty of latecomers, though. Everyone needs a bit of Dutch courage!'

'Thanks.'

Anticipation and eucalyptus hang in the air. I help myself to a white-wine spritzer and smile at a girl with a Devil1 sticker caught in her unruly dark hair. It's greenhouse hot in here and I feel like I'm going to pass out. There's no sign of Darth Vader, just an atrium of strangers making mindless chitchat.

A lady with the yellowy-green shine of a recovering black eye taps a metal spoon against a glass and ushers us into the basement for speed dating. At least it's several degrees cooler downstairs. The tables are dressed with scented candles and love-heart confetti. She and the barman have a bit of a hoo-ha about whether the devils should stay at their table and the angels rotate, or vice versa. He points out that, either way, angels won't meet angels and devils won't get to meet devils;

something they appear to have overlooked, having only ever run straight events previously. She holds up an acrylic nail whilst thinking it through, and it's like watching someone trying to work out whether the clocks are going forward or backward, or whether the tide is in or out. Eventually we're mixed up, a scramble of angels and devils.

My first date is Devil3, who smells of Deep Heat and explains that she can only stay forty minutes and doesn't really expect to meet anyone. I refrain from agreeing with her.

The bell rings a few minutes later, punctuating the arrival of my second date: a girl in a laced corset, who moans about the one-way system around Ponds Forge, and then has a sneezing fit. My third date comprises a nostalgic run through what chocolate bars were popular when we were kids, allowing me to ascertain that she is three decades older than me.

I'm ready to go home by the time I'm on to the fifth date, until she proves to be a black-cloaked figure in a Darth Vader mask.

'*May the force be with you.*'

'Angel3?' I readjust my feathers.

She gathers her cloak, revealing a killer figure silhouetted by a tight black roll-neck and skinny jeans. She wears fuck-me heels and has an aura of self-assurance; maybe it's the cloak. Slowly, she sits down opposite me and presses the button underneath her mouthpiece.

'*Luke, we meet at last.*' Her breath smells of Parma Violets. A few seconds go by.

'So, Angel3, what do you sound like without the Darth mask?' I say.

'Like this,' she says, in a very familiar voice.

310

A strong metallic taste lingers in my mouth. 'Lorna?'

'Billie.' She removes her disguise.

I rip off my mask. 'But you said you were American!'

'I said nothing of the sort!'

'But, but . . .' Heat travels from my breastbone, branching out across my chest and creeping up my neck until it feels as though I'm wearing an invisible itchy scarf. 'You said you were an artist and you spell 'color' without a "u."'

'American language settings, and I am an artist. You've known me for years and never asked how I spend my spare time. You've never asked what my favourite chocolate bar is. Whether I've ever been speed-dating. You've not once shown any interest in me or taken the time to understand who I am,' she says, her neck reddening.

I assess her like you would a new pound coin, looking for everything that's changed since its last version. 'I'm sorry.'

The speed-dating hostess looks over and taps at her face to suggest we should put our masks back on.

Lorna gathers her cloak. 'I think we need to talk!'

'I think you're right.'

We get up and leave, much to the delight of the barman, who springs to life, opening doors for us and winking.

We stumble out, pumped up and confused.

The nearest pub is The Graduate, a dimly lit establishment full of students hammering flavoured cider around a jukebox and snogging each other over the pool table. A stag party of twenty-somethings in printed polo shirts with wacky nicknames jeer and clap as Tiddler, their groom-to-be, freebases a dubious cocktail of something dark brown provided by his rotund sidekick.

'Vodka?' I suggest as we reach the bar.

'Double.'

I feel a bit like you do when you discover Father Christmas isn't real – everything slowly falling into place: the different wrapping paper, the different writing on the tags, the disappearance of mince pies and sherry. The carrots for Rudolph with teeth marks. I feel a bit foolish and can't quite catch up.

She ties her mousy-blonde hair into a ponytail and smiles, freckles dancing on her nose. 'I didn't have much time,' she says apologetically, tugging at her top.

I pull myself onto the stool next to her. 'You look great.' I think about her online personality. How hot-headed and witty she sounds, yet how cold and aloof she can be in the flesh. Polar opposites meshed together on a bar stool in front of me.

'You too,' she says. 'I've never seen you in a dress.'

'OK, so I'm still playing catch-up.' My halter-neck digs in around my neck each time I shift. 'What are you doing at a gay singles night?'

The barman places two large vodka and limes in front of us.

She picks up her tumbler. 'Sorry?'

I smooth the scratchy material of my dress over my thighs. 'Well, you've always been quite anti this sort of thing.'

She knocks back her double vodka in one go and slams the glass back on the bar. 'What sort of thing?'

'Being gay and single.' I sip my vodka, wondering how she did hers in one hit, the bitter-sweet fire burning the back of my throat.

She laughs. 'Billie, I've been gay and single for most of my adult life!'

I squint at her in a way that you might suddenly question the spelling of a familiar word. 'What about Guy?'

'He's my partner. My *business* partner.' She pushes her glass towards the barman and gestures for a refill.

I stare at her. Every detail of her face suddenly seems more important. 'But you live together?'

'We flat-share,' she says, accidentally triggering Darth Vader's electronic voice.

I confiscate the mask, throwing it under my stool. 'I'm sorry, I'm still . . .' I shake my head, thinking it all through. Lorna asking me about my girlfriends. Lorna turning her nose up at Joely. And at Neve before that.

'I like to keep my personal life private,' Lorna says, dusting her finger in a bowl of roasted peanut crumbs. 'You wouldn't believe the amount of village gossip that does the rounds. It's honestly easier when people think I'm with Guy. You met Jessica, though.'

I think back to the hoof-trimming accident and my bleeding hands. 'You were going out with Jessica?'

She nods.

'I thought you were just friends!'

Lorna laughs as I bristle at the thought of her with another woman, realizing that for years I've dismissed Lorna as some minor annoyance, based on her brusque comments and curt put-me-downs, when all she was trying to do was flirt.

I finish my vodka and look at her. 'We probably need to talk about that kiss.'

'We probably do.' She looks me straight in the eye, her face all perky and fresh. 'Though I don't want to get in the way of you and Joely.'

'Me and Joely?'

'This is where I ask *you* why *you're* at a gay singles night.'

'I'm not with Joely, if that's what you're getting at.'

Her eyes narrow.

'We split up pretty much the moment I took on the farm.'

Her face hardens. 'Not true. She was sending flowers and postcards not so long ago, and after you kissed me, you told me you felt like a dick.'

'The flowers were from my friends, and Joely had already finished with me before that postcard arrived in the snail mail from Korea.' I move my glass around the bar mat in circles. 'Never post anything home from Seoul – it takes weeks! And for the record, I said I felt like a dick because Guy saw us and I thought you were together.'

She studies me. 'So, you don't have feelings for her?'

Feeling nothing for Joely is like the average woman feeling nothing for Don Draper. 'We're not right for each other,' I reply diplomatically.

'Did you pop the question?' she says.

My eyes widen. 'Pop the question?'

'I saw the ring box,' she says. 'Addressed to Joely Goddess.'

'It wasn't a ring,' I say, almost too quickly. 'I bought her a ladybird pendant for her birthday, which I never gave her. Turns out she hates ladybirds.'

'Bullshit. Nobody hates ladybirds.' Her eyes shift around the room. 'OK, so here goes. I get tongue-tied around you because I like you, Billie. I've always liked you. I think you're bloody brilliant. That's why I say and do the most inappropriate things around you.'

An overwhelming sense of happiness glows inside me.

314

'So, what do we do now?' She squeezes my knee.

I reach under her cloak and slide my arm around her waist. She tenses up, her back straightening, her collarbone rising. I feel like liquid. Thick and sludgy at first and then, as I lean towards her, everything dilutes, sloshing and swirling out of control. I press my lips against hers and kiss her.

Ten stags raise their glasses to us and cheer.

We kiss again.

## CHAPTER NINETEEN

# KAT AND BEAR'S WEDDING

A few days later, and Lorna and I have agreed that we are 'seeing where it takes us'. Today has taken us back to her flat, which, contrary to preconceptions, is not a wall-to-wall shrine of rosettes and show-jumping trophies, but contemporary cool with retro neon signs, statement sofas and shedloads of vinyl. Her loft conversion bedroom has a living area and an en-suite, which means that the only time we risk bumping into Guy is when he's in the kitchen, which is not very often as he's not the most culinary of men. He does, however, think up every excuse under the sun to come upstairs in the hope of catching us 'at it'.

'Lorn, do you have a hot-water bottle?' he booms.

She looks up at me, her head in my lap, her legs dangling over the arm of her two-seater sofa. 'Just ignore him. He's a pervert.'

'Do you actually get on with him?' I say, tucking her hair behind her ears.

'I think I feel sorry for him.' She sighs, staring at the ceiling and hugging a pillow to her chest. 'His parents don't know who he is, and at times I'm not sure that he does. They're in a home. Alzheimer's.'

I run my fingers over the scar on her forehead. 'You know I always thought you disapproved of me.'

'How so, Shit Angel?' She strokes my arm.

'Outing me to all Grandma's friends at bridge club for starters.'

She sits bolt upright. 'I thought they knew!'

'Only Grandma and Beatrice.'

'Shit, I'm sorry,' she says, burying her head in her hands.

'Then there was that newspaper article on London gay saunas you gave to my dad, remember that?' I say, rolling my eyes.

'No?'

'It wasn't that long ago!'

'I remember cutting out an article on genomics for you.' Her face crumples. 'Oh Jesus, is that what was printed on the other side?'

'You have no idea how much anguish you caused my dad!' I laugh.

Then within seconds, something inside me switches and there it is: the elephant in the room that is the bull sperm incident. Part of me wants to bury it deep inside and pretend it never happened, but it's too late, I've projected the thoughts now and the atmosphere has become tense. I stare at the carpet. 'We should probably talk about the time when—'

'I never breathed a word,' she blurts. 'It was all Andy.'

Quick as a flash I turn to face her. 'Andy didn't go to our school!'

317

'No, but his mates from judo did.'

I throw myself back on the sofa. 'You realize there are people who still think that's why I'm gay?'

'What do you mean?'

'My auntie June maintains I'd be straight, had I not been so traumatized by the whole sperm experience.'

'No disrespect, but your auntie June is bat shit.'

It's only when she laughs that perspective sets in and I realize I've been carrying around this dead weight of humiliation for the best part of seventeen years, whilst nobody else has given a damn and the only people who can remember are not exactly the benchmark for 'sane'. A ball of shame on an invisible chain. All those moments I thought Lorna had one over on me. All those times I imagined she was thinking about it. I've allowed the whole thing to grow completely out of proportion. Talking about it out loud, all these years later, I know I sound ridiculously tetchy. At the end of the day, Andy Pickering was just some bored, hormonal teenager and Lorna just happened to be there. She didn't start the rumours. She didn't find it funny. She just witnessed it; guilty by association. And as for Andy Pickering, his reputation will forever be in the gutter since he got charged with sheep rustling.

Lorna rolls against me and pulls her fingers through my hair. 'You know, there were so many times I wanted to kiss you.'

'Example?' I trace her face with my forefinger.

We lie facing each other, propped up on our elbows. Our eyes are now inches from each other's, our mouths a fraction closer. 'When I was deworming the cattle and you had a little cry. At the Ridgecroft Country Show in the pantomime cow suit. At your auntie and uncle's vow renewals.'

'I seem to remember thinking I repulsed you then.'

'Why?'

'That dirty look you gave me when—'

'When you were kissing Joely?'

'Yes.'

She chews her fingernails. 'Yeah. I didn't much like that.'

'I can't imagine you being jealous,' I say, taking her hand and placing it on my waist.

'There was another time, which you probably won't remember, but I'll never forget.' She closes her eyes and grimaces at the memory. 'At the #SaveOurDairy event in London and I had to present you with the Milker's Booby Prize rosette . . .'

'And practically stabbed me in the chest!' I say.

She opens her eyes. 'I know it was awful. I was awful.'

I look into her big, grey eyes and wonder whether 'taking things slowly' is a solid enough foundation for asking her to accompany me to Kat and Bev's wedding. The Louis de Bernières passage that Bev and Kat want me to read talks about love being a volcanic temporary madness followed by an enduring friendship once the passion subsides. Are my roots entwined with Lorna's, or am I in love with the idea of being in love? Did the Queen have this dilemma when she started dating Prince Philip?

I run my fingers across the horseshoe-shaped scar on her forehead, which has been there ever since I've known her, but I've never asked her about.

'How did you get this?' I say, studying the silvery pink line. 'I mean, I know you got kicked by a horse, but . . .'

'A foal.' She lifts her hand to it. 'I was thirteen and got way too close. You never came to the livery, did you?'

319

'I've never felt a connection with horses,' I say. 'Give me cows any day. You know where you stand with cows. They're less temperamental.'

A row of paintings hangs on the wall next to the bookcase. Watercolours of sand dunes. Poppy fields and oak trees. A march hare in long grass.

'Is this your stuff?' I say, and then momentarily panic that I've just revealed myself as an art philistine and that this is the work of a famous artist I've never heard of.

She nods, thank fuck.

'They're great,' I say. 'Do you have any more?'

She gets up, takes a heavy hessian-bound book off the bookshelf and plonks it on my lap. The hard, scratchy cover pulls at my tights. I open it. Sketch after sketch of women entwined: women entwined on the grassy edge of a brook, women entwined in a Victorian bathing pond, women entwined to form the gnarly skeleton of a dead tree, women entwined on lily pads floating on a green-blue pond. All of them naked. They're amazing – art gallery amazing. The sort of paintings that transport you places and make you feel that you too are lying on a river bank on a summer's day, surrounded by nymphs, long grass tickling your back, your bare feet touching cold, wet rock.

She peers over my shoulder at her work. 'Eighteen months ago, I had a bit of a midlife crisis and decided I'd had enough of sticking my hands up cows' bottoms. I started applying for Fine Art courses all over the place.'

'And?'

'And I got on a course at the University of Washington,' she says.

'Washington DC?'

'Yes.'

I turn to face her. 'You're going to Washington?'

'The course started three months ago. A vet from Hathersage was going to buy out my half of the business and I was going to start afresh but . . .' She stares at the carpet and chews on her lip. 'OK, you were a big part of why I stayed.'

'Really?'

Her eyes flick back to mine. 'I got cold feet about leaving. I love this part of the world and the business was going well. And then there was you. You'd just found out about your dad and leaving didn't feel right.'

Warmth fills my core.

'I was supposed to sign over the business the day I was deworming your cattle, but I couldn't.' She looks into my eyes. 'I do think rather a lot of you, you know.'

I feel fuzzy inside, a bit like I did when Dad said I could have my first pet. 'Thank you.'

'Lorn?' Guy's voice booms from below.

She ignores him, which I figure gives me carte blanche to slide my fingertip under her bra strap and trace the contours of her collarbone. She kisses me. My finger zigs and zags down her sternum. Her chest rises as I brush my hands over the curves of her breasts, and she kisses me harder.

'Lorn!' Guy bangs on the door. 'Belinda's car's blocking me in.'

We giggle like schoolgirls.

'One sec,' I shout, kissing her again.

When I get outside, I realize the Land Rover's got a flat tyre. I manage to reverse enough for Guy to get his car out, but it pulls hard left and feels all baggy. Lorna taps on the window. 'Have you got a jack?'

'I've no idea.' I instantly feel like a moron.

She opens the boot, rummages under the fake floor, locates both the spare tyre and a drawstring bag containing a jack, and has the Land Rover hoisted and secured within seconds.

'Pry bar wrench?' she demands, holding out her hand.

I tentatively hand her what may or may not be a pry bar wrench and am relieved when she crouches down unquestioningly and removes each lug nut, one at a time.

'Spare?' she says, blowing dirt off her hands.

I roll the spare tyre over to her, which she fits before I've got the flat one back in the boot. She's bloody amazing. A-Team amazing.

'Thank you,' I say. 'And if you don't mind, I've another favour to ask.'

'Shoot.'

I look into her eyes. 'Would you come with me to Bev and Kat's wedding?'

She throws her arms around my neck. 'I'd love to!'

Everything seems to have clicked into place with Lorna. She's relaxed. I'm relaxed. It feels so good not having to walk on eggshells, constantly worried about my appearance, my lack of polish, my lack of interest in glossy magazines and designer homeware. Looking back on it, dating Joely was pretty exhausting. Straightforwardness is so refreshing. Why have I pissed away so many years second-guessing girls?

*

When Dad finishes his course of radiotherapy in early December, we buy a lopsided Christmas tree from a man on the corner at Longshaw in celebration. The dusty box of decorations on top of Grandma's wardrobe comes up trumps with garish baubles and squashed pinecones spray-painted gold. At the bottom of the box, in a bed of blue tinsel, sits my mother's painted metal nutcracker – devoid of arms, legs and facial features. The golden thread that once stemmed from the centre of his tin helmet has been replaced with a loop of pale blue cotton. I pick it up and press its cold body into the palm of my hand and wonder what my mother would look like now.

I would like to think that she'd be one of those cool mothers who dress like a rock star, swear with carefree abandon, and don't dye their hair. She'd have great taste in music, educating me on the latest indie bands, inviting me to gigs, swapping vinyl. She'd love Dolly Parton, for sure. We'd talk about anything and everything over a pot of tea: travel, politics, our plans for the future, Dolly. She'd be perky and fun. As much a friend as a mother. She'd be sixty-one years old.

'How's about fish and chips tonight?' Grandma says, trying to rescue tinsel from the jaws of Speedo. 'I could get Bea round and we could make a bit of a *do* of it. You could ask Lorna.'

'Sounds good,' I say, untangling a box of fairy lights. 'Anyone you'd like to invite, Dad?'

'Not really,' he says.

I sort through a pile of Christmas cards as he affixes the plug to the end of the tree lights. One from Charlie, wishing the three of us the merriest of Christmases 'in spite of it all.'

A cheap one from Uncle Pete and Auntie June with a close-up of a bauble. One from Tazzy, featuring a hedgehog in a duffel coat and red wellies. An Oxfam snow scene from 'everyone at Birchover Farm'. Two penguins kissing under mistletoe from Bev and Kat. A jolly Father Christmas signed with 'love' from Marjorie and Graham. And a single robin on a snowy tree stump from 'Pat', the lady from the bowling club, who sent him a 'Get Well Soon' card, another pyramid of kisses under her signature. 'What about Pat?'

'Pat?' Four creases appear in his forehead.

I pass him the card and underline the kisses with my dirty thumbnail.

'Interesting.' His eyes twinkle. 'Though I'm going to have to be a killjoy tonight. I'm too bloody exhausted.'

We decorate the tree with red and gold baubles and a set of lights with half the bulbs dead. Dad looks up, his forehead wrinkled in contemplation as I place the demonic angel I made at primary school on the top. Grandma and I wait patiently, thinking he's going to say something life-changing, but instead he says, 'I can't wait for fish and chips to taste like fish and chips again.'

As I'm pegging Christmas cards onto gold-flecked thread, I realize Dad's just like me. Or at least, I'm just like him. He puts up barriers because he doesn't want to get hurt. He lost Mum, and he doesn't want to lose anyone else. He's happy to give, but not to take, because that way he owes nobody. On the face of it, it's so simple. Beneath the surface, though, there's a complex web of logic. Farming may have chosen Dad, but Dad also chose farming. Not just as a profession, but as an all-consuming lifestyle. A lifestyle that legitimizes never having the time for romance. Never having the space for loneliness. Never having to verbalize your feelings. Cows understand without having to do any of that.

However, judging by the way Dad is now standing at his laptop in the kitchen, browsing 'Pat Gillingham, Baslow Crown Bowls' on the local Sportsfield Trust website, it looks like he may be lowering his barrier. And, you never know, fish and chips might taste like fish and chips again one day.

I pack my battered leather carry-all with wedding essentials (constituting a lot less gear than I deemed necessary six months ago) and get Grandma to dump me at Chesterfield station on her way to the big Sainsbury's.

'Are you not taking Lorna?' Grandma pulls up on double yellows.

'She's joining me tomorrow.'

She nods. 'Have fun! Hi to the girls!'

I walk through the ticket office, the taste of freedom on my lips. A bedraggled acrylic Christmas tree stands next to the entrance to the platform, looking as though it's been crammed into a suitcase between annual outings for a good few years. I think about how it will feel to walk back into my flat and sleep in my bed once again. I think about the girls and the infinite choices that London offers, whether it's things to do, places to eat or people to meet. I board the train, excited and nervous, like a new mother spending her first hour away from her baby. I'm sure the agency staff will cope, but I just wonder what the cows will make of it all.

St Pancras looks different when I get there. Bigger and glossier than normal. Rows of pigeons line the blue metal arcs supporting the glass roof, cooing and fluttering above the gold gilded clock, whilst people cuss and dart below, as if operated by remote control. A crowd-drawing thirty-foot Lego Christmas tree stands on the floor below, commanding spectators from every level. Elaborate yuletide window displays line the thoroughfare. Golden cuckoos pop out of wooden clocks with shiny presents in their beaks, and miniature glockenspiels chime 'Silent Night'. A man in a Starbucks apron offers free samples of caramel apple spice latte, gingerbread cappuccino, eggnog mocha and crème brûlée hot chocolate. Infinite beverage flavourings on one small tray. In London, anything is possible. I feel alive.

I take the Northern Line to Elephant and Castle, where a temporary Christmas market flogging translucent wrapping paper and cheap gadgets sprawls across the entrance to the defunct shopping centre.

'Give us a smile, darlin'!' a man in a duffel coat yells as he empties a bowl of bruised satsumas into a brown paper bag. 'Ten for a p'aand. Ten for a p'aand.'

The streets smell of raw haddock, a fishmonger slinging bloodstained ice out of a bucket, which crunches underfoot.

'Any bag a tenner, darlin!' A lady selling knock-off designer handbags at market prices jangles her money belt.

I make my way along the Old Kent Road, ducking behind a row of shops selling African root vegetables and mobile phone covers. A cat fight has broken out between two women in Aztec leggings, just next to our tower block. The stairs to the third floor smell of piss. Home sweet home.

'Phantom of the Opera' blares through the windows of my flat. Maria comes to the door dressed in a black silk kimono and fluffy pink mules. She holds a plastic pink flamingo watering can in one hand and a Curly Wurly in the other.

'Bilbo!' She hugs me, dripping water down my spine. 'Sorry,' she says, gesturing to the watering can. 'It's for the benefit of the gay couple opposite. We've got a bit of a competition going with "balconies in bloom".' She makes her way over to the windowsill and waters what look like fake petunias.

'Aren't they plastic?' I say, gesturing to the flowers.

'Yeah,' she says.

I've missed Maria. Inside, it doesn't feel like much has changed. The furniture is as I left it, save the new zebra print throw on the sofa. It smells the same. Draughts creep through the same cracks. The tea stain on the hallway carpet is still there. The bathroom door still opens out the wrong way.

'So, I won't get to meet Darius this weekend?' I say, noticing that a couple of framed photos have appeared on the hall walls. Maria all liquid-eye smitten, and him all Mediterranean sex.

She shakes her head. 'His shoot doesn't finish until Sunday and then it'll be Monday by the time he can get on a flight from Adelaide.'

'Shame.'

I open my wardrobe door, and a bonier, older version of the girl I last saw in this mirror stares back. What used to be shoulder-length hair, layered at the ends, is now long, unkempt and ragged with split ends. My face is harder somehow, my skin more brittle. My hands are the worst – dry, wizened old lady's hands with gnarled veins and skin like wrinkled stockings.

My maid-of-honour dress hangs on the door – a silver silk

evening gown with spaghetti straps. I try it on – what fitted me perfectly a few months ago now hangs off me. It's also so transparent that the birthmark above my belly button is visible. I search for appropriate undergarments to make it inoffensive, but the only thing that really works is wearing my swimming costume underneath; inside-out, so as not to reveal its fluorescent block-brick pattern.

We share a dinner of M&S sandwiches, and Maria puts on the fairy lights and reaches for the Disaronno. The square black cap crunches, dislodging flecks of crystallized sugar onto the carpet. Dolly Parton blurts out '9 to 5' from the record player. It's good to be back, but at the same time, I've forgotten how to relax: I'm already worrying about Basile and her eye-worm. Will I ever be able to reintegrate into society?

Sleeping in my own bed is like a *Star Wars* prequel: pretty underwhelming. Despite the opportunity of a lie-in, my body clock won't allow it and I'm up at six.

**From: Lorna Parsons**
B, I've been called out to perform an emergency caesarean on a Hereford. Really sorry but I'll be late to the wedding xxx

**To: Lorna Parsons**
Good luck with the C-section. Don't worry, I'll have matron-of-honour duties at the beginning anyway. Come when you can xx

I get out of bed and pluck a shrivelled Post-it note off my foot.

## New Year's Resolutions:
## Get PhD Scholarship

The whole PhD thing fills me with dread. The thought of having to go through the process all over again. Ingratiating myself to professors. Filling out page after page of application forms. I stick the Post-it note on the inside of the wardrobe door and shut it.

By ten o'clock, I've been for a run, and am showered, dressed and wrestling with eyeliner when Maria appears along with the smell of hairspray and Stella (the perfume, not the lager). She looks great in her dress, like the heroine of a Jackie Collins paperback romance. Freshly curled tendrils are piled on top of her head, with carefully selected ringlets cascading down each side.

'Just nipping to the corner shop for tissues and confetti,' she says, touching up her mascara, and whisks out in a puff of perfume, the front door slamming behind her.

A minute later, the doorbell rings.

'Didn't you take your key?' I holler without moving, mid-tricky-eyeliner application.

The doorbell rings again.

'Give me a sec!' I pad through the living room and make out the silhouette of someone taller than Maria through the frosted glass. I open the door.

'*Bonjour, ma petite Anglaise!*'

Honeysuckle pervades the air; my blood goes hot and the world stands still.

'*Pour toi.*' Joely smoulders in a figure-hugging black dress, handing me a bouquet of red roses as her eyes take me in from top to toe.

'What are you doing here?' I finally find my voice.

'You look beautiful.' Her chocolate eyes devour me. 'Can I come in?'

My innards go all pulpy. The smell of her perfume triggers a flashback of nudity between Egyptian cotton sheets. I look over her shoulder and open the door. 'Very quickly.'

She follows me to the lounge, her eyes skimming the walls to assess what has changed since her last visit.

'I knew you'd be back for the wedding,' she says.

I scratch the back of my neck, making eye contact with the floor as she lowers herself onto the arm of the sofa and removes leather gloves with her teeth.

'What do you want, Joely?'

'I think about you all of the time.' Her hand reaches for my arm, which almost ignites at her touch. 'I'm so sorry for everything.'

'You—'

'I was denying our relationship to myself because I couldn't tell my family. I didn't see how it could ever work and then . . .' Her skin glows with an effervescence you can't bottle. 'I found the courage.' Her hair is silky soft. 'I knew you'd be here for the wedding and I had to take a chance.' She runs her fingers down my arm to clasp my hand.

I stare at the carpet, her touch doing peculiar things to my ovaries. 'Joely, I barely heard from you. You ended it. Things have changed. I've changed.' The words to tell her about Lorna stick in my throat, and I can't swallow. What's wrong with me?

'That's the problem, *ma petite Anglaise*.' She waits until I look up, at which point I'm forced to remember how crazy beautiful she is. 'I can't forget you.'

'I . . .'

'Let me show you something.' She taps at her phone. 'It will take only one minute, I promise.'

I have an out-of-body experience as Joely plays a video clip of a couple in their sixties, sitting on a cream chaise longue, waving at the camera. The man, tanned and refined, has a pastel-blue pullover slung around his shoulders and holds an unlit, filterless cigarette; the kind of perfect white stick with two mint-green bands that a villain would smoke in a Bond film. The woman next to him wears a cream rollneck. Her auburn hair is scooped into a chignon, accentuating her chiselled jaw and high cheekbones; an ex-ballet dancer perhaps.

EX-BALLET DANCER

Hello, Billie!

BOND VILLAIN

*Bonjour*, Billie! We are the parents of Joelle. I am Jean-Luc and my wife, Claudine.

EX-BALLET DANCER

We look forward to meeting you. Joelle talks very much about you. I know she is very sorry to be so late to explain but we hope it's not too late.

BOND VILLAIN

It's never too late. Come and have a drink with us in France!

We hope to meet you soon, Billie. *Bisous*!

Joely looks at me, her eyes deep pools of melted chocolate. 'I'm ready to do this.'

'You came out to your parents?'

'Yes.' She brushes my hair out of my face. 'I'm free now.'

The door rattles. 'Bilbo?'

'One sec!' I shout.

'I want to be with you, Billie,' Joely says.

My stomach does that elastic yoyo thing and my legs feel like jelly as I walk to the front door to let Maria in.

'I forgot my keys. What's up?' Maria says, clocking my raised eyebrow, her eyes travelling to the lounge, to the sofa and then to Joely. 'Holy fuck.'

'Billie?' Joely gets up and wanders into the hall. 'I know I have been an insupportable species of shit.'

'You said it, sister!' Maria says, barging past her.

'But I didn't feel I could commit until I told my parents,' she continues.

'Come the fuck on, Bilbo!' Maria shouts.

The ridges of Joely's ribbed black jumper dress accentuate the contours of her body.

I grab my clutch bag. 'We've got to go.'

Joely smiles. 'You really do look beautiful.'

'Thank you.' I feel my cheeks go hot and my body turn to melting wax.

She saunters out of the living room, her heels tapping rhythmically on the laminate flooring of the hallway. When she reaches the door, she turns round. 'Call me.'

I can barely move.

From: Lorna Parsons
I'm so sorry, Billie. I've got a life/death situation on my
hands with this cow and I'm not going to be able to
make the wedding. I'm really, really, really sorry. I know
this is totally shit and I'll make it up to you when you get
back xxx

Remembering Kat's tiered wedding invitation list and her
dozens of backup guests, I message Bev to let her know I
won't be using their 'plus one', in case they want to invite
someone else last minute.

**From: Bev**
Bit late. You must know one person who would kill to
come to the lesbian wedding of the century?

I consider this for a moment and realize I *do* perhaps know
someone after all.

'A lesbian wedding?' Dave says, no doubt with an immediate
hard-on.

'I know it's probably a no-go with last-minute childcare but—'
'Hell, yes!' He hangs up.

Dave lingers outside Islington's Screen on the Green in a light
brown suit and a white shirt with a small blue clover print
– an improvement on his lab coat. Red and black canopy
lettering spells out 'Bev & Kat's Big Day' and passers-by
rubberneck for a glimpse of the brides.

'Good to see you, Dinosaur.' I kiss him on the cheek.

'You too, Shitbag.'

Bev's sisters shimmy up the entrance steps in figure-hugging silk.

'This is my idea of heaven,' Dave says, his head twisted towards them.

Retro metal signs with 1960s slogans line the walls of the draughty foyer. A circular 7UP lamp cranks out just about enough light for us to make out three young flower girls handing out popcorn. In the dimly lit auditorium, guests of all ages mingle in the aisles and huddle at the bar sipping champagne.

'Psst!' Kat's head pokes out from a heavy ceiling-to-floor velvet curtain.

I nudge Dave. 'Back in a sec.'

Maria follows me behind the curtain, where Kat shivers in a plunge-back ivory silk gown, her hair swept back with a single white rose. 'Please tell me I don't look a tit, Bill.'

'You don't look a tit.'

'Maz?' Kat twitches.

Maria takes Kat's hand. 'You don't look a tit.'

'Ballade pour Adeline' plays in the background. How can an instrumental piece of music sound so beautifully French? I think of Joely, her skin, her smell, the taste of peppermint. The way she pronounces *Anglaise* like it's a cream-smothered dessert.

'Fuck, I'm nervous.' Kat twists and turns in circles, clutching a bunch of pale pink roses.

I rub her back. 'You'll be fine.'

'Ladies and gentlemen, please be seated for a short film by the bride and groom.'

'Bride!' Kat yells at the ceiling. 'Bride and bride!'

The three of us peep through a side curtain to watch Bev and Kat on the big screen as they playfully contradict each other in a pre-wedding interview filmed in their kitchen. The audio is littered with bleeps as Kat fails to keep her language in check.

Good old Dave is sitting right next to some redhead in a low-cut red dress. It's only when she turns to talk to the person next to her that I realize it's Neve! Neve, who was in my life for three years. Neve, who I don't think about any more. Neve throws her head of auburn curls back with carefree abandon, laughing in all the right places. How can today be such a hotbed of ex-girlfriends?

'Neve's here!' I elbow Maria. 'Does that mean Nic is too?'

'No!' Maria whispers. 'They split up last month.'

I shouldn't feel anything, but it stings. How can this nugget of information have possibly slipped the net? How can such monumentally significant news to one person be so 'so what' to another?

'Nic wasn't feeling it,' Maria says. 'Neve was ready to have a baby and it was all moving way too fast for Nic so . . .' She shrugs. 'Poor Neve.'

I can handle my friends still being friends with Neve. That in itself is OK, but when your ex (Neve) breaks your heart by running off with their mate (Nic), the only anecdotes you want to hear from mutual friends are ones of misery, regret and an undercurrent of 'she'd have been so much better off with you'. Anecdotes are not meant to incite sympathy for the cheating heartbreaker, who wants babies with the newer, better version of you.

I start to sweat. I haven't thought about Neve in months. I don't even care about Neve, and now she is somehow all over everything. I'm quite happy with Joely, thank you very much. *Lorna*. I mean *Lorna*, for fuck's sake!

'Ladies and gentlemen, please be upstanding for the bride.'

Through a kink in the curtain, I make out Bev waiting on the stage. She's dressed in a blue trouser suit and a white shirt dotted with small humming birds. She wears an enormous grin.

Maria looks to Kat. 'Ready?'

'I've been ready for ten years,' Kat croaks.

Debussy's 'Clair de Lune' floats gently through the jam-packed auditorium. Another beautiful French classic. *Why am I still so ridiculously attracted to her?*

Maria and I peel back the heavy curtain. There's no wedding-dress train to hold, so we simply walk either side of Kat, following the tiny floor lights marking the central aisle, not knowing what to do with our hands. Ladies whoop, gentlemen cheer and my heartbeat can't seem to settle the fuck down. *Turning up like that, with all those roses.* Kat gathers her floor-length dress up on one side to negotiate the stairs up to the stage, where Bev adjusts her silver toucan cufflinks and runs her hands over her neatly trimmed Mohican.

The registrar, a squat woman in a green skirt suit, ushers Maria and me to one side while she completes the ceremony preamble. We climb down from the stage, tiptoe back to our seats, and watch as Bev and Kat take their vows. I sit and snivel, Maria providing a steady supply of paper tissues.

The audience claps, flinging popcorn in place of confetti as Mrs and Mrs Leason-Mellor walk back up the aisle, the room pumped with love. The auditorium lights go up and everyone is ushered out of the building for photos, Bev's uncle juggling lens caps in the central reservation of Upper Street and trying to stage us all under the cinema canopy. We huddle in the drizzle, all goose bumps and frizzing hair, waiting for double-deckers to pass until he can get the perfect shot.

Dave crouches next to me. 'I thought living in the countryside was supposed to chill you out,' he says.

'I had a weird start to the day,' I say.

He smiles. 'Me too. I was on my way to bootcamp and now I'm at my first gay wedding!'

The chime of a bell marks the arrival of a flower-adorned cycle rickshaw, which pulls up on the pavement. The chauffeur, a young man in top hat and tails, helps the happy couple over the metal spokes of the large wheels and onto the back seat.

'See you at the pub!' Kat yells, tossing her roses over her shoulder, which Dave catches with a 'why the hell not?' shrug.

The Angel smells of hops and burgers. Bev's mothers hand out tall flutes of champagne to a steady flow of guests. The function room is surprisingly light and airy considering the low ceilings and overhead beams. Music mixes with raucous laughter and the hum of small talk. A crowd forms around two bride hedgehog cakes with chocolate button spikes and sugar paper veils. *Joely Chevalier wants me back.* I feel a bit light-headed, my vision becoming pixelated and everyone's voices slipping away.

'Let there be cake!' Kat squeals as Bev drives a breadknife through a hedgehog.

Dave wanders over with two slices. *She can't have thought it was over, not if she then came out to her parents.* Bev makes a speech, reciting 'The Owl and the Pussy Cat' with a 'find and replace all' *Owl* with *Bear* slant. I snivel into my slice of hedgehog's bottom, blowing my nose on a chocolate-crumbed napkin.

'Seriously, what's up with you today, Shitbag?' Dave leans over the bar and takes another slice of cake. 'I get that weddings are emotional, but you're like Gwyneth fucking Paltrow accepting an Oscar.'

I sip my champagne. 'Sorry, I'm just a bit all over the place at the moment.'

'A bit?' he says, handing me the double Disaronno that Bev's mother has passed him for my consumption.

I take a gulp of the sweet almond liqueur from the tumbler in my other hand. 'Joely turned up at the flat this morning.'

'Hot, French, KSG Joely?'

'Yes.'

'And this is a problem?' He practically spits his pint across the bar.

'Yes.'

'Why?'

I shrug. 'Too little too late.' I press my back against the cold wooden bar, staring into the crowd. 'I met someone up north. Lorna. She's a vet.'

Dave pops his steel-framed glasses onto his nose. 'And where is Lorna-the-vet now?'

'Performing a caesarean on a Hereford cow.'

'Gotcha,' he says, leering at a gaggle of girls comparing garters. 'And where's hot Frenchy right now?'

'She left. I was practically on my way out of the door to come here.'

Neve wanders over with a plate of canapés, her red dress billowing above a floor vent. She has a playful look about her I haven't seen since we first met. 'Hi!' Her steely-blue eyes seek me out. 'Mini Yorkshire pudding?'

She looks annoyingly perky for someone recently dumped.

'Thanks,' Dave says, favouring roast beef and horseradish over quinoa and beetroot.

She places the tray down on the bar and beds in for conversation. 'It's good to see you again.' She touches my elbow.

'It's been a while,' I say, accidentally sending a piece of spittle flying. Why do things like that only happen when it matters? Why is it so unfathomably essential to come across as a devastatingly beautiful, serene, intelligent, articulate, funny, easy-going and infinitely superior goddess when involuntarily thrown into conversation with your ex? And why, when all of this is so hugely important, do you never fail to regress to a spitting, snorting, gibbering wreck? I don't even like her any more, for fuck's sake. I've moved on, twice.

She leans in. 'How's your dad?'

'It's your round, Shitbag,' Dave interrupts.

'Neve, this is my friend Dave.' I smile, trying to regain exterior splendour.

'Nice to meet you.' Dave kisses her hand.

I look to Neve. 'My round apparently. Would you like a drink?'

'A piña colada would be grand, thanks,' she says.

I readjust my swimming costume and lean over the bar. 'Three piña coladas, please.' I hate piña coladas. Why am I ordering myself a piña colada? Why am I pretending to be someone I'm not? And who exactly am I pretending to be?

Neve chats to Dave while I wait. I can't work out whether I'm still attracted to her or not, deciding whilst she's generically attractive, she no longer exudes that *je ne sais quoi.* I can admire her beauty as I would an oil painting – once every couple of years and against my will.

I hand Neve and Dave their drinks and drift into a daydream as they compare the miles-per-gallon petrol consumption of their respective cars. *Joely and I are on a beach. We sit in the sand dunes and stare out at the sea. Sun dances on our skin, our toes digging into the warm sand. Her head lies in my lap. We say nothing.*

I try to imagine the same scene with Lorna, but can't visualize being on the beach with her. I can't remember what her toes look like, or whether I've even seen them. Does this mean our roots aren't entwined? I panic, only calming once I can vividly picture Lorna and me sitting on my dad's haystack, mud-spattered and happy. I pick up my phone to send Lorna a text but it's dead, and I'm not far behind.

A cocktail of amaretto, Prosecco and piña colada sloshes around in my gut and all I want to do is throw up. The DJ has set up behind a mishmash of flashing lights and sits on a stool reading a paperback thriller whilst his amps do all the work blaring Bowie's 'Let's Dance'.

'Fancy a dance?' Neve asks.

I couldn't be less in the mood for a dance, but sobriety and sense have long departed, and I've got nothing better to do. That, and I'm determined to portray myself as a winning warrior woman with moral high ground. Everything swirls and sloshes as Neve swings me under a mirrored disco ball. The room becomes a blur. Dave morphs into Bev's mothers,

Kat into Bev, and Bev into Kat, the two hedgehog cakes becoming one. I should really stop drinking.

'Shame they didn't have a hen party, otherwise we could have got all this awkwardness out of the way earlier,' Neve shouts over the music.

My head is pounding and I don't have room to either agree or disagree.

'It's weird,' she goes on, 'that we knew each other so well and for so long.'

I try not to throw up on her dress.

'I'm sorry for the way it ended,' she shouts, filling my mind with images of her and Nic going at it on an IKEA futon. 'But it was because you wouldn't let me in. Not properly.'

'How do you mean?' I mumble.

'You were too scared of letting me down, and then, in the end, I let you down.' She puts her hands on my shoulders and I sway under her grip. 'You OK, Billie?'

'Ladies and gentlemen, please come upstairs to be seated for your banquet.'

We amble upstairs. It's almost too late for food, having already hit the dance floor. Bev, Kat, Maria, Dave and I are ushered to the top table, the five of us seated in a row over-looking everyone else like *Hello!* magazine royals. For some reason, everyone is handing me glasses of water and asking if I'm OK.

'What's up with you, buddy?' Bev says as I gulp down another glass.

'Joely turned up at the flat,' Maria explains, leaning around Kat.

'What the fuck did she want?' Kat says.

'A new start.' I reach for one of the waters I can see, knocking over the other. 'She's told her folks about me.'

'Yeah, right!' Kat says sarcastically.

'She really has,' I mumble as a plate of melon is placed in front of me.

Bev picks up her napkin. 'Tempted?'

I could do with everything just staying still for a second.

'She's way too fit to pass up,' Dave says. 'If you want male perspective.'

'I can't hear you properly,' Maria shouts from the end of the row. 'But if we're talking about Joely, she's flaky as hell, Bilbo!'

Kat leans in closer. 'What about Lorna?'

'Lorna, who isn't here?' Dave says, tucking into the bread rolls.

'Lorna, who would be here if she wasn't doing an emergency C-section,' Maria counters.

I fiddle with my cutlery.

'This is the girl that dumped you, Bill!' Kat says, just as a microphone is handed to her, the whole room now listening. 'She dumped you and had her hands all over that beefcake!'

'I know.'

'She left you for dust and then decides she wants you back when she sees you all over the newspapers in a bikini?' Kat rages, causing the room to gasp in horror. 'How do you turn this fucking thing off?'

The room undulates. I run my fingers over a small silver spoon, its smoothness calming. 'Maybe things have moved a bit fast with Lorna,' I say.

'Here.' Bev takes the microphone and presses mute.

'Too fast?' Kat protests. 'This has to be the slowest-burning romance of all time!'

'Can we talk about this another time?' I suggest. 'It is, after all, your wedding.'

'Hell, no!' Kat grabs more Prosecco and fills her glass.

'I can't hear you from down here,' Maria yells, bringing her chair round to sit opposite me, her back to the wedding guests.

I feel like I'm not really at the wedding, like I'm floating somewhere in orbit. Like none of this is really happening to me, but to another Billie Oliver on another planet. 'I don't think Lorna will ever move from her life in the countryside.'

'Have you asked her?' Kat says.

I feel very queasy. 'No.'

Dave smirks. 'Is she good in the sack?'

'Are we talking about Lorna or Joely now?' Bev says, innocently.

'Either!' Dave laughs.

'Well, say what you want, but I'm rooting for Lorna,' Maria says.

'Me too,' Kat says, sawing through a slice of cantaloupe with extraordinary force. 'Bear?'

'Sorry, Kitty Kat, but it is pretty bad form to bail on the actual day of a wedding. I know she took a long time, but she got there in the end, so I'm with Joely.'

Dave reddens. 'I've always been with Joely.'

'Billie, it has to be Lorna!' Maria says, infuriated.

'Joely is beautiful and has told her parents she's in love with you,' Bev says.

'Joely's a flake!' Maria says. 'Lorna would rescue you from a fire that Joely would have probably started.'

'Harsh,' Bev says.

'But fair!' Maria says.

'Do you still have Joely's number in your phone?' Dave says.

'Yes.'

'Then you still have feelings for her,' he says.

Maria wrinkles her face at him. 'That's bullshit. I've still got three ex's numbers in my phone that I don't give a bloody monkey's about.' She turns to me. 'Do you know Joely's phone number off by heart?'

I ponder the relevance of this question for a moment. 'No.'

'Then it's not true love,' she concludes smugly.

'Ladies and gentlemen, please raise your glasses for the bride and bride.'

I fill myself with buttered bread rolls and water, and try to sober myself up for the reading.

'And in breaking with tradition, before we have our main course, a poem from the bride to the bride.'

'To be continued,' Kat whispers as she turns on the microphone, retrieves a script from her bosom and clears her throat.

> 'Love is like tea at the end of the day,
> It takes time to brew and is much better GAY,
> Everyone's tea is to their own taste,
> For love and tea are no copy and paste.'

Kat is good. Her poem is good. I am up next with my Captain Corelli volcano piece and am close to throwing up.

> 'Bev ordered ice-cream, not tea when we met.
> A large ninety-nine. How good does it get?

We both wore flipflops, we both wore a hat,
Two kindred spirits with a load of chat.'

It was all OK when it was merely the challenge of delivering it loud enough for Maria to hear over the vacuum cleaner, but now, in front of Neve and . . . my head spins. The door opposite swings open, sending a free-standing silver ice bucket clattering to the ground. Everyone's eyes are drawn to the tall, slender latecomer who hovers in the doorway.

'But it wasn't your perfectly scripted rom-com,
for I was an ovary ticking bomb,
and I knew that Bev was my cup of tea.
She ran for the hills as quick as can be.'

It isn't the way she swaggers to the empty seat next to Kat's mum, fanning herself with a drinks menu. It isn't the way the duck-egg-blue silk dress I bought for her birthday sits perfectly on her hips. It isn't the way her chocolate-brown eyes flicker across the room until they single me out, but there is something disarming about Joely Chevalier.

'Ten years on and we've found our own blend,
of stubbornness and compromise, for let's not pretend,
it's all rosy lee with a flowery feeling,
For neither of us are the perfect Darjeeling.'

Joely whispers something to Kat's mum, causing her to look at me and smile. I try to decide whether gate-crashing a wedding to reclaim an ex is an act of true love or the act of a psychopath. She throws her head back and flicks off her pashmina, exposing elegant shoulders and the suggestion of a cleavage. The dress fits her perfectly.

> 'We're practically married, we come as a pair,
> I am your Kitty Kat, you are my Bear.
> The last ten years have been a retainer,
> now marrying Bev is a total no-brainer.'

I begin to feel toilet-searchingly sick. Patches of my face disappear, and my skin feels clammy. I can neither focus on Kat nor Joely as the room spins round, Neve appearing in flashes somewhere between the two of them.

> 'I'm marrying Bev for her buzzard blogs,
> for rescuing eagles and fostering frogs,
> for making me laugh a lot in life.
> Bev, I'm honoured to be your wife.'

Rapturous applause fills the room, the clapping and whooping continuing as Kat kisses Bev and sits back down.

'Ladies and gentlemen, please welcome our maids of honour, Billie and Maria, for a reading from *Captain Corelli's Mandolin.*'

I hold the wireless microphone under my chin and take the reading out of my bag, willing it to stop wavering in my hand.

'Hi,' I say, addressing the room but looking straight at Joely.

'Hi,' she mouths back, flicking her hair off her shoulder.

'This is a piece written by Louis de B . . .'

The room rotates and consciousness slides away until I am a shell of a person, reading on autopilot. All eyes are on me, including Joely Chevalier's, and as much as I want this to be over, I don't know what I'm going to do when this reading ends.

## CHAPTER TWENTY

# GiRL VERSUS GiRL

The Angel's basement bar is open to the public and consequently packed to the rafters with Christmas shoppers, hats, bags and coats. The dull beat of Pulp's 'Common People' from the wedding party upstairs can be heard over the slow croon of 'White Christmas' from the jukebox.

Joely sits at a small table next to a window enveloped in condensation, her nose in a copy of Baudelaire's *Les Fleurs du Mal*. She sees me and stands up, duck-egg-blue silk caressing her hips.

'Thanks for agreeing to listen.' She kisses my left cheek and something inside me ignites, my heart somewhere in my mouth.

The ten-minute time-out alone in the fresh air has sorted me out, and I feel a lot more alert. 'I've got to get back to the wedding in ten minutes.' I peer over my shoulder to check I'm not being followed.

Her eyes meet mine, and I'm reminded of our emails. The flirting, the thrill, the *will she, won't she?*

'You once said that every coming-out story deserves an audience,' Joely says, picking up her champagne. 'I wanted to tell you mine, but first I need alcohol.'

We make small talk about big things: Dad's health, her parents, her promotion at KSG. Big things that are somehow reduced to a fraction of their worth. I can't really explain about Dad because she didn't know him, not like Lorna does, and so the whole thing gets tied up in some neat, little 'benign-now-recovering' package.

My head thumps.

She tops up her glass with more champagne. 'OK, so my parents expected me to marry Christophe—'

'Recently, or when you were seeing him before?' I feel like I've been prodded with a hot iron.

'We have not dated recently,' she says matter-of-factly.

'That's not what it looked like in the photos!'

'You can read anything into photos, Billie.' She smiles at me. 'They expected me to marry Christophe when I was younger, but I couldn't. I knew I would sabotage a marriage with him. It would be too perfect, and I'd explode.'

'Right.' A simple *no* would have sufficed.

She plays with the menu. 'I explained that life doesn't work like that, and I'm actually in love with *une petite Anglaise* who has no money!' I try to stifle my disappoint-ment at the brutally accurate portrayal of my status. 'At first my father said nothing and then he went crazy, saying I've disappointed him *et patati et patata*,' she says, gesticulating wildly and knocking over her glass, which luckily bounces rather than smashes. She picks it up and refills it. 'It was traumatic. I was crying, my mother was crying.' She puts her hand on my thigh reassuringly, though nothing about it is reassuring.

I'm flooded with flashbacks. *I rip off her clothes in my hallway. We writhe around naked in her bed. We kiss at Waterloo station. We kiss in the lab. Her hands over my thighs. We kiss. Her hands between my thighs. We kiss some more.*

She takes another gulp of champagne.

'Easy, Joels,' I say, unsure as to whether I'm trying to slow down her drinking or the hand on my thigh.

'And then my mother says she and my father are responsible, because they don't present a great image of true love between a man and a woman, and then she starts to shout at my father for licking the mussel of the lady in the apartment next door.'

'Licking the—'

'It's very vulgar.'

'OK,' I say, conscious that I should be back upstairs now.

'And my father wants to know how long I've been interested in the female form and I explain that it's not always the gender that counts. It's the individual. And he says these are the words of poetry, not real life.' She twizzles the stem of her glass. 'And then my mother says she just wants me to be happy.'

'I needed you when I was on the farm,' I blurt, emotion gurgling at the back of my throat. Everything comes flooding back. The feeling of slowly sinking and crying out for help that never comes. The helplessness. The desperation. The loneliness. That overwhelming feeling of being let down whilst she's in complete control of her life. I'm power*less* and she's power*ful* and the longer it goes on, the more pathetic I feel. 'I needed the moral support.'

'I'm sorry,' she says, her doe eyes looking up at me. 'I was a coward.'

And now here she is, all vulnerable and out of control. I'm drowning in emotions I don't even understand. I know I'm in too deep, but she has this gravitational pull on me. 'I need to go back to the wedding,' I say.

She grabs my hand and squeezes it. 'Can I come with you?'

I should say no but there's a big part of me that wants to say yes. She's mesmerizingly beautiful. 'Sorry, Joels. I don't think it's a good—'

Her eyes sparkle. 'Please.'

I become conscious of my heart beating loudly.

She circles her fingertip on the back of my hand. 'I promise, it will be worth it.'

'It's too late.' I get up, checking that I've still got the silver beaded purse I'm not used to carrying. 'Things have changed. I've changed.'

'*Ma petite Anglaise.*' She stands up and places her hands on my hips. Her breath is hot and heavy, her perfume intoxicating. It's all I can do not to kiss her.

'Joels, I've met someone.' I'm unsure as to whether she hasn't heard or whether she's just choosing to ignore it, but the words don't seem to register. Instead, she leans in and kisses me, and this time there's no way I can hold back. Her lips are soft and taste of strawberry lip balm. My stomach flips over and over as her tongue finds mine. 'Joels?' I pull away. 'I can't. I've met someone.'

She looks into my eyes. 'We have something special, Billie.'

'I can't.' I grab my bag and make to leave.

'You remember this dress?' She steps backwards dramatically just as an elderly couple try to squeeze past. 'You bought it for me only a few months ago.'

'Of course, I remember the dress.'

'And now it means nothing?'

'Joely, you're the one that ended our relationship.'

'And now I'm here, saying sorry. Telling you I'm totally committed.' She wobbles, steadying herself on the back of her chair.

'Sorry, may we just get past?' The lady standing behind Joely smiles nervously.

I feel like I'm living in some art-house film where sense and reason are sidelined for raw emotion; instead of moving out of the way, Joely only serves to box in our spectators further by puffing out her arms and, to my horror, starts to unzip the back of her dress.

'Joely!' I hiss.

'Here!' She peels her shoulders out of the dress. 'You can take your dress!'

'Joely!' I yank her dress back up as diners from the surrounding tables suspend conversation.

'You bought it, so it is officially yours.' She tries to wriggle out of it.

'Good grief!' the elderly man next to us mutters.

My eyes dart around the restaurant. 'You're making a scene!'

She pulls down the straps. 'You don't find me attractive any more?'

'That's very nice, dear but we've a tube to catch,' the captive lady says, finger tapping her non-existent watch.

Joely sways from side to side. 'We had plans, Billie.'

'Which you reneged on!' I say, trying to weave my way past her.

Joely lowers her dress another inch.

A small, neatly presented waiter hurries over from the bar. 'Excuse me, madam!' He clasps Joely's lower arm with a tea towel. 'You're in Islington, not Benidorm!'

I manoeuvre myself out of the way and head for the exit, heads turning as I go. I should never have followed her down here.

Outside, the cold drizzle, exhaust fumes and inner-city grime feel cathartic against my face. What on earth was I thinking? I get out my phone, forgetting it's dead, and contemplate getting a bus away from all this when a familiar figure in an unfamiliar soft cream coat and high-heeled ankle boots steps out of a cab and walks towards me: Lorna Parsons has arrived. Her hair is styled with a side-parting, her fresh face awash with freckles, her lips accentuated by red lipstick. Her grey eyes sparkle.

She grins at me. 'Sorry I'm ridiculously late.'

'Lorna!' I wrap my arms around her.

'What are you doing out here?' She frowns. 'You're not a covert smoker, are you?'

'I was just . . . it's busy in there. I needed some air.' I look over my shoulder, willing Joely not to make an appearance.

'How's about you introduce me to the happy couple?' she says, grabbing my arm and leading me back into the wedding.

Back inside, the party's in full swing. Dave flings two middle-aged ladies in low-cut blouses around the dance floor to 'Stayin' Alive'.

Lorna removes her coat to reveal a jade cocktail dress.

I hug her. 'You look fucking amazing.'

'You don't scrub up too badly yourself,' she says. 'We got him out, the Hereford calf. Little boy. All healthy.'

'That's great,' I say, aware that the person I was six months ago would've glazed over at this sort of detail, unable to relate to any part of it. Six months ago, I was a different person. God knows which one is better.

I feel a tap on my shoulder. Lorna's smile dissolves into a look of horror, her body becoming brittle. I turn round to see Joely, who has at least pulled her dress back on. I grab Lorna's hand.

'*Ma petite Anglaise.*' Ignoring Lorna completely, Joely threads her arm through mine.

Lorna's face drops. 'Billie?'

I try to flick Joely's arm away, which only makes her cling onto me.

'Why is she here?' Joely slurs, hanging onto my elbow.

Lorna grits her teeth. 'I could ask you the same question.'

I peel Joely off my arm and try to grab Lorna's, but she keeps both hands firmly welded around her bag. 'I didn't invite Joely. She just showed up,' I say.

'Nobody just shows up to a wedding,' Lorna says, walking away from me towards the bar.

'Nobody except Joely,' I say, following desperately, Joely slumping into a chair behind us.

'*Nobody except Joely.* You say it like she's something special. And meanwhile, I'm just some sort of comfort blanket? Good old "get you out of jail" Lorna?'

Neve looks our way and does a double-take when she sees Lorna. Lorna squints back and then returns her frown to me.

'Jesus, Billie,' Lorna says. 'Just exactly how many people did you have on stand-by?'

Then, before I have time to do anything about it, Lorna charges back through the room and heads straight over to Joely. I watch them exchange a barrage of words, which leads to Joely showing something to Lorna on her phone. I hurry over in trepidation.

'Just showed up, huh?' Lorna waves Joely's phone in my face. On her screen, a photo of the wedding invitation looms large.

Joely smells my desperation and capitalizes on it. 'You invited me, Billie.'

'Months and months ago, when we were together!' I say.

'Spare me the bullshit, Billie.' Lorna turns on her heels, the muscles of her bare back flickering as she retreats to the main door with her coat.

'Lorna, wait!' I rush after her, negotiating tables, umbrellas, coat-stands and waiting staff, the double doors slamming in my face.

She trots along the pavement, teeth chattering, arms folded tightly over her chest, holding out her arm in the hope of stopping a cab.

'It's not what it looks like!' I shout. 'Nothing happened with Joely.'

She takes off her ankle boot and shakes out a stone that skims into the road, her big grey eyes boring into me. 'Did you really need to humiliate me like this?'

'I haven't humiliated you!' I say.

'I'm going home. I don't want you to contact me.' She hails a taxi.

'Lorna, wait!'

The door clunks shut behind her.

'Lorna!' I scream, but she's gone.

Maria appears at my side. 'Where the bloody hell have *you* been? Bev's uncle's looking for you.' She looks at me. 'Bilbo, what's the matter?'

'Lorna's gone.'

'Lorna?'

'Yes.'

'Gone where?' she says.

'Home. Away. Anywhere. I don't know.'

Dave appears next to us. 'I think your femme fatale might need a bit of help.'

Maria rolls her eyes and drags me back inside where Joely Chevalier is slumped against the wall in a pool of vomit.

'Can you move her outside?' Bev's uncle says. 'I can't afford to lose my deposit on the venue, what with Christmas only around the corner!'

I look at Joely and want nothing to do with her, but she's now my responsibility. I want to tell her to go fuck herself. That she's ruined everything. But what's the point? She's too paralytic to understand what I'm saying. Maria helps me bundle her into the Ladies', where she slumps over the washbasin, head lodged under the soap dispenser, dress stained with red wine and diced carrot. I peel off her dress at arm's length and shove it into a pedal bin bag we find under the sink.

Maria hands me a peach table cloth. 'It's the only thing I could find!'

I wrap it around Joely, mummifying her in tableware. We call for a taxi, but when one arrives, it won't take her. In the end, Dave has to bribe the wedding rickshaw man, who's been taking wedding guests with small children round the block for a tenner all evening, to pedal her home. And as she disappears out of sight, I sit on the dirty, wet kerb, trying to make sense of everything, headlights reflecting in oily puddles, a pigeon pecking at some congealed chewing gum.

Maria sits down next to me. 'Fucked up there, Bilbo!'

We both stare at the pigeon in contemplation. Were we smokers, she would've definitely handed me a cigarette and we would have sparked up in silence, drinking in the nicotine-infused world, but we're not, so she doesn't.

'No shit.' I peer into the gutter. 'And my fucking phone's dead, so I can't call her.'

Maria dips her hand into her diamanté handbag and pulls out her phone, its screen full of app icons sitting on top of a photo of Dolly Parton. 'Do you know her number?'

I picture the eleven digits emblazoned across the Parsons-Bonneville SUV and punch them sequentially into her phone.

Maria smiles. 'Maybe there's still hope.'

But Lorna's phone goes straight to voicemail.

If there is hope, it is not meant for today.

# CHAPTER TWENTY-ONE

# UNFUCKiNG THE FUCK-UP THAT iS MY LiFE

Christmas Eve arrives and Derbyshire is tinselled by sleet. The bookies bank on a revival of Cliff Richard's 'Mistletoe and Wine' being Christmas number one and slash the odds on a White Christmas as weather forecasters predict 'Snowmageddon' across northern Britain. I prepare the farm for the worst, gritting the lane, digging out snow chains and stocking up on tinned baked beans, chocolate and anti-freeze.

In a parallel universe, I am mid-Winter Wonderland romp, frolicking in fresh white powder in the style of a boy band Christmas video, playfully throwing slow-motion snowballs at a giggling, rosy-cheeked Lorna Parsons. In this universe, I'm dragging on wellies and stomping solo in an inadequately lined parka to the milking shed, painfully and resolutely single. It's been almost two weeks since the wedding and Lorna has rebuffed every attempt I've made at contact. I've left voice-mails, put notes through her letterbox, been turned away countless times at her front door by Guy, and skulked around the village, hoping to 'just bump into her'. It's like she's dropped off the face of my earth.

A semi-inflated Father Christmas buffets against the entrance to the barn, his neck tethered by fairy lights, his reindeer spattered in wood-pigeon poo and flecked with mud. The wind howls. Hallam FM churns out Mariah Carey's 'All I Want for Christmas Is You', and I have never missed Lorna Parsons so much.

I log onto Dad's computer and type her name into the search box. The results are impressive. She's a regular speaker on the veterinarian circuit, a pioneer in bovine podiatry, a co-inventor of the Cowslip, a tough plastic shoe used to treat lameness in cattle. Her headshot is a close-up of her freckled face, caked in mud and smiling. Winner of the National Vet Award three years ago. Runner-up the following year. You name it, she's got it.

I type 'Billie Oliver' into the internet, which returns umpteen online profiles and several obituaries for Billie Olivers who accomplished great things with their lives: freedom fighters, drug barons, Bodacious Woman Award winners, but nothing related to me. When I hunt hard enough, I eventually stumble across a thirty-five-page case study I wrote at Durham University on 'Barriers to Reduce Toxaemia in Women with Pre-Eclampsia'. Other than that, it's just the business-as-usual neglected job profile and a couple of sporadically updated social media sites.

From: Dave Aspinall
Subj: Happy Christmas!

Happy Christmas Eve, Shitbag!

How's it hanging? Just wanted to tell you that Queen's Secret Santa lives on in your absence! Today's exchange of presents included:

Me: a piece of plastic sick from the local joke shop.
New intern: a 'Keep Calm and Eat Pizza' fridge magnet (probably from the joke shop).
Arlene: a plastic dog poo (definitely from the joke shop).

I miss our post-match analysis. It's not the same without someone to laugh about it. You've been gone for a fucking age. So long, in fact, that 'the boss' packed up all your stuff the other day and sent it to you registered post for fear of not adhering to some HR handbook clause about proprietary rights.

Thought you also might like to know that your eclampsia case studies got published alongside some video clips KSG put together. Links below.

Have a Happy Christmas and keep the faith!
Davo x

I click on the links. The first video shows a woman with known pre-eclampsia in full-on labour. She lies on a hospital bed, her legs splayed, the bloody, matted crown of her unborn child's head appearing and disappearing between shudders and shakes. The mother's muscles spasm, her body jerking and juddering, her neck twisting this way and that. She throws her head back with exhaustion. The midwife passes her a canister of gas and air, which she snatches, biting on the mouthpiece as her head pulses left and right and her body is seized once again. These are no ordinary contractions. She's practically vibrating. I think of my mum and can't watch the rest.

When I press 'stop', the image freezes on a close-up of a doctor's gloved hand poised with a needle of calcium gluconate.

'Billie?' Grandma hollers from downstairs.

'One sec!' I close the lid of my laptop. At least, not knowing the outcome, there's a chance she didn't die.

'Can you pick up your auntie Bea?'

It's tradition in the Oliver household that Beatrice comes over on Christmas Eve and stays until New Year, so that we can all get on each other's tits and feel recharged once everyone is firmly back under their own roof. It's also tradition that we have Christmas dinner on Christmas Eve, so that we can go to the Cavendish Hotel for a meal on Christmas Day and pretend to be posh. This is Beatrice's 'treat' to us all, for taking her under our wing, though truth be known, Dad and I would prefer to stay at home and watch telly.

'Sure,' I say. 'Did a package come for me?'

'No, but we got a slip through.' She fumbles behind the toaster and drags out a 'Sorry we missed you' card, which says I've got to drive to some Royal Mail depot in the arse end of nowhere to pick it up. I have no idea which belongings I left at the lab, but don't really want to leave it until after Christmas in case it gets lost, so I take a detour.

The man at Raleigh Park depot hands me a heavy cardboard box. 'There's £2 postage to pay,' he says. 'Looks like they under-provisioned.'

That's Queen's for you. I bite my lip and slide a £2 coin over the counter.

It's not until I've managed to lug the package over to the car and drag it into the boot, that I open it up, slicing open the brown parcel tape with the car key. The package contains:

- One box of Tampax
- One skanky pair of size 4 Fuji Attack Asics
- One greying sports bra
- One pair of age 12 boys' jogging bottoms
- Deodorant
- A KSG baseball cap
- A KSG stress ball
- A printed biography of Joely Chevalier
- An unopened box addressed to me from KSG containing twenty-four boxes of calcium gluconate-based product samples

I drive to Bakewell wondering how much it cost Queen's to send all this shit.

Beatrice's bell doesn't work. It takes a good ten minutes of thumping on the front door before footsteps descend the staircase. She appears in the holly-and-berry print dress she wears every year with a built-in red belt. With unsteady hands, she crayons on lip-liner in the hallway mirror, primps her pink-tinted hair and slips on a snow-wash denim jacket.

She reaches for a leopard-skin print scarf and her handbag. 'Sometimes, you have to compromise warmth for fashion,' she says, tucking a five-pound note into my pocket. 'It's Christmas. Buy yourself something nice!'

Grandma and Dad are busy arguing over the food safety of defrosted turkey when we get back to the farm. The smell of roast potatoes fills the kitchen. Grandma kisses Beatrice on the cheek and shunts us in with a rolled-up copy of the Christmas *Radio Times*.

'Why is this house always so freezing?' Beatrice squeezes her stockinged feet into sheepskin slippers. 'Anyone'd think it were the North frigging Pole.'

'South Pole, more like,' Grandma says.

'What's the difference?'

'Penguins.'

'Well, penguins or no penguins, it's like living in a barn,' Beatrice says.

'Seeing as it's a special occasion, we'll put the heating on!' Grandma goes into the pantry and rummages for the boiler, which has been in the utility room for eleven years. She comes out holding a bottle of San Pellegrino at arm's length. 'I guess everyone enjoys a bit of sparkle at Christmas.'

Dad turns on the television, which screens some appalling quiz show with minor celebrities dressed in Santa hats. I set the table and wonder what Lorna is up to. Whether she's with her parents or at her brother's. Whether she's with Guy. Whether she's on her own.

The four of us sit down to turkey roast with all the trimmings. Speedo whimpers under the table, letting out turkey farts. The sausages are burned to a frazzle and the parsnips are soggy, but nobody says anything.

'Happy Chuffing Christmas!' Grandma shouts over a shit cracker.

'Happy Christmas, everybody!' Beatrice chuckles. 'Thanks for having me again.'

Dad stands up, holding onto the table. 'Happy Christmas, all!' He raises his glass. 'They say behind every good man is a good woman. I'm just lucky I've got a team of women behind me. I couldn't have got through the year without you, I really couldn't.' He raises a glass to Grandma and me. 'So, Billie. There's something I'd like to talk to you about.'

Grandma peers at him from under her cracker hat. 'Is it wise to do this now?'

He sits down. 'It's about the farm, Bilberry. I think the time may have come for me to hang up my boots. The tumour's been a bit of a wake-up call, if I'm honest, and . . .' Tears spring to his eyes.

'It's OK, son,' Grandma says, cupping his hand in hers.

Dad fiddles with his cracker whilst Grandma rubs his back and pours him a glass of sherry. We prod at the vegetables until he regains his composure.

'I know I'm only going to be able to sell for a fraction of what the farm's worth, what with the number of years on the lease dropping, but it's only going to lose value the longer I hang onto it. I'm not getting any younger and, as you know, farming's a very physical job. Billie, you've been a star, but they're not going to keep your job open for ever. It's time for me to sell up.'

I feel as if someone's just stabbed me. 'What about your dreams of keeping a small plot of land and a couple of cows?' I try not to choke on the pig-in-blanket I'm trying to chew covertly.

'That would still be the dream, Billie, but I have to be realistic.'

I want to say I'll take on the farm, but I can't. I don't have the capital to buy him out, I can't make his business profitable and, selfishly, I have my own career to pursue.

He leans on his elbows and puts his hands together, his fingertips touching. 'There's a chap in Bakewell who's already expressed an interest as a cash buyer.'

'Not the one who wants to turn the farm into a Christian retreat?' Grandma frowns.

'A Christian what?' Beatrice says.

'Retreat,' Grandma says. 'He wants to open up a Christian centre for the rehabilitation of Young Offenders.'

'Young what?'

'Offenders, Bea!'

'No need to shout!'

'What about the herd?' I say, looking over at Dad, who looks like he's just buried a loved one. 'Is this what you want?'

'It doesn't matter what I want,' he says quietly. 'It's what's best for business.'

'Is rehabilitation even a business?' Beatrice says.

'Apparently the government is big on grants for that sort of stuff,' Grandma says, dabbing bread sauce on the side of her plate and spattering it up Beatrice's sleeve. 'Though heaven only knows what good it'll do, letting a bunch of convicts chat to God in a barn.'

'You'll have to lock your stuff up, all right.' Beatrice gives her hairdo another pat.

'You're not helping, ladies.' Dad chews his turkey. 'As you well know, dairy is an all-consuming beast.'

'It's a profession of hope, is farming.' Grandma reaches for the gravy boat. 'What was it that Mahatma Gandhi said?'

'"Where there is love, there is life"?' Beatrice quotes innocently.

Grandma stands at the helm of our Christmas spread; a matriarch sent by the Angel Gabriel. '"The cow is a poem of compassion".' She slams her fist down on the table, causing our plates to chink. '"We must defend the worship of the cow against the whole world."'

'I think he meant that as a devout Hindu,' Dad says curtly.

'Hindu, Muslim, Christian, Jew, a cow's a cow at the end of the day,' Grandma says.

Beatrice looks baffled. 'Since when have cows been religious?'

Dad grabs my hand. 'It's obviously yours if you want it, Bilberry. You've done a brilliant job, but I don't expect you to stay. You've got dreams of your own and that's the way it should be.'

'I'd stay for longer only Lorna's not speaking to me,' I say, aware that I sound like a child.

Grandma slings another Yorkshire pudding on my plate. 'Whatever it is, I'm sure it's fixable.'

'I'm not so sure.' I push broccoli around my plate with my fork.

'She'll be at the carol thing this afternoon,' Grandma says. 'Why don't you catch her there and talk to her?'

'What carol thing?' I say.

She gets up, reaches behind the toaster and passes me a

flyer for the Agricultural Society's Camp Christmas Carol Concert at Ridgecroft, a handwritten footnote apologizing for the printing error in omitting 'fire'. It starts in half an hour.

'Can I borrow the car?' I say.

Ridgecroft is like something out of a Christmas Brit-flick; a stately home illuminated by dots of gold and silver. Neon reindeer gallop across each turret of the house, its doors decorated with a thick wreath of winter greens and scarlet berries. A handsome fir tree bedecked with red ribbons and fairy lights stands proudly in the courtyard. The smell of cinnamon and cloves carries on the air. A brass band in white tuxedos trumpets 'Hark! the Herald Angels Sing', whilst people full of festive cheer huddle, their breath laced with mince pies and mulled wine. I look around for Lorna.

Thanks to the printing faux pas, a whole new demographic has been introduced, and it appears that Lorna and I are in no way, shape or form, the only gays in the village; far from it. There are homosexuals from Hathersage, Hope and Harewood Hall. Two butcher-than-butch butchers from Bamford have arrived in matching Christmas jumpers and are flirting outrageously with five jolly gents from St Mildred's choir, who are not shy of a sausage pun.

Doreen and Tazzy make their way over.

'Mince pie?' Doreen offers me a warm, greasy paper bag.

'I'm full, thanks,' I say, becoming conscious that she's not so much wanting me to sample her patisserie but take notice of the writing on the paper bag, which reads 'Peterson's Pastries'.

'Thanks for being the only one with the gumption to tell me,' she says.

I crack a smile. 'Though Buns and Baps did have a ring to it!'

More men in tuxedos spill out of a minibus, slipping and sliding over the path with tubas and trombones. 'O Little Town of Bethlehem' gets underway as the first proper snow-flakes fall.

There's still no sign of Lorna.

A smaller version of the Wolf, his younger brother perhaps, takes to the microphone in a tartan kilt, knee-length socks and a cropped black jacket, his arms wrapped round a spindly lady with ash-blonde hair and a soft grey coat. 'Ladies and gentlemen, boys and girls.' He smiles. 'Jemima and I would like to wish everyone a healthy and hearty, Happy Christmas! Help yourselves to refreshments. Be jolly, be merry, have a great evening. And, in keeping with tradition, may I hand you over to my father, Wolfgang Huxley-Lipyeat, better known to some of you as the Wolf.'

Muffled applause comes from the crowd. It's hard to clap in gloves.

A voice shouts from the back. 'He's in the cowshed! Bit of an emergency!'

It occurs to me that Lorna might be in the cowshed too, if it's a cow emergency. I weave my way through the crowd, pardoning and excusing as I pass the fairy-lit fir trees and the wreath-bearing outhouse. Past a security guard who stands, arms folded, in front of a huge log cabin, but there's no sign of a cowshed. Unless the guarded log cabin is the cowshed, on account of its pedigree bovine inhabitants? I double back.

'I'm here to see the Wolf,' I say to the security guard.

He looks me up and down. 'The cow girl?'

'Yeee-es,' I say. Technically, it's the truth.

'Calf's on your left. Mademoiselle's at the back.' He stands aside.

The barn is heated and smells of freshly chopped pinewood. It takes my eyes a few moments to adjust to the glare of the strip lights rigged under the roof. A girl with a face full of cold sores feeds the calf; a tiny creature with evenly spaced markings: 'Mademoiselle V', according to the sign. At the far end of the barn, the Wolf and his wife stand knee-deep in straw at the side of Mademoiselle. There's no sign of Lorna.

I walk towards them. 'Congratu—'

Their faces are sunken and solemn. Mademoiselle twitches, her neck collapsed in an S shape. She fights to straighten the kink, but the weight of her head is too heavy and crashes downwards. Her wide, dilated pupils stare trancelike at nothing.

The Wolf looks up. 'Is the vet with you?'

'No.'

Penelope feeds a tea towel repeatedly through her tiny fingers. 'She was on fine form yesterday. Excited to be a mother again, dancing about like a wind-up toy, and now she's got nothing left. Won't even feed her calf.'

The Wolf eyes me angrily. 'In case you hadn't noticed, now is not a good time.'

Mademoiselle's muscles spasm. She grinds her teeth, jerking this way and that, shuffling her back hooves under her bulk, and I'm reminded of the countless videos of women with post-natal eclampsia I've watched; muscles flinching, limbs jerking. I've read hundreds of case studies, including my mother's, and if I know one thing, I know this: Mademoiselle has eclampsia, milk fever in cows. Unless treated, she's about to slide into a phase of hypocalcaemia, which is a lot more serious. Seizure-serious. Deadly serious.

I look at the Wolf. 'You say you've called the vet?'

'Several,' Penelope's voice wobbles. 'But being Christmas Eve . . .'

I call Lorna, but of course there's no answer. Unauthorized, I walk over and touch Mademoiselle's ears. They're stone cold and her legs aren't much warmer.

'She needs calcium, fast,' I say.

'There should be nothing wrong with her calcium levels,' the Wolf barks. 'We've been supplementing her calcium all the way through her pregnancy.'

I want to tell him that this is the exact opposite of what he should have done. That by upping her calcium levels, her body will only dispose of it. A divine paradox. But that's not going to help right now. 'Where's your first-aid kit?'

Penelope lifts a small bony finger towards a hook on the wall. I open it up and rummage through the contents for calcium gluconate or magnesium sulphate, but there's nothing. And then I remember the stash of KSG samples in the boot of the Land Rover.

'Back in one sec!'

I stumble through the snow to the car. I can't let Mademoiselle down. The world can't lose another mother. My feet are wet, and I've lost all feeling in my little toes. A ridge of white powder falls to the ground as I open the car boot and reach for the cardboard box stamped with 'Queen's

College' in red ink. Inside, boxes and boxes of liquid calcium gluconate in KSG packaging sit one on top of the other. Dozens of ready-made solutions. I pick out twelve packets. The average cow weighs in at ten times the average woman, so it's going to take a mega-dose. I hug it all to my chest while shutting the boot and slip and slide back to the cow shed. The security guard acknowledges me with a dip of the head. I throw the boxes down onto a hay bale and look at the Wolf. 'Can you get me a sterilized needle?'

'Oh no, you don't!' he growls. 'You're not going anywhere near her with a needle.'

I look to Penelope. 'This is what I specialize in: eclampsia. She's got eclampsia. We need to act fast.' I run my fingers over Mademoiselle's back. 'I won't go in intravenously. You'd need a vet to do that. It'll need to be subcutaneous.'

'Get her the needle!' Penelope finds her voice.

Reluctantly, the Wolf grapples for the first-aid kit, tossing everything out until he finds a needle in a sterilized pouch. 'Here!' he says, presenting me with a needle so big, I don't trust myself.

'Is there a smaller one?'

He hands me a smaller package.

'How much does she weigh?' I try to calculate how many sachets I need.

'1,550 pounds,' the Wolf says.

Of course, she does – optimal weight, statistical perfection. I empty out sachet after sachet of KSG product. Mademoiselle slumps further, her head now resting on the ground. She starts to fit, her head vibrating in one enormous shudder, nostrils flaring, tongue hanging out.

'Can you get a bucket of hot water?' I say. 'I need to get the solution to body temperature.' I get out my phone and surf the internet for 'subcutaneous injections in cattle'.

Penelope and the Wolf share a look of concern, but she hurries off and is back in barely a minute with a full bucket.

'Thank you. We need to prop her up, too, so she doesn't collapse. They'll do!' I point to the hay bales in the corner of the barn.

'You'd better know what you're doing, missy,' the Wolf growls, as he heaves them into position.

We arrange the other hay bales around Mademoiselle like blocks of Lego, bolstering her stooped shoulders, her crooked neck, her sloping backside, until the needle is warm enough.

Nervous as hell, I place my hand on the skin of her shoulder, spread my fingers out wide, and move down Mademoiselle's backbone by a further spread hand's width.

'Here we go!' I say, holding the needle at a 45-degree angle whilst feeling for the layer of skin above her fat. I need to avoid her muscle.

'Are you sure?' Penelope bites her lip.

My hand jitters and my mouth dries. If I screw this up, I cost the Wolf a smooth million and unquantifiable heartbreak. What would Lorna do in this situation? Cool, calm, collected Lorna. The internet is telling me to hold the skin in one hand and push the needle hard with the other. Instinct is telling me to go to the toilet. Without thinking, I press the needle through her skin. 'Yes.'

Mademoiselle shudders and tries to stand on her front legs, which can't quite support her weight, her backside sliding back down again.

'Come on, come on, come on, lassie!' the Wolf shouts, at Mademoiselle, rather than me, presumably.

I waggle the needle to ensure it hasn't gone through to the muscle. Then, placing the rubber cap of the flutter valve over the bottle, I tilt it upside down in the air, the orange brown fluid bubbling and sliding down the tube, into the needle.

I massage the skin downward and away from the needle to disperse the liquid – something I've seen both Dad and Lorna do countless times to speed things up and make sure it doesn't get pocketed in the tissues, but I can't articulate this. I can either talk, or continue with what I know needs to be done, but somehow can't manage both simultaneously.

'What are you doing now?' the Wolf barks. 'Billie?' he says forcefully as the fluid drains away.

I pull out the needle, sticky with dextrose, and rub her skin. Mademoiselle shudders and I quietly crap myself that she's about to drop like a stone. I've read that if she's going to recover, it should be pretty fast. She should stand within twenty minutes.

'Talk to me, lassie!' the Wolf says crossly. 'What happens now?'

My heart beats violently. I look down at my sticky, torn, grime-infested fingers. Her life is in my hands. 'I . . .' If she dies, I'll be guilty of cow-slaughter and no doubt named and shamed in the national press, which will mean it's all over for our farm – the Wolf will make sure of that. 'We have to wait.'

There I am, crouched in the corner of the pen, eyes closed, trying to think reassuring thoughts and stop that fucking 'Lightning Tree' song playing over and over in my head. And there the Wolf is, looming above me with a bucket of water, sponging Mademoiselle's neck. The clock is ticking.

'Wait for what?' Penelope's voice trembles.

'Just give it a minute,' I say, unable to look at her.

The Wolf paces up and down through the straw, fists clenched. 'Come on, come on, come on,' he mutters under his breath.

Two minutes later, Mademoiselle struggles to her feet and stands unaided. Her eyes regain focus, and although she stumbles at first, she stands.

The Wolf throws his arms around her neck. 'You fucking champion!' He presses his nose against her cheek and I would swear he is nearly crying. Penelope definitely is, having sat down heavily on a hay bale as Mademoiselle found her feet. She now has her head in her hands, sobbing loudly, while murmuring 'oh, thank God' over and over again.

Mademoiselle plods over to the water trough and I become aware of a pulse in my ears, blood pumping loudly. My skin tingles and the scent of fresh pine smells stronger than ever. It's only now that I realize that I'm shaking like a leaf, tiny tears of relief escaping from the corners of my eyes. A feeling I haven't experienced since the march surges through my veins: pride.

'Come here!' The Wolf throws his arms open to me. 'Well done, lassie. Well done!' He pats my back over and over, and I try not to notice his dandruff on my sleeve.

'Thank you,' Penelope squeaks through cupped hands.

The Wolf picks up Penelope as you might carry a small child to bed. 'She's alive! Alive!' He twirls her around, kicking up straw in celebration, as she grips his shoulders and laughs through her tears.

Mademoiselle swings her head round from the trough and looks at me with doleful eyes. Eyes that don't blink or flicker, waiver or stray. Rock-steady, grateful eyes. She takes two steps towards me and bows her head without breaking her gaze. I hold my hand out to her and she snorts, sweat glistening on her nostrils. She plods over and presses her wet nose on my neck, cow dribble matted in my hair.

The Wolf chuckles. 'You've got a friend for life there!' He watches me for a moment, Penelope sitting next to him, before dragging out a silver hip flask from the inside of his jacket and unscrewing the lid. 'A toast!' He holds up the hip flask and thrusts it in my direction. 'To the Cow Girl.'

'Hear, hear!' Penelope claps her hands together.

I raise the silver flask to my nose and am met with the strong, oaky smell of hardened spirit. Whiskey, or brandy perhaps. I take a swig, the taste of burned rubber lingering as I swallow, my throat feeling on fire. Bourbon.

The Wolf laughs as I fold at the waist, shielding my mouth with my forearm.

'Got a bit of a kick, hasn't it, lassie?'

He takes back the flask and offers it to Penelope, who politely declines. Three gulps later, he screws the top back on and looks at me. 'You wanted to negotiate on the freehold?'

'Yes.'

'Out of the question.' His jowls shake.

It's all I can do not to jab the needle repeatedly into his small, piggy eyes. After everything I've done. After everything that's just happened. I feel cheated. Hollow. Wronged.

'Consider it yours. You've earned it, lassie!' He extends his hand to me, his enormous sausage fingers squeezing mine.

'Thank you.' My voice shakes with giddiness.

'No. Thank you, Billie.' He squeezes my shoulder. 'You'll have confirmation in writing by the time you get home.'

I'm so pumped with adrenaline I swear I could burst. It's a weird sensation – I feel empty yet replete. Weightless yet complete. I want to tell Lorna everything.

I place my hand on Mademoiselle's neck. 'Well done, lady,' I whisper.

I gather my things with shaky hands and, as I make my way out of the barn, I hear the Wolf say, 'Who'd have thought it? A biochemist from London.'

It's snowing heavily outside. I trudge through the soft white powder back to the carol concert in pursuit of Lorna, but no matter how many huddled groups of duffel coats and bobble hats I infiltrate, she's nowhere to be seen. Reluctantly, I leave, 'The Holly and the Ivy' chiming in the distance.

The Land Rover takes a couple of attempts to choke to life. I crunch my way through the gears, windscreen wipers going like billy-o against the flurry of snow. I could go straight back to the farm, but I need to find Lorna. The clock on the dashboard suggests it is eight o'clock on Christmas Eve. She's possibly on her way here, but fuck it, if you don't try, you don't get, you've got to be in it to win it, and all those other clichés.

I trundle along at twenty miles an hour behind a gritter. It's no longer snowing by the time I reach Blackamoor, and the cold night air hangs black and silent. I somehow miss the turn to Marstone Crescent and have to double back on myself, eventually pulling up outside Lorna and Guy's flat, which pays homage to Christmas with a simple wreath of twisted ever-greens.

I get out of the car. Lorna's bedroom light is on. Snow creaks under my boots as I make my way up their path. I ring the Parsons-Bonneville buzzer and take a step back.

Guy comes to the door in a Christmas jumper, jodhpurs and odd socks. He holds a miniature Christmas microwavable pudding pot in one hand and a teaspoon in the other.

'She's out, I'm afraid.' He smiles aggressively.

'I really need to see her,' I say, eyeing up the stairs and wondering whether I can rugby-tackle him and gallop up them. I can hear her hairdryer going. She must be ten metres away from me at the most.

He plunges his spoon into his pudding and takes a mouthful. 'Sorry,' he says, dribbling suet over himself. 'Have a Happy Christmas!'

The door closes and that sky-high feeling of euphoric elation drains away, lead-heavy dejection setting in.


Everyone's already in bed by the time I get home. Even Speedo's bark is only half-hearted when he hears my key in the door. I pluck a foil-wrapped chocolate decoration from the Christmas tree and mull over the thing with Mademoiselle. If that isn't 'thinking out of the box', then I don't know what is. I turn on the Christmas lights, pour myself an amaretto, grab my laptop and don't stop writing. Once I've finished, I have one final email to send before bed.


**Subj:'Thinking Outside the Box' for PhD in Eclampsia Research**

Dear Professor Williams,

I had the pleasure of meeting you earlier this year at the KSG Obstetric Abnormalities Conference. You kindly gave me a lift to the station and advised me to apply my research to real life and 'think outside the box' before applying for a scholarship for the PhD in Eclampsia Research. It's taken me a while, but I believe I've now achieved that.

Please find enclosed my real-world case study, showing how calcium gluconate can not only treat eclampsia but also milk fever. Note: Mademoiselle is not a woman but a pedigree cow.

Wishing you a Merry Christmas and all the best for the New Year.

Yours sincerely,
Billie Oliver

And now it's gone midnight, one final text.

**To: Lorna Parsons**
Lorna, I know you still hate me, but I still miss you like mad. Just wanted to wish you a very Happy Christmas. Love Billie x

It's Christmas Day and another four inches of snow have come down overnight. It should feel magical, yet winning the freehold without winning back Lorna doesn't feel right. The sweet taste of victory isn't so divine without a loved one to share it. Still, I can't wait to tell Grandma and Dad once they're up.

Hallam FM declares Cliff Richard the Christmas number one. An ex-Pussy Cat Doll is interviewed live from the Bahamas on what it's like to have 'the perfect beach body for Christmas', and the inflatable Father Christmas tethered to the roof of the cowshed has popped, a hollow corpse swinging back and forth in the breeze.

I pull on wellies and trudge across the unspoiled, glittery white blanket of snow to the barn. The herd greet me, their groans and grunts faithful to our everyday routine. There's something comforting in the whole milking process when you're feeling shit. It's just me and the girls, and it's better that way. Although animals can harbour resentment and hold grudges, it's always short-lived. They may be demanding, but they're always fair. Treat them with respect and they'll respect you. 'Happy Christmas, ladies.'

**From: Maria**
Happy Christmas, Bilbo Baggins. Love you long time xxx

**From: Kat Leason-Mellor**
Happy Christmas, Bill. Hope you have a cracker! We've got Bev's mums over until Boxing Day. Wish me luck!!! Still, not as much oestrogen as at your place. Send our love to the cows. Love and moos, Kat and Bev x

Back in the kitchen, Grandma is loosening grapefruit segments with a serrated knife. 'Happy Christmas, Billie Goat.'

I peel off my damp welly socks and drape them over the radiator. 'Happy Christmas!' I hug her tightly and smile, deciding to keep the news until we go out for dinner, where I can make a moment of it.

At 11 a.m., as tradition demands, Grandma wheels her Japanese ash hostess trolley festooned with flapjack into the living room. She turns on the television, navigating her way around More4 to find *Countdown*. She takes a seat in the Tudor orthopaedic armchair she inherited from her mother.

'Of course, the *Countdown* clock ticks quicker than what it used to,' Beatrice says, helping herself to a honey granola chunk.

'I know,' Grandma agrees.

'Disqualified.'

'Shouldn't have been.'

It's good that Grandma has a partner in crime. It's been thirteen years since my grandpa died, and that's a long time to be alone. I just wish Dad had someone. He's been on his own for longer than he was with Mum and would enjoy a companion.

'Shouldn't have got three points for that.'

'Were about to say the same.'

We exchange presents at midday. Grandma gives me thermals and an urban dictionary, which she and Beatrice pore over, tittering at words like 'White Walling' and 'Facebortion'. Dad snores, surrounded by socks, Jelly Babies and brandy.

The clock strikes three, which signals Christmas dinner at The Cavendish. I'm about to get ready when an email comes through.

From: Professor N. Williams, PhD, MD
Re: 'Thinking Outside the Box' for PhD in Eclampsia
Research

Dear Billie,
Now that's what I'm talking about. This is genuinely
exciting!

I'd love to be part of your PhD journey and help you on
your way. May I suggest you pop in and see me at
Sheffield University in the new year and we can talk
through your application form.

Wishing both you and Mademoiselle a very Happy
Christmas.

Best wishes,
Nigel

I feel all floaty and possibly like Buddhists do when they reach
enlightenment.

Grandma fixes her hair in the hallway mirror. I'm bursting
to tell her but Speedo's throwing up yesterday's turkey over
the lounge rug and I figure it deserves a bigger moment, along
with the freehold.

'Remember it's very posh, dessert fork as well as a spoon.'
She says the same thing every year.

We arrive at The Cavendish, an upmarket hotel with white
starched tablecloths and silver cutlery. A 'please wait to be

seated' sign greets us in the entrance to the restaurant, where Christmas carols play over the chink and clink of cutlery on china.

'We've a reservation under the name of Oliver,' Grandma announces proudly to the waiter in her poshest voice.

'Mrs Oliver times four,' the waiter confirms, looking at his booking sheet and then at my footwear, as if it's broken some sort of law.

The door swings open behind us, letting in a gale. 'Would you mind making it five?'

Lorna Parsons beams from ear to ear, fresh-faced and perky.

'Lorna!' I squeal, wrapping my arms around her. 'How did you know . . .'

'You come here every year,' Lorna says.

My dad kisses her cheek. 'Why don't the pair of you join us in a second?' he says, walking Grandma and Beatrice over to the table.

'Thanks, Dad,' I say, still beaming.

Lorna pulls me back into the foyer, pushes me against the door and kisses me, long and hard. 'Happy Christmas,' she whispers.

I study her face. Her kind eyes, her dancing freckles, her pretty pink scar. 'You know, nothing went on with Joely.'

'I know.' She kisses me again. 'I've been reassured a few times now.'

'By who?'

'Maria and Kat both wrote to me. I wasn't in the right frame of mind for it back then, but I've had plenty of time to think it through and . . . well, it was actually Guy, really.'

'Guy?' I say, realizing I've got mud on my boots.

'He said you looked like a lost puppy on our doorstep yesterday and I should forgive you.'

'Fuck, I've missed you,' I say, taking her hand and interlacing my fingers with hers.

'I've missed you too.'

She smiles. 'I guess we'd better not keep the old girls waiting.'

We go through to the restaurant. Lorna squeezes in beside me and pinches my knee as Grandma flits between foie gras (pronounced foy grass) and duck à l'orange on the menu.

'You don't even like duck, Kathleen!' Beatrice mutters.

'I do when it's French,' Grandma says, folding her menu and dusting imaginary crumbs off her knee.

'Everyone likes anything when it's French,' Lorna smirks.

After a momentary flirtation with nut log, the five of us order roast turkey. The waiter lights the log fire in front of us, which crackles and glows. Lorna slots her hand into mine under the table and everything feels warm and right.

'I'd like to make an announcement,' I say, squeezing Lorna's hand. 'Yesterday, I secured the—'

'Red or white?' the waiter leans over and lights the candles on our table.

'I think we'll want a bit of both, won't we?' Grandma says.

'I'll not have a wine, but I might manage a spritzer,' Beatrice says.

'A bottle of each, please,' Dad says.

I take a deep breath as the waiter shuts his notebook. 'Yes, so yesterday when I was at the carol concert—'

'Actually, I will have a wine,' Beatrice says.

'OK.' The waiter flips open his notebook and changes the order.

I run my fingers over the silver serviette ring. 'I was at the carol concert and Mademoiselle, the Wolf's pedigree cow was—'

'Although I'll regret it in the morning,' Beatrice says, turning back to the retreating waiter. 'Sorry, love. I'll stick to a white-wine spritzer.'

'I've got the freehold!' I shout.

Everyone in the restaurant stops what they're doing and looks at me. Lorna has instinctively let go of my hand and my whole family is staring at me.

'Yesterday, I got us the freehold to the farm,' I say.

'For how much?' Dad says.

'For nothing,' I say, fiddling with my fork. 'I saved Mademoiselle from an eclampsia seizure, and in return, Wolfgang Huxley Knobhead has given us the freehold.'

Dad says nothing and gives me the same look he did when I came out to him.

'I'll believe that when I see it in writing!' Grandma says.

I take my phone out of my pocket and enlarge the text. 'Here.'

She puts on her reading glasses. 'Well, I'll be damned!'

'Let's have a look,' Dad says, taking the phone. 'Fuck me!'

The only time I've ever heard Dad say, 'fuck me' was when Donald Trump came to power, though that was accompanied by a look of horror, whereas now he looks caught between amazed and enraptured. 'Jesus, Billie. You're one in a million.'

'Bloody hell!' Lorna finally gets hold of the phone as the waiter fills our glasses. 'I'm so proud of you.'

'Not as proud as I am,' Grandma announces.

'Nor me!' Dad says, standing up and inadvertently

addressing the room with a raised glass. 'To my brilliant daughter!'

'To Billie!' Grandma and Lorna clink glasses.

'I'm not following,' Beatrice says, looking at me. 'Are you getting married?'

Grandma realigns her cutlery. 'She's got the freehold to the farm.'

'The what?' Beatrice says.

'It's worth hundreds of thousands,' Grandma says.

'So, which one of you is going to carry the egg?' Beatrice persists.

'You probably don't need an egg these days, Bea,' Grandma says.

'Of course, they didn't acknowledge lesbians back in our day,' Beatrice says. 'And there were none of them trans-whatsits around either.'

'Transvestites?' I suggest.

'Women with meat and two veg,' Beatrice says. 'You don't mind so much if it's some hairy man in fishnet stockings and a mini-skirt, but tampering with what Mother Nature gave you? That's just plain wrong.'

'Not for . . .' I trail off as Lorna squeezes my knee under the table.

'Never know what you're getting these days,' Beatrice says. 'There was a lady down our precinct, who were seeing a man, who turned out to be a woman. Went out for a jacket potato and came back with a steak and kidney pie.'

'It's early days yet, Grandma.' I smile, my roots well and truly entwined with those of Lorna's. 'We haven't even been out on a proper date!'

'You'd better get your skates on then,' Beatrice says. 'You don't want to leave it until you're both in your seventies.'

Grandma takes hold of Beatrice's hand over the table. 'No, you don't want to make that mistake.'

Lorna's jaw drops slightly, and she nudges my leg with her knee, the cutlery jumping. I look at her with a face that says, *Come on, you knew, right?* and she looks back at me with one that screams, *No!*

'What's wrong? Cat got your tongue?' Grandma looks at Lorna.

Lorna blushes. 'Sorry, I just . . .'

That's the thing about being in your eighties: companionship doesn't need classification. Friendships don't need boundaries. And relationships don't need outing. Love is love, whether it's sleeping together, holding hands, or living alongside someone, playing Scrabble. Why ruin it with a label?

It's New Year's Eve. The girls are on their way up. Grandma has defrosted a shrimp and macaroni casserole, which Dad has declared too adventurous for his pallet and is sticking with sausage and mash *thank you very much*. Bev is bringing Manfred, an injured violet-crowned hummingbird, who traditionally winters in Mexico but this year will be holidaying on the Derbyshire/Yorkshire border with the heating on. Kat is bringing her laptop and has a work deadline. Maria is bringing five family packs of extra strength verruca cream, now that she is the face/foot of Bazuka Verruca Removal Gel.

'Do you think you'll stay up for midnight?' I say to Dad as he clicks shut the padlock to his shed.

'I think I might.' He drops the key into his pocket.

I take a handful of leftover toffee Quality Streets from my pocket. 'We'll prod you if you fall asleep.'

'Thanks, but you won't be there.' His eyes twinkle. 'I'm going out for a drink with a lady friend after dinner.'

I grab his arm with excitement, releasing my grip when I see him flinch. 'Really?'

'Pat, a lady from the bowling club.'

'Friesian-card-with-the-kisses Pat?'

He smiles. 'The very one.'

'Brilliant!' I squeeze him until he can't breathe.

Lorna presses her nose against the kitchen window, and I realize I'm late for our haystack reunion.

'You'd better be off,' Dad chuckles.

Rain drums hypnotically on the corrugated-iron cowshed roof. My head lolls onto Lorna's shoulder as the two of us lie entwined on top of the haystack. I stare at the small rectangular space in the roof where a panel is missing; a casualty of the storm. It feels good to be back on the haystack with Lorna, making idle chitchat, my head propped on her shoulder, listening to the howling wind while we're safely sheltered, Parsnip chomping on hay next to Jupiter II in the pen below.

'I'm glad you don't hate me any more.' I chew on a piece of hay.

Lorna smiles. 'So, forgive the lesbian angst, but what happens now?'

I tilt my head to one side and grab her waist. 'How would you feel about me moving to Sheffield to do a PhD?'

She rolls over so that we're face to face. 'Serious?'

I run my fingers over her pretty horseshoe-shaped scar. 'It'd mean getting a flat somewhere in Sheffield.'

She stares at the roof, pulling her coat tighter around us and running her fingers over my thigh. The barn door rattles in the wind and the light flickers. Parsnip shuffles Jupiter II closer to her and groans.

'But what about your life in London?' Lorna says. 'Your friends, your—'

'My friends will always be my friends, no matter where I live. We can visit London whenever we want. You're up here and so is the PhD. It's a no-brainer.'

Lorna smirks.

'What?' I say, digging her in the ribs.

'You'll make a brilliant doctor,' she says, plucking a coarse strand of hay out of the bale we're sitting on and tracing my face with it. 'But you'll always be my cow girl.'

Parsnip moos. Lorna's ladybird pendant catches the light and I know that everything's going to be OK.

# ACKNOWLEDGEMENTS

Thank you firstly to Adam for surfing the highs and lows of writing alongside me, for championing *Cow Girl* from the very beginning and for reading countless drafts and shouldering a multitude of meltdowns.

Massive thanks to Helen Lederer and all the wonderfully witty women involved in Comedy Women in Print for setting up an award that recognizes comedy writing as a craft in its own right, and to the judges, Jenny Eclair, Susan Calman, Fanny Blake, Lara Marshall, Martha Ashby, Jennifer Young and Karen McPherson, of the Unpublished category, for selecting *Cow Girl*.

Thank you to Martha, at HarperCollins, for guiding me through the editing process with precision, humour and the odd pet anecdote – always felt on the same wavelength – it's been a blast.

Thanks to my agent, Felicity Trew, who loved Billie enough to take a punt on me, and to everyone at the Caroline Sheldon agency.

Thanks to Jacq Burns at the London Writers Club for her invaluable critique of *Cow Girl*. Jacq, your LWC sessions are solid gold for debut writers and provided an introduction to Felicity.

And not forgetting a HUGE thank you to my writer friends, who read my early drafts, encouraged, critiqued and provided constructive feedback – especially to Clare Lydon, Loretta Milan and everyone on my CBC writers course, after whom I've named a cow. Oh, and to KT for being a muse and Susie for her unfaltering support.

*Cow Girl* by Kirsty Eyre was the winner of the Comedy Women in Print's Unpublished Novel 2019.

Comedy Women in Print was set up by Helen Lederer to shine a light on witty women authors and is the first literary prize to bring forward the next generation of witty women authors as well as shine a light on those with established comedy writing careers.

Entry details for the Published and Unpublished prizes are here https://www.comedywomeninprint.co.uk/how-to-enter

Become a friend https://www.comedywomeninprint.co.uk/friends-of-cwip

At last, female comedy writing has a place within the canvas of literary prizes.

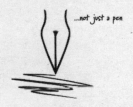

...not just a pen